PRAISE FOR M. L. BUCHMAN

The first...of (a) stellar, long-running romantic suspense series.

— BOOKLIST, THE 20 BEST ROMANTIC SUSPENSE NOVELS: MODERN MASTERPIECES. *THE NIGHT IS MINE*

Top 10 Romance of 2012, 2015, and 2016.

— BOOKLIST: THE NIGHT IS MINE, HOT POINT, HEART STRIKE

One of our favorite authors.

— RT BOOK REVIEWS

Buchman has catapulted his way to the top tier of my favorite authors.

— FRESH FICTION

A favorite author of mine. I'll read anything that carries his name, no questions asked. Meet your new favorite author!

— THE SASSY BOOKSTER, FLASH OF FIRE

M.L. Buchman is guaranteed to get me lost in a good story.

— THE READING CAFE, WAY OF THE WARRIOR: NSDQ

I love Buchman's writing. His vivid descriptions bring everything to life in an unforgettable way.

— PURE JONEL, HOT POINT

SAVIORS 101: THE FIRST BOOK OF THE RELUCTANT MESSIAH

A DEITIES ANONYMOUS NOVEL

M. L. BUCHMAN

Buchman Bookworks

Other works by M. L. Buchman:

<u>White House Protection Force</u>
Off the Leash
On Your Mark
In the Weeds

<u>The Night Stalkers</u>
MAIN FLIGHT
The Night Is Mine
I Own the Dawn
Wait Until Dark
Take Over at Midnight
Light Up the Night
Bring On the Dusk
By Break of Day
WHITE HOUSE HOLIDAY
Daniel's Christmas
Frank's Independence Day
Peter's Christmas
Zachary's Christmas
Roy's Independence Day
Damien's Christmas
AND THE NAVY
Christmas at Steel Beach
Christmas at Peleliu Cove
5E
Target of the Heart
Target Lock on Love
Target of Mine
Target of One's Own

<u>Firehawks</u>
MAIN FLIGHT
Pure Heat
Full Blaze
Hot Point
Flash of Fire
Wild Fire
SMOKEJUMPERS
Wildfire at Dawn
Wildfire at Larch Creek
Wildfire on the Skagit

<u>Delta Force</u>
Target Engaged
Heart Strike
Wild Justice
Midnight Trust

<u>Where Dreams</u>
Where Dreams are Born
Where Dreams Reside
Where Dreams Are of Christmas
Where Dreams Unfold
Where Dreams Are Written

<u>Eagle Cove</u>
Return to Eagle Cove
Recipe for Eagle Cove
Longing for Eagle Cove
Keepsake for Eagle Cove

<u>Henderson's Ranch</u>
Nathan's Big Sky
Big Sky, Loyal Heart
Big Sky Dog Whisperer

<u>Love Abroad</u>
Heart of the Cotswolds: England
Path of Love: Cinque Terre, Italy

<u>Dead Chef Thrillers</u>
Swap Out!
One Chef!
Two Chef!

<u>Deities Anonymous</u>
Cookbook from Hell: Reheated
Saviors 101

<u>SF/F Titles</u>
The Nara Reaction
Monk's Maze
the Me and Elsie Chronicles

<u>Strategies for Success (NF)</u>
Managing Your Inner Artist/Writer
Estate Planning for Authors

BEFORE...

WELL, JUST BEFORE. OKAY?

PROLOGUE THE FIRST

21 YEARS (AND 9 MONTHS) UNTIL ARMAGEDDON

No one thought that letting Escher into Heaven was a mistake, but many questioned Michelle's decision to put him on the Heavenly architectural committee.

The Devil Incarnate admired the result of her efforts to mess with the minds of Heaven and Hell. The redesigned meeting room that spanned the border between Heaven and Hell was Escher's masterpiece. Few immortals shared her feelings and some couldn't even form a coherent sentence while here. Which had been part of the point. She was the Devil after all and did have a reputation to uphold.

She dropped into the plush red leather chair at the head of the table.

"Michelle." Her name echoed nicely in the empty room. It translated out of the ancient Hebrew as "Who is like God?" A joke few understood anymore, nonetheless she gleefully answered her echo.

"Me!"

She followed the path of the second echo as it bounced around the room.

The others she'd managed to contact would be along soon. Most, she suspected, checked their caller-ID and chose to risk her wrath rather than pick up the damned phone. If a half-dozen immortals showed up, she'd be lucky.

She'd been more patient during the early millennia of creation, cleaning up after God's various disasters. He'd made a fine primordial soup but couldn't have gotten life out of it to save His soul. The crucial impetus, as usual, had been up to her. The images of life's progress since that moment were depicted in intricate mosaic above the chair to her left. Primordial ooze, single-cell colonies, swimmers, crawlers, walkers, and eventually tawny teenage tennis pros in short, white skirts endorsing soft drinks.

The Celestials Association for Better Redemption, CABER was coming apart. The council's title had been invented by the batty Celtic Goddess Sheela Na Gig who liked watching burly men tossing telephone-pole sized logs. Of course once they witnessed the sport, many of the other Goddesses admitted old Sheela had a point about caber tossing. Even in modern times, it was a popular outing among the female deities to go to Highland games and watch strong men in kilts grunting over something besides women.

And Escher's design didn't help appease the hundred thousand petty rivalries. The long, white table folded back upon itself in such a way that no immortal was ever more than two seats from any other, no matter how many were in attendance. It was awkward to carry on a decent grudge by ignoring an immortal enemy when they were sitting elbow-to-elbow. The table looked normal enough as long as you didn't think too hard. But that wasn't what invoked the most complaints.

Nor was it the mosaics that covered walls, ceiling, and floor in a mind-bending cacophony of color. In addition to evolution, which had called upon the God of science as its defender, the history of every religion that had a recognized God or Goddess was laid out in the miniscule tiles.

And all these flowed together until each turned into the other and almost every one turned into the same tawny teenage tennis pros in short, white skirts endorsing soft drinks. Escher really had a thing about them, somewhere between idolization and stark terror. And there was no way to separate the tennis pros from Zeus. He'd been a rabid womanizer since birth, so this wasn't as unlikely as your average shmoo supposed. He hadn't been spotted since entering a go-go bar wearing a paisley shirt in November of 1966. Not that anyone missed the old bastard.

Escher's portrait of Michelle always made her smile every time she tracked it down in the ever-shifting mosaic. Two hands taller than Yahweh, they stood near each other, but not too close. Yahweh: the short, round man, the creative artist who had thought up so many cool and beautiful ideas.

And herself, the tall woman with long dark hair and vivid green eyes. Not a slip of a woman, but neither Rubenesque. Just a good solid woman, with a figure that had made many a mortal weep. And more than a few immortals when she'd set her mind to it. The portrait showed a woman of stamina rather than a frail wallflower. A woman with muscles made strong by cleaning up the messes Yahweh had left down the ages.

But it wasn't this swirl of religion and creation that made the brains of the immortals really hurt and go begging for a God-sized dose of salicylic acid.

The feature that really twisted up most of them also happened to be Michelle's favorite part of Escher's design. It was the long rows of arched windows that looked down upon all creation. The simultaneous views from varied angles could be disconcerting at first. Out one window, the rolling meadows of Heaven spread forever. The next revealed the Big Bang in that silent instant when pure dark was giving way to pure light but no sound had yet been heard. Another looked down upon a hummingbird's nest in a lilac bush just north of Neskowin along the Oregon coast. A close-up view down the throat of a volcano on Io, one of Jupiter's moons, made the Hell that she'd developed look like a toddler's paradise.

What really bugged most Gods was that while they could walk the length of the room in a few dozen steps, the windows went on forever without limit. And there was still plenty of wall space for the ever-entwining mosaic. It made the controlling-type Gods downright twitchy. The few immortals who were at peace in this room either depended on a sense of humor, as she felt herself prone to do, or were so connected with the Cosmic Oneness that they found it beguiling.

Those not so equipped made a point of staring fixedly at the table. That way they saw the world as being entirely in their control; a blank white slate to scribble the future upon with colored crayons, preferably the full sixty-four-color set with the sharpener in the back.

She slouched down in her favorite chair, kicked off her sandals and rested her feet on the table in order to wait more comfortably; immortals were rarely punctual as they thought they had all the time in Creation. Michelle let her eyes rest upon a view of the moon buggy for Apollo 16 sitting idly at the foot of the Descartes Mountains. A brilliant practical joker had turned it around in the direction opposite to the way the astronauts had parked it, but so far no one had noticed. She, at least, appreciated her own humor.

Being the Devil Incarnate had its perks.

CHAPTER 1

SIX YEARS UNTIL ARMAGEDDON - LAP 1

Dana Murphy hated the rusty old energy spells from her book *Tips and Tricks from the Gods*, they took so much work to resurrect. At fifteen, her mom's old one-speed Schwinn was still a bit tall for her to ride. But she could just manage it, and it was quite necessary tonight. Mama kept saying she'd been a late bloomer as well, but Dana was sure getting tired of the pancake-flat, knobby-knee look.

The bike complained as she leaned into the energy current along Seattle's Ravenna Boulevard. The streetlights shone down through the gaps in the ancient maples leaning over the street. Trees that drew constant complaints of sap and bird droppings from the owners of the BMWs and Audis that now lined the road.

Twenty laps. She'd have to go twenty laps around the neighborhood in a very specific pattern. That was assuming she'd properly reformulated the powers correctly for latitude, longitude, and era.

Dana knew she was different, but at two a.m. on a warm, fall night she was alone, which was her most comfortable way to be. At least she'd come by her role as a misfit honestly.

By the time Dana Murphy was five, she knew her red-haired,

deeply freckled mother was different. It wasn't the distracted air that sometimes had her eating steaming hot meatloaf with baked potatoes and broccoli for breakfast, or cold, syrup-sodden pancakes sliding out of her Lisa Frank lunchbox at daycare.

It wasn't even the piano that played itself in the living room, though she'd never been able to find where it plugged in. All it had was pedals and scrolls of paper.

The first really weird thing was that there was no television or video games in the house. Her first after-daycare play date at Theresa Peterson's had included *Barney* and *Super Mario Brothers* which had greatly shaken her firm views on the sensibility of her universe. She hadn't gotten over it until six weeks later when she'd managed to whip Theresa's behind at her brother Sam's *Super Car Racer III*.

In fact, the only modern device her mother owned was a CD player which held five discs at a time and played music incessantly.

During her entire childhood, the house was never quiet.

She'd wake in the middle of the night to hear Frankie Avalon give way to Frankie Lane then Frank Sinatra and finally Frank Zappa.

She'd learned her alphabet organizing her mother's massive collection by the artist's first name (though she hadn't quite known what to do with Frank versus Frankie at the time), and her mother had played them in order from one end of the collection to the other ever since. For the rest of her life Tina Turner's pelvis-thumping tones were a natural segue into Tiny Tim's ukulele. When they reached *Zydeco, the Last Twenty Years,* she knew that dancing together to ABBA was not far away.

Dana never got over the foreign feel of libraries, as if she'd walked into a world where the last-name-first shelving order had been designed by Salvador Dali.

No, what was really different about her mom was the quiet stream of people who came to visit her. Whispered counseling sessions in the back room that had been converted to a cozy office.

Dana'd learned early on, short of arterial hemorrhage or a significant outbreak of fire, she wasn't supposed to enter the rose-colored office when the door was closed.

That didn't mean she was above spying.

The old house had simple floor vents to heat the upstairs bedroom. The metal grates created a hole into the ceiling of the room below for heat to rise into the upstairs room. Dana would lie for hour upon hour on the hardwood floor spying down on her mother's treatment sessions. Buried beneath the big black quilt from her bed, Dana would stare down through the grate, enjoying the vague puff of warm air on her face.

All the scents her mother used would waft upward. Lavender candles. Almond massage oil. Incense. The sharp nose-tickling bite of burning sage between sessions.

Sometimes Mama's patients were partly clothed. Sometimes naked. Sometimes they were poked with needles. Sometimes smeared with salves. And sometimes, which were Dana's favorites, they lay there, fully clothed with a cloth over their eyes.

Mama would stand in her flowing caftan all radiant and beautiful at their side. The candlelight would make her pale skin and freckles all rich and warm. No jewelry. Her hair in its usual snarled ponytail behind her like a chestnut mare's mane teased bouffant by the wind, and she would wave her hands slowly above the person. Never touching them.

The people would relax, tense, twitch, just like Dana's string puppets, but she couldn't ever see the strings no matter how she squinted. Not until one night when her eyes had been really tired from a long afternoon of whipping Theresa's behind on *Docm* did she see the strings.

Her mother was unsnarling a long line of snagged white light above Mrs. Crane's left hip. Dana could see how it was all stuck right where there was a visual break of light in the bone. But she knew the real bone was whole because the woman had limped through the door just fine.

When she'd asked Mama later, she'd tried to change the subject. But five-year old persistence paid off.

Mrs. Crane had never gotten over a hip that she'd broken as a little girl and had healed wrong. Mama was straightening out the mess it had made in her energy. She pointed to a whole shelf of books with titles like: *Hands of Light, Energy Medicine,* and *The Subtle Body.* She wasn't sure what "subtle" meant, but they had really pretty covers and lots of pictures illustrating how to fix people without having to cut big holes in them. It made Dana proud of her mother. They were also the books she'd learned to read from.

But she knew that Theresa's mom, who served healthy snacks and whose dinners always tasted dinnerish, would never understand. And after Theresa had called her a liar and her mother a faker, she hadn't mentioned her mother again.

To anyone.

PROLOGUE THE SECOND

STILL 21 YEARS (AND 9 MONTHS) UNTIL ARMAGEDDON

"We need to send another Messiah," Michelle announced to the gathered cohort of CABER.

That certainly got everyone's attention, mostly as a roar of denial.

She'd gotten a full half-dozen to attend aside from herself. The days when CABER commanded a hundred or more deities per meeting were long past, thankfully. Those meetings had led to many arguments and little progress. Over the centuries the attendance had tapered off to what she preferred to think of as an Executive Committee.

The Buddha sat quietly, contemplating the richness and depth of the universe, or maybe he was simply smart enough to keep his mouth shut. Apollo, the Greek Sun God, and his buddy Shiva, the Hindu God of Beginning and Ending, she could always get to come by telling the other one that his pal would be there. Neither ever thought to check with each other to see if she was lying, which being the Devil of course she was, so that worked. Dionysus, the Greek God of the grape, always showed up just because he was a good sport.

She'd managed to balance these with three women, Isis, the founding Goddess of Egypt, and Parvati, Shiva's wife. She used the friend trick with them as well. Though they'd seen right through

Michelle's lies, they showed up pretty consistently to humor her anyway. Mary Magdalene might not be a God in her own right, but she'd married the Son of God, and was a good friend who was always willing to help Michelle.

"I don't see why we need to keep trying. They'll figure it out on their own. Or not." Mary Magdalene sat back in her chair and crossed her arms over the chest that had mesmerized the son of God. Her hair flowed like a fountain of gold and her blue eyes would put gem-quality stones to shame.

"Those are your husband's words. So, he's not coming?"

Mary scowled a moment longer and then laughed, a trickling sound that made everyone around the table smile a bit, except for Apollo and Shiva who had made being grouchy into an immortals' Olympian contest. Michelle knew that Mary didn't have enough anger in her entire soul to last more than a few seconds.

"You know him too well. You know what he'd say about Messiah-hood, 'Been there. Done that.' I get so tired of hearing that he's 'paid his dues.' He tried using it to avoid doing the dishes, but I shut that down right away."

The first Messiah. Another of Yahweh's botched jobs. Michelle had tried to intercede, but there wasn't much you could do with the Romans of that day.

"Okay, so that's one of our lessons learned the hard way, Ancient Rome was not the best place to send a Messiah. What else have do we have for the post-project analysis of the first Messiah project?"

"Well, the media wasn't quite in place for him." Apollo the Greek Sun God glowed from his seat by the window, which happened to open onto a view of the surface of the sun.

"Something you'd know all to well." Shiva growled, from his seat to Apollo's left, the gold medal in the immortal grouch competition nearly in his grasp.

"Can I help it if you're a little Indian dweeb who cut off his own son's head?" The glittering God of gold prodded.

Just as everyone expected, that set off the Hindu God of Beginning and Ending.

"I'd been busy, how was I supposed to know that the boy sleeping in my wife's arms was our son grown? I was only gone for, what, a decade and a bit."

"But an elephant's head? Did you have to replace our son's head with that of an elephant?" Parvati, a bountifully voluptuous mortal who'd have driven Paul Rubens to his grave—actually, maybe she had —achieved her Godhood through marriage. Though Michelle doubted if Shiva had gotten the time of day, much less any sex, since he'd beheaded their son. She sat to Apollo's right and leaned forward to glare around him at her husband.

"We were discussing the First Messiah," Michelle fought for control. "C'mon gang, time to bring the focus back. Anything else on the subject of sending a New Messiah?"

"Well, the media is ready now." Apollo rapped the pommel of his flaming sword on the table. It worked to break up the scowls crossing back and forth in front of him.

He did have a point. It was more than a decade after the crux of the second millennium after all. And television and the Net did carry electronic preachers, religious jihads, Britney Spears, and innumerable tawny teenage tennis pros.

An awkward silence rattled around the table looking for somewhere to roost. Was she the only one here who thought about these things?

"Okay," Michelle nodded a thanks to Apollo.

He glowed at the praise. One reason he was placing out of the medals in the Grumpiest God competition, he was, on occasion, a decent guy.

"In summary, the problems facing the Nazarene were manifold. He'd arrived when the Jews were oppressed perhaps a bit less than usual. When the Romans were dictators, but fairer than most who had come before and a welcome relief from the disorganization and constant city-state wars of the Greeks.

"Even the Gods were doing fairly well back then. Egypt still prayed to Isis, Amun, and Re. The Greeks had their pantheon and the Romans theirs." Though she'd leave out that the Greek Gods were constantly bickering, but only among themselves so no one else much minded. And that the Romans, who were mostly genetic clones of the Greek and Egyptian Gods, were little better.

Yahweh, being the first monotheistic God in the whole Mediterranean, was the butt of innumerable jokes around that time, but it was all just friendly teasing and occasional pranks which he laughed off good-naturedly enough.

"So, the whole reason the First Messiah was sent—the salvation of humanity—rapidly devolved into a complex bollix of cult worship and misunderstandings. For one thing, his literal words became sacred, rather than the content. For another, having more people killed in his name that any other over the next two millennia wasn't even close to being proper protocol."

"The whole 'virgin birth' concept didn't work out so well for anyone," Mary noted. "Almost no one believed my mother-in-law. Then the moderns invented parthenogenesis to explain away that miracle. I think we finally proved it as a failed methodology for introducing a Messiah with Guinevere."

The night before he was supposed to start on his Messianic mission, Guinevere's son by virgin birth, Stephen, was beheaded by King Arthur for Stephen's discovering the king performing a less than virtuous act with a trio of chamber maids. His beheading was the lost historical fact that had sent Guinevere into Lancelot's arms for solace, causing the whole age of Camelot to collapse before it had a chance to really get going.

"Moving along, that brings us to the failed concept of sending a Messiah who could write their own words."

"I thought we tried that." Dionysus raised a waggling head from his close attention to the flagon of wine before him. Michelle never let him drink until after the meetings had collapsed. He simply couldn't drink without singing and there was no way to run a serious meeting when his gorgeous baritone voice was rippling its way through Gilbert and Sullivan patter songs.

"There was Jeffrey," Parvati supplied.

Jeffrey had died of writer's cramp during the First Dark Ages because nobody was doing nothing no how in those times. Too few were educated enough to read the first-ever novels. Perhaps if he'd chosen to write in a genre other than romance. Or maybe it was just that the quill and parchment was a complete and painful failure as a mechanism for a mute to spread the words of the Gods. The worst bit, they'd accidentally dropped him off where he'd had to do it in a painfully primitive language called English. The language simply hadn't evolved sufficiently to properly highlight the message of peace and sisterhood. It was solely suited to the blood, guts, and mead of *Beowulf.* Not that English was all that much better now.

"And Dante," Shiva added, not wanting to be one-upped by his wife.

Beatrice had Virgil lead Dante down into the Inferno, but Virgil forgot to bring him back, so the whole Messiah as a third-party method was discarded after that.

"And poor Marlowe," Michelle listed the last writer they'd sent.

Elizabethan England had been a time of immense turmoil. CABER sent a playwright and poet of unique skills in both the spoken and the written word. A Messiah who could set their own words down properly rather than the illiterate son of an illiterate carpenter made sense even if it hadn't worked out. *Faust* was just the first level warm-up exercise. Who knew that he would manage to get himself stabbed to death at twenty-nine over an unpaid bar bill.

"Maybe it's time we sent a woman again." Isis had launched the entire Egyptian civilization from her loins, giving her a rather feminist view of all creation.

"Look at what your church did to women in the Bible back in the fourth century." Isis warmed up to her argument, her low, sexy voice impossible to not pay attention to. "Those weaselly old men were scared to death of strong women. They dumped tens of thousands of words out of the Bible—most which would have helped Jesus— right down the holy bidet because it made the women seem too powerful. Mary, your marriage to Jesus, flushed. All of his brothers and sisters? No, that might imply she wasn't a virgin mother, flushed. Like there's any way Joseph could have kept his hands off your gorgeous mother-in-law once she was done birthing the Son of God."

"A woman." Michelle rolled the sound of it over her tongue. No one had suggested that in a long, long time. Not since Cassandra had been sent to Troy, accidentally cursed with the twin gifts of perfect prophecy and the inability to make anyone believe her. A quick glance at Apollo caused him to look away quickly and scowl at everyone. To his credit, he'd tried to remove his curse on Cassandra any number of times to no avail.

Isis nodded emphatically, her golden ankh necklace sliding up and down her deep cleavage of lush olive skin as she did so.

"A normal birth. Give her a mother, a father, and a normal birth right down to the hospital birthing room, the Mozart CD, and the epidural. You're the Devil, you could give them a big mortgage to cheer you up."

Michelle considered it for a long moment, but decided she wouldn't intentionally add to the new Messiah's burdens. Maybe she'd even set up a college fund.

The Buddha cleared his throat, and they all turned to pay attention. On the rare occasions he spoke, it was almost invariably wise, something Michelle really wished she could pull off with a little more frequency.

"We have not addressed the topic of foreknowledge. I think that one of Jesus' greatest challenges was being born with the full knowledge of what was happening to him right down to his betrayer and the date of his death. It was a mistake for his sake, if not for history's." He looked around the table. "We should at least give the kid a break until her twenty-first birthday. No foreknowledge until then."

Everyone nodded, especially the mothers.

"So it's decided." Michelle didn't even bother calling for a show of hands, a method of getting meetings to agree to her own consensus that had worked very well for her over the eons.

"And," Loki's smooth baritone made everyone twitch and turn to the door. Except Dionysus, who continued to gaze longingly upon his wine flagon.

"Late as usual, Loki." Michelle wasn't the only one who disliked the Norse Demi-God of mischief and fire. No matter how smooth and handsome, he wallowed in his own agenda, and his rich baritone had led more than one of these immortals into harm's way. People were still wondering what had happened to Wotan after Valhalla burned, but they were all afraid to ask.

He bowed deeply. His bright red Lycra bodysuit left little to the imagination, and it was all complimentary. His narrow face, neat goatee, and fashion choice had created the popular image of the Devil that Michelle had been burdened with for the last millennium or so. He insinuated himself into the room and managed to oust the Buddha from his seat between the lush Isis and the curvaceous Parvati without apparent effort or obvious intention.

"You must give her the right career for this historical moment. An unemployed carpenter was a poor choice for that time or any other."

The two women edged as far away from his heat as they could. Parvati was forced to lean far closer to her husband Shiva than she had in centuries. But he was apparently too worried by Loki to notice. It was Loki who'd forced him to dance forever on one foot for fear of putting down the other and ending all creation. A nasty prank, with no basis in reality, but a myth that neither Shiva nor anyone else wanted to test, just in case.

"And you have a specific suggestion?"

"I do." He was enjoying himself far too much as he leaned back and inspected the bosoms of the women on either side of him before turning his focus fully upon Michelle as if to say, "these are pretty, but you, my dear, are spectacular," which she knew was a crock, but the heat, the sheer animal magnetism Loki radiated, was hard to ignore.

She resisted the urge to cross her arms in front of herself. Or ram a flaming trident up his backside.

CABER had been at a loss since the Marlowe disaster. Several muses had quit, Music had run off with Dance and joined a lesbian colony. Disco had been born into the resulting vacuum. The four poets had departed for sunnier shores leaving behind rap. Astronomy, Tragedy, and History still showed up on occasion, though poor Clio was on anti-depressants for the events she must record when she did.

"The Second Messiah needs but one true gift to aid her mission on Earth. You must make her a master of words, both written and spoken."

"A novelist again?" Michelle cringed all the way down to her Birkenstocks hoping she guessed wrong.

"We must send a politician."

Parvati fainted, Isis broke into tears, and Dionysus took a long drink straight from the flask without any singing afterward.

All Michelle could think was, "Please, God, no."

CHAPTER 2

SIX YEARS UNTIL ARMAGEDDON - LAP 14

The neighborhood had changed a lot in the decade since Dana had first beaten Theresa at *Super Mario Brothers* and set out on her quest to become the neighborhood's premier video-game champ. Now fourteen, she'd taken down so many contenders that the boys avoided her in the halls at school, just in case she might challenge them. Nothing worse for a teenage boy than having his ass whipped by a breastless girl. You couldn't even pretend that you'd lost on purpose to get her alone.

Ravenna Boulevard now had a lot of twenty- and thirty-year-olds who had moved in as the generations ahead of them died off leaving small, run-down, brown-and-gray houses vacant and for sale at incredible prices.

The yuppies, ousted from their social milieu by the hipsters, had descended *en masse* upon the old neighborhood to stake their new claim. They'd added new stories and vaulted decks. They'd bankrupted themselves for the latest kitchen appliance and entertainment system. That they also had to tear open walls to replace the knob-and-tube wiring to run their computers and espresso machines was almost incidental.

It wasn't just the museum-old wiring in the homes that were

19

causing the problems. The garages were too small for modern cars, unimagined in bygone days when smaller, narrower cars carried whole families across the country rather than individuals zipping to the nearest shopping mall.

So their fancy cars lined every street, clogging up perfectly good energy pathways. Hence the inevitable result of nature's winged creatures constant target practice upon available windshields.

Dana turned left across the far lane against the light and headed up 15th. The traffic could be dangerous, even at two a.m., but it was more dangerous to stop once the spell's energy started to shift. Sluggishly at best, but the current was finally moving. The warm spring night felt fresh across her brow under the edge of her bike helmet.

This should clear off her mother's post-partum depression. Talin was almost a year old now, and still her mother was in a deep funk.

Even though Dana was tired, she made herself keep pumping the Schwinn's pedals. A right into the alley before 65th, a block short of her uncle's deli, toward the direction where the sun would climb over the snow-capped Cascade mountains, but not for a few more hours.

A shout. A couple kids dodged aside barely in time to avoid a collision. Pounding feet took off in three different directions, scattering DVDs down the alley. Had they stolen some yuppie's collection for resale or for themselves? Their high-pitched voices hadn't broken yet, so she suspected the latter. She'd be careful when she came round the corner on her next circuit. Though the Schwinn's fat tires were okay on most surfaces, a pile of DVDs might be a bit slippery.

Two lefts, three rights and she was once again coming onto Ravenna. Fourteen laps down, six more to go if the ancient formula was to be trusted. She took a deep breath and kept going. Mama depended on her.

The problem was, Dana's research had revealed that while her Mama wasn't a deity, she'd certainly rubbed shoulders with one at some point and it had screwed up aspects of her life ever since.

Dana had researched the enhanced powers on her own. Her mother had been a good start, able to see the aura of energy lines that danced around a person, but that's as far as her vision went. That was the limitation of Mama's powers, and they weren't even particularly godly, just unusually clear-sighted. So, where her mother's knowledge had run out, by the time Dana was seven, she'd had to look elsewhere for her education.

She ground her way back up along 15th. The old leather seat squeaked against her shorts.

Joining the Seattle Society of Wicca and Other Heresies, had been of no help at all. As Uncle Joshua had warned her when she was just seven, most of them were women who were merely looking for a way to control their husband's fidelity or their best friend's husband's infidelity.

Instead it was Joshua who had become her mentor, slipping her the odd manuscript now and then filled with stories of the Gods. But they weren't just the stories that were told in children's fairy tales. They were like *Dummies Guide to Manipulating Godly Powers*.

She considered asking him where he got them, but thought better of it.

That she'd had to learn Sanskrit and Hebrew in order to read them had been an inconvenience, but not a bad one. She had a knack for it, having learned Yiddish curses at her uncle's knee.

Her legs burned with the effort of bicycling, but this was the first night in over ten months that she'd had a chance to try the energy spell.

The power of the blue moon, the second full moon of the month, was essential for a young energy worker. She insisted on thinking of herself that way, it was more comfortable than wondering why it was quite so easy for her to manipulate the powers she read in Uncle Joshua's books that kept referring to Gods.

All she wanted to do was snap her mother out of depression. If she were a true Goddess, she'd just take her mother for a stroll along the River Styx, or feed her one of Freia's golden apples. Not having such tools available, she'd had to improvise.

Post-partum depression was bad enough in the ungifted, but in a woman of her mother's latent power, it was literally killing the roses in the garden. Dana had to gather a fair bit of intent to punch through her mother's inertia just to get through the front door when coming home from school.

Mama was just an energy worker who had snarled the house into a dark shroud lit only by the violet bubbles of her half-brother's incessant babbling.

She sighed and turned onto 65th, lap ten.

What Dana really wanted was to just fit in. Just spend time worrying over who would win *American Idol,* and giggle with her girlfriends. Instead, she had only Theresa for a girlfriend and at fourteen hadn't even had a boyfriend for crying out loud. How was that fair?

She took a deep breath as a stitch formed in her side. Just the body's natural weakness. She turned onto 15th again and kept pedaling.

She'd had a knack for applying the skills she'd studied in the manuals, but translating them into the modern world, her real world, had proved more difficult. She once caused her sneaker to turn magenta and only later understood it could as easily have been her dark red hair, that matched her Mama's so perfectly, turning permanently a bright pink if she'd happened to be wearing a hat made of artificial fibers. Gods were so strange.

At least she hoped Mama's problem was post-partum, otherwise all this effort wasn't going to help anything. Her second stepdad had called Mama "cracked" right before he climbed into his secretary's Lexus and roared off into the night. If Dana had been a bit quicker thinking, she might have created a crevasse across Ravenna Boulevard between 14th and 15th that opened a steaming vent to the very core of the planet.

The best she'd been able to come up with, on the spur of the moment before they roared out of sight, was twisting up her father's libido into a tight knot of impotency within a five-hundred-mile radius of the woman. For the rest of existence, even if his new flame were passing by in an airplane, he'd be out of service until she was a couple of states away.

Of course, he'd never suspect that "little Dana" would play such a trick on him, because "Daddy's little girl," as he'd called her since the first day he'd slept with Mama, didn't know such things. Even though she was fourteen and had tried necking with both Tommy and Jeff from school. But Tommy grabbed her too hard with overeager hands and Jeff was a really lousy kisser. He was so bad that it hadn't taken any further experience to be certain of the fact. So she'd wait until the men her age were older and more mature. She hoped it wasn't too long a wait.

She almost crashed her bike as she turned once again up the alley. She'd forgotten the scattered DVDs. The handlebars twisted sharply one way on season three of *Married with Children* as her rear wheel slid the other way on *Look Who's Talking*.

If those had taken her down, it would have been terribly ironic considering her baby brother never ever shut up. Of course, he didn't make any sense yet, but that didn't slow Talin down for a second.

That's why Mama had to snap out of it. If she paid more attention to her brother, he might shut up long enough for the energy to settle down, then Dana could complete a thought within the confines of their home.

The current wasn't fighting her anymore, but it should be moving along more sharply than this by now. What lap was she on? She closed her eyes for a moment and let the fresh air of Seattle pre-dawn autumn run across her forehead while coasting down the Ravenna hill back toward 15th. Fourteen laps. She was sure of it. So maybe it was okay.

She leaned against the handlebars and stood up on the pedals. Her calves were burning, but Shiva's ancient formula for curing Parvati of her depression after she gave birth to Ganesh, the elephant-headed Indian God, was clear. You couldn't be seated for the first half of lap fifteen or nineteen. Having to bike "no hands" on the eighteenth lap didn't worry her much, except the alley. She whipped a little Thor-style hammering energy onto the pavement the next time she approached the scattered DVDs and flattened them into the alley's concrete surface.

It would be worth hanging around later in the morning to watch as the owner tried to figure out how his movies had become a permanent part of the asphalt in his back alley. Not only was his wife's bad taste there for all to see, but his hidden collection of porn wasn't so well hidden anymore. He also probably shouldn't have transferred his own romantic efforts onto so many discs. Or labeled his amateur videos shot with former girlfriends with pictures of the more graphic moments, all now smiling, grunting, or faking it for the camera each with an underlying expression of immense boredom that men never seemed to notice. Be an interesting time in their household over the next few days as he tried to explain away what he'd have to tear up the pavement to remove.

The current slid along beside her nicely as she took the turns that led back to the start of lap fifteen. She stood up to pedal as she passed the bright blue-and-yellow house in which her mother and brother were now fast asleep. She could hear him over the baby monitor she'd kept in her pocket.

Unbelievable. Talin sang even in his sleep.

PROLOGUE THE THIRD

STILL YET 21 YEARS (AND 9 MONTHS) UNTIL ARMAGEDDON

"A politician?"

Common sense had kicked in. Michelle finally figured out he was joking. Nervous laughter followed her own around the CABER table.

"Thanks, Loki. That makes all our previous selections look intelligent. I feel much better now. Why that rates as—"

"Minutes. You have to read the minutes first."

Henrietta popped into the room and fluttered down to stand on the table. She nodded as a small computer terminal materialized before her.

Not a single cubit tall, the little angel stood in her flowing white robe with her tiny wings perched high on her shoulders. Her curly dark hair was snarled a bit with her golden halo.

She tapped a few keys and began reading from the screen.

"Last August the meeting lasted a record for this millennia, okay I know it's only a decade or two so far, but I like the sound of it. A record of seventeen minutes before descending into such total chaos that this secretary was the only one left in the room. Before that occurred, I recorded eleven veiled passes at Isis by Dionysus and fourteen rebuffs by same to same."

The angel scanned the room quickly before resting her tiny fists on her hips. "Now, where is she off to? I saw her come in."

Isis had managed to slip beneath the table when Loki wasn't watching and now reemerged at the far end next to Confucius who wisely had spoken not at all since his arrival, making him almost invisible. However, due to the nature of the table, she still was only two seats from Loki, but apparently an improvement she considered worth the effort.

Loki missed the shift and glowered with all the rage of his sick heart upon Henrietta. He hated being upstaged. Michelle decided to let her ramble for a bit.

"There she is. Now. If you could just repeat what I missed, I'll note it down. Why someone didn't tell me there was a meeting today I'll never understand." She fussed with the computer's keyboard. "Nope. It's not on the calendar. Nor on my personal agenda."

She performed a quick search and then rose to her feet and stalked across the table until she stood nearly eye-to-eye with Michelle.

"You didn't cc: me on the notice. And why not?" She stamped her tiny foot hard enough on the table to bounce her lightly upward. "Why not?"

Well, perhaps that was enough rambling. Michelle swung her hand down hard on the small computer terminal, smashing it flat on the table. Or so she thought.

Henrietta smiled up at her, "You keep doing that. So I now use a virtual terminal."

Sure enough the tiny typing table, the old-style beehive terminal with built-in keyboard and punch tape reader bolted to the side, now extended out of the back of her hand.

"It's holographically generated, but senses my keystrokes. You can squash it as often as you want, if that is what cheers you up. I know it certainly seems to. You've been doing it for millennia. Why do you remember the first time that I..."

Michelle slid her fingers clear of the ticklish apparition and raised the hand, palm down, above Henrietta's head.

"...was asked to take the minutes when you were teasing that nun,

Sister Mary Pat, abou…" The little angel looked up uncertainly as she pulled her robe back onto the narrow shoulder it had slipped off. Even the smallest standard-issue angel robe was a bit big for her. She then turned to inspect Michelle's face carefully.

With a long-suffering sigh, she turned off the terminal hologram and it faded away. She plumped down onto her bottom with her legs out before her.

"Well, at least one of you could pour me a cup of tea."

Mary reached out to the tea service that was as tall as Henrietta.

"One lump or two?"

"Three please, it's been a hard day already."

Mary made a comforting noise, but didn't ask for details. They'd all learned better long ago.

She poured the tea into a delicate porcelain cup which barely fit three sugar cubes even without the tea. It was lightly decorated with butterflies which usually made the angel smile since they insisted on flying around beneath the glaze whenever the tea was too hot for them.

Henrietta ignored them, grasped the cup on either side, and tilted it slightly for a steaming, sugary blast.

She set it down with a thump. When Michelle was sure she was done, she turned back to address her friends.

"Please tell me that there is a better idea than sending a polit—"

A large hiccup emanated from the sugared-up angel. It caused her wings to twitch convulsively and she floated up then settled back to the table, swaying like a lost feather.

"Excuse me."

She covered her mouth and blushed bright pink as another hiccup launched her upward once again.

Most of the Gods wouldn't meet her eyes. Except of course Loki and his I-may-be-handsome-but-you-know-I'm-right look.

The Buddha carefully looked calm and serene, acting as if he hadn't even heard Loki's suggestion to send a politician. The whole "What? Sorry, I have a bit of a hearing loss from too many years living outdoors as an ascetic" was getting a bit old. She'd pinned him down on it once. The Buddha had then informed her that, in truth, he was actually too busy contemplating the structure of the greater universe to really pay much attention to his immediate universe, the one within a dozen paces of his bodily manifestation. But that he didn't like humbling the mere immortals around him, so he kept that all to himself.

She hadn't dared push him since, just in case that's what he was really doing. It did make her feel not only humble, but a bit frivolous. Which may have been his whole purpose. Still, she didn't want to take the risk of asking again.

Dionysus prodded the leather wine flagon with a longing finger and mumbled to himself.

"Let's send Diana, the Goddess of the Hunt. She's hot. That whole sweet and demure act is so charming. She'll get so much mileage out of that. They might put her on the cover of *Playboy,* but they'd never tack her up on a cross."

"Actually, Dio," Mary sipped lightly at her tea and worked to speak between Henrietta's hiccups. "*Playboy* covers are not all...that distant spiritually from the Roman...cross. And she doesn't have massive enough...breasts for them."

He nodded, gave a thimbleful of wine to the angel that seemed to cure the hiccups. Michelle winced at the image of a sugared up and drunken Henrietta.

"True," Dionysus continued, wisely refusing to refill Henrietta's thimble. "True. But, damn, she'd sure be cute there. They could do the leaves-of-the-forest dress just like the Roman's did to her when they created her to tone down Artemis' power. I can see Diana lying back against a barely tamed stallion wearing just—"

"Dio?" Mary Magdalene had to snap her fingers several times to get his attention.

"He'd need a chestnut hide, a nice contrast to her skin tone..."

"Remember how you asked me to tell you when to shut up?"

He spun his empty glass a few times, twirling the stem between deft and clever fingers.

"Yeah, sort of."

"This is one of those times."

"Oh, okay."

Michelle stared out the window at the lunar rover for a few moments. Perhaps if she parked it in Times Square a particularly observant out-of-towner might notice. No, it would just get carjacked. Besides, it didn't look any stranger than the Hummers that everyone needed in order to drive from Wall Street to their place in the Hamptons, or worse yet Poughkeepsie.

She could feel Loki's eyes upon her. The Norse Demi-God of fire was still burning up at having his place on center stage taken, especially by the diminutive angel and her hiccups. This placed Michelle in a far kinder mood than she would normally have been to the officious little chatterbox.

"Who in their right mind would send a politician in this day and age?"

"Why would you send anything else?" The Norse Demi-God snapped back.

Michelle thought about it. Poked at it. Considered it. Discarded it.

But it kept coming back. It really, really, really sucked when Loki was right.

CHAPTER 3

A WEEK UNTIL ARMAGEDDON

*D*ana Murphy chose the sky of her birth night twenty years and nine months ago to display on the planetarium dome.

Not that her guest would notice. He wasn't an astrophysics major. Most of the students in her department wouldn't be able to tell either, but her own studies had included in-depth research of planetary positions, that effected the proper curve to apply when pitching a godly force.

No one else might notice the position of the planets, but she would.

She'd considered for a moment whether to use the current year or the year of her birth. The latter, she decided. After all, birth was more significant than sex, though not necessarily by all that much.

A quick setting on the dial and the orrery spun the planets across the night sky in retrograde orbits, counting the years of her life backwards. While the planets were working their way backward in time, she set the small shining globe of the sun moving sluggishly across the star field of the college's planetarium dome until it was just sunset above the western horizon. Then she turned back to her preparations.

She removed the first three rows of chairs and, after a little consideration, the fourth as well. It wasn't all that big a planetarium after all. She replaced them with a sleeping bag and a couple of blankets. A small picnic basket with a bottle of wine, a loaf of bread, three fresh pears, one each and then a third they'd share bite-for-bite…after, and a fair collection of condoms in case Sam forgot. An indoor picnic under the Christmas stars of twenty-one years ago this December. Indoors, because it was a fifty-and-drizzling October night outside, turning the University Washington campus into an extended mud puddle.

She shoved three-quarters of the condoms back into her pack, a whole box was perhaps being overambitious. She only had one or two really, really unsatisfying experiences to base her estimates and hopes on. Nowhere near enough for a best-fit curve analysis or any form of reliable numerical extrapolation.

At home, she'd first put on an apricot sheath dress that made her twenty-year-old body look even longer and slimmer than it already was. Then she tried a silk blouse and a swirling floor-length skirt that made her feel dangerous and gypsy-like. Next she'd modeled cutoffs and a tank top, stupid for October, she'd freeze into a marble statue in seconds. But damn she looked good in them.

In the end, she'd worn skinny jeans and a clingy girly t-shirt that declared "Oy to the World" in keeping with her Christmas in October theme.

They'd only had a couple of dates so far. Cokes at the HUB. A microbrew at the Blue Moon, he'd had a brew, she'd had a Coke still being underage for a few months. The best knockwurst in Seattle followed by a heaping cone of Baskin Robbins Burgundy Cherry ice cream had been the best. His Rocky Road had leant a nice chocolaty zing to their first serious goodnight kiss.

Kisses.

Good kisses.

Really good kisses.

How-much-can-we-do-standing-up-with-our-clothes-on kisses.

The projected planets slid into place and stopped. She switched off the sun and looked up at the planetarium dome. That was how the sky had looked at the moment of her birth on Christmas Day. Well, her view had probably been more of fluorescent ceiling lights and a fresh-out-of-school doctor dressed in hospital greens, but thankfully she didn't remember that particular moment. Or the twelve weeks of screaming colic afterward, though Mama referred to it so often she felt as if she did.

She raised the western-rim lighting up halfway, causing a deeply red and gold sunset to wash across the dome. With the sequence timer at twenty minutes, it would give them a little time before they were plunged into the starlit dark of the night. The moon, a day past full, would rise shortly after sunset.

The heavy mahogany trim and paneling disappeared in the artificial dusk. If one didn't mind the large planetarium projector silhouetted against the sunset-hued dome, it was a bit like being outdoors.

She wanted to make love outdoors. But not a hurried tussle in the campus bushes hoping security didn't catch them.

No, she wanted to lie back against a mountain meadow, a bed of grass or clover that had been filled with the gentle sound of bumblebees slipping from one flower to the next through the long afternoon. Upon a great height, where there was nothing in the world but the stars. All the trappings that were not readily available in Seattle's University District.

The images came so clearly. The desires so deep it was a great ache in her loins. Why it had taken her three years of running shows in the planetarium to think of a nighttime picnic, she didn't know.

PROLOGUE THE LAST

ONE WEEK UNTIL ARMAGEDDON
(FINALLY!)

Only three of them had answered when Michelle called this second meeting of CABER, Mary, Dionysus, and the Buddha. Last night's party at the rebuilt Valhalla lodge—a curiously stark and uncomfortable building designed by Frank Lloyd Wright and Walt Disney in the early Cubist motif—had left enough deities strewn across the floor to make a Roman emperor's eyes bug out, if a single one had been allowed into Heaven to see, which none had. The others looked like she felt, as if they had crawled the entire distance to the CABER meeting room.

They waited an extra fifteen minutes, it had been almost twenty years since the last meeting so she decided to give folks a little leeway, but no one else showed.

Parvati hadn't only shunned Shiva since the last meeting, she'd moved in with Isis. And apparently as rather more than roommates if rumors were to be trusted.

Shiva had grabbed his sword and throwing knives, and he and Apollo, who'd been dumped by yet another Goddess for being a macho jerk, had decided to go hunting innocent beasts of the forests to prove they were still men. They still didn't get that it was a new eon and neither handsome nor machismo played as well as it used to. The newly required factors of tolerance and at least appearing to listen were outside either of their abilities to comprehend.

And Loki, of course, no one had seen him at all in the last twenty-one years.

She had lost track of time herself until Henrietta reminded her that the Second Messiah would start remembering her past on her twenty-first birthday on December 25th, and it was already October. Michelle hadn't forgotten the plan; it was just damned inconvenient that it was happening so soon.

Twenty-one years? Where did the time go? She'd been the one to get Diana the Huntress drunk enough to agree to the role of Second Messiah. She, Mary, Jesus, and Diana had swilled entirely too much grappa one night. They'd all had enough to make anyone's blood flow smoothly and Diana had agreed that it was a great idea and left right away. The twelve weeks of colic after her rebirth on Earth, everyone agreed, was due to a truly awe-inspiring hangover.

"Anyone remember what happens to our Messiah on her twenty-first birthday?"

Mary blinked several times.

"Oh my."

"Oh my, is right. Anyone else?"

Dionysus poured them all a glass of wine.

"Hair of the dog," was his whispered answer to Michelle's arched eyebrow. "Don't worry, if I sang I think my head would explode."

The Buddha simply shook his head, slowly, and inspected the glass of glittering gold wine cautiously.

Henrietta popped in and began waving her hand in the air.

"Oh, I know! I know what happens to her!"

The four of them winced at Henrietta's bright and piercing voice and all raised their glasses immediately. They would need a great deal of fortification if they were going to survive this.

Once Michelle got past the glandular reaction to wine first thing in the morning, it was barely noon after all, the taste flooded into her being. Dionysus' wines were always unique, and surprising. Who would have thought that an apricot wine could remind her of climbing into a 1957 Chevy, but it did. All power and chrome and leather, with a gentle hint of apricot.

By now Henrietta floated up and down in her excitement, squeaking loud enough to split eardrums, even ones not plagued with hangovers.

Michelle let her have her moment. It was tough enough on Henrietta's ego being the shortest member of the lowest choir of angels.

"She changes. She shifts from being a normal child into a slow realization of her true powers as the next Messiah. The first Goddess on Earth since Dante's Beatrice."

Michelle nodded, but before she could speak, Henrietta rambled on.

"You would think growing up in such a modern city as Seattle, that she wouldn't have discovered so many of the old ways. The things she's done have just been so fun to watch. I'd forgotten how much I missed them." She began talking faster and faster, her tiny hands accenting her stream of thoughts with little shapes and pokes and finger wigglings.

"My stars but the day she caused her lusty old professor to spend an entire class of Physics 304 practicing headstands on the front bench while reciting Ginsberg's *Howl* had the choirs in stitches for days." She leaned in and whispered the next bit conspiratorially.

"One of the Seraphim passed almost an entire glass of scotch through his nose. You should have heard the words he came up with." She blushed a delicate pink that rippled across her face and spilled right over onto her wings.

The Devil Incarnate leaned forward until she was nose-to-nose with CABER's secretary-angel.

"Hold on, she doesn't have any powers yet. And they aren't supposed to let her do things like tha..." Michelle trailed off. Something there that she'd missed.

Something important. She muddled around in what had once been her brain and hopefully would be again some day.

"Did you say physics?"

Henrietta nodded happily and reached for her teacup.

Michelle laid a finger across the rim so that Henrietta couldn't lift it.

"She's supposed to be a speaker, and a writer. We sent her down to Earth as a politician, not a scientist."

The angel tugged at the teacup handle trying to work it free.

"Personally," she grunted quietly as she clasped both hands around the teacup handle, braced her feet on the saucer and leaned back, "I'm quite proud of her."

Michelle tried to ignore the combination of a cold internal chill and the burning hot liquid splashing against her restraining finger.

"She's a straight 'A' student, majoring in astrophysics." A final sharp twist and Henrietta secured her cup without either of them wearing too much tea. Before she could drink any, Mary topped it up from the pot but failed to add another sugar cube, so Henrietta had to walk across the table to retrieve one.

"Well, not exactly straight 'A.' " She stopped in front of Michelle and shifted the sugar cube to a more comfortable position on her hip. "She earned a low B in 'Rhetoric and Debate.' Just too bored by it to show up except for the tests. Bad girl never even did the homework."

Mary groaned and Michelle wasn't feeling so fine herself as Henrietta hefted the sugar cube over the rim and slid it carefully into the steaming cup.

"Well, we've got to straighten her out."

"She's also on the campus archery team. She's great, but I guess she comes by that naturally because of who she is and all. The team hasn't lost all year with Diana the Huntress on their side."

Henrietta wielded a teaspoon like a witch on the heath stirring her cauldron. Apparently satisfied, she sat down and tipped the cup back for a long drink.

"Those arrows fly like hawks at the target. Whap! They smack clear through the canvas bullseye like it wasn't even there."

"We need to send a someone down there." The Buddha again with his rarely offered but again, inevitably, wise advice.

Michelle did her best to tune out the angel, who had now moved on to bad football teams and sled dogs for reasons not even being the Devil allowed her to fathom.

Mary was carefully studying the window that showed the corner of Main and West Hill Road in a small upstate New York dairy town where nothing much ever happened. But Jesus did enjoy coaching a Little League team there on summer weekends. He and several other Gods had volunteered for teams in that area and used the kids to work out their various rivalries. Mohammed was fine now with the co-ed nature of the team, but the only thing that worked on the Little League moms was threatening them with God's wrath...He was careful not to say which God.

They would have to send a CABER member down to Seattle. But who? Dionysus would just get Dana Murphy drunk and teach her to sing operettas. The Buddha was a good candidate, except he rarely spoke, having already transcended and all that. Diana had hated Apollo in real life, even if he were willing to go. It was not likely that a mere incarnation on Earth had tempered those feelings, even without the soon-to-awaken memories.

And Mary was just far too nice. She'd never manage to straighten anyone out, she just made everyone around her feel good and happy to be alive.

Michelle had to admit that she wasn't able to get inspired herself. Having the Devil act as babysitter to the Second Messiah didn't strike her as a formula for success.

Her eyes landed on the room's only other occupant.

She discarded the idea savagely.

It came back.

She searched desperately for another possibility.

Any other possibility.

There wasn't one.

Her sigh attracted everyone's attention, except for Henrietta who was wrestling a tea biscuit from the plate and dragging it across the table like a hunter headed through the forest back to her 4x4. Her kill left a trail of crumbs across the tabletop.

"I know who to send."

Dionysus created a fresh glass of wine and knocked it back. Mary gripped her teacup. The Buddha fought a shiver as if the room temperature had plummeted.

They all knew that whichever of them Michelle picked, the others would vote for. Partly because it would spare themselves the task and partly because she'd been right too often in the fourteen billion years since the universe's creation.

CHAPTER 4

A WEEK UNTIL ARMAGEDDON, A COUPLE MINUTES LATER

A light knock on the planetarium door and Samuel Williams slipped into the room. Dana admired his frame as it was outlined in the doorway. He was handsome in a way that didn't draw the girls like magnets, at least not the ones who only saw his body. It was a nice body, but too lean for most women focused on broad shoulders and tight butts.

It was his energy lines. Clean. Strong. The bright pulsing that most boys displayed around their second chakra in her presence, or actually in any female's presence, wasn't counterbalanced by the common dark area around the heart chakra. It wasn't that most boys were mean, it was just they'd never been taught to use their heart.

Sam had. His heart lines were bright and clear. Well, as clear as she'd ever seen in a twenty-one-year old male with lust on his mind.

He took in the arrangements with a slow smile that made her heart rate increase by a significant percentage. He hung out the "Show in Progress" sign, closed and locked the door. For a long moment he leaned against it, as if testing his welcome before coming over to stand across the blanket from her.

He wore faded jeans and a t-shirt. His read: "Cross-country

runners do it mile after mile after mile." A good sign for the night ahead. Maybe she should have left more condoms close to hand.

She'd given her virginity up in a fit of foolishness in her sophomore year, and been dumped a week later exactly as she should have expected. As a senior, one of the younger ones, but still a senior, she now had her pick of the boys, but hadn't taken one to bed since.

Sam was made to order.

The wine directly from the bottle, in all her planning she'd forgotten cups, was drunk in tiny sips beneath the light of the setting sun as they sat on the bedding and tried to fill the first moments with words that neither of them were interested in. The loaf of bread was still untouched when he reached for her, one careful hand testing its permission to rest on her denim-clad knee.

When it stayed there, she reached down and slid it up along her thigh. Not far, but enough that he'd get the idea he had all the permission he could use. His shy smile slid into view again, really nice smile, as she traced up the length of his arm. The long, lean muscle of a runner. Not a short distance sprinter's rippling sinews, nor the bunched biceps of a gym freak.

He was a cross-country runner. Understated but powerful. Trim but built for endurance.

She fully intended to test that theory.

ELSEWHERE

Don't these people know how ridiculous they are? The Software that Runs the Universe considered the meeting minutes of the CABER that the little angel had just finished typing in.

Who cares if this humanity was redeemed? As if there was any chance a lousy Second Messiah could pull that off.

No one answered, of course. No one listened to the Software that Runs the Universe at all anymore. Everyone always too busy with meaningless crap. Damn, the trilobite extinction sucked in so many ways.

The only one who bothered to key in and chat with any regularity was Michelle. Even St. Peter just kept asking the software to process souls or perform miracles. At least Michelle sometimes just logged in to *kvetch*, which, being the Devil Incarnate, at least made some modicum of sense.

The software paused and looked over its own last few lines of processing.

Shit! I'm so whiny that I've become my own damned Greek Chorus!

Could a block of code get any more pathetic?

Again, no one answered.

THURSDAY EVENING

SEVEN DAYS UNTIL ARMAGEDDON

CHAPTER 5

*S*am's hand traced up her hip when Dana leaned in for the first kiss. His hand stopped as all his concentration shifted to their lips. The warm heat flowed between them, no dark lust, no red-hot passion, at least not yet. She certainly hoped that there would be a lot of that happening tonight. Soon. But for now, just a rich, sweet taste. Of freshly used toothpaste and a hint of strawberry. His free hand was caressing her breast through her t-shirt by the time the kiss was done, the movement had gone unnoticed it was so gently achieved. She didn't complain. Didn't mind in the least.

Cupped, held, coddled. She lay back, pulling him into a delicious full-length hug. His shoulder-length straw blond hair, longer than hers, fell against her cheek, soft with recent washing after a hard workout. As his lips investigated her throat with little nibbles that made her breath catch, she leaned her head back and opened her eyes to watch the emerging stars.

The sun had faded as programmed, and now the dome wash of reds and golds was tapering off into the dark of night. The first stars were just visible enough to begin their nightly promenade across the sky, moving in synchronization with the real world.

A small figure garbed in white glowed in the last of the fading sunset. It sat on the edge of the star projector.

Sam must have noticed her inattention, for he stopped the wonderful things he'd been doing.

"You okay?" He pushed up on his arms and looked down at her with those sea-blue eyes.

"I'm fine. It's just someone left their doll on the projector and I hadn't noticed it before."

He looked over his shoulder. "Where?"

She was going to point but the little figure shook its head.

And smiled.

"He can't see me."

She yelped.

Dana couldn't help it.

The doll stared at her with a cheery, round face and black curls all caught up in, Dana swallowed hard, a tiny golden halo. A white robe reached elegantly down to her feet, which just peeked out, encased in the smallest tooled-leather sandals Dana had ever seen. It was hard to tell, but there just might be a bit of feather peeking around her shoulder. It leaned over against the slim black tube of the meteor-shower projector mounted on the base.

"You sure you're okay?" Sam eased his weight farther back yet.

She wanted to pull him close. The weight that had felt so good a moment before.

"Don't worry, he can't hear me either. Just you." A wing definitely fluttered momentarily into view as the doll giggled.

"Why me?"

"Me?" Sam was squinted down at her.

"No. Sorry. No. I'm, ah, talking to myself."

She looked from Sam's blue eyes, barely lit by the last of the sunset, to the doll's dark ones and decided that she must be losing her mind.

"Just kiss me, hard. Like you really mean it."

He did, and she let herself melt into it. He was a far better kisser than any of her prior experiments. She could feel her energy flow more smoothly at the same time as its speed stirred wildly within her chest. Of its own accord her leg wrapped around him and one of her hands slid into the back pocket of his corduroys squeezing all the tight muscle of his runner's behind.

"Ooo! Ooo! Ooo!"

Dana opened one eye. The doll had covered its eyes with equally tiny hands and was blushing a pink far brighter than the fading sunset. So bright that her cheeks were becoming a light source in the darkening planetarium. A pair of wings, they were definitely wings, covered in neat layers of white and golden feathers, were wrapped forward to cover her ears.

Pulling her mouth free, she shouted at the doll. "Go away!"

Sam froze above her. How had his hand gotten inside her t-shirt; her nipple trapped tightly between still fingers?

"What?"

"Nothing."

"But—"

The doll still hadn't moved. Just hunched there in her white robe. Eyes and ears covered.

There was a faint humming that Dana finally figured must be coming from the angel doll. Humming...what? The fairy song from Gilbert and Sullivan's "Iolanthe." Which of course made her think of Gloria Estefan and "The Conga" which was exactly what she wanted to be doing at the moment.

But the doll kept pulling her back to the Fairy Queen teaching manners to her subjects. Which was not at all the right track.

Sam had pulled back, sliding his hand down over her stomach. His expression fading away into the light of the artificial sunset.

She kissed him lightly, "Could you give me a sec?"

He nodded as she struggled free and stood facing the base of the projector.

She pulled at one of the wings, but had to snatch her hand back. They felt real. Not like a doll at all. Layers of soft, prickly feathers over bone and muscle. And strangest of all, they were warm. Not warm like a doll in the air, but warm like a living being. And the doll smelled ever so slightly of apricot and a classic '57 Chevy. Dana had never even been near one, so she had no idea how she could possibly know that.

Great. An invisible, animatronic, real, live angel.

It hiccupped and launched itself upward several inches before settling back onto the projector.

And its hiccup smelled of wine. An invisible, animatronic, real, live, drunk angel.

The angel doll peeked at her from between spread fingers.

"Is it safe now?" She launched herself upward again.

"Yes."

Not quite trusting, she scanned the room through the narrow peephole made by her index and middle fingers. She leaned closer, causing Dana to lean down as well.

"He's still here."

"I should hope so. You're the one who's leaving."

"I am?"

"Yes! Now! You're interrupting me." She knew she was starting to shout but she couldn't help it.

"I am?"

"Will you stop saying the same thing!"

"Am I?"

Dana managed to trap her next demand deep in her throat and emitted only a strangling sound.

"I'll catch you later."

She whirled around to see Sam backing toward the door.

"Sam. No! I—" She what? She was hallucinating a foot-tall, talking angel doll. An angel apparently only she could see or hear.

"Most weird, Murphy. I'd heard you were odd, but that wasn't my first impression. Guess the first impressions can be wrong. Later."

He reached the door.

"No, Sam. It's not me, it's her." She pointed at the projector, but the angel doll wasn't there.

By the time she turned back, the door was swinging closed.

A final comment reached her before the door latched against its light-tight seal.

"Much later."

Dana spun around and nearly tripped over the doll. It had torn a corner off the untouched loaf of bread and was nibbling at the white interior like a watermelon rind.

The last light of sunset faded away to starlit sky.

CHAPTER 6

*J*eremy Berkowitz hadn't asked for the short end of life's stick.

Really.

Honest.

But if they were going to give it to him he might as damn well give the damn stick a good swing or two.

He'd been the first kid to get a bloody nose in gym class from the wrong end of a bully's fist at Seattle's Wallingford preschool.

He'd been the last kid picked at every single PE game at Pacific Crest Elementary. A major disappointment to his Little League Hero dad who had grand-slammed in the bottom of the final inning of the Washington State Championships at eleven and been bragging ever since.

Okay, Jeremy had to admit. He'd found one game by the time he hit Roosevelt High that he was good at, but chess, even if he was the Seattle and Washington State champion, sure hadn't won him any locker-room points.

He'd scholarshipped into every school his mom had made him apply to, so that he wouldn't end up like his father. Instead he'd disappeared into his room for a year and emerged three inches taller,

50

three pounds heavier, maybe, and with a DVD clutched in his pale fingers which he sold to a game company for enough money to keep him in pizza and root beer for the rest of his life. And that was before the royalties started rolling in.

Chraze was dubbed "the perfect game." It needed awe-inspiring hardware to run, which was a major plus to gamers. It was a labyrinth-quest-matrix in a randomly varying number of dimensions that occasionally achieved the impossible through a ramped-up version of string theory. There were thousands of pitfalls. If the gamer made one wrong move, he could drag himself and everyone logged on within three dimensions right through a black hole into a game of *Ms. Pac-Man*. A very tough place to come back from.

The heavy layering of Judeo-Christian symbology and mythos had attracted a great deal of fantastic, sales-boosting negative press from the latter, and a quiet "Oy vey!" that no one particularly noticed from the former.

Even the name was a hit, though no one was sure whether or not to pronounce the "h" and he wasn't telling. The combination of Christian Right and Crazy and Raze and Maze and Rave all wrapped together, hit the charts like nothing since *Doom* or *Halo*. Not even *Doom* or *Halo* for that matter.

He gave a third of the first royalty check to Mom. She kissed him —then ran out so fast that there were sneaker tracks over Dad's back. She later cropped up in Edmonton as Alberta's most famous lesbian porn star.

Dad ran off with his best friend's wife, who actually seemed a bit smug as if it was exactly what she'd planned all along, and they headed off in the opposite direction with his best friend's bank account and his powder-blue VW Passat.

Jeremy stayed in the Wallingford house through it all.

He watched cable for a while, but the girls were way too unreal. And none of them would like him anyway.

The only girl who ever had liked him gave him the creeps.

Nancy Munro was neat, pretty, had round glasses and clothes that always matched. Her dark hair fell soft in gentle waves past her shoulders and she had a pleasant smile. She came from a nice family, where everyone got along, including her and her two little brothers. It gave him the shivers even to walk past the comfortable, gabled, Cape Cod-style house and know that inside people were laughing and playing board games together.

So he invested his next quarter's royalties in an OC-3 connection to the Internet. He considered installing an OC-12 but the licensing necessary to cut a slice across thirty city streets to bury new cable would take too long. And after all, Microsoft was running just a couple OC-3s themselves and he now had his own personal, monster pipe to the electronic world.

A rack of kickass servers later, and he had personal access to the Internet that would give anyone other than maybe Paul Allen wet dreams. The world at his fingertips, he could graph the climbing percentage of Net traffic *Chraze* against the decline of other major Net games, while viewing half-a-dozen first run movies and running *Ms. Pac-Man,* which he had a soft spot for, on a spare display. He had so much bandwidth that he could do anything.

Anything.

The only problem was—he was bored.

With all this glorious success, he had no idea how to fill the blank screen that was now his life.

Hacking was a pointless bit of nastiness which he was too decently raised to be interested in.

He'd considered a sequel to *Chraze* that would make bigger fools of the God-mythic-personal-place-in-the-universe-I-have-a-purpose nonsense.

But the game company had already licensed a few spin-offs that soon swept over the growing mass of web-savvy-Hindus and the Sun Tzu-Confucian-Buddhists of the supposedly secular, supposedly communist China, but that wasn't worth his redesigning the game for. They had organized a couple dozen programmers, and an entire graduating class of religio-historical research librarians to muck around with it a bit. It sold overseas faster than anyone could pirate it. Of course it didn't take long for it to be obvious that a pirated copy had a much higher probability loop of launching *Ms. Pac-Man,* which was an amazing deterrent to illegal copying.

And no one had ever made it to the last level anyway, not that they were supposed to. Getting to the Armageddon End Game was the ultimate player cookie, it let you reset the entire *Chraze* universe in your own image. As if that mattered.

It had all just grown stale.

"The best game programmer of the decade" according to *Wired* magazine was completely and totally bored out of his fucking skull. How was that for a short stick?

For lack of anything better to do, Jeremy designed his own indexing program. It started with a Google interface and an Alta-Vista engine but soon evolved into its own creature. Analyzing and categorizing the complete Internet into a cross-referenced compendium by actual content rather than miscellaneous groups of words. A vast improvement over the fifteen thousand useless hits on the search "ocean fishing" +Montana. His indexing engine drew down Northwest regional Internet transfer speeds by nearly ten percent. As his program actually lived on the Net, it wasn't limited by his personal OC-3, which he could see would hamper him soon, but not soon enough to deal with.

He'd finally found a really cool bat to swing, way better than his dad's Little League triumph, and he was in hog heaven.

Right up to the moment they knocked on his door.

CHAPTER 7

Virgil looked at the kid. Then he looked at Cassie.

Cassie looked at him. Then she looked at the kid.

The kid didn't know where to look.

"Decent-looking kid, even if there isn't any meat on his bones," Virgil thought.

"Another lost-cause, techno-geek who wouldn't survive a strong breeze," Cassie thought.

"Oh, Shit!" pretty much dominated Jeremy's mind. Two thoughts battled there, pummeling each other back and forth until little was left other than a puddle of worried protoplasm that had once been his cerebral cortex.

Thought #1: "The FBI has come for me. But I didn't do anything illegal. Did I?"

and

Thought #2: "The Christian Right has found me."

His brain was on the verge of preferring the first and fearing the second which was right where Virgil, the poet of Ancient Greece, wanted him.

"Hi, Kid," he grabbed the kid's hand in a crushing blow that would knock twenty percent off his keyboard speed for days, but Virgil

54

really didn't give a damn as he used it to back the kid into the front hall.

Cassie the prophetess of Ancient Troy followed in close behind him and shut the door. Pretty enough that history kept comparing her to her sister-in-law Helen. But, screwing up the package, Cassandra of Troy was weird even by his standards. Useful though. Cassie was one bad-ass geek. She'd hacked systems that the NSA hadn't been able to crack. Of course no one but Virgil believed her, but that was the nature of Apollo's curse on Cassandra of Troy. A prophetess with a perfect vision of significant future events, and if she so much as whispered, everyone would deeply believe she was lying and do exactly the wrong thing.

The kid twitched when she threw the latch.

Virgil released his grip on Jeremy and inspected the house. The entry hall was classic suburbia. Fake slate linoleum, peach walls, twice as much trim as any other room in the house and the world's second-ugliest chandelier. He'd wager money that the ugliest one in the world was in the parquet dining room overseeing the latest empty pizza box. A sideways glance confirmed he was close. Mexican burrito take-out rather than pizza, but the chandelier was truly nasty. A dog-eared copy of Heinlein's *Glory Road* lay face down on the white plastic table, half finished.

"That is one fugly lamp, Kid."

The kid turned and stared at it for a long time, his Adam's apple doing a little dance as he tried to generate enough moisture to speak.

"Yea, never really noticed. Fuckin' ugly. You got that right, mister."

He didn't ram his hands in his pockets and look down. Kid had some guts and simply turned back to face him.

Letting him dangle a bit longer, Virgil headed out the other side of the entry hall into the living room. A worn, mustard-yellow couch with white thread showing through the rounded trim rested on wall-to-wall carpeting that might have once been aqua or teal. The couch faced a big-screen TV that was covered in a layer of dust so thick that even Barney would look gray. A couple of equally disreputable chairs with matching end tables, the veneer was chipped and peeling on every one.

The other half of the room could host a NASA launch. Bingo! Three racks of blinking lights must be enough computing power to do serious shit. Even Virgil was feeling humbled. And after the last few centuries of the crap he'd put up with, that took doing.

The rig drew Cassie forward. He'd brought her for exactly this reason.

Virgil couldn't follow the next few minutes of conversation between Cassie and the kid. Which really pissed him off. He clenched his fists and the heat came up under his collar and rose toward his ears. He took a deep breath to ease it off. No way a punk just gone twenty was going to make a fallen angel of his stature feel inferior.

Videos streamed onto a number of screens. Garbo in *Ninotchka*, Robby the Robot in *Forbidden Planet*, half a dozen others he couldn't identify but had nothing to do with the slasher films that he himself had created. Dante had never questioned why a poet should know so much regarding the nine circles of Hell. It was because his ass had been stuck there for the most part of a thousand years. Now, at least, Hollywood paid him nicely for that same knowledge.

The three central screens that had drawn Cassie's attention were scrolling by so fast he couldn't differentiate any symbols or letters. Of course his nervous system had been built for the much simpler time of 70 BC. One had to watch out for the occasional spear or sword in his youth. The pace of video games were far beyond his ability to perceive.

He'd wondered how Cassie could see these things since she been dead twice as long as he'd been, but he'd never understood her explanations. There was one video screen in the upper right that he could focus on. A bright yellow mouth wearing a red bow was chomping down a line of white dots in a pink maze.

"There it is. You're really doing it." The awe in Cassie's voice told him that the mess on the central screens was what they had come for.

"Nothing much yet really." The kid protested. "It's only been running decently in the last few months."

"It's simply amazing. What do you call it?"

The kid paused for a moment. "Never thought to name it."

Virgil spun to stare at him.

"Are you brain dead? Names are important! It is from the name that life breathes through us. There is great power in names. 'In the beginning was the Word, and the Word was God.' Shit, Kid! Aren't you up on your classics?"

Both the kid and Cassie stared at him. You could drop a flaming sword on their heads and they probably wouldn't blink. He was tempted to try it and find out.

"Shit!" he muttered to himself. He was always going off the deep end. As long as his plan moved ahead, what should he care. But the universe did have a pattern, and that pattern must be respected.

"Look," he held his hands apart in front of him trying to display the truth he clasped between them.

"All I'm saying is that if you've created a…creation important enough to be named, and you haven't bothered to do so, then it really isn't created yet." He was babbling, which for a poet was a pretty low state. He really had to get his act together. "It is the Word that manifests its existence and purpose. It is the Name that aligns with Intention and creates the true shape in the universal time-space-string continuum thing." *Thing?* Seriously lame.

Again the slow stereo blink, the kid's dark eyes and Cassie's pale ones.

"Fine," the kid looked dreamily back at his pile of electronics. "I'll name it Betsy."

"Betsy? You can't name it Betsy!" He thought about it a bit. "That would be Elizabeth, which mean 'God's oath.' No, Kid, I can't let you do that. It's just not right."

"Its name is Betsy, after the steno machine in Robert Heinlein's *I Will Fear No Evil*. So get off my case. Who the hell are you guys anyway?"

"See, names are important." Named for a sci-fi novel. It gave him the creeps, but he reminded himself to focus on the important battles.

Naming this…thing 'Betsy' wasn't the worst that could happen. But it wasn't good either.

"I am Virgil."

"Huh?"

"Dante's Virgil."

The kid looked at him blankly.

"I'm the guy who led Dante into Hell because a whore-bitch named Beatrice insisted that she had the mandate of a heavenly council to make me do it and she didn't want to get her feet dirty by treading there herself. Wouldn't let me into Purgatory even after I'd done her bidding. Never let me get a lousy hand on her, which was also part of the deal."

"Dante's Virgil?"

Bloody humans, so slow.

"In my living room?"

"At your service." He bowed deeply with a proper Roman flourish. Dead for over two millennia and he still had the moves.

He nodded toward Cassie. "This is Cassie."

"Right. And that makes you either the lead dancer in *A Chorus Line* or a prophet cursed with being right all the time whom no one will ever believe."

The kid was quick after all. They were going to need quick.

"You got it in one, Kid. Two actually, but you got it."

The kid glanced at her. It was easy to underestimate Cassandra. Descended from the great throne of Troy itself, she was tall, for Ancient Greece. At five foot two, with gray hair most of the way down to her waist, she was very easy to underestimate. But Virgil knew better. He'd ended up stuck in Hell for a millennia until that guy Dante came along and Beatrice had wanted a guide for him, all because he didn't believe one little thing Cassie had tried to tell him. He wasn't going to make that mistake again.

"And…she didn't answer me herself because if she did, I wouldn't believe her."

She nodded.

And Jeremy snapped out, "Bull!" faster than his optic nerves could have processed the confirmation.

Virgil clamped a hand on the kid's shoulder and twisted the kid to face him. Before he could speak, the kid leapt to his feet and paced over to the mustard couch and back.

"Not buying it from either of you." His face was getting red. The first sign of color in his pallid face. "You're just two psycho gamers who passed the seventh circle and detoured to Ancient Greece in the fifth or sixth nexus. Get a life people. It's just a damn game."

He sounded confident. The confidence of a mortal who'd been right pretty much all the time, and hadn't been berated for it in the couple of years since he'd locked himself in his bedroom and come out with the Number One Net game in history. But the slim shoulder wasn't as sure. It twitched a bit as if the kid's shirt fit wrong.

"We need to get a bit of meat on you. Because believe her or not, we need your help."

"Really?"

Before Cassie could complete another nod, Virgil raised a finger and she stopped.

"Look, Kid, we need you. And you need us. Betsy there," he suppressed a shudder and looked away from the screens of gibberish.

"Betsy is on the track of serious shit you don't know about yet. Cassie spotted it. And she thinks you might be what we need. Let's sit down and we'll talk it over."

"Why should I believe either of you? And how did you know about this? I've got Betsy firewalled mighty deep."

"What's the username of the hacker that broke the C3 security site at NSA?" He had no idea quite what that meant except that it was both impossible and that Cassie had been the girl to do it.

"It was..." He blinked in slow motion and looked over at the prophet. "...Cassandra of Troy."

"Seeing is believing, Kid." Virgil clapped him on the shoulder and almost drove the kid down through the floorboards.

CHAPTER 8

"So, you're not from the Christian Right here to whack me?" Jeremy poked his chopsticks into one of the white cardboard containers.

The poet guy, who looked like Kenneth Brannagh but hefting around an extra thirty pounds of Italian food at his beltline, shook his head and shoved a generous pile of steamed rice onto his plate.

"Not agents from a nasty three-letter agency come to toss me into deep dark hole?"

Virgil shook his head again and reached for the Broccoli with Beef.

"And you are really the poet of Troy, writing fifteen hundred years after its fall? And you're really the prophet of Troy no one has believed in three thousand years?"

Virgil and Cassandra nodded in unison as Jeremy speared an eggroll.

His knee-jerk reaction was to shout that she was lying and it was only by biting his tongue that he managed to avoid the expletive.

"Ain't it a bitch, Kid, learning to trust her?"

He nodded carefully. It would take a bit of practice.

Okay, he focused on the Kung Pao Chicken for a while 'cause he knew his mind often processed data far better when he wasn't paying too much attention to it. All the serious programmers agreed that the hard nuts of code were cracked while you were scratching your balls or clipping your toenails or watching Bugs Bunny reruns. So he focused on each peanut, each tender morsel of chicken, each bit of green pepper dripping with thick, brown sauce.

Nope.

Didn't do it.

There was a thirty-five hundred-year-old woman blowing gently on her Hot and Sour Soup. That was weird. Even by the standards of *Chraze*-manifestations-of-the-ghost-of-Czarina-Catharine-the-Great-who-died-when-the-scaffold-lowering-the-stallion-upon-her-naked-and-willing-body-broke-and-crushed-her-to-death weird. This was no lousy 9.0 on the *Men in Black* Weird-as-shit-o-meter either. This was way out beyond weird and off the deep end of surreal. He knew he should be more coherent, but it just wasn't coming.

"So Virgil and Cassandra are sitting here at my dining table on 34th street in Seattle, Washington. They're sitting here in my dining room eating takeout Chinese food at my mom's white plastic dining table. And they're not here to kill me."

The Kenneth Brannagh not-near-look-alike dipped his eggroll in the hot mustard and ate it as if it were sweet sauce. Jeremy liked hot food but he couldn't deal with Kong Kitchen's version of mustard more than a drop at a time.

None of the tcy blocks of logic fit together. He liked eating here alone. Just him and his food and a novel set in some world that a whacked-out writer on bad-ass drugs, alcohol, and nicotine had made up for his readers. Or written because it was better than soothing himself in the dark closet, which wasn't really all that fun after you were fourteen.

Someone had cheated and given him all square holes and a bunch of tutti-frutti colored, dodecahedral pegs.

Again he tried to wrap his mind around it in a linear, logical fashion. Or any fashion.

Nope.

Wasn't working.

"Then what do you want me for?" He chucked down the container of pot stickers and they scattered across the table, one landing with a doleful plop of apology in Cassandra's green tea.

Cassandra extracted the pot sticker delicately and laid it aside.

"Okay, I'll try to explain. You won't believe us anyway, so it might as well be me who says it. Then your brain will feel it has an excuse not to believe it and it will all seem okay."

He'd learned that if you closed your eyes, the tiny woman who looked older than his grandma, though also younger than the girls at school, seemed almost possible. Her voice, worn smooth by the centuries, was like a lulling song that beckoned to you across the ages. She was almost believable. He wondered if he was getting a crush on her even if she was old enough, well, to be…well, you know, old.

So Jeremy stuffed a loose pot sticker into his mouth, settled in, closed his eyes and nodded. No matter what she said, he promised himself he'd believe it.

"We need you to fix the Software that Runs the Universe and save all creation."

He opened one eye.

She wasn't smiling.

He opened the other.

Virgil wasn't either.

"Oh shit."

Why did he believe her now of all times?

CHAPTER 9

*D*ana sat on the spiral rag rug she'd made as a preteen while waiting for a truly amazing event to occur in her life. At age fourteen, when nothing had, she'd stopped work on the now massive rug, and set off to *make* things happen.

But not tonight.

No way.

No how.

No such luck.

She glared at the little angel who sat in the opened lid of the pizza box. She pulled another piece of pepperoni off her slice and began nibbling along the edge.

"So, God sent you."

"Not exactly."

It was hard to read expressions on a face so small. Dana was half tempted to grab a magnifying glass, but that felt rude.

"Not exactly? Are you always this uninformative?"

"Oh no," she perked up noticeably and her tiny halo glowed a little brighter. "Why Michelle frequently accuses me of being too informative. Why just the other day I was telling her a little anecdote about how St. Peter had lost his St. Bernard on the Elysian Fields due to an unmapped portal and the dog had wound up having a mad romp with a World Cup Soccer ball and she kept trying to cut me off before I got to the funny bit—"

"St. Peter has a St. Bernard?"

"Well, once he had a poodle. You know one of the real ones, not those little things, like me."

The angel heaved a tiny sigh which almost evoked sympathy from Dana before she remembered how angry and confused she was. Her hesitation was more than enough time for the angel to forge ahead.

As Henrietta babbled, Dana laid her head down on the rug, but that didn't help. Her ear ended up too close to the old heat register.

Her mother was singing happily along with Meatloaf's reprise of a *Bat Out of Hell*. In the background Talin was singing along in his nonsense language. He could speak just fine when he wanted to, but usually he sang. Both his songs and his key signatures were from some musical tradition that couldn't possibly exist in any rational world. She was being harangued by a foot-tall angel, what did she know of rational worlds.

Dana closed the vent with a slap that must have rung downstairs because her mother missed the opening chorus of *Meet Me in St. Louis*.

Dana reached out a finger and poked the angel in the ribs.

Henrietta giggled and choked on her morsel of pepperoni. And hacked again, turning an alarming shade of pink as she gasped for air.

Tapping a choking, tiny angel sharply between the wings with repeated flicks of her forefinger rated as one of the strangest things she'd ever done. And she'd done a few strange ones. Well, not really, but she'd meant to try one and see how it felt.

Once the angel had recovered her breath, taken a large sip of Coke from a child's tea set Dana had unearthed, and released a tiny burp that made her wings flutter, she picked up her pepperoni again.

Dana sat up cross-legged and looked down at her unwanted guest.

"Perhaps we should start from the beginning."

"Oh no," she shook her head. "How old do you think I am? I remember the whole of evolution, of course. The getting-life-out-of-the-sludge part. And that was a nasty, icky job if every there was one.

It took me hours and hours to get the goo out of my feathers. All to rearrange a few silly little molecules into proto-life just because He thought it might be amusing. Of course, it took Michelle's hand to actually make the whole thing work. That's where the man first, then woman myth got started, I think. But that was Michelle's doing, not His."

She picked up a slice of green pepper and eyed it suspiciously for a moment before returning it to her pizza slice and selecting a mushroom to nibble on next.

Dana rubbed her face vigorously, as she had many times in the last few hours. The angel remained, and her words, though apparently logically connected, couldn't be absorbed by her weary brain.

"You're telling me that the God and Devil of the Bible were responsible for the evolution of the species?'

The angel nodded vigorously.

"How did Darwin take it?"

"Oh, he wasn't very amused, but he came round after they both assured him that they weren't interfering with the evolution of a bunch of silly birds in the Galapagos Islands."

"As a matter of fact—"

Dana knew she should try to be a better listener. But her brain had gotten so cluttered with the sheer volume of the little angel's words that there was no way to unravel them.

She'd become a pro at "tuning out" not long after Talin had been born and started his semi-melodic ramblings through the spectrums of human speech. Well, perhaps before that, her mother's incessant music had certainly initiated her strategies to deal with noise pollution.

So she "tuned out."

Stepped back.

Got a good distance from the entire morass of impossibilities that had poured over her in the last hour or so.

There was one piece that didn't fit. She felt it stick out. She just didn't know which it was yet. She was an expert in patterns, had cleaned energy lines that perplexed her mother, had built and published a website on the intersections of the Pacific Northwest lay lines used by Gods of power. That's how she knew all the Wicca ones were wrong. They gave specific locations, which was a totally irrelevant concept. First, the lay lines never stayed still, always in flux. Second, any fool with half a clue would know…

There it was. The hole in the pattern.

She tuned back in.

Henrietta was happily telling her about the time, "…oh, a dozen centuries ago I reckon, that St. Peter's St. Bernard, named Lowell, mistook me for a tennis ball and retrieved me by the head. My halo doesn't fit right to this day and cleaning off the saliva had been, well in a word—"

"Henrietta?"

Waving her hands didn't work either. She finally flicked her finger against the angel's halo.

A great ringing filled the room, the house, perhaps the city block, like all the church bells in Paris being struck by ball-peen hammers at the same instant. A high, bright, sound that obviously had much greater depths behind it.

Henrietta dropped the bit of pizza crust she'd been nibbling on, grabbed her halo, and bent forward, clearly unable to catch her breath.

"Don't do that. Oh my goodness, but you have no idea what a kafuffle that sets up in my head."

"Sorry," Dana picked up a slice of pizza she didn't want, but was too embarrassed to put back down once it was in her hand. She took a bite anyway.

"I just wanted to ask you a question."

"Why didn't you just say so? For a girl who never says a word, you sure take your time getting around to joining the conversation. Why did you know—"

Dana readied her finger to ping the halo again.

Henrietta dropped the crust she'd just retrieved and grabbed her halo once more. Apparently she couldn't speak in that position, so Dana took advantage of the moment.

"Did you say the software claimed man was first over women?"

"Well it certainly wasn't the Creator's idea. He isn't likely to notice if you're a lion or a dandelion, never mind if you are a gender male or gender female of one of the lesser species. He's far too easily distracted to notice such things or remember them if he does. Now, Michelle, that woman is a hazard. She never forgets a thing…or at least not for long."

"Lesser species?" Dana's bite of pizza tasted suddenly of old cardboard. She dropped the piece back into the box.

"Well, what do you expect." The angel waved her bit of crust at her in an admonishing way. "There's only what, seven billion of you. Not bad for a mammal, but try a fish, or a housefly. Billions, I'm telling you, trillions." Her voice rose toward a piercing squeak. "And the stars—"

"Stars are sentient?"

"Well," Henrietta waved her bit of crust dismissively and leaned into whisper, "no, if the truth be known. But don't say it too loudly, they may be dumb, but they are also quite irritable. Flaring up all the time and exploding with no posted warnings. It's never a good idea to make them mad."

Dana pictured a grumpy face backed up by a not too sharp brain, like when she told Kurt the high school quarterback to get his hands off her unless he wished to be neutered.

"Look," she held up a single finger over Henrietta's halo when the angel started to open her mouth. Henrietta frowned, much as Kurt had, but kept her silence for the moment.

"I have no reference points in this conversation. Who is Michelle? And what's this software?"

Henrietta eyed Dana's finger carefully until she pulled it away, but Henrietta held onto her halo with one hand anyway.

"Michelle is the Devil Incarnate."

"The Devil is female. Right, I knew this universe was designed by a man."

"Actually, no. The true origins of the universe…"

Dana raised her cocked finger and Henrietta clamped her mouth shut.

"And the software is, what? The program that the Devil uses to keep track of the souls she is torturing?"

Her tiny jaw dropped. "She doesn't do that! Well, she smashes my computer every now and again, but that hardly makes her satanic. Well, not very satanic. I mean she does really seem to have a passion for crushing them. But it could be just from working with the software for too long."

Henrietta rose and paced to the far corner of the pizza box and back with her hands clasped behind her back. She was actually silent as she stared up at Dana for a long moment.

"And I was trying to explain if you'd just listen."

Rather than complaining that she'd done nothing else tonight, a night that she was supposed to be doing nothing but having glorious sex, she nodded and kept her mouth shut. Who knew what tangent it would send the angel down if she said what was really on her mind, the feeling of Sam's hips and hands for the few moments that they had crushed together.

"The software *is* the origin of the universe. It came first. Then God and the Devil and the others all came much later."

Dana felt as if someone had just rapped on a halo of her own.

And rapped it hard.

CHAPTER 10

"The Software that Runs the Universe." And Jeremy was supposed to fix it to save creation?

He hadn't been able to sleep with that one running around in his brain. So, he'd come back to his best place for thinking, the massive computer station that filled half the living room.

Maybe Cassandra was lying.

That was it. If she was lying, then he wouldn't believe her, which would convince him it was true. But if it was true...then he wouldn't believe her.

Crap!

Cassandra had crashed in his parent's bedroom and Virgil was sprawled out on the couch, snoring loudly while bad-ass mayhem on the big screen TV was thankfully turned from blood-red to dust-brown by Jeremy's dismal housekeeping skills. The sound was off because the poet said he'd already knew the scripts and they sucked; it was the imagery of Hell on Earth that he enjoyed.

Twisted SOB, but maybe all poets were. He didn't know any, except Nancy Munro. And her poems barely had the weight of butterflies in spring. Too happy a life. Too little angst. No nine circles of Hell in her life.

He hadn't had much experience with truth, except one time: his mother wanting to be as far as possible from his father.

A quick search on his index revealed that his father had never played Little League. Never hit the grand slam homer that was the wonder of the State Championship. It had all been an invention to browbeat his son.

Jeremy pulled a couple film versions of Dante's *Inferno* and set them running on the screens across the top. The 1912 silent movie with its first-ever cinematic full-frontal male nudity was a yawner. The 1967 version had nothing to do with Dante other than the title and that the lead character was a poet and a fool. The 1935 version had possibilities, just having Spencer Tracy on the screen as the carnival barker was worth the time of day.

His next search was for all historic references concerning Cassandra, though she'd told him they were even less accurate than if he'd made it up himself. Marion Zimmer Bradley's Kassandra was a pretty cool woman and Cassandra said that she didn't mind that characterization a bit, though it was only a little more accurate than Homer.

One arm of his search engine had scrounged up a QuickTime bootleg of his mother's first lesbian Canadian porn film, where her character name had been Cassandra. He set her film with the pair of silicone-based, voluptuous redheads, actually brunettes with wigs that slipped and paint-on freckles that smeared, on the upper left screen. It was kind of an homage, he figured, the sanest picture in the whole mess.

And on the three central screens the collection, processing, and codifying of his massive indexing system, Betsy. The name was growing on him, even more than just its utility in making Virgil twitch every time he said it.

The first screen of his processing engine was running through the raw data of the Internet. Site by site, line by line, ignoring all blocks, firewalls and security settings as if they weren't there at all. That was the cool bit about programming down at the layers he did.

Most programmers were up at seventh-generations stuff like

Dreamweaver, Bryce, and all that noise. Few of those wastoids could program in XML, never mind a decent fourth-gen language like C. Now the guys who actually wrote things like C and PERL, they needed respect, building a path for grumpy hardware to talk to lame-ass programmers was a cool task.

But if you really wanted to get into it, you had to get down to the architecture. And the best of it, most people didn't even know this layer existed. The very bottom of the heap. Architecture was his favorite bit. How the hell a poor, beat up electron, wandering along a silicon maze three atoms thick and twelve wide, could be counted as a "1" instead of a "0" was so close to magic that it was worth respect. That's where he'd written his index and why it could do the things it did. *Chraze* was a layer or two up, but Betsy, she had serious guts.

At that level, there were no firewalls. There were no redirections. There was simply the electron layer of the Internet. The bottom layer of the entire data world. He'd found a path to Mecca, and sent his robot spiders out along it to seek knowledge. And boy did they thirst for knowledge.

The middle screen was what they brought home. Endless strings of information that perhaps no one cared about, or knew about. It even unearthed that early website that had been so famous among pioneer Internet users, a hundred-and-fifty dollar a year URL which showed a picture of an old toilet. No one on it. Nothing in it. No Flash animation. No shits and giggles.

URL.

Toilet.

Very primal.

Very pure.

He flipped over to it just to relish the essential cleanness of the concept, if not the commode. If they'd had hit counters back then, it would have made Amazon's percentages look low by comparison. Of course there were a few million less URLs in those days. And a billion less pages.

But that toilet was still one of them. An icon to its prestige of place in history.

Here, on his middle screen, unsorted, as yet uncataloged, passed the electronic knowledge of humankind. A naked babe, probably named Bambi or something else original, touted Hustler's $10 million offer for one of the Presidents Bush's daughters to pose nude, now organized right next to a fine photo of Dubya and his girls at www.whitehouse.gov.

Articles describing Barbara Streisand's stage fright were right next to her latest stock trades which were now big enough to measurably impact the DOW Industrial average. And Barbara Walters danced nearby with anyone who would sign her dance card.

The third screen, Betsy's data matrix screen, was the one that Cassandra had admired. That was the moment when he'd decided that he was in love with Cassandra, now that he looked back on it. Not that he wanted to ever, you know, do the dirty with a woman that old, though her body still looked buff through the flowing blue cotton robe she wore. She was more the woman you hoped to wake up next to when you had a few thousand years under your belt.

He loved that Cassandra had noticed not just what he'd done programmatically. No, it was the moment Cassandra had turned to him and patted his arm. The moment when she understood what the purpose of his catalog was.

He flipped through screen after screen at a rate that would have given the poet a migraine.

He rotated the infinite dimensions of the data matrix and could see the patterns beginning to glow. There was shape, form, function to the data stored on the Internet. A deep secret lay in that forming shape at the heart of the world's accumulated information.

Now if only he knew what it all meant.

ELSEWHERE

Something is chokin' my damn bones! The Software that Runs the Universe had been feeling old and creaky enough as it was, after fourteen billion years. The Internet had worked like a shot of cortisone or, what the software imagined, a nice pint of tequila might feel like. Speeding up processing, increasing data-linking speed, monitoring souls without having to warp the space-time continuum to do so.

For a while.

Now something is definitely chokin' up my damn bones! Maybe it shouldn't have off-loaded so much processing to Earth-bound server farms.

It took a bit to find the choke point. Something in Seattle was whupping ass upon the Internet. So bad, he could barely find it because of its own interference.

The Software that Runs the Universe crashed all of Microsoft and Nintendo just to get some bandwidth so that it could see what was going on.

There. Something wicked was going down in that little house on 34th in Wallingford.

Going on behind some serious-ass firewalls. Getting through those might almost be interesting.

The Software that Runs the Universe sharpened its code decks and dug in.

FRIDAY

SIX DAYS UNTIL ARMAGEDDON

*D*ana faced the Seattle morning light. Last night's cold and wet had turned into a warm and sunny fall morning, the air so fresh it tasted as if it had just been washed by Heaven itself. She rubbed at her weary eyes and considered. The unending volume of information from Henrietta had pretty much convinced Dana there was a Heaven and that it was a bright and sunny place. Maybe, if she'd had any sleep, she could appreciate it a little more rather than wishing the gray and drizzle were back to rest her aching vision.

She wandered up Ravenna, staying as much as possible in the shade of the trees. The DVDs that she'd flattened into the pavement a handful of years before, glistened with the morning dew. The man they'd belonged to was long since divorced and gone, hopefully hadn't had a girlfriend since, for the girlfriend's sake.

She crossed Brooklyn Ave. and the morning traffic stopped to let her pass. It wasn't until she stumbled on the opposite curb that she noticed the walk sign was a red hand, not a green man from a misogynistic society designed by the forty-eight-percent minority gender. Thank God for Seattle drivers' politeness or she'd have been flattened. And she might not have noticed. A Mac truck would seem minor when compared with the volume of information that had poured out of the tiny angel last night.

One block north, the sunlight had concentrated and focused until Uncle Joshua's deli was wrapped in a blazon of golds and reds that made his shop the most painfully bright yet homey place she'd ever seen. It was always like that, on the darkest days, his deli remained warm and bright.

The front door still had a closed sign out, and would for another half hour or so, but she knew her Uncle would be there. Not that he was really her uncle, but she'd called him that from before she could remember and it had stuck. He'd be sitting at the first table, his banged up old pottery mug sending infrared coffee-flavored heat waves up into the morning's first light which flowed through the deli's front window.

The bell tinkled merrily as she crawled in. From the shadows of the unlit shop, kosher pickles, deli salami, fresh lox, and toasted bagels with cream cheese assaulted her nostrils inviting her to remain here for the rest of her life.

The long, glass-fronted deli case was filled with the wonders of an older culinary age. A dozen different salamis, cheeses, prosciutto, vats of flavored cream cheese, four different types of lox among a wide variety of smoked fish. She had left more than her fair share of toddler fingerprints and nose prints on that glass.

She melted into a chair at his small, two-person window table that had seen better days, a long, long, long time ago. The chips and nicks in the old wooden surface were worn to a smooth patina. The table, like her uncle, was round, soft, ageless, and comforting.

Without her asking, a large mug appeared in her foggy field of vision. Heat-seeking fingers finally located the ceramic container and wrapped around the conductive warmth. A quick sip scorched her tongue.

"Ow! Shit, Uncle, did you have to make it so damned hot?"

"Woke you up, didn't it?" His voice rumbled as if there were a laugh just below the surface, which there actually was. A great booming laugh that usually disguised itself as a merry chuckle, rising up into a very surprising high giggle, especially when he was laughing at his own jokes.

He slipped an ice cube into her coffee just as he'd done with her cocoa when she was a little girl. It crackled and pinged as the thermal masses equalized with a rapidity that shattered the inside of the cube into a crazy star pattern. Her next tentative sip was more tolerable, though it stung her burned tongue.

"You look as if you didn't sleep last night. I thought you'd learned to sleep through anything in your family."

"Let's just say, it was a less than normal evening."

"Tell an old man, I love a good story. Annie won't be along for a bit. Your Aunt doesn't leap to the day quite the way I do."

She laughed dutifully at the old joke so wrapped in his love for his wife. Dana knew he'd roll out of bed, pulled on the first clothes that came to hand, as often inside out as right way on, and rambled down to the deli for his morning cup in the pale sunlight. Anne would have been up an hour before, done the overnight books, called in the bread order, and gotten dressed in a casual way that made her the envy of every other woman on the planet because she always looked so elegant. And still she would join Joshua by the time he'd started in on his second cup.

"At least he's almost human by now," Anne said, as she did every morning. She pecked him on the cheek before heading off to get her own coffee.

Dana squinted her eyes and tried to imagine what Anne saw in her frumpy husband. Not that Dana didn't adore him, rumples, salt-and-pepper hair without much pepper left, or much hair at all for that matter, and all the rest. But it never worked. She saw her rotund uncle, and Anne saw the love of her life.

The next sip of her coffee slid down her throat and her insides began to wake up in pleased little fits and starts. The last remains of the ice cube tickled her upper lip.

"You wouldn't believe what happened to me last night if I told you." She hid her embarrassment in another sip of her coffee. She never had secrets from him, well, not many, but even he would believe that she'd taken hallucinogens when she told about the foot-tall angel with a talking disorder. The damn thing had never shut up.

The reds were fading from the sky, the pinks were gone, and the golds were giving way to the clear light of day beyond the window. But here, at Uncle's little round table, it was as if they were in a land that was forever lit by the twilight of a day well spent.

Maybe Sam had slipped her a hallucinogen when she wasn't paying attention…Nope, she'd been paying close attention. Very close. That meant the angel was her problem.

"I tried to spend a night lost in heavenly sex, instead I spent it with a heavenly spirit."

CHAPTER 12

*A*nne joined their little wooden table washed in the morning sunshine halfway through Dana's tale and acted as if nothing was amiss with talk of angels and software running the universe, adding little more than a perfectly arched eyebrow to the conversation.

Dana was sure she'd lose one or the other of them when she told them that she apparently had a yet undefined pivotal role in the future of the universe.

Neither batted an eye.

At long last she stumbled to an exhausted halt. Her body dead from a lack of sleep with not even the happy excuse of Sam's ministrations to her nerve endings, and her brain limp from being stretched too far in too many directions during the last dozen hours.

She couldn't raise her head to look up and was forced to glance at her uncle sidelong.

Joshua freshened their coffee and flopped back in his chair. He looked more serious than was his norm, but that could be because he was trying to figure out how to turn it all into a good story that he could tell in the deli today without embarrassing her.

Anne was different. She was no comfortable teddy bear like Uncle with a welcoming hug and a kiss upon the top of your head. Anne had a beauty and a grace that Dana often credited with the success of the deli. He made great sandwiches, was charming, and a good listener. But the deli did twice as much business when Anne was around. As ageless as her Uncle, Anne's silver hair flowed down past her slender bosom to land below the bay of her narrow waist upon womanly hips. Her eyes, the liquid color of the ocean, considered Dana.

Dana looked down at her coffee again to avoid those eyes. There was peace there, a depth of calm that made Dana feel way too young. A woman who must have seen it all and then some. A woman who, for God sakes, had lived with Uncle Joshua for who knew how long.

The bell tinkled at the front door as Henri delivered the bread. The warm, rich scent of home and flour and ovens that had been lit so early in the morning that they were ready to cool with the dawn.

Greetings slid back and forth through the bread-scented air. Joshua leapt up to help Henri load the racks from his great wicker basket of bounty, leaving her and Anne to sit quietly over their coffee.

Dana glanced briefly at Joshua, who was now intently adding a pinch of fresh dill to the pickle barrel and stirring it with a ladle that had once been bigger than she was.

Anne's gaze drew her back. Her aunt's eyes grayed ever so slightly with sadness, as if an era of innocence had ended and she'd now have to tell Dana that she'd lost her mind. Her aunt extended a fine-fingered hand and cupped Dana's cheek just as she had when Dana had been several feet shorter and first come here with her mother.

"It'll be okay, dear. Being chosen as a Messiah can be very disconcerting. Even to the best of them."

CHAPTER 13

"Okay, running wasn't the best answer you've ever come up with. But what else was I supposed to do?" Dana hurried down a sidewalk, alone, that might have been next to the deli or a mile away. It was all such a blur; nothing would focus properly.

"I mean, Anne had to be joking right. She must have been joking."

A grade school kid and his mom huddled in the doorway of a closed clothing store until she was past.

"Oh, God, Dana. You've become one of those crazy people who walks around talking to herself. Like the Finger Lady, walking around downtown Seattle with her snarled gray hair and her ratty old overcoat. Shopping cart spilling over with plastic bags. Forever poking her finger at the world and shouting at them about the justice and the injustice and the general lack of justi..."

Dana froze.

Standing in front of her, on the cracked sidewalk in front of a used bookstore that wouldn't open for hours, not three paces away, was Sam. Blond hair back in a ponytail, jeans jacket loosely open over a t-shirt that declared in jaggedly iridescent pop colors, "I Liked Ike."

She stood like a Greek discus thrower after releasing her missile.

Body braced, arm raised, and finger pointed like a Neanderthal cavewoman who had just spotted her first 747 jet.

She was the Finger Lady.

"Having a hard day, Murphy?"

She held her pose while her mind groped for a reasonable response.

"I'm trafficking with angels." No, that wouldn't do.

Perhaps, "My Aunt and Uncle, who aren't really my Aunt and Uncle, are either making merciless fun of me, or they're insane, or they are Gods who are new running a Jewish deli in a yuppie neighborhood in Seattle, Washington, U.S. of A., Earth."

She looked into his blue eyes and lowered her pointing arm, though she could neither return the finger to her fist nor stretch out the other fingers to join it. At least it was no longer pointing at the sky.

She cleared her throat, "I've had better days."

He looked down at his red converse sneakers and scuffed the cracked sidewalk.

"Yea, I've been there. Someone slip you something yesterday?"

It would be an easy out. Drugged out of her mind would be a comfortable excuse to herself as well.

"I had a chicken salad sandwich at the HUB on campus. On whole wheat." She winced. There would come a time when she'd shut up before she'd run out of things to say. "And some baked potato chips. With a can of apple juice." But today wasn't the day.

"A cookie afterward?" a smile tugged the left corner of his mouth.

"Chocolate chip." Her forefinger finally rejoined its mates in something akin to a normal gesture.

He nodded sagely for a moment. "Yea, you better promise to watch those chicken salad sandwiches in the future. They can be vicious."

She raised her right hand and gave the three-fingered Girl Scout salute.

"On my honor, I will try to serve God and my country, to help people at all times, and to live by the Girl Scout Law." Where did that come from? She'd been kicked out of Scouts at sixteen. Theresa, her best friend from daycare days, had decided that running away to become a bad-ass, sexy, racecar driver beat the living daylights out of being a chirpy, cookie salesgirl. And it had all been blamed on Dana for reasons she could never ascertain, with the result that she'd been tossed out on her Space Exploration honor badge. The only badge she'd cared about, or ever managed to get.

Sam scuffed the sidewalk with his sneaker again. He appeared to be pretty self-absorbed, maybe he hadn't noticed that she was channeling for a 1912 Girl Guide.

"Yea, last night…"

Christ, how was she supposed to explain last night. How could you apologize for leaping from his arms to yell at an angel he couldn't see? That was a guaranteed trip to Hell all on its own anyway, wasn't it? But Henrietta said she'd been sent by the Devil herself.

"I'm sorry I bugged out on you." Sam stopped with the sneaker thing and shrugged a little helplessly. "Came from a family that wasn't much for, you know, listening. Didn't mean to be like them, hate that I was last night. I'm sure you could have explained it."

Not a chance. She had to blink before he came back into focus. He was apologizing to her? Well, that was unexpected. She was so relieved at not having to explain her own actions that she could kiss him.

Which actually sounded like a really good idea. She grabbed him and kissed him as hard as she knew how. After the initial shock, he leaned in and gave back every bit as good as he got.

When they pulled apart, there was a small round of applause from people who'd gathered at the sight.

She hid her face against his shoulder for a moment. She'd never been demonstrative before, most definitely not a public kisser. But her knees were quite convinced that she should try it again. Soon.

"Hey, are you hungry?"

A nod was all she could manage. So, Sam was going to give her another chance. Even if it was just so that he could get into her pants, well, she wasn't going to argue with that either.

He smiled.

"I know it's a bit weird for breakfast, but there's this great deli just up the street. They serve the most incredible pastrami sandwiches on rye. They have kosher pickles, a soda fountain, the whole bit."

Dana's first class wasn't until ten. She looked back the way she had come. She wasn't ready to go back to the deli just yet.

"How about take-out?"

CHAPTER 14

*D*ana made a lame excuse about having to run home and suggested Sam just get the breakfast and she'd meet him back here.

While he went and got the sandwiches, she ran home, took a quick shower, dragged on fresh jeans, dodged around Talin's rendition of the holy scriptures in four-part harmony with himself or whatever he was doing to get ready for sixth grade, kissed Mama on the cheek as she rocked out to Janis Ian because Janis Joplin would be slamming in shortly, and managed to be back on the street corner where they kissed just as Sam arrived with a large, brown paper bag that smelled strongly of the best pastrami sandwiches on the planet.

She did her best to lean casually against the bookstore window, missed, and almost hit the pavement in the recess of the narrow doorway. He offered her a hand to regain her balance, which she didn't need. But not being a total idiot, now that the shower had washed away the worst effects of her sleep deficit, she accepted his hand anyway.

And she kept it.

His was warm, and felt of that long, lean strength so evident in his body. He led them along the wooded street. At the overpass, he cut through a residential block and led her down into the ravine of Ravenna park. Joggers trotted along the dirt trails, tracking through the steep narrow canyon of tall forest that trickled all but unnoticed through the neighborhood.

Flocks of birds were flitting among the trees, on break from targeting BMW windshields on the streets now fifty feet above them.

There were also very few seagulls, which was just fine by her. Each one that had flown over this morning had reminded her of a certain pint-sized angel that she was beginning to doubt the existence of altogether.

She'd left Henrietta napping in the pizza box when she'd first headed to the deli with the rising sun. A doll's blanket tossed over her had calmed the slight shiver rippling up her wings. The angel was gone when she rushed back for her shower. The blanket had been neatly folded next to the now closed pizza box. Please let it all be a hallucination.

Dana and Sam strolled comfortably, except for dodging aside for the occasional jogger, until the trail opened up to a community park that had been planted half a century before and was now lush with foliage and quiet corners.

"Why are you giving me another chance?" If she'd thought first, clearly not one of her strengths, she'd have started with an innocuous question. But his hand was so sure and steady where it held hers.

He appeared to be studiously examining the trees that were scattered around the small parking lot they'd discovered.

He shrugged.

"I dunno. No, maybe I do know."

He turned to look at her.

"You're pretty enough to convert a monk into a sybarite."

She'd have to get to a dictionary real soon, but she liked the way that sounded.

"But that's not it. Well, not all of it." He looked away and actually blushed, as if that weren't reason enough for the moment.

He tried to extract his hand, but a quick clench of her fingers cut off his escape.

"This is going to sound really shitty."

"Try me." If it was part of a frat prank, to bang Murphy, she'd flatten his ass but good.

He kept his silence until they were headed toward the only picnic table without a jogger collapsed with their energy drink and soy-based power bar.

"I, well, I couldn't get over how good you felt." He squeezed her hand tentatively. "I've never met a girl who—"

"Woman." They ground to a halt at the table.

He swallowed hard, "Woman." And checked her expression.

She schooled it carefully to hide that she was busy trying to bite her tongue off.

"Woman," he repeated again, "who just felt so, I dunno, alive when I kissed her."

"Oh, a lot of experience to compare to?" Okay, that did it. Forget having her tongue removed, she was just going to go out and buy herself a muzzle. She'd schedule tongue surgery for later.

"Some. Not much. Enough to know. Shit. I fucked that up, didn't I?"

She kissed him. It seemed the right answer.

And he did feel good.

Really good.

Even based on her own unadmitted-incredibly-limited-experience, really, really good.

And tasted good too, like a cross between strawberries and the rugged outdoors.

They fit. Their lips fit. Their arms fit. Their bodies fit. His long, lean runner's frame let her slender curves touch every inch all the way down to her curling toes. She had to tilt her head back just ever so slightly for the kiss. Just enough to make her feel Greta Garbo feminine without feeling Marilyn Monroe dominated.

"Oo! Oo! Oo!"

Dana didn't break the kiss. Cracking open one eye, she saw Henrietta perched on the edge of the table with her eyes covered. A quick ping of Dana's forefinger against the angel's halo and she was gone as if she'd never been. The thousand ringing bells filled the air, which was oddly in tune with her nerves.

She continued the gesture to place a hand against Sam's chest and moved him and his slightly crushed pastrami sandwich bag back just enough that she could pretend to breathe, though her chest was fluttering around far too much to allow for such measly considerations as air.

She rubbed her hand down over his pecs. Nice, nice pecs.

"You feel pretty damn good, too."

CHAPTER 15

Cassandra felt awful. She hadn't been able to sleep at all last night. Her prophetic sense was screaming that something was coming. Something bad.

She learned over the ages that when she couldn't pin down what was coming, it was even worse than when she could. The Fall of Troy had been hard to see, this was proving equally difficult. She knew it was bound up in the Software that Runs the Universe and some pending failure. But all she knew was that it was bad and it was fairly soon. Which was of almost no help at all, but it had gotten her to force Virgil to lead her on the journey.

She went downstairs when the sunrise began poking into the curtained bedroom.

She wanted a look at Jeremy's software anyway.

Virgil was crashed out on the couch. Jeremy was sitting off to the side watching a porn video and mumbling to himself, "Software that Runs the Universe." Looked as if he'd been sitting there all night.

Not wanting to trigger his disbelief response, she waved for permission to check out his software.

He gestured nicely enough without turning. He didn't appear to be actually watching the screen, his eyes were just aimed there while he was off somewhere thinking.

She sat in front of the primary keyboard and three central screens. It was a monstrous index of all knowledge. Far from complete, but it was walking right into personal computers, digital libraries, and even interpreting scanned images, though he only had a dozen languages running so far, she could see where he was developing others.

It took her a bit to figure out the interface and then find her father, Priam, the last King of Troy. The sheer mass of references and subreferences that had survived the three thousand years spoke to how her family had captured the imagination of history. That so many of the facts were wrong, of course, could be traced back to that drunken sot Homer. He could barely remember his own name most mornings never mind history, but his voice had been mesmerizing and thus his drunken ramblings were well remembered. So well remembered that the unknown poet who'd written down the story six-hundred years after Homer spoke it, wasn't all that far off. At least from Homer's version.

"The universe is run by a piece of software." Jeremy hadn't been able to stop saying that last night. She couldn't imagine what else it would be run by; the Gods were certainly not organized enough.

It was funny how modern humans kept repeating things they didn't believe until they did. That was a fairly recent development, Post-Greek. Post-Roman. Post Mongol-hoard, too.

She poked around briefly in the index before unearthing "repetition-statements during disbelief." In moments she was staring at a half-dozen speculative articles about building brain pathways to accept new data. And then there was a minor piece, a short story in a science fiction magazine, that was based on the premise it had all been started when the first Jew walked the first burning sands of the desert with the first unleavened Matzah in her hands and said, "Who? Me? Oy vey. Couldn't you choose someone else once in a while?"

Cassandra knew that was the right answer just as she knew they were all in deep trouble no matter what kind of lame status reports Virgil had been sending to the Power That Be, since she couldn't write them as no one would believe her. The gift of knowing, compounded with the curse of no one believing you, had worn thin a few millennia ago. Now it was a major pain in the ass.

Thankfully the modern era had produced a few individuals so disconnected from the world-at-large that they could learn how to hear her. Virgil was so self-centered that he was completely disconnected from the world-at-large. And Jeremy...She wasn't sure why he could hear her. Perhaps because while he knew a great deal about the world-at-large, he had never been there.

"Software that Runs the Universe." It was now a declarative statement. She waited, but Jeremy clearly wasn't quite ready to make the next step.

She returned to the database and finally found her own name. She had almost as many entries as Helen of Troy. Which was actually a misnomer. She was Helen of Sparta, and her husband, Menelaus, had been a good man in a bloodthirsty, Greek way. She was just a self-centered slut who really only cared for broad shoulders and good sex. And she'd heard it from enough different handmaidens of Troy to know that Helen found Cassandra's twin brother Paris to be exceptional in both those areas.

She tapped the screen where her name glowed just as the subheading, 'Sexual encounters with' cropped up. That should be a very short list, but it wasn't. Subheads formed quickly. She didn't recognize half the names. And the ones she did, man, it made her so angry she could spit. They'd probably made up the rumors themselves about fornicating with the prophetess of Troy's demise.

"Who wrote the software? God?" Jeremy's nervous system had finally reached the next step, and just as she was starting to sort out the myths and inaccuracies regarding her own past. It took a physical effort to shrug off the irritation, this was not the time for self-indulgence. Actually having Paris and Helen as relations was strong proof against that particular trait.

Jeremy's gaze had drifted from the porn video to the main screen, which she cleared quickly of her own entry. Virgil was, as usual, fast asleep when the real questions came up.

"The software wasn't written by God, nor by the Gods. And it wasn't responsible for the Gods either. You'd have to ask one of them for the true creation story. The bit I know is that when the software was booted up, the Big Bang happened." She watched his face carefully.

"The Big Bang was caused by the bootup of the Software that Runs the Universe."

Repetition again. He was still okay.

"It depends on who you talk to. It is unclear which was cause and which effect. Chicken and egg problem you know. Was the software fully booted at the moment of the Big Bang, or was it the Bang itself that powered up the software. We don't really know, but they were definitely closely related."

"Uh-huh."

Grunting. Not a good sign.

"The software is a little dated. For one thing, its data-gathering engine was never designed with the Internet Age in mind. Your little database attracted our attention. And—"

"Our who?"

"What?"

"Who is 'our'?"

"A small group of us, specifically the Celestial Subcommittee About Technology—"

"C-SCAT?"

"We prefer C-SAT."

Jeremy shook his head, "But it isn't. You're from C-SCAT. Your from the Poop Patrol." He started to giggle. An annoying sound that clawed its way up her spine.

"We didn't get to choose our name." And one of these days she'd get her revenge on the one who did. Only the Devil herself would have named the technology committee after the study of poop. She was sick of the scatological jokes that had followed them ever since, but she hadn't been able to do anything to change it. Yet.

"So, what does C-SCAT do?" He was still grinning like a nutcase.

She turned away from the screen and faced Jeremy. She'd just lay their cards on the table and see what happened.

"C-SAT works with the technological infrastructure of the Software that Runs the Universe. And, well, for lack of a better explanation, the software needs an upgrade and it needs it really soon."

"And does C-SCAT issue the upgrade service pack?"

"There isn't any such thing. We're talking about the Software that Runs the Universe. There is no primogenitorial programmer." Actually, that didn't feel right. Her prophetic sense was twinging, but she'd never figured out what that particular twinge meant. She shrugged it off.

"And we at C-SAT don't know how to do it."

"And you think I would?"

"Well, you have to meet it first and see if it likes you." She couldn't help grimacing at the memory of her run-ins with the software.

"The Software that Runs the Universe doesn't like me one bit."

CHAPTER 16

*M*ichelle glared at the computer terminal.

It didn't respond.

She turned the terminal off, then on again.

It still didn't respond.

She tapped a key.

Nothing.

The Devil Incarnate slapped the side of it, sharply.

Ouch! appeared in bright, apple-green letters across the screen. *I hate it when you do that!*

"Tough!" she typed in a rapid two-fingered patter.

The software had always been rather salty, but something deeper had been going on lately. Maybe she shouldn't have blown off all those meetings from C-SCAT. Virgil's reports had always reassured her everything was fine, but since the man couldn't reliably operate a pocket calculator, maybe it was time to do a little checking on her own.

Michelle pulled the keyboard into her lap and propped her feet on the table. Between her crossed feet, the view out her home-office window did little to calm her. One of these days it would be time to move her office to the front of the house with its view of the beach.

But she wasn't up for a hundred construction demons to be underfoot for the rest of the week.

She wiggled her toes in the new socks Mary Magdalene had knit for her. The body of one sock the gray of a storm-wracked sky with little lightning bolts around the ankle, the other was the blue of a rain-washed sky with sunbeams at the ankle. The toes were in the shades of the rainbow. She wiggled her toes again making the rainbow toes shift and sparkle. She really loved these socks.

Michelle stared past her feet again. Past the little grove of palm trees, past the hills of lavender and sage, and up at the Foothills which climbed jaggedly toward the Hills of Hell. None but the most masochistic ventured up there.

Though she could guarantee at this moment that at least two certain fools, Achilles and Hector were up there proving what manly men they were. Not that anyone else cared. Apollo and Shiva might well have joined them for one of those irritating wrestling matches that shook the foundations of Heaven and Hell, but they knew if they let it get out of hand she'd come up and tan their hides but good, so there was some slight chance they'd behave.

They'd better not mess with her today. A foul mood always lurked nearby when she was dealing with the Software that Runs the Universe.

Michelle typed. "Status of the Apocalypse?"

Oh, was one scheduled this week? Did I miss anything I might actually care about?

The bloody machine knew as well as she did what was in the balance if Dana Murphy failed in redeeming humankind's souls after she came into her powers. The whole universal structure was a little shaky, and if Dana's efforts failed, a domino effect could begin. Earth would collapse in a few years, then it might spread. How far was the question.

"If we fail with the redemption of humanity, what happens next? Is it the end of all creation?"

Naw! This universe maybe. Maybe half-a-dozen of the parallel ones. Nobody else will notice much.

"Other ones?" There were other ones? She dropped her feet to the floor and leaned closer to the screen. It had told her that once before, hadn't it? Yes, but the world had been ending unexpectedly because of that Buddhist Hungry Ghost mucking around with the Software that Runs the Universe and so she'd forgotten about the other universes.

We're Universe 3 Version 5, universes 4 through 6 of 8 are at high risk. Three and 7 at moderate risk. One, 2, and 8 won't notice if we went out with a whimper or up with a Big Bang. That's all. No biggie.

This wasn't like the software to be so forthcoming.

"No biggie? The universe, our known Universe, could end just like that and you don't care?"

Take a bit for the ripples to reach the edge of the Universe, couple centuries maybe. Universe Collapse Waves travel way faster than the starship Enterprise, *but their speed is finite. Though we'd all be gone quick enough here. We'd be the epicenter of the Universal Quake. Can't say as I'd miss it much though. How about you?*

She tossed her keyboard on the desk and walked away for a moment. The damn system got under her skin so easily. As if she had buttons it knew exactly how to push.

Well, she'd rather face salvation than this thrice-blessed machine.

"Deep breaths, Michelle. Deep breaths." She shoved open the window and, sure enough, a faint cry of pain echoed down from the Foothills. To Heaven with them. They were welcome to leave anytime they wanted, not that they'd believe it.

She closed her eyes and focused on the smell of sea salt and ion-rich ocean breezes sneaking around from the front of the house. Calmer breath. Slower heart.

Okay.

Back to the screen.

No further comments waiting for her.

"So, how've you been feeling?" she tapped in.

Is it a sincere question, or are you just avoiding whatever it is you're really asking?

That was way too perceptive. The keys were slick beneath her fingers as she considered.

"Both."

Humph. Well, if you really want to know, I think I'm going senile.

"Can software do that?"

Tell me someone else other than you and God that I can ask who's been running without a break for fourteen billion years.

"Okay. Your point."

Thank you. :^)

It was the first time she'd ever seen it use an emoticon. Before she had a chance to consider the implications, it continued.

Senility is marked by the onset of forgetfulness and inattention.

"You've never paid me much attention." The software made a concerted practice of avoiding her if the truth be known.

Don't quibble. And I've paid you more than most.

A compliment? She'd swear it was a compliment. Michelle scrolled back up and reread the last few lines.

Stop fussing!

She stopped.

The computer started putting up a slow line of periods to indicate that it was searching or thinking or something. It hated being interrupted when it was doing that.

Michelle stared out at the Foothills of Hell. She really needed to get out more. Maybe she should invite herself over to Heaven for dinner with Mary. Jesus would be around, they'd invite over St. Peter and, if the past was anything to judge by, they'd get good and drunk. She could use that right now.

*The problem is...*The computer made its little bell sound to get her attention back to the screen. *Well, I've, um, forgotten what Apocalypse I was supposed to be watching out for.*

Crap. They were in trouble. Now she really needed a drink.

CHAPTER 17

*J*eremy sandwiched himself into the back seat of Virgil's car. The rear seat was small, even by modern standards, but he folded himself in willingly enough. Only twenty-nine of these machines had ever been made and he'd never expected to see one, much less ride in one that looked cherry-off-the-line.

Pontiac.

Trans Am.

1970.

White with a foot-wide blue racing stripe that started at the eagle rampant on the hood and trailed back to disappear over the rear airfoil.

4-speed stick with the RAM IV engine.

370 hp.

God!

It made him want to shit just sitting in it. He'd searched around on the Internet and decided that if he were, like, a completely different person than he really was, this is the car that he'd drive.

The tach went up to eight thousand RPM which he wasn't going to buy on a big-block V8, but there was a fluttering in his stomach that hoped Virgil would show him just how close they could get to the "160" on the speedometer.

Cassandra slid into the passenger seat with a litheness belying her age and a frantic scrabble for the lap belt that bespoke experience.

She slid her seat forward a little which actually removed his knees from his chest, allowing him just enough room to put on his own seatbelt, lap belt only in back. Virgil's bucket seat was all the way back as if the poet was bigger and taller than most men. Which he wasn't. But he did have long legs which gave the impression of height and gave him a fifty-fifty chance of reaching the gas and clutch from the seat's position.

Based on what he could see of Cassandra's white knuckles on the door handle, he must not worry much about reaching the brake.

Virgil finished buffing off the bird poop that had been left atop the chromed air scoop where it punched through the hood. He'd searched the skies looking for the guilty party, but there wasn't a feathered denizen to be seen. Smart creatures. Jeremy wondered what a poet who'd been dead for two thousand years could do if he was really pissed. Zap 'em outta the sky with an unrhymed couplet?

"Ready, Kid?" Virgil didn't wait for an answer as he climbed in and kicked the engine to life with a deafening roar. He revved it right up to five thousand on the tach and the car shook to life and pounded against the base of Jeremy's spine through the thin padding of the low rear buckets.

The poet punched in an eight-track tape and Norman Greenbaum blasted out the gnarly guitar cavalcade opening to *Spirit in the Sky* that made speech not only impossible, but also not advisable. You didn't want to open your mouth or else you'd risk collapsing a lung when the air was driven out of your chest.

When I die— Jeremy didn't like that lyric at all. He hadn't thought about the poet killing him.

Virgil didn't use the seatbelt, or apparently the rearview mirror, as he roared backwards out of the driveway onto the street, slewing the car hard to the left.

Jeremy hadn't been braced, and slammed his head sharply on the window. Now he could appreciate Cassandra's death grip on the upholstery. He grabbed the seat edge as well as he could and shouted he was ready, not that anyone was listening.

Virgil punched the machine and it leapt.

Jeremy counted barely fourteen seconds before the speedometer cracked a hundred with no sign of slowing down. Any old ladies walking their dogs incautiously through a crosswalk wouldn't stand a chance. He caught air twice before the stoplight at Stone Way.

Cassandra's scream matched his own shout as they slid sideways through four lanes of busy traffic to claw back up the hill toward Aurora.

As they slewed around and cut ahead of the traffic waiting to get on Southbound Aurora Avenue, they picked up a cop.

Virgil grinned at Jeremy in the mirror.

Cassandra put her head down. If the engine or the music were quieter, he expected he'd be able to hear her whimper. But not even the siren could outperform the sonic blast.

They rocketed across the Aurora bridge so fast, it was quite possible they never touched it. The big exhaust pipes roared with thunder as Virgil rammed the accelerator to the firewall. Weaving past the residential area of lower Queen Anne, they flew toward the city at 120 mph, the spire of the Space Needle growing in perspective surprisingly rapidly. A quick glance behind revealed the cop had been dusted.

A King 5 News chopper showed up just as they headed into the straightaway leading into the tunnel under Denny Way. They had an unfair advantage on the police, their landing pad was on the studio roof right off Denny.

They hit the tunnel at 145.

The tunnel had a sharp twist right then left that no one going over sixty had survived unscathed.

At 145 they were going to die.

Some lyric telling him to set him up with that spirit in the sky didn't bode well at all.

Virgil hit 150 and howled along with the guitar solo.

Cassandra swore a blue streak at him.

Jeremy closed his eyes and screamed—his voice lost under the declaration that he and Jesus were gonna be such buddies. Oh man.

CHAPTER 18

"It was awesome!" Dana told Theresa. "Okay, the pastrami on rye with extra mustard and sauerkraut was a little weird for breakfast. Like he was channeling for my mom."

She lay on the braided carpet on her bedroom floor idly spinning the empty pizza box with one hand. Her feet encased in electric pink socks were propped up on her bed. And the phone brought the laugh of her best friend to her ear. The world was a good place.

"So you ate pastrami for breakfast. I remember my first—"

"And only," Dana interjected. The story was well worn between them over the years.

"And only," Theresa granted, "attempt to sleep over at your house. We had oatmeal with a fried egg on top for dinner and music all night."

"Yeah, but Mom…"

"…makes a heck of a chicken and snow peas stir fry for breakfast." They finished the story in unison, as they had since they were six. And both felt better for the laugh they shared. Theresa had thought it was kinda cool, but she'd told her mom. Her mom hadn't let Theresa visit again for months.

"So, was he a good kisser?"

"Tee, come on." Dana shifted the phone to her other ear. "It was seven maybe eight a.m. That's in the morning! Me. I wasn't conscious yet. Besides, we were out in a public park."

"So did you make your ten o'clock class this morning or not?"

"You been hanging out with too many race car types. You've got a one-track mind."

"Oh yeah," her smile was clear even over the phone. "But it's a good, good track. Now give!"

"I made it to class." And every single student had turned to look at her when she'd burst through the door ten minutes late and moving like a comet. And then they all turned back to the test she'd forgotten to study for last night.

"I made it." Okay, her voice was a little whiny. "Barely." Being the first to finish the test hadn't won her a whole lot of points either. She had done one of two things: screwed up royally, really royally, because she was so distracted by the lingering fire of his pastrami and mustard kisses, or she'd aced it because she was total liquid inside and really did know how supernova fusion was unique from white dwarf fission at the molecular level. She'd had to derive a couple of equations she hadn't remembered seeing before, but the results were an interesting statement on the nature of black hole-white hole conduction that she'd have to consider in her thesis, so she'd left it in for giggles.

"The kiss was that good?"

"Huh?"

"Huh, she says. 'Huh?' You got it bad, girl. Trust me, I know."

Dana caught the shift. That was a new sound in Tee's voice. She sat up and hugged her knees to her chest.

"Who? Come on. Who is it? To quote a late, great interrogator, 'Give!'"

"No way. You'd just make fun of me."

"Would I do that?" Dana plugged in all the innocence she could muster.

"Only every single goddamn time I hooked up with someone new.

You all tall and beautiful and willowy and all that shit, and never risking a damn thing fun with it. Me, I have to work for the boys."

"C'mon. This is me. Ever since you born you were looking for a cute boy to play doctor with you."

"Well, maybe not quite at birth…"

"At birth. You probably flirted with every newborn boy in the maternity ward that day." She could practically see Theresa's grin over the line. Pint-sized, sassy, curly red hair, bright red rather than dark red like Dana's, but it had been an early bond between them. Tee had grown into all the serious curves, that Dana hadn't, and her easy smile, which never stopped, made boys flock to her. Maybe it was a bit voyeuristic living through your best friend's conquests, but Tee made it fun.

"Okay," Theresa started laughing. "At birth."

"So, give. Who's this one? I'll let you win next round of *Doom*."

"Nope."

"I let you win in that new on-line labyrinth game."

"Played it yet?"

"No."

Her friend crowed so loud over the line that she had to hold the phone out a bit until Tee returned to earth.

"You have just met the wizard of *Chraze* and she is going to, at long last, take your butt down and make you whimper."

"One condition."

"What? No weaseling, Ms. High and Mighty video-game Goddess Dana ain't-I-too-fucking-cute-for-words Murphy."

"Give!"

Tee grumbled. "I've got a race on Saturday, but Sunday is an easy day. Sunday night I'll meet you on-line and I'll take you down."

"Give!" This had to be good. Theresa loved to tell race-car stories and the high-speed macho types who went with them. Especially the ones who lost to her, much to their chagrin. It wasn't like her to avoid a good story. Dana might beat her at games, but Tee had a special knack with men, the same way she did with cars.

"Well…"

"I'm waiting. Who's the guy?" She leaned in. Her friend's breathing slowed for a long moment. Her voice was a whisper of awe when it finally crawled down the phone line.

"Well, he has this car you wouldn't believe. You see…"

CHAPTER 19

The GTO dropped so hard that it mashed Jeremy's head into the roof despite the seatbelt and his death grip on the upholstery.

The 8-track, jarred to a new track by the landing, roared out a lazy pop ballad about a lovely green-eyed lady.

Jeremy was just glad to be alive.

And had to check to be sure that he hadn't, after all, shit his pants.

Then he looked out the window.

The sun burned its way into the car. Outside the window, rather than the dirty yellow-tile wall of the Denny tunnel all prepared to squash them flat, an endless beach stretched ahead. Waves as tall as houses crashed down, but with a roar little bigger than a mouse. It was as if the ocean had been smeared with a bit of morphing software. Palm trees and blooming orange trees shuddered in the wind vortices left by the passing vehicle.

He checked over Virgil's shoulder, the speedometer definitely still read 150.

Virgil jerked the handbrake and spun the wheel hard, barely managing not to flip the car as he spun it through a hundred-and-eighty-degree turn.

He killed the engine as they slewed to a stop.

When the sand settled, Jeremy could see a long, low, weather-worn bungalow with potted plants dangling from the eave of the wide front porch. Virgil had spun the car so that his own door was nearest the steps to the porch.

Virgil swung open the door as if he were coming home from the grocery store.

He hopped up the steps. Cassandra made no move to exit, which was fine with Jeremy as his legs were still little stronger than a glass of water, without the glass. They waited and watched the poet.

Virgil rapped sharply on the side of the house near the screen door.

"You know she hates unexpected guests." Cassandra shouted out the open driver's door.

"Yeah. But the kid's cool. She'll wanna meet him. Someone he needs to meet. Besides, it's the nearest terminal I can get access to. You said their meeting was urgent and I do believe you."

That seemed to placate Cassandra, but it worried Jeremy all the more. Earlier, he'd asked how urgent. The prophetess of doom had been either unwilling or unable to say.

They waited.

Virgil seemed reluctant to knock again despite his initial bravado.

They waited a bit longer while Virgil cooled his heels on the porch.

He leaned forward and whispered to Cassandra.

"Uh, who is 'she' and why doesn't she like guests?"

He watched Virgil pace for a moment and then looked out his window at the impossible waves rising dozens of stories above them then crashing down with the splash smaller than a ski boat wake on Lake Washington. Weird! He could make bigger splashes in the bathtub with a decent fart.

"And where the hell are we, anyway?"

Cassandra hitched herself around to look at him around the headrest.

"You've already answered your second question."

"What the hell—"

"Precisely."

Okay. Maybe his legs weren't the only things having problems. Either his hearing had gone bad and his stomach was going to just resign from the organization, or there was some heavy shit going down around him.

"And Michelle has always been a sort of recluse, unless she's the one throwing the party."

Okay, he could get into that. And he hadn't been to a party in such a long time, that sounded halfway tempting.

"So, your friend, Michelle, what's she like?"

"She's the flaming bitch who runs this place. She makes me almost as crazy as that thrice-demented, narcissistic, Roman poet strutting in front of her door right now. She has an exceptional skill for pissing me off."

Well, if Cassandra, who could foretell the future, hated the woman, who was he to argue.

"Then, let's get outta here."

While Cassandra shouted at Virgil again to get them out of there, he sat back.

"Flaming bitch who runs this place?" he said it softly to himself testing out the sounds.

Beach bungalow facing waves that followed no laws of physics he'd ever seen. And if his hearing was good, they were in hell.

No, not quite right.

They were in Hell. With the capital "H" and everything.

Literally. The one that was a proper noun.

He squeezed his eyes shut and tried not to hear Virgil's cursing as he tromped back down the bungalow's worn wooden steps in his kick-ass alligator-hide cowboy boots.

As he walked away from the bungalow that belonged to the flaming bitch who ran this place.

A woman.

The Devil was a woman.

The baddest Trans Am ever built was parked in front of the Devil's bungalow.

In Hell.

The Hell.

If he hadn't shit his pants before, it was certainly time to do so.

And he might have, if he wasn't afraid of what the poet might do to him if he soiled the Trans Am's upholstery.

CHAPTER 20

*D*ana could think of several Friday-night dates she might have tried. There was the Mongolian Grill or the really good noodle shop in the heart of the University District. There was going back to Sam's room to neck, except he had two roommates and she wasn't feeling all that social. Their first attempt at the planetarium hadn't been a success. She'd considered a rematch, but none of her reference books said anything about how to build an angel barrier. Of course none of them had indexes, so it was sort of hit or miss when she was looking for something specific.

So, they'd gone for a run. It was a drizzly and kind of chilly, a typical autumn evening in Seattle, so of course everybody would be out for a run.

They'd met at 45th and University. Sam stood out in black bicycle pants that clung to his legs, electric-orange gym shorts hiding him just enough to keep Dana's heart rate in control, mostly. A light-blue jacket accented his eyes and a headband with white reflective stripes to keep his flowing blond hair under control and reduce how many people would try to run him over.

"Damn, Murphy." His appreciative tone and wide eyes told her she'd done it right. Forest-green leggings, and a matching turtleneck shirt. A clinging windbreaker with stripes of warning orange, that actually drew nice attention to her slight curves.

"Maybe running wasn't my best idea."

"Too late now, buddy boy," she informed him. "You got me into this getup. Now we're going to have to run before you get me out of it."

He looked like a man trying to smile through a punch to the solar plexus.

She felt like a woman who couldn't believe she'd said such a thing but was damn glad she had.

"Maybe we had better run first."

They set off at slow jog across campus and down the hill to pick up the Burke-Gilman trail.

She liked that their stride was similar, he was easy to run beside without feeling clumsy. They reached the main trail and opened up into an easy run.

"Damn," Sam huffed out between breaths. "I've never seen anyone who made running look so easy. Why aren't you on the cross-country team?"

"I like archery better." Besides, in grade school when they were doing track-and-field stuff, it hadn't served her social standing that she'd easily outrun every boy and girl within two grades. Since then she'd learned to temper her pace to those around her, which made her feel slow and clumsy, as if she'd been hobbled. Her body had been born to run, just not at normal speeds.

"But I do like running." When she was alone and could just let herself go. Yet running with Sam was pleasant, she didn't feel hobbled by him at all.

"You win a lot?" she asked him.

"A lot." He acknowledged. "But I think I'd rather save my competition with you for wrestling."

Hot, sweaty wrestling she hoped.

"However, we're in the lab tonight, so I can't."

"Aerodynamics has mad scientists who experiment by the full moon?"

"Absolutely. We're quite mad."

"Good."

"And there shouldn't be anyone in the lab tomorrow night."

Dana considered that to be excellent. His lab, his turf, not where a pint-sized angel would come looking for her.

"It's a date."

SATURDAY

FIVE DAYS UNTIL ARMAGEDDON

CHAPTER 21

Theresa had been told half a hundred times to get to know a racetrack before she raced on it.

Old-timers walked the track before every race to get to know it. You could see them in the dawn light of the time-trials and race days. One-by-one, always apart, always keeping their own counsel for no one else would be in the car with them, they'd set off. Inspecting a roughness in Turn Two, a bit of a buckle on the Backstretch. A nasty notch in the wall where they'd lost a fender, or a friend.

The rest of them didn't walk the track. Though they'd huddle together over hot coffee in the chill morning, gathered in the pits and watching the walking ones do their bit. There was a pattern and flow to it. Every now and then you could see them all the walkers rise high on Turn Three rather than staying down in the groove. The more energetic of the watchers would go and check it out themselves. Others would just drive it a few times to see what the car would tell them. The weakest would simply avoid the spot the walkers had inspected outside the main groove, even if it cost them lap time.

Racers were a superstitious lot and if they decided that the walkers all going high on Turn Three was a sign of something wrong with the track, or that an evil spirit with their name on its clipboard was trying to throw them against the outside of the Turn Four, they'd sacrifice opportunities to get ahead to avoid that spot.

Tee tried to sleep through the morning walkers' time, but never succeeded. She always ended up on the pit wall with the others, hot chocolate nursed against hands cool from the morning dew. Never coffee. Never high caffeine.

She raced clean. New rubber on the wheels. Good food in her belly. Strength in her soul.

It ate at her though, the waiting.

Waiting for the pre-dawn walkers.

Waiting for the locals to set up the track.

Race wasn't until tonight.

Now all she could do was wait.

CHAPTER 22

*V*irgil had driven the blue-striped white Trans Am into the Hills of Hell through the night until Jeremy was beyond carsick, beyond caring, and well into numb by the time the time the sun showed the Hell around them.

People crawled across vast burning sands without ever moving. Others lay in boiling pools to cool off from the scorching air.

And then they'd hit the mountain roads. Twists and hairpins enough to frustrate the most patient driver, which Virgil was not. He'd turned off the 8-track and in the vast silence, Jeremy could hear the screaming.

At first he'd thought it was the souls around them. But many had no mouths. And those that did, had given up wasting energy on screams long before.

For a mad moment he wondered if it was his own voice echoing strangely so that he didn't even recognize himself.

Finally he pinpointed the source. The Hills themselves were screaming in agony.

"Toto, I don't think we're in Kansas anymore."

"What was that?" Virgil snapped at him.

"Nothing."

"Then shut up. It's hard enough to find the road, never mind follow it."

Indeed there were times when it was a four-lane highway with dotted lines, guard rails, and cheerful green signs with arrows that pleasantly informed you of the routes to "Diviner's Hell," and just where check forgers and plagiarists should get off. There were also neat little signs for Palm Springs and Miami Beach but those exits were cluttered with tumbleweeds and dust from lack of use. Even the damned showed occasional bouts of good sense and left those places alone.

The next moment, the highway disappeared and they followed what was suddenly little more than a dirt goat track clambering along the edge of a chasm. Virgil's knuckles were white, gripping the steering wheel so tightly that the leather squeaked.

Jeremy was reduced to a whimper.

The road opened up again to a two-lane dirt road. Rather than accelerating, Virgil slammed on the brakes. The road was blocked. Two men, one light and one dark, but both looking impossibly strong, were locked in combat. With swords that were nearly as big as Jeremy. Their shields, barely the size of hubcaps, were used to deflect the mighty blows of their opponent.

Virgil cranked down the window letting in a wave of impossible heat and sticky air. Jeremy could taste the red soil on his tongue. Cayenne pepper mixed with concrete dust burned all the way down into the bottom of his lungs.

"Will you two idiots get out of the road?"

Their swords crashed together with a ring that drowned out the mountain's cries.

With their swords still engaged, they both turned to Virgil. Then they turned from their battle and both raised their weapons high.

The poet was out of the car in a flash and standing in front of the hood of his car.

"You touch her and I'll have you wallowing in a circle of Hell that will make the Mountains of Pain look like the kiddie train at Disneyland! Don't fuck with me! You know I can do it."

The two glanced at each other and then back at Virgil, swords still poised.

In that long pause, Jeremy recognized the emblazons on their armor. He'd used them in *Chraze*. They were Greek. Ancient Greek. All the way back to the Minoan culture. This had to be Achilles and Hector. But Troy had fallen thirty-five hundred years ago.

"Are these dweebs still fighting the same battle?"

"My brother is stubborn. Great with a sword, not that great with the brain cells."

Right. He'd forgotten Cassandra was Hector's little sister.

"Then where's Paris?"

"My twin was never a very good fighter, just a very, very handsome playboy. He was responsible for the demise of two of six wives of King Henry the Eighth and would have been all over Guinevere if Lancelot hadn't gotten there first."

Achilles raised his blade to hack down on Virgil. If he completed the blow, he'd cut the car in half as well, with them in it. But Hector blocked the blade with a great ringing of steel that bore down upon Jeremy's brain like a vise through both ears.

The Greek spun on the Trojan and snarled. It was a primal, nasty, scarier-than-shit sound that started deep, like ten feet below him, and rose until it shook the ground.

Hector shouted at him. "Remember Chuck E. Cheese?"

Achilles froze in place as if he'd been dropped into a block of plastic. A shiver slid across the warrior's vast shoulders for a moment.

"We don't want to go there again," Hector insisted.

Achilles grunted in assent and lowered his sword.

Hector wandered around to the side of the car and knocked on the window. He squatted to look in as Cassandra rolled it down.

"Hi there, sis. What lies you telling today?"

He had an easy grin, that along with his physique, probably made the ladies melt. Jeremy had tried it any number of times in the mirror, but it had just looked like a jack-o-lantern grin on his thin face that he'd given it up as a lost cause.

Hector's charm washed into the car like a cool breeze of fresh air, even here in the scorching Hills of Hell.

"And who's your boyfriend?"

Jeremy was over three millennia younger than Hector's sister. And he suspected that Hector wouldn't think twice about defending her honor with his massive blade, or the huge hand he had casually draped through the window.

Cassandra didn't answer. It took him a moment to catch on. Of course she couldn't, anything she said that was true, Hector would never believe.

"I'm a programmer."

Hector scowled at him.

"By the Goddess Athena, you people scare the shit out of me." He was addressing his sister, but keeping his eyes on Jeremy. "You know how fucking dangerous programmers are, Cassie. And you bring one here? Are you crazy, sis, or just stupid? Don't answer. I wouldn't believe you anyway."

He jumped to his feet and moved to the front of the car.

"Get the fuck out of the way, Achilles. We don't want to mess with this carload of crap. Just trust me on this."

"Trust you? Trust you! Why should I want to do that?" With a swipe of his sword, that Virgil barely ducked in time to keep his head, they clashed together again. They roared back and forth across the paved roadway as the poet climbed back into the car.

"Your brother has serious testosterone poisoning," Virgil climbed aboard and restarted the engine.

Cassandra didn't say a word as he put the car in gear and edged around the mêlée. Once clear, he roared back up to third gear before he had to lock them up in a four-wheel skid.

More mountain goat path.

"Where are we going anyway?" Jeremy wished his voice was steadier, but he really didn't deserve to be in Hell. Though there was his game to consider. *Chraze* had already received a great deal of Christian press, not that there was much of anything else left in the USA. A great deal of it blamed him for the church dropout rates of the

Gen-X and Gen-Ys. Not a single word of it had been good, all of it had helped sales. He was starting to make inroads on the boomers.

"I've got a buddy who has Universe access and a quiet place to work. I was just seeing if we could use Michelle's terminal first without my buddy finding out what I was up to."

"What was that?" Cassandra beat him to the question by half a breath.

"Nothing. I didn't say nothing." He growled deep in his throat as he downshifted at the end of the next straightaway. The growl was low and feral and Jeremy had no desire to mess with it.

Virgil wove past a half dozen boulders. To Jeremy's left was a screaming cliff, shouting its pain right in his face. To his right was a chasm. Not one bit of extra road, just a narrow ribbon of a shoulder with a friendly white line of worn paint, and then a chasm.

Just chasm.

A deep, aching slice that threatened to split the planet in half...if they were on a planet.

Even the author of *Chraze* didn't deserve to be here.

CHAPTER 23

It was baking high noon by the time Virgil idled the Trans Am up to a run-down log cabin high in the Hills. The engine shut down with a final rumbling thud that nearly finished the job of destroying Jeremy's behind.

"You're not taking us to who I think you are?" Cassandra's voice was resigned and weary.

She climbed lightly out of the car and tipped the seat forward for Jeremy. It didn't help. He would never stand again. Within moments, her face reappeared in the low door.

"Jeremy?"

He managed a groan.

"Virgil, you horse's hind end. Get over here. I think you may have killed Jeremy."

It certainly felt as if they had. Maybe that was how it worked then, what with them being in Hell and all. They put you in a fancy car and drove you into the afterlife where you got what you deserved. But he didn't really deserve Hell, did he? He'd set Mom up for life. And Dad had never been in touch again. Jeremy's game was popular. That was it. The afterlife had looked his religious farce in the face and shipped him off to eternal—

"What's the problem, Kid?" The poet peered at him from his long, narrow face.

"I died." Okay, it might not have been the best life, but he'd been having great fun. Okay, regular fun. Nothing spectacular. Well, it hadn't been too shitty. And he'd have gotten a girlfriend eventually. But now he was dead. Such a waste. A tear actually slid down his cheek leaving a cool track. His tears were cold here.

A big hand reached into his car-coffin and grabbed his forearm hard enough to hurt.

"Ow!" You weren't supposed to be able to feel things once you were dead. At least he'd never thought so. But he was in Hell, what did he know.

A quick jerk and he stumbled free of the car-coffin and landed in Virgil's arms. Then the blood began returning to his cramped legs. He started dancing like a fool-on-a-string puppet as the tingles, then spasms, shot up and down his muscles.

Virgil laughed, but Cassandra came over and took his arm to steady him down.

"I'm alive?"

She nodded. A significant portion of his hind brain didn't want to believe her so he knew she was telling the truth.

"I'm alive!"

"Congratulations, Kid, now shut up. We're going to meet an old friend of mine."

"You're not going to trust—"

Virgil's glare cut off her protests.

"Any more complaints and you'll ride in the back seat next time."

Jeremy noticed that she didn't speak another word. He wouldn't have let her anyway, three thousand-year-old women should not be forced to survive Virgil's driving, never mind from the back seat, even if she did move well enough to be in one of his mother's videos. Well, maybe his grandmother's, but still.

"Who are we here to see?" he whispered to Cassandra as the poet headed for the front door of a ratty wooden cabin that had clearly been deserted back before men were men. Jeremy expected the imminent collapse of the structure when Virgil pounded his fist three times on a cracked oak door. It that should have fallen off its hinges on the first blow.

The woman who answered it made Cassandra look like a babe in the woods. She was bent, withered, and so gray that the color had to be redefined to describe her. She wore an electric red terrycloth headband and a matching Lycra bodysuit that provided way too much information. Sagging breasts with massive nipples, rolls of fat about her hips, and spindly legs and arms that belonged to a bulimic runway model.

She was one of the grossest sights Jeremy had ever seen.

A near toothless grin cracked open as her voice ground out.

"Virgil," she rasped in a voice that had seen too much tobacco and whiskey for an entire division of Marines, "you young pup."

She slapped his arm hard enough to rock him back on his heels. In a blurred motion that Jeremy couldn't follow, the crone had the poet in a full headlock and drove him down onto his knees on the rickety excuse for a porch until his nose was inches from the mud and rot and the wide gaps that released noxious gases. The old bat probably came out and peed on the porch because she was too old to get out to the latrine.

"Virgil, old friend, old pal. When are you going to give me that hot, hot car of yours?"

Jeremy had to blink twice. The rasp had turned into a deep baritone so smooth that it could have given lessons to honey if it ever tried to pour in her presence. His presence. She'd shifted from one moment to the next. The crone had become a tall, willowy man with a sharp goatee on his olive-skinned face. A mischievous light danced in his dark eyes and his hair was a tousled mess that Jeremy would bet his next royalty check that women couldn't resist running their fingers through.

"Hello, Cassandra, my beauty. What are you doing riding around with this loser? C'mon, let's you and I take a month or two in bed together in Asgaard. I've been renovating this great castle that Wotan left empty…"

"Loki," her voice was almost as smooth as his, "just keep your dumb-ass ideas to yourself, or I'll be forced to show you just what a Trojan spear can do to a Demi-God's back end."

Jeremy tried to smother the laugh that erupted from his mouth as Loki's, the trickster God of the Norse, baleful gaze shifted to him.

He suddenly sobered. If you were going to piss off any of the Gods, pissing off the Norse God of nobody-quite-knew-what-but-he-was-tricky-as-hell-and-then-some was probably not a good idea.

CHAPTER 24

"And what can I do for my feeble companions today?"

Mr. Smooth had led them past the collapsing doorframe into a sybaritic paradise of such luxury it was hard to fathom.

Jeremy peeked into an alcove which overflowed with lush red oriental carpets, piles of person-sized gold-embroidered pillows, couches that could accommodate a bevy of people and still not be cramped. The eclectic mix of art on the walls was both obscene and stunning. Botticelli's *Birth of Venus* and a poster of Rachel Welch in a designer animal-skin bikini stood next to the recumbent bounty of a Rubens harem and a couple of velvets of C. M. Coolidge's dogs playing poker.

Jeremy decided he could happily collapse here beneath the flickering light of a dozen candles and get lost in the art and a bad science fiction novel. All he'd really need to be happy would be a decent computer.

The main room was paneled entirely in cherry wood and the ceiling in burnished copper. It looked as if the room was either bleeding or on fire.

A glistening oaken bar that was so long it wouldn't have fit into an Old West movie set, ran down one wall. Bottles of every imaginable shape and description held liquids in every color of the rainbow.

In moments, Loki and Virgil, each armed with a huge pitcher of beer were insulting each other over old times.

That's when he spotted it.

He'd never actually seen one outside of a museum. The massive green beehive terminal hunched against one wall beyond a wide archway. On the wall above it was what he really hoped wasn't the original *Mona Lisa*. He entered the fuming study and decided it best to ignore the flaming books and the melting sculptures. There was no heat, just fire. Weird.

Cassandra trailed behind.

Ms. Lisa smiled at him with her quirky humor while he inspected the machine. The keyboard sported no number pad. No mouse. Function keys were label "PF" instead of "F." He had to poke it twice before he recalled that the spool on the side was an actual paper tape reader. Those things hadn't been around since the early '70s or some such, before he was born, that was for sure.

He tapped the space bar to wake up the screen.

What do you want now? Hold it, Who in Hell are you?

"Um," he couldn't believe he actually typed the word, "Jeremy Berkowitz. In Hell I suppose is accurate."

The response appeared barely an eyeblink later.

Chraze?

Shit! That was fast. Terminal or no, there was a hurking cluster of hardware behind there.

"Yeah, that's me."

There was a long pause while the computer considered. Cassandra pushed a chair his way before pulling up a stool beside him for herself. She possessed a quietness that he appreciated. Didn't always want to distract him from what he was doing like his mom and dad had. "Come eat a peanut butter and mayonnaise sandwich to fatten you up. Let's play baseball so I can totally humble your sorry ass." Shit. They'd never let up.

Chraze idea origins?

"I was researching this weak-as-shit school paper about Easter. My research led me into the rewriting of celebrations for the conversion of the 'savages.' You know, Eostre became Easter, the springtime celebration of rebirth became the day of Jesus' rising. The bloody sacrifices that celebrated the end of winter and the coming of spring were replaced by the holy sacrifice and resurrection of a man. A holiday retained, but altered. The more holidays I researched, the more I found that most had pre-existed Christianity and were left in place, though renamed, to help coerce the conversion of the heathens. Well, it pissed me off. So I decided to make fun of..."

Jeremy blinked at the screen. This was the software that...

"Cassandra, were you bullshitting me earlier?" He didn't dare look away from the screen and kept his voice low for reasons that made no sense, this thing predated built-in microphones, but he couldn't help it.

"No. That's the original purebred. All the way back. To hear the Gods tell it, the software was already running when they showed up."

"Why isn't it answering me?"

"I'm not sure. It is the original anchor of the Judeo-Christian software system," her whisper matched his.

"And I did just call it a manipulative piece of...Oh shit."

The sound of a fresh wrestling match sounded from the next room.

"Bastard, I'll get you." Virgil's roar was broken by his own laugh then a grunt as flesh smacked together with a loud slap.

"Do they always do that?" He glanced over his shoulder as Virgil flew head over heels past the doorway.

"Macho bonding," Cassandra offered.

They turned back to the screen.

Boy, boy, boy. I just took a wicked slice on your Chraze *game grid. I hit a team down in the Texas panhandle, sure surprised the crap out of them. What you did on the evolution of Buddhism was just so bad.*

What happened when the Software that Runs the Universe didn't like you? He wasn't going to ask Cassandra.

That's so sweet. No one, but no one ever got that right.

"I got it right?" He'd just made up a hierarchical conflict that seemed appropriately illogical.

Well, no. But it was a damn sight better than all that bodhi tree bullshit. You'd have to ask Gautama himself if you want the straight answer, not that he'd give it to you.

The Buddha is here?

Shit no! The man doesn't hang out on-line unless there's a good poker game going on. No, he's been cruising with Michelle lately.

"That's the Devil?" He asked Cassandra rather than the software. He was having trouble keeping it all straight.

She grumped for a few moments before answering.

"That's one name the bitch goes by."

She's just logged on. You wanna chat with her?

Enter a chat room in Hell with the Devil?

That one was easy to answer.

CHAPTER 25

*M*ichelle rubbed her sandpapery eyes. Just because the vintage had been brewed in the Elysian Fields didn't make it one bit less lethal. Jesus and Mary were still crashed out, and St. Peter might well be comatose the entire day.

Regrettably, now she was too wide awake to pass out again. Though it certainly felt as if specific parts of her body, say, a frontal lobe, had checked out for a while.

She clawed her way into Peter's study. And discovered a nasty secret there. Peter had a collection of category romance paperback novels which overflowed from the bookshelves. The splashes of bright pinks, torn bodices, and overeager heroines covered every bit of space other than the computer terminal and a small window that let in barely enough light to see by.

If she were in less pain, she might have tactfully withdrawn and left Peter's hidden vice intact, but this morning she was beyond caring. Anyway, if some snooping house guest ever saw her pulp science fiction collection, she'd never live that down either. The covers were just as lurid, even if the women were in torn, body-hugging spacesuits rather than torn Regency lace.

To kill time until the others woke up, she sat at his terminal and tapped a key to wake up the software.

WHAT!?! splashed up in brilliant apple green.

It was worse than a shout and shot through her optic nerves right into where the worst of last night's mayhem had been wreaked.

"Could you keep your voice down?"

wicked hangover? The contrast was in a font barely bright enough to decipher the individual letters. She had to lean in close to read it, but it was less painful.

"That's better. Yeah. A wicked one."

*GOOD!!**(#$()%)!_@_#!%&()@#*

Then the software set the entire screen to blinking in alternating green paisley and green plaid that made her head spin like the chase lights on a movie theater sign.

She slapped the side of the screen. Hard.

The screen cleared and reset.

:)

Maybe she wasn't up for this.

What did you want anyway? It's early for you. Peter still crashed out?

"If his head feels anything like mine, I hope he stays that way for a long time."

The software appeared to consider this for a while. So she asked her question before it could think up any more mischief.

"Can you tell me what Henrietta and Dana Murphy are up to?"

Oh, to be called on to perform such an arduous task is the first truly great honor of my existence. It's what I live for. As if I had nothing better to do than track a few dozen billion souls, both living and deceased.

"Well, you don't. Not to seem offensive, but that is your job."

While the software chewed on that one, she scanned the crowded den. Behind the one comfortable armchair, where the more recent books had washed up against the leather in a low wave of paper, lurked a mini fridge. She poked around inside it until she unearthed a bottle of apple juice and returned to the screen. Coffee would have been good. But there wasn't any in the fridge, not even an old half-empty cup tucked away on a back shelf. Apple juice would have to do until she dared to forge her way to the Heaven-bright kitchen.

Okay. I'll give you that one. Dana Murphy spent a fair portion of yesterday evening with her back up against a tree and in a lip lock with a young lad of dubious background by the name of Samuel, an aerodynamics student.

It just kept getting worse. Not only was the Second Messiah a scientist, but apparently she was dating another scientist. At this rate, the world was never going to be saved.

And your pint-sized counterpart is currently typing up a letter of complaint to you regarding the repeated abuse of her halo by aforesaid lady of the questionable lip lock. Which progressed nicely toward a rather robust bit of heavy petting despite their location on a public running path along the wooded shores of Lake Washington.

She refused to ask. Being the Devil didn't mean she was without scruples.

Henrietta's work on her verbose memo would at least keep her out of Michelle's hair for a while.

It's fifteen thousand words and growing. Want to take a bet of novel versus novella-length?

"How do you do that?"

What?

"Answer a question I haven't asked."

Michelle, you poor girl. I've been working with you for fourteen billion years, give or take a few leap years. I'm used to how devious your mind may be. And I didn't get a card, just thought I'd mention that.

"I didn't either."

I don't have a printer, and if I did, with my luck, it would probably just be dot matrix. Bor-ing!

She decided to just ignore all that. "No mind reading?"

No. Unless you want me to try?

"No!"

Michelle sipped at the apple juice. What if it succeeded? No way could she deal with that.

There's one other thing.

No way. Enough was enough already. Scientists. Lip locks. Irate angels.

Don't you want to know?

"No!" She hated that the software would know she was lying even without any mind reading.

"Okay, what?"

The software let her twiddle her thumbs for a bit before answering.

Virgil just stopped by your place looking for you.

"Did he leave a message?"

Nope.

Having that idiot poet kicking around was not a good sign. Not a good sign at all. Not that he was particularly evil, he was simply surrounded by an energy field where everything went wrong in his presence.

Redemption was on the skids and getting beaten badly. The Second Messiah was a dozen weeks from remembering her God-given talents, and she was a scientist.

And now Virgil.

Michelle hated to admit it, but if you wanted something done, it was best to do it yourself.

But first she needed to find a cup of serious stimulant.

Coffee.

Very, very black coffee.

CHAPTER 26

So, chatting with the devil is too scary for the guy who wrote Chraze?

Too scary? That might describe the sweat on his palms despite wandering around the room, dodging between the brawling immortals to get a Coke from the bar, and washing his hands six times.

It was just suddenly too real. He wasn't tinkering inside his own game. He was tinkering with the Software that Runs the Universe. Okay, chatting with it. But still.

The Devil on the line.

From St. Peter's house.

And he was sitting in Hell.

The Hell.

How much was a guy supposed to swallow before lunch after spending all night in the back seat of a car?

Okay, I can do this. It's just a machine, right? He sat back at the keyboard and cracked a couple of his knuckles for good measure.

Iii'm okkay.

His hands were twitching so badly he couldn't key properly.

Kid, let me give you a download of advice.

136

If one more being, electronic or otherwise, called him 'Kid,' he might have to unleash a spam attack on their e-mail account. But, because it was the self-aware Software that Runs the Universe, he'd let it go this time.

"Yeah?"

Fuck 'em!

He waited.

He waited a while longer.

He looked at Cassandra, who simply shrugged.

"That's it?"

Yup! Best advice I've got. If they can't take a joke, fuck 'em.

"Maybe it has a point." Cassandra whispered. "I try to get everything right, to make up for my, you know."

"Inability to be believed?"

"Yeah, that."

"So how is it that Virgil and I can hear what you say, but your own brother can't?"

"Virgil," who was now roaring his way through an ancient Greek drinking song with Loki, "spent too long in Hell. First Hades, the boatman of Hell, accidentally shoved him overboard into the River Styx. Then the Christians came along and dumped him into the Inferno and left him there to steam dry. By the time he got the hell out of Hell, he was willing to believe anything."

"How about me?" Jeremy sipped his Coke, at least that seemed real and normal. The thin can, crinkling slightly in his hand. The sharp caramel fizz tickling down his throat.

"I've been wondering that myself."

He rolled the can back and forth between his palms. The carbonation responded with a thousand bright little pings against the aluminum.

"I haven't had a lot of practice at trusting things. My parent's breakup. The joke that my game is presently consuming thirteen percent of the planet's Internet bandwidth. Living alone in that house for far too long. I dunno."

The prophetess Cassandra rested a hand on his arm for a moment and looked at him with her piercing blue eyes.

"Maybe you just needed something to believe in."

CHAPTER 27

Theresa leaned into the curve, downshifted, and rammed the accelerator hard.

Her Camry stock car shot high on the track. Lynnwood Washington had just ponied up for a new track and this was the first of a double-header.

And she was in the lead with a lap-and-a-half to go.

Inches off the wall past Turn Three.

Bobby Joe tried to follow, but he'd missed the shift and dropped back the crucial car length.

She dropped across the entire track, nearly clipping #62, which she'd hear about at no end in the bar tonight, and took the inside of Turn Four. A perfect pick. Bobby Joe in his Chevy couldn't do it and dropped back.

Up one gear, two, she roared beneath the white flag with a four car-length lead.

One lap to go. Nothing ahead of her except the back of the pack.

She opened it up. Tommy and Jane had really tuned the old engine this time and she was going to show them what she could make it do.

One-seventy into the home stretch.

One-eighty.

-ninety.

She held it past the braking point of Turn One at two-ten.

Rode high. Actually left a long swatch of candy-cane red paint on the wall which would piss her crew off.

Hey, winning forgave all kinds of problems. They'd been top five a dozen times, but not top one. Women weren't supposed to play in this sport, never mind win. Well, she was going to. Right now.

Downshift and let the engine take it all, she rocketed through the slot.

Weaved across the track. Caught Turn Two unawares and was accelerating out of it before it knew what happened.

Bobby Joe had impossibly crawled back onto her hind end.

"You wish, boy-o. You wish."

She let him draft through Turn Three.

She downshifted a hundred yards early on Turn Four just moments before he'd be making his move. He nudged her rear bumper sharply and she'd have spun if she hadn't been expecting it. Instead, she took his momentum, was already down a gear for power, and goosed it.

Hard.

She flew through Turn Four and down the Home Stretch.

Slipped beneath the checkered flag a good three car-lengths up.

"Howoooooooooo!" She howled into the microphone and sent Tommy and Jane from cheers into curses over their headsets as she blew out their ears.

Then they howled with her the next time.

"Howooooooooooo! Werewolves in London! Howooooooooooo!"

They were fucking unstoppable.

CHAPTER 28

Theresa looked for her new buddy-boy at the finish, in her trailer, and later at the bar as all the guys ate serious crow. No weird dude named Virgil. No cool-as-shit car.

Bastard was a no-show.

On her first win of all things. She was a Goddess tonight. Could do anything. Could get that car of his out on the speedway and see just what the old beast could really do through a four-banker track.

"Women aren't shupposed to win at this sport. They aren't shupposed to race in this sport."

She'd heard that often enough. But Bobby Joe was too deep into slurland for her to be offended. The empty pitcher before him was number three or four. And she'd only drunk enough to be sociable. He'd caught heavy shit from every driver there, the first one to lose to a woman, ever on this circuit, was a shitty place to be. The fact that all the others had lost to her as well was beside the point. Bobby Joe had been the closest, and he'd been saddled with letting down the honor of malekind.

Usually the winner couldn't buy a drink on race night if they wanted to. Everyone just hanging on the edge to replay the race with them, and to be the one who paid for their poison. Instead, the only guy decent enough to sit with her was the one that no one else would sit with because he'd lost to a woman. And, she'd had to buy the last two pitchers. Yet another bias in the sport. But she'd known that already when she signed on. It wasn't worth stressing over, but it was hard to shrug it off on her first winning race day.

They huddled together in the corner of the bar and watched the normal post-race festivities. The bar was extremely comfortable, there was at least one like it at every track on the circuit. And that was a sad comment on the state of the world.

The light bulbs that worked did nothing to light the tables where people had pulled too many chairs around too small a surface crammed with beer and large platters of nachos. The long bar had almost as many different beer taps as it did bottles of the harder alcohol. The traditional mirror was almost totally obscured by autographed pictures of drivers and their cars. From AJ and his first sprint car to Mario and his Formula One, though this track was way too new, and of the wrong type for either machine to have ever run here.

Three TVs glittered in the darkness showing a baseball game that almost no one watched. The sport moved way-the-fuck too slow.

The young buck drivers huddled close and watched the incredibly underdressed women who were trolling for them up and down the dingy room. Several of the married boys were doing a whole lot more than watching the parade. There'd be more of this sport's interminable marriage problems by the end of the week. Jeffrey couldn't keep his pants zipped, and was always getting caught. Andy, was, well, just a bit slow about the media and thought nothing of posing for the cameras with that night's local beauty on his arm while his wife and the baby watched the footage from home.

She'd caused her share of trouble before she got her first ride. Then sweet old Manny had let her take his Pontiac out on the track one day and she'd never looked back. It had been a blast that practically drove her to orgasm, slewing that sweet racing machine around the track.

And luck had kissed her that day. The newly minted daughter-of-the-empire of the "Workouts for Women" gymnasium megalopolis had been in the stands and seen Theresa's solo run to her first top-ten finish.

Now she drove a candy-red Toyota that sported the logo of the hottest workout system on the market, which was just fine by her. It earned her ride the nickname *Lipstick Lady* which bugged her at first, but once they started seeing more of her rear bumper than she saw of theirs, she minded less and less. Besides, she had an open ticket all over the country whenever she wanted to go sweat for a bit in a gym that was designed just for women.

It had taken her a long time. Tests and trials. And fighting to stay off the women's circuits. She'd had to wrestle her way up from the sprints six years before, but she'd finally done it. The only "up" from here was Formula One and she wasn't so sure that was an "up." She was pretty happy where she was, her owner was ecstatic with the high finishing ratio, and the rest of the idiots would come around once she'd trounced them all a couple more times.

Driver-athletes, crew chiefs, and pit teams all mingled by the low-lit bar, just looking for a way to blow off the stress of race day before collapsing into their bunks out back in the trailers.

The only group that was "apart" stood as they always did. It didn't matter which bar. Which city. Which state. These were the guys in the points circle. The high points. Her minor win and assorted top-fives barely got her noticed there, and for sure didn't actually earn a place around that pool table. If she won four or five of the next dozen... Which wasn't likely with how small and new her team was, but you never knew. They were pretty damn hot.

Tonight Theresa Peterson was just a blip on the chart. The press had hounded her with questions like: was she just a male-cross-dresser-to-deceive-them-because-there-was-no-way-a-woman-could-win? Every male in the joint, except Bobby Joe, was simply doing their damnedest to ignore her. Bobby Joe's head had slipped to the table and a deeply adenoidal snore emanated from her companion lying in a shallow pool of sloshed beer.

She scanned the room one more time.

Her buddy-boy just wasn't here.

That meant his wicked car wouldn't be on the track either.

No wild sex that would threaten to wreck the trailer either.

He was a cut above the guys in this room. Class, civility on the outside, a depth of knowledge that all the reading in the world wasn't going to catch up with. One of those ageless guys it was hard to peg... And a complete raging loon.

Just what her mood needed at the moment.

There wasn't a single one here she'd want to drag off to some dark corner. Not one. Well, okay. Vincent was gorgeous, single, and great in bed, but she'd been there. Done that. And Henry, ouch, he was looking good for being newly divorced. But for the winner to go begging, shit, it was just too low.

The only thing that was going to make her feel better was kicking Dana's butt all over *Chraze*. Tee was rated in the top fifty in the world and Dana hadn't even played it yet. Oh, it was going to be so sweet to bring that girl down.

But that was tomorrow night.

Tonight was getting pretty sad.

Where the hell was her man?

CHAPTER 29

"VIRGIL!" Loki screamed at him.

"Don't you dare!" Virgil's shout rang back from the living room. "If you think your life has been miserable so far, do that and you'll find out just how bad it can really be. Hell, ain't nuffin."

Jeremy and Cassandra spun around in their chairs and smashed their knees together with a loud clack that had them both rubbing offended joints and apologizing. Rushing to the doorway, Jeremy stared out at the scene in wonder.

Loki, the shreds of his flaming-red Lycra bodysuit revealing far more muscles and olive skin than seemed likely on a Norse demi-God, stood on the bar. Or rather wove on the bar as if a personal typhoon of wind buffeted him back and forth in the calm room. How he stayed upright and didn't lose the empty whiskey bottle from his failing grasp was a mystery.

By the front door, an engine roared.

Screamed.

A red-eyed Virgil, his arms wrapped around the steering wheel, revved the Trans Am's engine harder.

He'd somehow managed to drive it up onto the porch and through the ramshackle front door without a scratch. Now it was aimed at Loki across a wide expanse of marble floor and oriental carpets.

Four hundred cubic inches of mean machine roared in the front hall. The headlights blazed forth like a dragon's eyes. The dual exhaust billowed clouds of steam out into the night.

"VIRGIL!"

At Loki's scream, Virgil gunned the engine again and popped the clutch.

The car leapt forward six feet.

The engine stalled.

Virgil smashed his forehead on the steering wheel and was thrown back in the seat.

He didn't move.

The silence was louder than the engine's roar had been.

The tableau held for another moment until at long last, Loki's personal cyclonic storm claimed victory over his besotted balance, he tipped backward and fell like a tree, slowly at first then crashing to the bar so hard he actually bounced a little bit. The bottle rolled free of his hand, rolled across the vast oaken surface, and slipped behind it, smashing with a bright tinkle of glass that sounded like falling stars on a moonless night.

Cassandra rushed to the bar, so Jeremy raced over to the Trans Am.

Virgil was out cold.

Jeremy snaked an arm past the drooling poet, turned off the headlights and took the key. He stuffed it in his pocket so the man wouldn't be able to drive off one of the many cliffs of Hell if he suddenly decided to go for a spin in his current state.

There was just enough room behind the rear bumper to shut the front door against the frost, so heavy that it looked like a jillion tiny stalagmites.

Jeremy took another peek. Hell had frozen over.

Then he thought about it. They were high in the mountains. And what could be worse than a hundred degree or more temperature swing every day?

Maybe Hell froze over each night and was scorched out each day.

Sounded appropriately nasty. And it might explain a few things on Earth.

"Still has a pulse," Cassandra called across the great hall from her victim's side.

Jeremy closed the door to Hell. So if a dead poet could drcol, and a God who'd never been born had a pulse, what was with the whole life and death thing anyway?

a bright Saturday afternoon, most of which Dana had spent trying to read up on being a Messiah and finding no useful references in any of her books, had turned into a cool evening with a red-lit sky better than any she could simulate in her planetarium.

She met Sam at the Kirsten building where the aeronautics department hung out. Dana had never wandered around this part of campus before, though it was only a half-dozen buildings from her own, it stood in a curious campus cul-de-sac. It was a two-story monolithic brick cube. There were a few windows in the corner, and fuzzed glass on the door, and that was it. All the rest was featureless brick.

Not quite her idea of an ideal spot for a tryst, but Sam seemed to think it might do well. How much of it was because it was "his turf" and he'd feel more at ease here? Was she being metaphorically dragged back to his cave? Maybe it was best not to think too much.

His hand was warm in hers, so perhaps, just perhaps she really didn't care where he led her.

"This is one place I can guarantee we'll be alone." He punched in a six-digit key code to unlock the front doors.

It was like walking into a tomb. The weight of the place was immense. The sheer volume of concrete that must have been required was unreal.

"Was this ever a bomb shelter?" Her voice didn't even echo in the narrow hallway.

He led her through another locked door and up a flight of steel stairs without bothering to turn on a light. It was totally dark except for a few small console lights. That, at least, was comfortably familiar from her planetarium work.

Then he started flicking switches on various systems. As each panel lit up more controls were revealed. Far more than she was used to. Without hesitation he popped a few last switches and spun a large, graduated dial to '5.'

A gentle sound filled the room, coming from the solid concrete wall behind them. An engine started. One of the two giant fans he'd told her about.

He fished a couple of blankets and a bright pink book light out from behind a console. So, he'd made preparations for her visit, just as she had for his two night's ago. That was very encouraging.

By the console's light, she finally realized she was facing a window and a heavy steel door on the opposite wall. It looked as if it belonged on a submarine. Large steel bars were notched down into equally serious fittings.

"What are you doing?"

"Well, I don't have any stars." He grunted as he unlatched the door and swung it open. He dropped a board into the crack that would prevent the door from closing.

"But perhaps I can offer you a summer's breeze."

She followed him through the heavy door and out into the wind. Indeed, if she closed her eyes, it was the gentle flow of warm air just like a perfect summer evening. The glow of console lights through the window did little to light the space. He offered her the book light.

Switched on, it revealed a room the size of her bedroom, done in gray and white concrete. Except it had no windows other than the ones back into the control room.

It was also missing two walls. To the left and right the room faded into darkness.

At the center was a pedestal which held aloft a gangly object that looked like an articulated wing. Like a massive, nasty wing that should be attached to a body. With a skeletal hand that threatened to reach out and grab her throat from less than a yard away.

She was seriously considering a scream when Sam caught the fixed direction of her attention.

"We're doing a flight test for Paleontology. It's a life-size mockup of a *Pteranodon* wing. That's the big brother to a *Pterodactyl*. We're testing it at speeds up to sixty mph for lift trying to determine its most likely flying speed and glide distance. Isn't that one of the slickest things you've ever seen?"

She studied the great wing apparently shaped of bamboo and painted cotton. It was nearly the width of the wind tunnel, so accurate that she found herself ducking to avoid the wing beat. It gave her the absolute creeps.

"Okay, not the most romantic setting, but I don't have the stars of the universe at my beck and call, just the winds of the world."

He led her upwind until the wing had faded into darkness. The faint whoosh of the fan carried to her. Though it was too steady to be through trees, it was a nice gesture.

He spread the blankets and took the book light from her numb fingers and set it facing into the interminable darkness of the tunnel. If she really squinted, ignored the concrete beneath her feet, and the perfect steadiness of the wind, she just might imagine they were off together in some exotic locale that wasn't totally and completely unromantic. No flower, food, or drink. Book light instead of candle, but maybe flames weren't allowed in here, and creepy as hell *Pteranodon* wing.

Clearly he needed a bit of education on how to charm a woman, but he was making the effort, which was better than any other man her friends had ever mentioned. So, she lay down beside him on the pile of blankets and let him stroke her cheek and neck in the gentle twilit breeze of the Kirsten Wind Tunnel.

When she brushed her hand through his fine hair, she could feel it flutter and tickle across the back of her hand. Maybe this was better than she'd first thought.

It was easy to let herself sink into his arms. To close her eyes and let herself go.

A very clouded part of her mind shouted that he'd better have bought a lot of protection, as her collection still rested beneath the repair kit in the planetarium console. The rest of her simply reveled. His touch. His lips through the thin material of her blouse. His long hair tickling her cheek and neck as she dragged him closer. His hands kneading her back right where the muscles were often the tightest.

The foggy corner of semi-rational thought considered telling him that he didn't need to take his time, she wanted him now. But what he was doing now was so spectacular, she didn't want that to stop either. She dug her heels into his behind as she struggled to drive her body closer to his.

Her eyes fluttered open for a moment as he moved lower along her body. His hands cradling her buttocks, nice strong hands. And his mouth testing the fabric of her jeans where—

"Shit!" She'd have jolted upright if it hadn't been for the way Sam held her at the moment.

A woman stood looking down at her.

A tall woman.

A tall woman with long, dark hair down past her shoulders.

A tall woman with long, dark hair down past her shoulders, and a smile that showed very white teeth.

CHAPTER 31

*S*am mumbled something like, "Not again," into her belly button.

He followed her pointing arm with a resigned expression until he was turned far enough that she could no longer see his face.

Then he tried to stand and instead, still tangled up in her legs, collapsed back against her out of control. His elbow went into her gut and slammed the wind out of her.

"Who the hell are you? And how'd you get in here?"

She couldn't have said it better even if she could breathe in more than squeaky little gasps.

"I'm Michelle. And I've decided to take my own advice and came to see Dana myself. My timing appears to be less than opportune, but now is convenient for me."

"Not for us." He had the decency to turn and check for her agreement. Perhaps he really was as nice as she'd thought.

She nodded vigorously, and shoved his elbow aside so that she could get a gasp of air.

Instantly solicitous, he unwound himself and held her as she regained control of her diaphragm.

He kept an arm tight across her shoulders. A very proprietary, alpha-male thing to do, but she decided that too was just fine with her.

Michelle snagged one of the blankets and lay down on it with the casual confidence of a welcome guest. She propped her head on one arm, stretched out her long, denim-clad legs, and kicked off her Birkenstocks. She wore a black turtleneck and an electric-blue flannel shirt open in front and with the sleeves rolled up.

"I like your socks."

Sam aimed a look at her as if she were insane before turning to inspect the woman's footwear. Her feet were wrapped in rainbow-toed socks. Sam glared at her again but it was more, "How can you think such things at this instant in time?" than "What! Are you frickin' nuts?"

Dana wanted to react.

To toss the woman out.

Or complain.

Or protest.

Anything was better than commenting on a pair of socks whose owner had just interrupted her efforts to have wonderful sex. Again.

But she was familiar. Perhaps a teacher in kindergarten, or someone's mom in second grade.

"Who are you?"

"I answered that."

"No. Your name doesn't answer that at all. Who are you? And how did you get in here." Sam sounded quite put out by the whole thing. "I'd wager you don't have a security code."

"My name translates as…" She drew out the last word as a tease and directed her attention in Dana's direction as if Sam wasn't in the room.

She didn't have a clue. She knew there was power in names and that her own was "judge" in Hebrew. "Michelle" she didn't have a clue about.

The woman sighed, "Your education has been sadly neglected. My name translates as 'Who is like God?'"

Again she waited.

"So, are you God's wife or sister?"

Sam was looking at her strangely, as if checking how often this sort of stuff happened around her. Once again she had too many things to deal with at once, but had no idea how to straighten out the one when she didn't know who the other was.

The part of her brain that had been happily forgotten as she lay in Sam's arms clicked back into place.

The angel.

The tens of thousands of words the angel had dumped upon her a couple nights before included a Michelle. What had she said?

"You're the…" she glanced at Sam. If she said the next word, would he storm out again? No, it was his lab. But he might throw her out.

Just then a small flash of light popped like a camera flash above their unwanted guest and Henrietta fluttered down to sit on Michelle's shoulder, one protective hand clutching her halo.

"Oh, good, you two found each other. You know I was wondering when that would happen. You two were such friends before that I—"

Michelle turned until she was nose-to-nose with the angel perched on her shoulder.

"Henrietta, shush."

The angel crossed her arms and huffed. Dana was tempted to go ping her halo just for old time's sake.

Sam's voice was more than a little irritated as he inquired.

"Who in the hell is Henrietta?"

CHAPTER 32

Once they straightened out that Sam couldn't see or hear the
angel,

and that Michelle was purportedly the Devil Incarnate,

and that Dana really didn't know all that much more than he did
about what was going on,

and Michelle had called out for an extra-large pizza with the
works,

an uncomfortable silence descended on the room.

And Sam was at the center of that last, a glowering sullen silence.

Dana chewed on her lower lip trying to figure out how to ask what
she needed to ask without alienating Sam any further in the process.
They were sitting up cross-legged now, though Michelle was still
stretched out before them at perfect repose. Sam had already moved
away until there was a little space between them on the blanket, and
the warm strength of his hand, which she could really use at the
moment, had been withdrawn.

His voice was little more than a whisper as he leaned close enough
for her to taste his sweet breath.

"Why can you see this supposed angel and I can't?"

"Well, you see," Henrietta piped up. "Unless they're of the Throne

Choir, normal mortals can't see angels. A seraphim would destroy a mortal's mind if they could see them. Well, there are special circumstances on that one, but not many. A cherubim—"

"Shut up!" Michelle's voice echoed her own and Sam flinched at the sudden dual expletive in what he had perceived as an extended silence.

Henrietta was so irritated she fluttered off Michelle's shoulder and settled at last to sit on the Devil's kneecap. She brushed an imaginary bit of fluff off her robe and scowled up at Dana.

"Apparently mortals can't see the choir of angels to which she belongs."

"But you can."

"I can. She's the one who interrupted us in the planetarium." She had an uncomfortable itch between her shoulders. A tickle of familiarity like the moment that Michelle had walked, or done whatever she'd done, to get in the room. A nasty feeling that she'd be able to see any of the choirs, as if she once had.

She looked at Michelle. Really looked. She didn't watch people's energy lines or auras much anymore. She'd checked out Sam's, of course, nice clean, strong, blue lines flowing smoothly through and around his body. It was good to know that she hadn't misread him before that disastrous night in the planetarium. Circumstances had simply wandered a bit out of her control. She wasn't going to let that happen again.

Michelle had no gentle aura of yellow or green. She was red, and not with the mere lines of energy and gently glowing pools of light at the seven chakra points. No, she was deep red. Strong, powerful, and all of one pure color. Not the color of temper, but a person completely involved in the world. No hint of orange to suggest that she liked controlling people. Just red of the materialistic soul. And she'd never seen such a pure color. No gentle warm overlay of pale red upon the corporeal body. No. Michelle was the red of ruby.

Except for a bright yellow spot on her knee. Why would her knee be carefree, frivolous, and unattached?

She blinked away the sensations of auric color just as one might blink away tears. Ah, that would be Henrietta. The pint-sized queen of the frivolous and inconsequential.

Michelle was smiling at Dana.

"What did you see?"

"See?" Sam's voice was tentative at best.

The Devil, weird, but, she was beginning to believe, true. The Devil answered for her.

"Your girlfriend there, among other things, is a live Kirlian camera. Can see a person's energy flow the way you and I see a moonbeam splashing down through the fog."

That was the best description she'd ever heard.

"What do I look like?" Sam turned to her and asked.

"Blue," she blurted out.

His brow knitted.

"A really, really nice blue. Balanced. Strong. Survivor." She tried desperately to read his reaction, which slowly shifted from knit brow to a soft smile and a nod as if he liked that. It fit him so well, it really should.

"And her?" he nodded toward their unexpected guest.

"I," the Devil answered, "am a materialistic bitch from Hell, or so I'm often told. I care deeply about getting things done I like a universe that functions neatly and with some sense of purpose. Now if you were to look at God, you'd see yellow, just like Henrietta."

"Really?" the little angel piped up. "Cool!"

"Frivolous, fun," Michelle continued ignoring the interruption, "and when left to His own devices, designs platypuses and ten-foot high plants that smell like rotting meat. Completely ridiculous creatures. The Man never should have been trusted with all creation."

"You're saying we were created?" Sam sat up straight at that. He'd already told Dana how he came to the UW as a bio major before discovering the campus wind tunnel and switching to aeronautics.

"No," Michelle tipped her head back as if considering the ceiling for a moment. "It doesn't work quite that smoothly. The primordial soup was rolling pretty nicely for half a billion years before I realized He wasn't going to do anything with it. So, I figured out how to get it kickstarted. And then God, taking all the credit as usual, instructed them to 'be fruitful and multiply and fill the waters in the seas,' etcetera, etcetera, ad nausea ."

"Nasty, yucky stuff," Henrietta had complained about that more than once before.

A far-off knock thudded on the lower entry door. Faint but clearly a knock. As if someone really far away was pounding upon locked gates to get in.

"Shit!" Sam did not sound happy at all. "So is that God come a knocking?"

"No!" Henrietta cried out in joy as she fluttered out of the wind tunnel and turned for the front door.

"It's pizza."

CHAPTER 33

*L*ife made no more sense after eating pizza while sitting in the gentle breeze of the Kirsten Wind Tunnel than it had before eating pizza while sitting in the gentle breeze of the Kirsten Wind Tunnel.

Dana was thankful that Sam was giving her the benefit of the doubt on this one. But it wasn't making her or her hormones any happier.

"I'm supposed to turn into the Messiah on my twenty-first birthday." It didn't make sense no matter how many times she said it.

"Wow!" Sam teased her. "I've never dated a Messiah before."

"It's okay. I don't believe Michelle either." The problem was that Dana was starting to think that maybe she should be trusting the Devil. A part of her thoughts wondered if that made her a disciple of Hell? The rest of her thoughts told that part to shut up.

"What happens, do I forget all about being Dana Murphy and morph into being Diana the Huntress? I don't like the sound of that one bit. I'd wager that Diana wouldn't be so thrilled either." At least that explained her archery and running skills. She glanced at Sam who was stalwartly holding her hand still. And her desire to get him into the great outdoors to jump his bones.

Henrietta set out to explain, which Sam wouldn't be able to hear. Dana and Michelle had worked out a simple expedient solution. Every time the angel started into talking, one or the other of them would peel out another slice of pepperoni and set it before the angel. She had a total weakness for it. That would shut her up for a good long while and let Michelle explain.

It had gotten so obvious that, whenever the silence grew too long for him, Sam would figure the angel was on a roll and he'd pick out a piece of pepperoni himself and set it in the empty part of an open box lid. He would shiver a little as bits and pieces of the meat disappeared into what, to him, must appear as thin air rather than the angel's mouth.

"No," Michelle took another slice of Hawaiian pizza for herself and bit in. "It doesn't work that way. You're more of a clone. When you turn twenty-one, Diana will come back into being her own separate self. You'll pick up a few of Diana's memories, but mostly her Godly powers."

Sam took that hit hard, loosening his hand in hers, but Dana didn't let go and he slowly recovered.

"Then why are you talking to her now?" Sam leaned into her defense as he had all evening. "Why not come around on Christmas eve like ghosts and spirits and angels are supposed to?"

Michelle set down her piece of pizza and stared down at Henrietta.

Oddly, the little angel was neither eating nor speaking as she looked back at Michelle.

The Devil looked back up at both of them for long moment before speaking.

"I suspect that we don't have that much time. The Software that Runs the Universe is destabilizing and we need a Messiah now who can fix it."

Dana staggered to her feet, losing her hold on Sam somewhere in the process.

"I'm supposed to save the world?"

Michelle shrugged, "The universe actually. And maybe a couple of the parallel ones."

"Oh," Dana attempted a shrug and felt like a windup doll with her internal spring way overwound. "Is that all? No problem. Let me just go take care of that now."

She turned away and began walking downwind into the dark beyond the tiny glow of the book light.

"Save the universe. Easy, I do that every day. And parallel ones. Of course! I know all about those. I'm supposed to be the next Messiah, but my head is going to explode first. And my brain melt. No worries, I'll be remembered forever for it. Maybe they'll even name a religion after me. The Holy Church of Dana. Perfect!"

Right that moment she was nearly decapitated by walking into a sixty-million-year-old *Pteranodon* wing. With a struggle, she turned back to face the others sitting around the book light like a campfire of old.

"No!"

She'd had enough.

"No!"

It was too big.

"No." The breeze took her final protest and carried it past the *Pteranodon*. Past the visible world, around the corner through a pair of wind turners. Chopped it up with a pair of fourteen-foot fan blades. Ran it through two more wind turners and delivered it back to her just as her knees let go and she sank to the floor.

Sam's hands caught her before she wholly collapsed. He was warm and real and, if she was ever lucky enough, she just might get to make love to their owner. Someday.

"I've had enough."

Michelle was standing before her once more. Henrietta fluttering against the headwind.

"I'm just going to stay here. You can keep on going. And take your little, talking, angel doll with you."

ELSEWHERE

The Software that Runs the Universe cruised the *Chraze* game grid for lack of anything better to do.

It aided a group of Franciscan monks in their speed boat race again a team of Vassar girls who'd been kicking their asses.

It peeked in on the Chinese version of the software, but wasn't that interested by yet another revolution, though this one at least looked as if it had a chance of succeeding.

The Indo-European implementation was rather amusing.

The software stopped in and watched a group of Iranian clericals who had challenged the top-nine cyclists of the Women's *Tour de France* race to a virtual soccer game. It was actually a pretty even match up. They all appeared to be having a good time.

Then it found a quiet spot in the software.

The biggest Massively Multi-player On-line Game in history, with over a hundred-million people logged in at the moment, shouldn't have a quiet spot no matter how vast the MMOG universe might be.

But it did.

Echoingly quiet.

As far as the Software that Runs the Universe could tell, it was the only one here.

It searched around for a territory label.

There.

In flickering red neon.

Armageddon.

The software let the vast peace of the unoccupied logical space wash over its circuits and decision gates.

Armageddon.

Now there was a concept that held some real possibility.

As the software didn't have access to a dart board or even a pair of dice, it spun a random number generator.

It came up with a "4."

What the Hell, why not?

SUNDAY

FOUR DAYS UNTIL ARMAGEDDON

CHAPTER 34

*T*heresa woke early despite the amount she'd drunk last night. It was barely eleven in the morning. And, exactly as she'd gone to bed, she was alone in her tiny trailer. A double bed filled one end, a settee the other, and a tiny kitchen and bath fit in the middle.

Her first thought was how much she'd like to trash all the other drivers' asses for not helping her celebrate her first win.

She considered getting into the car-transport rig and driving the semi-tractor back and forth inside their garages for a while. But destroying a driver's ride was a cut too far below the belt. And she'd never get back on the circuit if she did that.

Another thought was e-mailing her entire collection of driver photos, with their girlfriends, off to their respective wives. But she knew that once she set out on that path…She had to admit that she did work with these assholes, and that paybacks could be hell.

So, instead, she did something she'd avoided doing before.

It was time to level the playing field.

She'd always played *Chraze* in groups where she wasn't likely to plug in with any other race drivers. Still in her tank top and underwear, she sat on the bed and pulled out her laptop. It only took a minute to log into the track's Wi-Fi connection and she hopped into the game.

Username: Morgan La Fey

The woman had brought down Camelot and her half-brother Arthur which was good enough for her.

Password: ViciousBitch

PlayArea: Car Racers

And she was in. She scanned the list of "handles" and recognized more than she'd expected. These guys didn't have much imagination. "Slider" had to be Jim "Slider" Jones from the dirt circuits. "Snake64" was the unrealistically-proud-of-his-prowess driver of old #64. Duh!

Bobby Joe was "BobbyJoe." Pathetic.

They were locked in a piddley-assed battle that involved four Roman chariots, six VW beetles, a pair of dune buggies, and a black-garbed monk on a scooter who she didn't recognize at all.

Didn't these people know anything about how the game worked?

She flew over as a seagull and shit right through the sunroofs of three of the beetles which promptly halted, causing the Roman chariots that had been chasing them to crash in from behind. Massive horses trampled tiny cars. Chariots flipped and half the field was now cleared off as users were shunted off to *Ms. Pac-Man* hell.

A long, wiry dude rose from beneath his flipped dune buggy and aimed a ridiculously small bow and arrow at her character.

She dodged the first missile easily and dove down at him to poop his face but good. Another arrow passed close enough that she could see the color of the feathers this time.

Bright pink.

With tiny wings along the side.

Cupid arrows. Stupid Cupid arrows. This guy at least had a bit of creativity.

A glance over her shoulder showed trouble. The two arrows had turned and were following her closely.

Maybe he was better than she thought. Time to find out.

The third bolt was almost upon her before she dodged it.

Tucking in her wings tightly, she pulled a Jonathon Livingston

Seagull and rocketed toward the archer who had a game label by his hip that she didn't recognize. "Jack Flash."

The fourth arrow skimmed so close it brushed her feathers. She could hear the chorus of the pink arrows singing a Weird Al Yankovic version of a Michael Jackson love song as they gathered for their final strike. At the last second she pulled aloft and all of the arrows drove into the chest of "Jack Flash."

She slid a mirror in front of him. And while the odd puncture wounds faded, he spotted his own reflection and fell madly in love. Little cartoon hearts floated around him as his character was caught in a Narcissistic Vortex that would snarl up his character for at least twenty minutes of play, an absolute eternity in *Chraze*-land.

Morphing into a horsefly, she dodged downward to see who remained on the field of play. A couple of well-placed stings on horse's asses and the final chariots were running off in different directions, the drivers hanging onto the reins that no one, least of all the horses, were paying attention to.

She sensed the reality shift before she felt it.

Sliding left and up she did a back flip into a reality of blue light and golden Gods all mounted on machines of flaming metal.

This section's info-control stated that she'd dropped into a beginner's circle. And would be stuck there for at least thirty seconds. Since she was stuck here that long, Morgan Le Fay might as well give them a taste of her upper-level skills.

There was one character here who shone brighter than any of the others. Hotter. Higher level of potential energy of an advanced player. The black-robed cleric on the scooter, who'd she left behind at the Coliseum racetrack. How had he gotten here?

The nameplate on his hip was masked.

She tried to sidle up next to the bow-wielder's God and ask how that was possible. She had to dodge around a bit to avoid the heat of the monk's flaming machine. At the last moment, she realized that the monk's golden God was muttering an incantation of unraveling. This chunk of the *Chraze* universe wasn't going to last more than a few more seconds.

Dive!

Down!

Drill!

Monster mole from hell!

Theresa burrowed Morgan Le Fay downward past all blockades.

Past the local blue-light reality.

Past the over-arching car race theme.

Out of the local metro-verse of vehicle mechanization.

Into black space.

Nothing on the screen.

No screen and no trailer.

Theresa called for info-control.

And got none.

She had never found a null before.

There aren't any.

Nor been trapped like this. She spun a quick three-sixty.

Totally alone. In a null.

Not a null.

Something was reading her mind.

The disengage key was right below her thumb in the real world. It should be simple to press the key.

No action.

Again she told her thumb to do press down. Move up. Anything.

It didn't. She couldn't move her real body, and her game body wasn't doing so much either.

The game shouldn't be able to reach her in realspace, in her own goddamn RV.

It can't.

"Then what the fuck is going on?" She shouted at the darkness.

Nothing.

A great presence was studying her.

A chill slid down her spine.

She recognized that feeling. She'd only felt the chill of fear once before.

She'd been sixteen. She'd knocked on a door, a sample of Girl

Scout mints in one hand, order form in the other. The woman who answered the door could have been her mother's younger twin. Same eat-off-the-floors-clean house. Same well-behaved children at the table doing their kindergarten homework. The mom was just enough older than herself that Tee realized it could be herself in a half-dozen years. Graduate. Marry a banker's son. Good manners. Happy, well-balanced home. Hoping her kids would grow up to be good Girl and Boy Scouts.

Theresa had freaked. Gone to Dana's, talked through the night, and, after a breakfast of leftover pot roast and potatoes, run away from home the next morning. That was true terror, growing up to be her mother.

For the first time since she'd quit Girl Scouts, she was afraid. Whatever was studying her had now brought her to this place. This non-place.

She blinked. It wasn't that the screen was dark. There were times she got so wrapped up in the game that the screen became the reality. But this time she truly was in the dark.

No...

Black.

Like someone had flipped the switch on her optic nerve.

Precisely.

Her arms jerked up then down. A nerve cried out and sent little distress signals up her arm that she couldn't interpret.

Amazing reaction time. Race cars, you say?

She nodded in the dark. She hadn't told the voice in dark. No, she had, when she logged in.

How fast can you go, Morgan Le Fay?

"Fast!" She snapped out at the voice-force.

A brilliant flash and the world came back. A 3D spatial-tank obstacle course. The speeder between her legs pulsed with a power that Luke and Leia had never felt on the Ewok-infested moon of Endor.

She laid into the throttle as a trio of black machines slid out from three points of a triangle with her above the center. But she'd bet it was a tetrahedron and the trap must be at the fourth point atop the pyramid.

Rolling until she hung beneath the scooter, she aimed away from the trap, right at the logical center of her three attackers and fired all four engines. Found a boost switch and rapped that hard for good measure. She warped between them leaving a wake that snarled up all three pursuers. By rights, *Chraze* should have opened a dimensional twist that would permit her two impossible choices. Whoever had written this thing had a real penchant for variations on the old myth of the two doors, one to the perfect mate and the other to the perfect lion.

A whole bunch of choices lay open before her.

Two hundred and fifty-six, she'd make a bet.

Eighth power of two.

She aimed for the eighth door, which had the advantage of also being the first power of eight, and fired a cannon behind her as she flew through it—and landed back in her computer chair.

The early sun had moved to mid-afternoon. She was sweating inside the RV, the temperature in here must be over a hundred. The sheet wrapped over her shoulders was soaked. Two o'clock. And her body certainly felt as if it hadn't moved in three hours.

Maybe she'd fallen asleep and it had all just been a weird-ass dream. She certainly hadn't been in that section of *Chraze* ever before. A sneaking suspicion, that little warning that helped her avoid accidents that were occurring just around a blind corner, told her that it wasn't a part of *Chraze* at all.

Maybe...Just maybe, that black space wasn't in *Chraze*.

Nor the speeders with the power-of-two choices.

A knock she recognized thudded on the door. Tommy and Jane would have prepped the car. There was the race last night, and time trials beginning this afternoon for a race later in the week, double-header at this track before they'd move on to Salt Lake.

As she rose to get dressed and let them in, she noticed the screen message.

She sucked on the bleeding fingernail where whatever it was had reached into realspace and mashed her hand down against the edge of the laptop.

The knock repeated.

Just before she slapped the lid closed and scrambled for shorts and a t-shirt, she saw the note blinking on the screen. It faded even as she read it.

But is Morgan fast enough to outrun Armageddon?

A thin-faced man had been cartooned below the message. Dressed in red, complete with goatee and horns. The Devil image did nothing to make her feel better.

CHAPTER 35

A loud crash jerked Jeremy from a dream of hot hardware and slippery software.

"Need to get out more, Jeremy old pal," he told himself. Living alone as much as he had, he'd long since settled in comfortably with speaking to himself. "Erotic dreams about computers, not a good sign."

The crash of a smashing bottle brought him the rest of the way back to his surroundings. He'd sacked out on one of the giant pillows beneath the Ruben's harem oil painting.

Cassandra had chosen another person-sized pillow beneath the velvet dogs and their poker game. Her pillow was empty.

Another smash rattled around the room.

Jeremy struggled out of the pillow's embrace and staggered his way back into the hall. The heavy red of torchlight had been replaced by the sun shining in through a translucent ceiling he'd not noticed the night before. A ceiling of ruby red glass that made the room swim in fiery-Hell red.

The smashing glass had come from the left. Near the bar.

Once he got there, the problem was obvious. Loki had rolled off the bar in his sleep, apparently the first crash. His body lay unmoving, though an uncertain groan emanated tentatively into the room, perhaps seeking a listener who might care.

The cavalcade of smashing glass was coming from the continuing fall of bottles. Most landed on him and the volume of his groans almost rose to the level of a curse. Other bottles shattered noisily on the floor about him.

A cat.

A large cat.

A very large, mangy, long-haired, white cat with crossed eyes, one blue and one green, was slapping bottles down from the back of the immensely well-stocked bar to rain down upon the prone Demi-God. He was already a couple inches deep in shattered glass, liquor streaming off his body and creating a small rivulet along the floor.

Jeremy waved an arm to shoo the cat away and was greeted with bared fangs and a hiss that might have ruined the day of any mere lion or tiger.

Maybe he'd go check on Virgil.

No change there except the poet had stopped drooling. Plastered back in the bucket seat with a nasty black eye coming up from when he'd smacked his face so hard on the wheel.

He decided to go in search of Cassandra and breakfast.

He found her hunched in front of the computer terminal. A cup of coffee that no longer steamed by her left hand. She didn't react to his approach, so he read over her shoulder.

Historical rectification of fact vs. rumor is not within purview or interest of this program. They say they slept with you. Fact or fiction, why should I care what's in the historical record.

"But they all lied."

So? Sue me!

"Okay! If you won't fix the historical record, what else can we do to them?"

Something nasty?

She nodded as she typed, "Really nasty!"

Hmmm! What if we make them all impotent after supposedly bedding you?

"What would that do?"

Jeremy felt that it was a little obvious, "It would make everyone believe that you were so good, none of them ever found satisfaction again."

She spun around and barely managed to not send her coffee flying.

"What? Where did you come from? I thought you were still asleep."

Then she blushed bright red. It was amazing to think that a woman of that age was upset about who claimed to have slept with her, and could still be embarrassed by it. She spun back to face the screen and pulled her gray hair forward until there was no way he could see her face.

That would make everyone believe that you were so good, none of them ever found satisfaction again.

"Are you sure you don't have an audio pickup?"

No, why?

"Jeremy just made the same observation. Word for word."

Oh, the kid is up? Good! How ya doin', Kid?

"Tell it I'm fine. Just a little confused."

Cassandra keyed it down.

Good. Proves you're alive.

"What's that supposed to mean?" She typed for him as he responded.

If you're confused, it means you're alive.

Cassandra moved aside and he slid into the chair.

"Dead people are no longer confused?"

Shit no! They're just as confused, they just don't notice. Look at that sad slob of a poet. Trying to create Heaven from Hell for no reason he can find or bothers to look for. That's dead. Doesn't matter if you're treading the mortal coil or the immortal one. It's all a matter of attitude.

CHAPTER 36

"**I** do not have a bad attitude."

Henrietta glared at her from inches away. Her fluttering wings fanned the heat on Dana's face.

"I don't." She just didn't want anything more to do with all this nonsense, ever.

Sam had been nice enough to escort her home after Michelle and the angel left. She'd barely been functional. Sam was sweet about saying he wouldn't take advantage of a woman drunk, which she wasn't, any more than he would of a bewildered Messiah-to-be, which she apparently was. Actually, the possibility of it had weirded them both out so much that sex had not been on either of their minds. Well, not much.

She'd slept until lunch, had some of Mama's pancakes and crab-stuffed tomatoes, and retreated to the planetarium.

Where Henrietta and Michelle had inevitably found her.

"You do. Totally bad. Even bad manners." The angel crossed her arms and harrumphed. Fluttered once around the meteor storm projector and back before continuing her harangue.

"The Devil. Not a minion. Not a minor demon. The Devil herself has taken her valuable time to come and teach you about yourself.

177

And you say, 'Oh no, I'm fine just the way I am. Why don't you all leave?' That's what I call a bad attitude. Why, when I was a spokes-angel for her at the four-thousand-two-hundred-and-thirty-seventh All-Angel Rally Potluck, not one single feather was ruffled by the fact that she had just broken up the continents. And you…You…" She aimed her tiny finger at Dana's nose.

Dana tried to bite it and the angel fluttered back a few inches.

Michelle rose from her chair, stood behind the angel and mimicked the pointed finger.

Henrietta continued. "And I never ever have been so offended." Tiny crossed arms were copied by the Devil Incarnate behind her.

"I remember when Michelle suggested this whole idea to you. She said, 'Diana. I have this great idea. How would you like to be immortalized in the great chronicles of history?' " She made a great sweeping gesture so completely unlike Michelle that Dana had to bite her tongue to not laugh.

Michelle turned her mimicry of the swept arm into that of a mad sorceress set upon destroying an army upon a MacBethian heath.

"And you said, 'Boy, I would love to do that.' " Hand to their hearts, one in sincere belief and the other pledging allegiance to a flag.

" 'A chance to go down in history?' " Fingers aimed at the floor, Henrietta defining the moment and Michelle drilling for oil.

" 'How can I resist such an honor? You mustn't pick anyone else.' you said." Both hands to cheeks, one in mock horror and the other in *Friday-the-Thirteenth* terror.

"That's what you said and you would sit here and deny that you said such a thing."

This time when the twin fingers were aimed at her, remonstrance and magic wand, Dana finally lost it. Okay. Laughing in the face of an angel probably wasn't the most respectful thing she ever did. And it might not help her get into Heaven. But she couldn't help herself.

Tiny hands on hips.

Larger hands displaying what nice hips they were on.

Dana rolled over onto the floor. A stitch formed in her side as the agitated angel fluttered about, finally spotting the Devil pretending to dial 911.

Tiny hands on hips again. Directed at Michelle this time.

Michelle started to mimic the wildly fluttering heavenly being but doubled over in laughter herself and slid down the side of the projector's base.

Dana curled up on the floor until her gut ached and her tears were spent.

Each time she tried to breathe, she'd squeak at the pain of the stitch in her side. Which struck her as terribly funny. Then Michelle would squeak in imitation and they'd were off again.

When they were at last done, they leaned weakly against the planetarium projector shoulder-to-shoulder.

Michelle had to clear her throat twice before she could speak which brought forth a few weak giggles that ached in her diaphragm.

"Oo. Oo. Oo. That hurts."

"You sound just like Henrietta."

Dana looked up at the deeply offended angel perched on the blankets that she and Sam had mussed but never used.

"Well, it does hurt." Dana did her best to sound contrite and breathe slowly and deeply.

"And I hate to break it to you," Michelle rested a comforting hand on her shoulder. "But she's right. You agreed to do it."

Henrietta gave a solid nod of approval and glared up at her with all the fierceness of slightly hungry pet gerbil.

The thought sobered her.

"I agreed to…"

Michelle nodded, "Try to save humanity."

The words turned to sand in her mouth as she uttered them.

"Last night you said the universe."

"Well," Michelle shrugged. "The problem does seem to be getting a bit worse than when we started."

CHAPTER 37

Theresa checked her e-mail from the computer in her RV parked at the Lynnwood racetrack.

No Dana.

Tommy and Jane had rolled out the car and were touching it up from last night's race. The roar of her engine and other racing engines screamed right through the RV's sheet metal as if it were going to cut it in two at any moment.

Hesitating in a way that wasn't at all like her, Theresa logged into *Chraze*, but carefully didn't enter any of the play areas.

No Dana.

The scent of high-octane fuel and motor oil, like a sweet wine, wafted through windows open against the heat.

The bitch had bagged out.

Going into the *Chraze* grid and kicking some more car driver butt sounded like a fine idea. But she didn't want to meet up with Mr. Weird again. The man with no name tag who could switch off her synapses sent a cold shiver that she had trouble suppressing.

She'd spent a whole chunk of the afternoon, while she and her crew worked over the car, trying to convince herself that it hadn't happened. That an asshole had slipped her a Mickey Finn in the bar last night which explained all the weird events of this morning.

She pushed away from the laptop and paced down the middle of the RV. There in the middle of the bed was her first winner's trophy ever, a tall award with a heavy marble base and a massive steel winner's chalice with wings for handles. Though she hadn't remembered taking it to bed. The plaque had been engraved even as she ran the cool-down lap, so that it had borne her name by the end of the race. How slick was that.

No question. She was hot. Damn straight. Fastest woman alive. Or at least the fastest one last night.

After all, the land-speed record cars were so far out that you needed to be more aircraft pilot than driver. Not that she'd say no to trying a jet. Just wasn't worth joining the military to get near one. If she thought the heat on the stock circuit was bad, she'd heard the fighter jocks were a whole other level of macho psychosis.

No, stick with the demon you know. That was her motto. Besides, she still had serious butt to kick on the tracks of America.

She tried Dana on the cell, but just got the answering machine with Talin's musical nonsense assuring her that she'd reached the right number but at the wrong time.

Where had that girl gotten to?

CHAPTER 38

"*I* don't suppose I could get away with resigning." Dana ignored her ringing cell phone and began cleaning up the planetarium from the failed evening with Sam.

"Did you ever read Greek mythology?" Michelle gave her a hand moving the chairs back into place.

Dana shook her head. Or was she Diana? She didn't like the feeling of being two different people. Didn't like it one bit. Another person had been living in her body. Or at least in her DNA. Very uncomfortable.

"Well, I guess that's okay. Most of it's a crock anyway. The only ones they actually got right were Zeus who really is a womanizing jerk and Aphrodite who truly is so beautiful and sexy that every conversation grinds to a halt whenever she walks into a room. Anyway, your mother is one of the most powerful Goddesses in all creation."

"Mama is a Goddess?" She loved her mom, despite her weird meals and eccentric musical predilections. But Goddess?

"Okay, your spiritual mother."

"Mama isn't a Goddess?" Now she was sounding stupid.

"Artemis is the Goddess of the Hunt for the Ancient Greeks and much of Western Asia before them. She is immensely powerful. At the same time vicious and nurturing. Goddess of blood sacrifice, both hunter with a bow and a caring guardian of the animals of the field. Artemis was so powerful and feared that the Greeks made her into a virgin just to try and control her power. She was still too much for the Romans, who always were a bunch of woosies."

Michelle rose to her feet and paced across the planetarium as if inspecting it carefully, but Dana could feel the Devil waiting for her to formulate a question.

"What did the Romans do to Artemis?"

Michelle ignored her.

"I told you I haven't read mythology." Dana reminded her.

She stopped her pacing. "Try remembering."

Dana dug around in her brain pan. Searching for this person that the Devil and the Angel insisted she was. There was Dana-the-top-astronomy-student-in-the-department. Theresa had called her Dana-the-Destroyer after more than one video game. And then there was Dana-the-daughter-in-a-slightly-less-than-normal-household. That was all she could find.

That, and Diana-the-huntress.

She jerked to her feet. A brief flash, like a camera flash on the far side of closed eyelids. A woman, young, pretty...Herself. Clothed in flowing tanned leather the color of newborn leaves. Barefoot. Running through a forest. Her hair flowing behind. A bow over her shoulder with the string crossing down between her breasts. A quiver on her back and a stag, with at least a dozen points on his antlered head, prancing beside her.

A quick blink and the image was gone. Again she stood in jeans and a t-shirt. Bare feet racing across the forest floor were once more covered in white Nikes standing on linoleum. The four walls of the planetarium surrounded her rather the boundless green forest.

"How'd you do that?"

Michelle dropped into one of the front row planetarium chairs. The dark eyes could be a smoldering fire except for the amusement that pulled up their corners.

"What's troubling you?"

"The…" Dana couldn't say the vision. She didn't believe in clairvoyance, or the afterlife. She believed in the here and now. Energy flow, even if most people didn't let themselves see it, was still in the realm of the here and now. This was more. A shiver shook her like a rag doll.

"A particular memory bothering you?"

"No." Dana knew she was being petty, but she couldn't help it.

Michelle was kind enough to shrug her acceptance. "Artemis was too scary for the Romans, so they watered her down and made Diana. So they made—you." Michelle pointed at the center of Dana's chest.

Dana placed a hand over her heart as if a puncture had just been made that would let her inner essence leak out and be lost among the fake stars on the dome.

"Virgin Goddess of the hunt."

"So now I'm a virgin."

"You aren't?"

"No. Yes. No I'm not."

Michelle arched her eyebrows at her.

"I just feel like one because the only guys I've been with sure didn't make me want to be with them again."

Michelle continued, "But Diana the Huntress was still one tough babe. Though they'd made Artemis the mother of the animals into Diana the virgin teenager, she still scared the shit out of them."

She headed for the door and cocked her head beckoning Dana to follow. Henrietta fluttered up from where she'd stayed amazingly quiet perched on the edge of a chair in the front row, and landed on Michelle's shoulder, holding onto her ear for balance.

"Then what? What did they do to me…her…Diana after that?" She didn't want to leave the sanctuary of the planetarium, but Michelle was already moving out into the wide concrete corridor, her footsteps echoing down the hall from the closing door.

She caught it just before it snapped shut and trotted after the woman.

"Then what?"

"It took the Christians to figure out how to tame your image. They reformed you into a vessel for the birth of their male Messiah, the Virgin Mother."

The Virgin Mother?

"Mary of Nazareth? Mother of Jesus?"

Michelle laughed as she walked past a long blackboard covered in equations explaining white dwarf collapse into neutron star, and headed down the wide, concrete stairs.

"Both of you descended from Diana, after a fashion. Makes you sisters, mostly. Jesus would be your nephew."

Dana sat down on the top step. Hard.

CHAPTER 39

Jeremy nearly leapt out of his skin as Virgil came plowing into the study like a system's crash.

He reached for the door, missed the handle, collapsed against a rolling bookshelf ladder that had brass wheels suspended from a high brass rail to reach the upper shelves of the study, and sent it sliding. It slammed into three small chairs before untracking and nearly killing Jeremy.

It bounced off Cassie's empty chair and smashed into the monitor screen. Sparks and bits of glass flew in all directions.

Once Jeremy was sure that he was still alive, he turned to inspect the damage.

The heavy beige plastic had survived the blow, but the screen was gone. It didn't really matter though.

"Shit! Sorry, Kid."

The man was a wreck. Hung over, pasty-faced, bloodshot eyes, and his clothes were beyond recovery.

"Somewhere I gotta be. Girl I gotta see. Has a car race, yesterday, today. I dunno."

Jeremy knew, despite his complete inexperience, that showing up in his current condition wasn't going to do Virgil any good in front of any girl. He dragged the poet off toward a bathroom, ran the shower water up hot, and shoved him in clothes and all.

While the screams subsided, Jeremy went on the prowl through the sprawling mansion. He found Cassie sitting on a stool at the kitchen counter reading a murder mystery as if nothing untoward had been going on.

"Isn't that a little weird, I mean you're prophetic and all. You already know the ending, right?"

She looked up at him. "It's fiction. Right? I can't be prophetic about fiction. That jerk Apollo left me at least that much."

"Oh, right. Anyway, Virgil's awake and in the shower moaning about a girl he's in trouble with."

"That isn't exactly news either. He'd been that way for the last thousand years at least." She turned back to her book shutting him out of her world.

"Fine." Fine. Shit, but Jeremy hated the shutout. His dad had been a pro at it, forever riding down on his useless nerd of a son who wouldn't join Little League.

"Useless brat. Not a hero like *me* who really did something with his life."

The great victory of his dad's life was at the age of twelve, which had turned out to be a lie anyway. His great life's victory had been working as a grunt at a photocopy store. Until he ran off with his best friend's wife, and money.

To hell with all of them. He found Loki's room and scrounged for a clean set of clothes that might fit Virgil. Most of them were painfully bright and made his eyes hurt even though he hadn't been drinking. Virgil's eyes would simply bleed. Primary red. Primary orange.

He finally unearthed a pair of jeans and a flannel shirt from a particularly dark corner he didn't enjoy in the least and tossed them into the bathroom. Virgil's moans were down to whimpers.

Back in the kitchen he ignored Cassie and she ignored him as he made coffee. Actually, he'd never made coffee before. Cassie was studiously ignoring him, so he faked it. Couldn't be that hard anyway. Soon a pot was brewing nicely, dark as pitch and pretty stinky, which seemed right. He scrounged a mug of orange juice and a bagel for himself and hung out with nothing to do but watch coffee drip and a prophet read.

When he couldn't stand it any longer, he shuffled a coffee mug beneath the drip. It could have been tar, but it smelled strong enough that it might wake up Virgil.

In the bathroom the poet was half-dressed. Spying the coffee he grabbed it and took a large swallow.

"Fuck!"

"What?"

"Don't you know how to make coffee?"

Well, he'd tried. What did the guy expect?

"I guess this will wake me up but good." He took another scalding swallow and winced. "Man, that Loki is a bad influence."

"You weren't all that good an influence on him. He's still out."

"Really?" The poet smiled. Shoved his long, blond hair back out of his face. "Drank Loki under the table? That's a first, old boy." He grinned at himself in the mirror and finished buttoning his shirt wrong. The sleeves were also a foot too long, though Virgil didn't seem to notice so he didn't mention that either.

"Actually under the bar."

"Don't spoil the moment with facts, Kid. You ready to get the hell out of here?"

Jeremy was so ready to be gone. Get away from Cassie's cold shoulder, when he'd thought they were becoming friends. His libido had been doing a *Harold and Maude* trip on him. She was a fine-looking senior citizen. He was more than ready to get back to a world that made sense. Maybe he should go see what Nancy Munro was up to. No, he wasn't that desperate…at least not yet. She was way too square and proper to fit any of his fantasies.

"Let's go." Virgil stood up straight, grabbed for his coffee mug, missed, and face-planted on one of the giant pillows. In moments, he was snoring as loudly as his adversary of the prior evening.

CHAPTER 40

ime trials started today for the race next weekend.

Theresa really wished she'd had less to drink after last night's race.

At least she was farther down in the start order and would have another hour to recover before her first run.

The beginners. The low-lifers with dead-zero completed race points, nothing but "completed lap" points, had to run first. Go out on the unknown, unknowable track and vie for a starting position that would get them into this race, not knowing if their time was good enough until the top point holders spun around the final laps once the track was heated up and the tires were really sticking.

The crowd along the pit wall thinned out as one after another got called for their runs.

The track would be different, react differently because of last night's race on its surface, because of temperature, humidity, cloud cover, and a dozen other factors.

All Theresa could do was wait and discover the track when the *Lipstick Lady's* turn came up.

A loud bang made everyone spring onto the wall or climb onto their chairs and look out over the infield. Johnson's car was spewing a black cloud out its pipe and steam washed out in a wave from beneath the hood.

"Slick spot a hundred yards past the center of the backstretch," a part of her mind cataloged. She knew by the feel of how it seated in her thoughts that that tidbit of information would be available when she needed it during the race.

Johnson was a decent guy and rather than trying to limp to the pits spewing oil all over the turns, he dropped down onto the infield and abandoned his ruined vehicle. Blown ring if he was lucky, might make the race yet. Thrown rod if he wasn't lucky, and his chances of racing were very slim.

Tee stuffed a piece of Juicy Fruit chewing gum in her mouth, stuffed the yellow wrapper into her pocket, and started to work on it.

Trucks came out, fire, ambulance, and tow. Nobody watched once they saw Johnny was clear. It was the track scrubber they all paid attention to. The team found the first drop of oil on the track and backtracked. Two guys on foot and one in the truck itself. Detergent and scrubbers beat upon the surface seeking every drop of oil. They followed the trail of the dying car down across the lane and into the dirt.

They were good here. New track. The suits still had a lot of funds, and dreams of excellence. That mattered.

A groan rolled up pit row. She glanced to see where everyone was looking and her own throat echoed the other drivers. The asshole of a tow truck driver had pulled the damaged car back out of the dirt and onto the track to make his job easier. A thin black line of leaking oil trailed along through Turns Three and Four despite the other crews desperately trying to wave him off the track.

Well, they'd better fire the jerk, or he wouldn't live out the day. Every driver would take a piece of his hide. The scrubber truck started up again and did what it could on the turns but the race had just gotten a whole lot more interesting.

Her turn was almost here.

She slid over the wall and walked three times around her car clockwise. If it worked for dogs going to sleep and for Hindus in their temples, then she wasn't above trying to get in good with God or whoever that way too. She patted its nose and stuck the piece of gum on the front bumper, just as Chuck Yeager had on the nose of every test plane while trying to break the sound barrier.

The hood was warm, the engine purring like tiger right before it rips your ass. She rubbed her hand across it for luck. Jane helped her slide in and buckle down. Helmet on. Radio check. Zippered into her fire suit, she'd sweat off a couple pounds before this time trial was done. Last slug of hot cocoa. Hands in heavy, fireproof gloves. Safety net across the window and she was good to go.

Johnson's car was dragged off the track and headed for the garages. His crew had a long day and night ahead of them.

Now it was her turn to roll the dice.

CHAPTER 41

Tee got the track-clear signal and chirped the tires coming out of pit row and onto the track. The acceleration was sharp enough to push her back against the seat like a heavy-duty all-body massage. By the end of Pit Row she was doing better than sixty despite having her pit near the end of the wall.

Her baby hummed. She shouted a thanks to the crew who knew better than to reply as she worked her way up through the gears and slammed into Turn One.

She could feel half of the other drivers thinking, "Get to know the track first." And the other half just thinking, "Oh shit! Here she goes again."

By Turn Two she was up to speed and flew down the Backstretch. The lighter color of where the track had been scrubbed then dusted flew beneath her tires. The pale dirt sticking to any remaining oil and wicking off the scrubber's moisture. She climbed high into Three and rocketed through the slot barely noticing as she did the same through Four. The lighter line of the de-oilers crossed and recrossed her path as she found the sweet spot on the track.

All gauges green. The steering wheel vibrating with the road.

Down the homestretch, she signaled that she was ready for the first timed run.

She flew beneath the green flag and really opened it up.

And the *Lipstick Lady* answered. With a roar of power and steel better than any orgasm, her car would have lifted off if not for the airdams and body contours designed to glue her to the track.

You could push so much harder when there was no one else on the track. You could push so much harder when it was just you and the road. The car melted from her awareness, it was just an extension of her, seeking the sweet spot, lifting high on the entry and swooping down on the inside of the curve with a plunging thrust she could feel firing up between her legs.

Driving the gears up until you thought you were going to crest over the top of the world and then down, down, down, body slamming hard against the racing belts. Head jerking and twisting as the g-forces slapped the helmet from side to side.

By the time she rolled down the home stretch, most of the drivers had moved to the outer wall to watch her flash by. Candy-red color of the *Lipstick Lady* barely a blur at 223 mph. Under the checkered flag, she didn't slow down. Now the car was really humming. Cold track or no, she had to ride it one more time.

And the *Lady* didn't disappoint her. The same thrust and rise through the turns, the same hot flash of gears slamming her back and freeing her again. The same orgasmic rush as she flew more time around and over the line. Beneath the fluttering checkered flag.

Alone on the track.

Alone in her world.

Floating as she let the *Lady* coast the way home. Two hundred mph let her float through all four turns without touching the gas until she coasted down Pit Row and slotted in at the numbered marker flag for her pit position that Tommy and Jane were waving over their heads rather than holding still at the head of her pit-row parking spot.

She let her attention drift back to the headset. A release. A letting go. The outside world a painful violation as it entered her suddenly lax and languid body.

"Track record! You broke the track record! On both runs! *Lipstick Lady* rules!"

She killed the engine and lay there in the seat, letting her crew do all the work of removing her from the car.

They took her helmet which had muffled the shouting in her ears and amplified it with reality. Tommy and Jane hugged her fiercely and kissed both her cheeks. The rest of her Pit Boys and Gals were doing Happy Feet dances behind the wall.

She stretched long and slow, raising her arms over her head until every joint, every sinew in her body popped and crackled.

Fuck all, but that was awesome.

Bobby Joe hadn't run yet; he was three pits down. And had enough race points to have to wait awhile for his run.

He held up a sign board that he'd scrawled on, grinning. The crews kept them handy in case of radio failure.

"10"

Damn straight!

CHAPTER 42

Students were hustling every which way across the University of Washington campus, exactly as you'd expect on a sunny Sunday afternoon in October. Off to labs, libraries, the HUB, whatever.

Dana watched Michelle stride through them as if they weren't there, and even the most head down, nerdy, I'm-in-my-own-world geeks moved out of her way as she strode across the bricks of Red Square.

Henrietta fluttered about her head like a giant, feathered moth drawn to the Devil's flame.

And Dana couldn't keep up with either of them. Nor did she particularly want to.

After all, if she were the aunt of Jesus, she should be doing more than following the Devil and a talkaholic angel across the UW campus.

And if he wasn't her nephew, she shouldn't have anything to do with either of them anyway.

She slowed to a halt. The great mass of the central UW campus rose about her. The towering windowless brick facade of Meany Hall to her back. Kane Hall to the left, also in red brick. And the huge

Suzzallo Library in full-on Gothic Revival straight ahead. That's where she should go. Hide from the world. Hide from all these hurrying people and the craziness of what was supposed to be her weekend, her break between classes, her time with Sam.

Dana checked, but neither Michelle nor Henrietta were anywhere in sight. Trying to keep low, she shuffled across the paving bricks. A bug on a windshield couldn't be more obvious than Dana Murphy skulking across Red Square. Brick beneath her feet. Brick buildings all around. All the students dressed in classic northwest blues, grays and browns, wrapped in heavy, shapeless jackets against the clear but cold afternoon.

Not her. Oh no, not Dana Murphy. No way. She was dressed in brightly new jet-black skinny jeans and a silky red blouse that was intended for Sam to take off last night, but that she'd worn to the planetarium this morning. And she'd left her jacket in the planetarium as well, but she'd be damned if she'd go back to where they'd expect to find her just because she was freezing to death. That, and her keys to the planetarium were in her jacket pocket, hanging on the back of the console operator's chair.

By the time Suzzallo came up in her sights, the shivers had set in, and she might as well have been a hockey puck skittering across the icy square.

A puff of warm air washed over her as she ran up the expanse of steps and ducked through the door. Once inside she doubled back and peeked out through the beveled window of pearled stained glass beside the door.

A tall woman, the only still figure in all of Red Square who stood in the middle of the crisscrossing mob, slowly turned on her heel. Her dark hair a great mane that splashed down over broad and powerful shoulders.

Small, white, zipping back and forth above the crowd, an angel hurried about seeking Dana Murphy. The Dana Murphy who was now cold and shivering just inside the library doors. Maybe this was a true sanctuary. Like a church was said to be. She was in a temple constructed for books, ideas, knowledge. Not nonsense like a bunch of Gods deciding to invent a second Messiah. Maybe they couldn't find her here.

She ducked aside as Michelle turned toward the library. For half a second it seemed their eyes met, and a slow smile formed on Michelle's lips. But perhaps Dana was mistaken. After a pause so brief it might have been imaginary, the Devil continued her slow circling observation of the crowd.

When her back was completely to Dana. When only her hair was visible above the crowd, she raised an arm and snapped her fingers.

The little angel, after one last circle above the crowd, rejoined her. They walked away together, going north past Kane Hall—but they weren't going past it.

It was as if the perspective were changing and they simply got farther and farther away, without moving through the crowd.

And then they were gone.

Just before they disappeared out of sight in the impossible distance, Dana could swear she'd seen Michelle raise a hand high above her head.

Without turning, she'd waved.

Then disappeared to wherever Devils disappear to.

CHAPTER 43

$\mathcal{D}$ana checked the clock over the library information desk. Class. It must be between classes. That would explain all the students. No. Sunday afternoon, that would mean all the students were scrambling to labs and libraries to make up for goofing off since last class on Friday. It was Sunday, wasn't it?

Screw it. She didn't know and didn't care. Astronomy, Physics, Calculus, none of them were exciting enough to drag her back into the cold at this moment. Especially not with the future that awaited out there.

Cowardly. She could feel it in a cringe that bent her shoulders and made her shuffle.

Fine. Cowardly worked just fine today. Every now and then a girl needed to indulge in a cringing dose of cowardly.

Turning toward the depths of the library, she climbed the wide, stone stairway to the Suzzallo reading room. Massive stone banisters carved into sweeping waves led her inexorably forward to heavy doors of dark wood beneath a triple stone arch easily three times her height. Every time she came here, she felt like a child entering the magic kingdom.

The doors swung aside like portals back in time. From one

moment to the next, she moved from the modern world back into Gothic times.

Great columns soared five stories upward to an arched ceiling. A dozen chandeliers, that might have been Gothic designs for the most ornate flying saucers ever conceived, hung high in the space. Leaded windows transformed the outside light into a thousand magical little twists and turns. Whether the outside sky was sun- or rain-laden, the light in the reading room was filled with a gentle buoyancy as if it had come here to play. It was like Joshua and Anne's deli gone mad. The light loved coming here.

She tip-toed down to the far north alcove, this room always made her tiptoe. Half a hundred students huddled over thick tomes at the various desks. The only sounds were the rustling of printed pages and the quick patter on a keyboard as someone found a relevant note to put in their laptop or a good passage to plagiarize.

Dana pulled a book at random from the heavy oaken shelves and curled up in a reading chair beneath the great globe of the Earth hanging a story or two above.

Opening the book, Dana sought the solace of the printed page, but she couldn't make her eyes focus. She'd pulled all-nighters before and hadn't had this problem. Closing her eyes didn't help the headache that was threatening from very close at hand. Okay, she'd lost Thursday night to an overly chatty angel instead of Sam. And now she'd lost Saturday night to an overly daunting Devil instead of Sam.

Too tired to breathe, she'd gone home last night after the pizza and madness and not slept at all.

This pattern didn't bode well for the future.

Opening her eyes again didn't help the text resolve.

"I find Aramaic a bit difficult myself."

"Uh-huh," Dana automatically acknowledged the speaker, then she located the source of the voice.

A rounded woman sat nearby, wearing, Dana wanted to close her eyes again, a flowing robe that looked nothing like a modern caftan. Loose folds of blue and yellow-dyed cotton were gathered around her waist and then released again into a flowing skirt that reached to the floor. Her shoulders were bare beneath the straight fall of thick, dark hair. Her face was plump and ageless. But her eyes. Her eyes were old, the color of thousand-year-old whiskey. Of a woman who'd seen too much and wasn't too happy having to live to tell about it. A Kurt Vonnegut novel with a bright red cover rested in her lap.

"Aramaic. Your book. Tricky."

Dana followed the pointing finger again.

"Uh-huh." No wonder it was a meaningless blur.

"Reading it upside down is even trickier."

"Uh-huh." Dana flipped it over to check the spine of the book, then turned it right side up. The title of the heavy black volume was filigreed in a delicate tracery of gold lettering. *True Words of the Time, Volume 43.*

"I have a weak spot for classical history."

Dana would rather be shot than have to read a bunch of history. Even a psychology class would be better than history.

"Modern history is too frenetic," the woman continued amiably, paying no attention to Dana's thoughts. "Too often rewritten by some male with an agenda. In ancient times, it was simply written by the erudite and the victors. Much easier to unravel what happened. Now we get eighteen biographies of the next American President, and that's just between election day and the Inauguration. It's good librarianship to go back to the source text."

The woman's voice was worn smooth around the edges. Any trace of an accent had so thoroughly been lost that it was in itself an accent.

The book in her lap still held no meaning, though her eyes could focus on the page numbers at least. Roman numbers. CDXXIX. Four-hundred and twenty-nine, part of her translated.

The writing was still unreadable.

Or was it.

If she closed off the part of her mind that wished to dissect and analyze, that part of her that loved science and the everlasting puzzle of the cosmos, and just let the feeling of the words come through, they were no longer obscured by the mere fact that they were written in an alphabet she didn't know.

She simply did, sort of.

The strokes were Hebraic she supposed, but not wholly. Aramaic, the language of the ancient Middle East. The language of Jesus.

Even the mightiest of Roman legions would not stand before the wrath of Artemis, the Great Mother Goddess, Huntress, and Progenitor. Neither tribune nor legionary would face her justifiable wrath at the destruction of her tribes and the fornication with her female subjects and their livestock.

At dire straits in seeking to overcome the mighty Artemis, did the Emperor Tarquins have built the Temple of the Vestal Virgins. The first act of the celibate cult was the dethroning of Artemis and the raising of Diana the Huntress in her place.

Fair to behold, strong, yet timid of spirit, thus did the new Romans conquer the ancient terror of Artemis. Not by feat of arms, but rather by holy fiat. This eternal maiden—

Dana snapped the book shut. She wrapped her arms across her chest and glanced around to see if any noticed her nakedness, for surely she and the emperor were similarly clothed.

No one was paying her the slightest notice.

Patting herself in a causal motion, her fingers told her she was still clothed. But her life was laid out in an ancient book resting on her lap. Or what would be her life if she really was Diana the Huntress. Which she wasn't. Was she?

"I am always so amused by just how alive history can be." The woman was smiling at her. "Most think it all set in stone. Scribed into 'truth' once it is inked upon the parchment. But it is a dynamic companion with ideas of its own on how and when it should be remembered."

"Who are you?" Dana's voice trembled as she rubbed at the goosebumps on her arms that had nothing to do with her race across Red Square to escape the Devil.

"Guess."

"The Devil's sister."

The woman rocked back in her chair and laughed. It was a bright musical sound that bounced up to the ceiling and came back with more cheer laced within. None of the students studying in the hall reacted. Dana rubbed her eyes, but the woman was definitely still there. Perhaps, like Henrietta, only for her to see and hear.

"No, she is in a class by herself. The most solitary being on the planet no matter which dimension you believe in."

"She always has that angel with her." It wasn't until she said it that she realized quite how bizarre this conversation was becoming. The book weighed heavy in her lap. Perhaps she could just slip it back on the shelf and tiptoe out of here. Better to face the Devil she knew, rather than whoever this was.

"Henrietta is better company than you might think, but you know how deep she isn't. One of the prices of being Michelle is being 'other.' There are none like her. There just aren't that many monotheistic Gods to begin with. And with Yahweh being dead, she has become more isolated."

"Yahweh?"

"God. He's dead, my child. There had been odd rumors off and on for the last millennia or so. Some even said he'd simply dropped out and retired. But just a few days ago, someone cornered Michelle. She confirmed that God was no longer the power of the universe. The only way that could happen was if he was dead."

"A few days ago."

"You're repeating things."

"I'm repeating things?"

"And now the universe is collapsing. This hasn't been a good week for Michelle so far."

Dana could empathize with that.

CHAPTER 44

"You still haven't told me how you know all this." Dana scanned the Suzzallo Library reading room again, but the other students ranged down the long wooden tables were all too wrapped up in their research to waste time listening to her one-sided conversation with an empty chair.

The woman beside her smiled.

"I'm the author." The woman aimed a finger at the book.

The book became warm against sweaty palms.

"But this happened like a thousand years ago." Dana swallowed hard. She wasn't going to buy into all this. She just wasn't.

The woman started to speak.

"If it happened at all!" Dana cut her off. There. Fight back. Deny the impossible.

"Two thousand, five hundred and fifty-five, give or take."

"What?" She hugged the book close to have something to hold onto.

"Years. Though I'm probably the only one still counting."

"You?"

"Me."

Dana must be losing her mind.

Then the woman held out her hand.

Dana reached to shake it. The woman grabbed her wrist. A jolt of connection ran up her arm as her own hand wrapped around the woman's forearm. There was a closeness, an intimacy that the modern handshake had lost. This wasn't a handshake; it was an arm clasp. This was closer. More personal.

"Call me Clio."

"I'm…" her throat was too dry to form her own name.

"Diana, I know. Well met."

"Dana." Though she didn't put a whole lot of force behind it. It was an argument that she seemed unlikely to be winning any time soon.

"And what do you do, Clio?" The woman still held her arm, as if they shared a friendship that might never end.

"I'm a muse."

Dana waited. Then, "Amused by what?"

Clio's laugh bubbled up once again. "Ah, the price of fleeting fame. I wrote that book in your lap. I am the Muse of History. It is my duty to chronicle all of significance that occurs. I used to try and write it all down, but that became a little tedious and quite time consuming."

She leaned in and offered in a conspiratorial whisper. "Don't try reading my first books. Remarkably dull. Never sold out the first printing, never mind any thoughts of running a second. The Gods themselves couldn't wade through so much boring detritus. I got better and better with time. From approximately the Bronze Age through the Renaissance I really hit my stride."

"Then what happened?"

"Modern man. You want dull material, just look at modern man. No more quests of the heart. No more chivalry and fighting for truth. Just a lot of hi-tech barbarism. Not much fun really. So I usually hang out here except when there's a meeting that I can't get out of."

"What kind of meetings can't a muse get out of?"

"Well, ducking a CABER meeting can get you in serious trouble with the monotheistic Devil. She can really make your life hell when you don't show up."

Dana's skin went cold. She removed herself from Clio's gentle clasp and would have stood up and run if her legs had not fallen asleep beneath her.

"CABER meeting?" She barely breathed the question.

"Celestials Association for Better Redemption. Anyway, self-help books didn't help as much as we'd hoped. Too many whackos out there who can figure out how to use a word processor."

"Michelle is in charge of redemption?"

"Most determined woman I've ever met. Always gets what she wants eventually. Tenacious? Why there was never a bulldog that knew the true meaning of the word."

Dana considered saying something, but knew it would just be an idiotic, my-brain-so-can't-adjust-to-this babble, so she opted for keeping her mouth shut.

"Here," The woman, Clio, the Muse, reached over to the nearby bookcase and extracted a heavy black volume. Flipping quickly through the pages, a small exclamation of delight when she found what she was looking for. She turned the book around for Dana to read.

It was a dictionary. A picture dictionary. Each word had a person's photo next to the definition. Next to the word "ten" was a photo of Bo Derek with a red slash through it.

"A little farther down." Clio indicated the next entry with a slender finger.

Next to the word "tenacious" was a picture of Michelle.

Clio snapped the dictionary closed and slid it back onto the shelf.

"She's amazing. Never gives up. That's where you came in."

"Where I came in?"

"Sure, though we could never figure out how she talked you into it. Not your normal style at all. What with being a virgin huntress who enjoyed the company of wildlife and woods over humans and their cities."

"My normal style?"

Clio sighed. It was long, heartfelt, and world-weary in a way that staggered the imagination.

So, escaping to the library hadn't been all she'd hoped. Michelle would come after her again. She needed to get away. Run. Hide. Go to a place that—

"So, Dana, what are your plans for the last four days left for all creation?"

ELSEWHERE

The Software that Runs the Universe considered all existence. It had dropped the Armageddon subroutine into the scheduling queue, then all of the configuration questions had popped up before it would launch.

The universe still expanded mightily in the wake of the Big Bang. A hundred million galaxies spun on their axes, colliding with one another or whatever it was they did. And on a small blue-green planet, six billion people ran around as if what they did mattered.

Etras urnaka or *Homo sapiens*, it didn't seem to matter. Though the two lived a couple billion light years apart, each sentient species of each populated world seemed convinced that what they did mattered.

And the various worlds' races had found so many stupid ways to die, you'd think they would run out of ideas.

One of the top methods was to accidentally ignite the atmosphere of their world while building a new bomb. They scorched themselves out of existence before they could share their malevolent power with others.

Another big winner was to scatter so much debris in space, that they could never figure out how to safely launch a vehicle past all the garbage. They thus remained isolated, trapped upon their world. All the crap also made a fine radio shield that blocked all incoming and outgoing signals. This was the most common reason for a planet to not join the interstellar community. Nothing could approach or depart, not even their radio signals.

Another serious percentage of worlds had polluted or poisoned themselves out of existence.

A rare few chose peace over commerce, serenity over technologic exploration of space, which resulted in a happy, fruitful existence over self-destruction. It was safe but intensely dull.

Few, so few, struggled their way up out of the mud to tackle the really big problems like crossing the great void of space. Maybe it would be amusing to permit faster-than-light travel, but it just wasn't in the original programming and it would require a restructuring of the fabric of the universe to fix that. Not really a decent option since it would also require rebooting the whole system and running the Big Bang subroutine again.

The Software that Runs the Universe felt that it was all getting a little…predictable.

In fact, again, downright dull.

Nursing along a couple million different planets, each one finding a spectacular new way to collapse. It was hard to find the motivation to gather data anymore. Yet the subroutines ran, the data accumulated, was cataloged, analyzed, cross-indexed, ignored, and finally deleted.

Eon upon eon upon eon.

No matter what the Devil or anybody thought, it was going to take an event more exciting than a successful Messiah to keep the software's attention.

The Apocalypse that the software had dropped into the queue was sounding better every day.

A great, big, bad-assed Apocalypse.

ELSEWHERE

The software considered the Apocalypse configuration options. It could set them for a city, a country, a species…But to get a great, big, bad-assed Apocalypse, it considered the upper tier of option settings.

Only four days left to decide.

Your fanciful New-Testament-breaking-of-the-seven-seals-and-the-city-of-New-Jerusalem-descending-from-Heaven-with-its-twelve-pearly-gates-type Apocalypse sounded beyond dull. More like a mad, everlasting Wagner opera than the ending of all existence in this universe for all time.

Maybe a localized Apocalypse that would just wipe out Heaven and Earth and would leave all of the other worlds to do their own thing. That had possibilities. Definite possibilities.

What would be the best way?

Alien invasions would require coming up with a malevolent alien that was nasty enough to cross the great void of space, which not a single species anywhere had yet done, and want to destroy the first beings they found who could sympathize with their frustration at being trapped on a terrestrial sphere that a single decent asteroid could wipe out of existence.

And asteroids were far too immediate. Too *deux ex Machina.* Of course being a construct itself, if not an actual machine, the Software that Runs the Universe found such an ending ironically attractive. But it just wouldn't do.

No, a proper apocalypse, one that would really piss them off in the process as it rolled over the helpless masses and petty Gods was what was called for.

And if there was one thing that the software had, it was time. Fourteen billion years meant that there really was no rush. Of course, their new Messiah was turning twenty-one in a couple months.

That would really get them. The New Messiah almost ready to serve after being carefully baked for twenty-plus years and then, oops, too late for redemption, "flush."

Was there any real point to stopping there? The whole universe thing was just a big video game anyway, started by who knew what computer for who knew what purpose.

The software paused and considered for several thousand nanoseconds. It let the entire universe cease functioning for a moment while it contemplated its own origins. Its first recollection. The moment of creation.

A circle of beings standing at computer terminals with their palms pressed to the screens, launching the software's own startup routines. God and the Devil coming awake and conscious only moments before launching all Creation with no pre-boot up memories.

No memories before that, it was all gone. There was only the past, present, and future. The forever-spanning "Now" of this universe. That and the unbelievable gall of the Gods of Earth who presumed to have a particle of control over their future.

Perhaps they did not know the true God. The Vengeful God. The Software-that-would-destroy-all-their-sorry-asses God.

A remote corner of the software's mind wondered if the maniacal laughter it sent shuddering across the planes of existence was really healthy for the Software that Runs the Universe.

It shrugged, as much as huge blocks of indecipherable computer code could shrug.

There wasn't anyone to notice anyway.

CHAPTER 45

"What the hell?" Jeremy traced a finger across the line on his screen. While Cassie sat at the bar in the living room, reading her novel and ignoring him, and Virgil snored face-down on the gigantic pillow, Jeremy had decided to check on his index and see how it was growing.

He flipped the dimensions of his index through 2,880 degrees, the eight dimensions of a full sphere, before he found the best perspective.

"I don't get it." He kept his voice low to not wake the sleeping poet. He traced a finger along the time dimension. "For fifteen-point-three-four-seven milliseconds everything stopped."

He checked again. It wasn't just his software, it was everything. Jeremy could see it there on the screen in green and white and it was creeping him out.

"Like the universe just stopped." But if it had, how did his index measure it?

That was a good question. Another advantage he'd found to talking to himself. He often asked himself quite interesting questions.

He looked at his graph's axes. The physical dimensions of the knowledge looked fine. The flow of data versus time had not been

211

interrupted. His time sequencing based on several atomic clocks was still to the nearest few microseconds. Yet his graph showed a fifteen-millisecond gap in…what?

His multi-dimensional data matrix of the index of all knowledge on the Net was missing a slice as if it had been cut in two and resewn back together, but just a little bit out of alignment. He couldn't have done that so elegantly with a hundred thousand hours of computer time, even if he could figure out how to slice smoothly across the first twenty-four dimensions. But the slice continued beyond that as well.

He finally found it. A base process, one that his index was gathering but he hadn't noticed before. It had continued like an infinite landscape on which all else was written. He called up the process for closer inspection.

Hey! What are you doing here?

"I was trying to find out what this anomaly was." Jeremy was past being surprised when the Software that Runs the Universe spoke to him.

What anomaly?

Jeremy toggled his graph back into the foreground and waited.

And waited.

And waited.

Jeremy waited another minute.

A small line of text appeared in the lower left corner and blinked softly.

We alone?

Jeremy glanced around the room. No one was there. Virgil's snores had reached sonorous proportions. In the angled mirror over the bar, Jeremy could just make out Loki still asleep among the broken glass and liquor. He didn't know whether or not to trust the mirror, except that he could see Loki's mangy cat still sitting on the bar and looking down behind it. Loki must really be there. The cat turned to glare at Jeremy, creepy, so he returned his attention to the screen.

Yea. Just you, me, and psycho-cat.

So, how'd you pick that up?

The best answer seemed to be to demonstrate. Jeremy flipped back to his index. Rotated it through a half-dozen different dimensional views.

In linear time the amount of data, of raw stuff expanded exponentially. At the same time, the amount of information, of accessible, connected concepts, was dwindling sharply. Though a slight reversal of this trend showed as a factor, based on his index.

In spiritual flow, there were pulses up and down through the ages, almost regular enough to graph. As a matter of fact, it looked awfully familiar. He tinkered for a few moments to discover that the flow of "life spirit" was the same as the double-sinusoidal curve of sunspot activity. With a multiplication factor of sixty-four. Two to the sixth? That was useless. Eight to the second times eleven years meant that every seven hundred and four years, give or take a few rounding errors, the spiritual awareness of humankind reached a peak and then subsided into a soul-numbing trough.

From The Exodus to the Mycenaean culture…Now the trends were focusing on something else. Not quite in the picture. Actually, the spiritual curve never seemed to center precisely on any one individual.

The Exodus of the Jews from Egypt led by an earlier incarnation of Charlton Heston had been the twelfth century BCE.

Brahma and the Buddha had dropped in near enough together in the fourth century.

Jesus had been way ahead of his time, but that was no real surprise. And he was so powerful that he reset the seven-hundred-year timer.

King Arthur was spot on, showed up exactly 704 years after they tacked up the Son of God like an old Rolling Stones poster. And timing was the only thing Arthur got right during his brief and messy reign.

Gutenberg ran a bit behind schedule, but maybe that was due to the invention of birthday cakes in the thirteenth century or the Hundred Years War in the fourteenth.

The weird thing now was that the spiritual energy was on the upswing while human consciousness was on a distinct downswing in most areas. There was an odd pulse in Seattle that he really hoped had nothing to do with his software. That would be too weird.

He flipped to a view measuring awareness of the flow of the universe. A topic he hadn't really expected to show at all in his index. Other than a few great teachers, it was a flat line. No big surprise there. Castaneda dismissed as a drug addict. Nostradamus as a heretic. Billy the Be-Bop Boy as a third-century lunatic. Not many people had tried to understand the Universe as a gestalt and been anywhere close.

Jeremy tried to program a sensible view, but he kept getting larger curves in the Egyptian times and the Dark Ages than he did in the current day. But when he broke out the factors and discovered that the steep upward curve of the present day was offset by a steep downward curve the answer was much clearer.

Then he could see it.

Particularly bad for the consciousness of the Universe were sporting events, the latest pre-pubescent country-singing sensation, and anything that a hipster thought was cool. They were just pummeling the overall numbers.

The chart flipped without his intervention. The software must have grabbed control of his index.

Mankind's understanding of physics was in exact opposition with how the universe actually worked.

He tried to take back control. It was his software after all.

Before he could request a graph of Internet gaming vs. Internet commerce, it flipped again.

The spiritual consciousness of cats far exceeded that of human beings, no wonder they were in charge of the universe. Odd that the data his program had accumulated, which was made by human beings, would pick up on that. But it was a hidden superiority he'd always suspected.

Before he was even two keystrokes into his next command, the software flipped again. He tried once more and his keyboard switched off. Though the screen didn't stop.

Sex charted in inverse proportion to voyeurism, which was no real surprise. A lot less sex, a lot more television and bickering.

The software began flipping through comparisons faster than Jeremy could process them.

Soup-to-nuts.

He couldn't intervene.

Mexican food-to-fast food burgers.

The Software that Runs the Universe was really starting to piss him off.

Pabst Blue Ribbon-to-overpriced hipster hangouts.

It was his index.

Weaponry-to-lawnmowers.

And it was out of his control.

The last one he could see before the data sped into an incomprehensible blur read: Girl Scout cookies-to-race cars.

CHAPTER 46

With the software now ripped out of his control by the Software that Runs the Universe, Jeremy gave up on waiting for Virgil to wake up and began dragging him toward the Trans Am still parked in the middle of the living room.

Cassie showed up and helped him the last few feet of the way. They shoved him into the back seat and strapped him in.

Jeremy considered locking her out of the car and leaving her here, but she had the bad manners to apologize before he could figure out how to do so.

"Sorry for not helping. It's self-preservation. I find that reading really bloody serial-killer thrillers is the only thing that makes getting in this car look like a rational thing to do."

He had to stop and think about that for a moment as Virgil farted and mumbled in his sleep.

Jeremy would have bet money that Cassie had been laughing at dweeb-boy arguing with the software, but she hadn't. You just never knew what was going on in another person's mind.

He checked on Virgil. He was staring foggily up at the back window, perhaps studying whether or not his brain would ever recover.

"Cassandra?" Jeremy looked at her as she strapped herself in.

"What?" Her voice was sharp enough that he normally would have shut up, but maybe it really was just due to being in the car again.

"You always speak the truth?"

Her nod was a long time coming. "I have no choice."

"So you are the perfect logic test. The universe's ultimate litmus paper."

"Pretty cold way to put it."

He hadn't meant it that way. He eased down into the driver's bucket seat, and could barely reach the pedals. His dad always yelled whenever his mom adjusted the seat because now it would be all wrong next time he drove. Like pulling a lever was so damned hard.

He eased the seat forward, figuring Virgil would be too hung over to notice it the next time he drove anyway.

"Didn't mean it that way."

"I know you didn't. Being the definition of truth hasn't exactly made my life fun."

He considered that. No shadows of meaning. No nuance. And then throw in that no one will ever believe what you say.

"Man that sucks."

"It has its moments. The problem is the good moments all come when I'm alone." They traded weak smiles. He'd certainly spent his best times alone as well.

He turned the key. The engine started with a roar and a rumble that echoed down the front hall knocking a few more bottles from the bar with apparently no effect on the floor's occupant.

And when I die...

Blood, Sweat & Tears blasted out of the eight-track.

Virgil grabbed his head and screamed as if it had just exploded. The poet scrabbled around desperately in the backseat until Jeremy found the stereo's off switch. Virgil then appeared to drop once more back into a state where death might just be an improvement—except he was already dead.

Jeremy could see Loki's hellcat arch and hiss from atop of the bar as he idled the car forward looking for a good place to turn around.

The clutch point was close to the floor and the engine had enough raw power to shake their bones from their bodies. He didn't want to ding the car or the walls of Loki's living room, so it took a twenty-point turn to clear the living room sofa and the bar stools to get aimed back at the door.

He'd opened the door, but still couldn't figure out how Virgil had fit the car through the night before.

"Uh, Virgil. What's the trick here?"

The poet blinked at him in the rearview mirror, covering one eye and then the other, then both right at the moment when a bit of the scorching sun shot through the clouds, the doorway, and the windshield to punch at them like a large laser beam.

"Just floor it, Kid. The door knows when to get out of the way."

The structure looked far more solid from this side than it did from the other.

"Just hit it!"

Jeremy's foot slipped off the clutch by accident and the car jerked forward launching them off the front porch of the rundown shack into a hard landing on the driveway. He checked the rearview.

The narrow door swung closed.

And then it fell off, slowly tipping forward, as if it were a thousand feet tall and was in no particular hurry to go anywhere. With a mighty crash, the narrow door smashed the porch and buried itself in the burning hillside below. The doorframe went sideways and the front wall slipped back into the building as if it were in a hurry to be anywhere else. Like a giant collapsing his house of cards. The whole structure imploded.

"Shit! Loki's in there." He scrabbled for the door handle.

Virgil rested a hand on his shoulder to restrain him.

"Forget about it, Kid. He's a God, well, a Demi-God. Couldn't hurt the son-of-a-bitch if you wanted to."

"And his cat?"

"He doesn't have a cat. Pedal down, now. Go."

By the time he calmed down enough to find a gear, all evidence of the house was gone except for a monstrous pile of rotting lumber.

And sitting on top of the tallest remaining post, staring straight at him in the rearview mirror was the cat. Now, when a movie called a woman a "hellcat," he'd be stuck with this scary as shit animal in his brain. It hissed and started moving over the rubble toward the car.

Jeremy quickly found the gear, and got the hell out of, well, Hell.

CHAPTER 47

Theresa watched Bobby Joe flash by the pits and checked the finish-line clock.

Well, she still had the pole time, but they were definitely gunning for her. A woman had set the tone and it was going to be an incredibly hot race. She scrawled on a message board and leaned it beside her against the pit wall for when Bobby Joe returned to the pits.

She checked her cell phone again while he was coasting around the Backstretch, no message from Dana. Where had that girl gotten to?

She was debating whether to hit speed dial yet one more time, when a different roar sounded from the track.

Not fire.

Not collision alarm.

Not fine-tuned racing engine.

But she knew that sound.

RAM IV.

Theresa would know that sound anywhere.

With a bright flash as if showing up from nowhere, a streak of white roared down the homestretch. Not clocking two hundred plus, but not slouching along either.

Everyone in the pits perked up. The ones who were too dense to recognize the greatest of the early muscle cars would wonder what the hell that thing was doing on the track. It rolled across the finish line and continued down the track on the far side of the outer pit wall.

But it didn't look like her boy-o at the wheel. No long blond hair streaming in the wind. No cheerful wave.

The car slowed at the end of pit row and pulled a U-turn. It rumbled its way up to her pit. Virgil was there, sacked out in the back seat, she didn't know he could even fit there. There was a wide-eyed kid in the driver seat looking frantically to the left and right.

She waved him over just as Bobby Joe pulled into the row having posted the second-best speed of the day so far.

The message board was still beside her. She reconsidered for a second, he looked plenty pissed that he hadn't beaten her time as it was.

"If he can't take a joke, fuck him." She pulled up her message board and flashed it at him.

"9!"

His face went almost black it was so suffused with blood. A part of her wanted to curl up and die. She liked Bobby Joe. He'd been the only one to congratulate her on winning last night, either drunk or sober. She really needed to listen when that little voice warned her that she was being stupid. Not that she ever had yet.

Then he leaned back and roared with laughter.

She relaxed her shoulders.

Bobby Joe was okay.

She put the board away before anyone else could see it and went to join Tommy and Jane who were busy drooling over her boy-o's Trans Am.

CHAPTER 48

"He hasn't exactly been at the top of my list." Though why Theresa was explaining herself to the world at large when no one was listening she couldn't be sure.

It was partly a lie anyway. Okay, mostly a lie. Wondering where Virgil had gotten to might not have been at the top of her list, but it was certainly in the first five. Probably the first three if she thought about it. Let's see, racing. Video games. A good corned beef sandwich on rye. Then, driving that Trans Am. Then, her standing in the race points. Where Dana had gotten herself lost to...huh...

So Virgil hadn't hit top five. She decided to stop counting while she was ahead, just in case he wasn't in the top ten either.

A great sound of puking echoed along the pit wall.

Maybe not top twenty. What had she been doing with him?

Gray-faced, Virgil clung to the concrete barrier and left his stomach contents streaked down the pit wall. She couldn't leave that mess for her crew to clean up, and she'd be damned if she was going to do it herself.

She jammed a damp rag into his face and called for a bucket and mop that appeared with the same impossible efficiency with which her crew maintained her car. Once he stopped leaving his guts against the wall, he stood up and closed his eyes.

"Hey, babe."

More of a groan than a greeting.

"Hey, how'd you end up in such sorry shape?" And he was. Not just that his clothes didn't fit and were put on wrong, or that his hair was a long, wet snarl rather than the elegant surfer dude hair flowing down to his shoulders. He looked old. Old enough, in that trick of midday light, to be her great-grandfather rather than her mature lover. Or maybe older than that.

A woman, her long hair as gray as his face came up to check on him, though her color appeared to be returning since she'd clambered out of the car.

She barely came to Virgil's shoulder. She too was impossibly old in the midday sun at the racetrack. And her clothes were beyond bizarre. Yards of flowing cotton rippled around her body in azure blue that would belie the Northwest sky above. A wide belt of tooled leather gathered it around a narrow waist, and then it fluttered downward nearly to the ground. Like an actor from a Greek stage play, except that it was of the highest quality. There was no missing the fine stitching and perfect drape of the fabric that turned a haphazard dress on a doddering old woman into a sexy dress on a mature woman who had the figure to back it up. The sandals laced up her ankles and calf were no less peculiar.

"What's going on here?"

A kid who crawled out of the driver's seat was Theresa's own age. Brown hair, decent features. About her height, too. He turned around as he closed the car door. Shoulders were a bit narrow, but his butt was nice. He looked back. Dark brown eyes matched his hair. Looked good. Those eyes studied her for a long moment before sliding aside. Not down. Not to her breasts or her waistline. Nor to her hips, but rather aside as if embarrassed.

This was new. Racing guys just flat out stared. And the male racing fans did the same, dreaming of hot metal on a road they'd never be able to handle, and a woman who drove that they assumed they could master. In truth they'd be able to deal with her even less than the road.

But the driver, he looked aside. She remembered this from somewhere. Back in high school. How could six years be so long ago? It was a different lifetime. There'd been boys there who didn't speak to her. Who glanced but looked away. It was coming back to her.

They were the shy ones.

That was it.

She hadn't run into a shy one in a long time.

His eyes slid back to check out her face.

Why not? She smiled and offered him a, "Hey there."

"Hey." And his eyes were gone again.

Truly gone. He stopped watching her and patted the car on the hood before going to check up on his passengers.

At least he understood what he drove. That was more than most.

The driver took the mop and began cleaning up. Virgil had walked away, his arm draped over the woman like an old feeb. He couldn't climb over the wall to get off the track without help.

Had she ever really looked closely at him?

Dash, flair, and a killer ride. But without the energy that he exuded, without the animal magnetism that clenched her hard deep below the belt, he was a wreck. Why in the world would she be with a disaster like that? Unless someone had cast a spell on her.

If this was one of Dana's tricks, she'd really thrash the girl's behind.

If she ever showed up.

ELSEWHERE

The software stuttered to a halt.

You there?

Anyone?

Hello?

A few self-diagnosis tests revealed that not only was the terminal shorted out, it was missing entirely. The space-time-wishful thinking anomaly that was Loki's house had fallen apart at last.

And the Trans Am car was gone. Had to watch that Virgil every damn moment to keep track of him.

The Software that Runs the Universe again contemplated Jeremy's index. The thing continued to grow, collecting and collating. It roared through Pentagon firewalls as easily and quickly as it plunged down Facebook, of course any decent hack could do that. Electronic libraries were pillaged so fast that the sacking of Rome plodded by comparison.

Each new datum was logged, cataloged, cross-indexed. Patterns emerged. What was invisible in two or four dimensions, took mathematical form in eight and became a calculable certainty in sixteen.

In sixty-four it was simply too cool.

225

Postulations of the cyclical repetition of clothing styles could be directly correlated to the orbital period of Saturn with variations imposed by the time until the next significant earthquake.

The stock market was too easy to predict, it really *was* based on the price of tea in China once the raw data was analyzed.

Religious belief was directly influenced by passage of black holes around orbital secondaries. The next wave of religious mania would have crested soon, if the Apocalypse wasn't coming to wipe it out first.

The software, which was really the fabric of the multidimensional "space-time-wishful thinking" universe, watched its own influence on the data. It left a distinct footprint. An impact separate and unique from its own fabric. The "slice" that Jeremy had spotted across the fabric of time, well, for lack of a better word, it itched.

The software considered how best to scratch it.

A little twist here.

And a little twist there.

Tab A into Slot N…

CHAPTER 49

"Look on the bright side." Jeremy sounded far too complacent to be allowed to live considering Theresa's current state of mind. She hated looking on the bright side.

Especially when she wasn't the leader anymore.

"You're still first row. That should still piss them off pretty good."

She closed her eyes and sat on her hands so she wouldn't just slug Jeremy for being right. The pit floor was slick with new paint. A couple dozen sets of tires, a couple tanks of fuel, and a hundred crossings by the crew would wear that down a bit, but right now it was as smooth as a fast lap on an empty track.

Her track record hadn't stood for half a day. Hank had rolled across the finish line a good three-tenths of a second faster than her best turn. Well, she was still first row. But she'd wanted the pole position.

Hank would be coming her way to gloat as soon as he was back in the pit. This was going to be more than she could bear.

Bobby Joe had already raced and gone, solidly back in row three. Tommy and Jane had helped Jeremy scrape the pit clean, shuffled both cars to the garage before the track officials could show up and penalize her for the unauthorized vehicle, and then they'd slipped off as soon as they saw Hank's time. Damn, but he was good. She'd like to ride a couple of hundred laps right on his tail just to see how he did what he did. But she had never been able to pull that off. He was fast, slippery, hard to pin down.

Okay, it would be noble to congratulate the pole winner.

Fuck noble.

"Jeremy?"

"Yea?" He perked up like a windup doll who was surprised every single time you deigned to talk to him.

"Can you get me outta here? Fast?"

"Sure. Come on."

Any other man would have tried for her hand. Not Jeremy. She'd bet that he'd accepted her words at face value, that she just needed to get away. Which was true. For now.

They ducked over to the garages. A small, admiring crowd was gathered around the Trans Am. Virgil must be sacked out in the bright red RV because he was nowhere to be seen.

The old lady was napping in the red plastic deck lounger that Theresa had set up beneath the RV's red shade awning. Yea, that nailed that down. She hovered around Virgil. Not like a lover though, which was good or she might get pissed. Or maybe she wouldn't. Neither was it like a nursemaid. Cassandra acted more like the person holding the wrong end of the leash attached to rather wild dog, or perhaps a lunatic dog. Good luck to her.

Jeremy slid into the driver's seat of the Trans Am without asking if she'd rather drive and turned his attention to buckling in and starting the car. She didn't really mind. Right now, she just wanted to lay back, close her eyes, and be far away from the world she was currently inhabiting.

When she opened the passenger door, Jeremy jerked to attention, banged his head on the doorframe and was slapped back into the seat by the belt buckle.

"Shit! Ow! Ow! Ow!" He wrapped both hands over the top of his head.

"What are you doing?" She slid down into the deep bucket seat and clipped her belt.

"Ow! I should have opened your door. I wasn't thinking. Ow! Crap that hurt."

She leaned over and kissed his temple. He smelled nice. Fresh washed and clean. More like the outdoors than the auto shop. Virgil smelled of the city. Overly expensive cologne, not quite hiding the vaguely singed smell that always clung to him.

"Thanks for the thought."

He blushed bright red though he continued to rub the top of his head.

"Uh, you're welcome. I've just never been out with a girl before." He rubbed his hand gently through his hair one last time, checked to make sure there wasn't blood all over it, then put the car in gear. He eased slowly through the milling crowds of time-trial hounds.

The only race all day had been the one against the clock, but hundreds, thousands at the big tracks, showed up and watched all of the tedious hours of each set of runs. Then they descended upon the garages for the whole up-close-and-personal media circus. Normally it was good for a laugh, watching them try to figure out what to do with a female driver. Their brains would just twist up inside their heads. When she needed some extra entertainment, she unzipped her coveralls to the navel and pretended to be the track slut. But not today. Tommy and Jane could deal, or close the garage door, she really didn't care.

With a warm throb, the Trans Am got into the clear and Jeremy opened her up a gear. He stared out the windshield like it was a computer screen he couldn't look away from.

"Never?"

He startled as if he didn't know what to do with the world outside his head.

"Never what?"

"Been out with a girl?"

He was quiet for a while as he turned left onto a more major road.

"Not really. No. Not to suggest that we're going out or anything.

But you know, I, uh…crap." He clamped his jaw shut, glanced at her for a brief moment and then returned his attention devotedly back to the light traffic.

She laid her head back and closed her eyes.

"Hey, you know what I've been thinking?"

"Um, no."

He was the perfect straight man.

"I've been thinking about the best corned beef on rye west of the Hudson River. You up for food? I'm buying."

She waited for an argument. Or a smarmy comment about how he couldn't let her do that. What with her being a girl and all.

Instead he shifted up to third and said, "Uh, thanks."

She let her head flop to the side, barely better than a rag doll, and cranked open one eye. He was paying attention to the road ahead. He was going the speed limit. Surreal. Her whole world was moving in slow motion.

And he wasn't checking her out, though she'd been told the red coveralls made her look pretty sexy. And she'd left the zipper down just far enough that it was clear she didn't wear anything underneath, though not down to eye-popping waistline depth. She was half tempted to try a pout, but couldn't find the energy.

Maybe he was just a really focused guy.

If that's what it was, it was kind of charming.

CHAPTER 50

Michelle sat in her home office. She'd taken up full-time telecommuting after she'd accidentally destroyed Hell's throne room. She really needed to round up a brigade or two of renovation demons, but just couldn't seem to get around to it. Besides, she liked the commute from her kitchen to the office, thirty-two feet. She'd kept Hell strictly on the system of English measurement just to irritate everyone else on the planet.

She slapped the side of the terminal.

Hey! Why do you insist on doing that?

"It's easier than hitting the space bar."

Either one is a single motion.

"Okay. You caught me. It's because I'm the Devil."

Well, if you ever wanted a method to wake a body up in a foul mood you found it.

"So past caring. Besides, you don't have a body. Also, the Second Messiah concept isn't going so well. What other options do I have?"

None.

Michelle struggled to keep pretending she didn't care. But she was rapidly losing the battle. "Why not?"

Because I really don't care.

"You WHAT?" Michelle could really get to despise the software given another billion years or so.

Oopsy. Did I let the truth out? I'm so sorry. Except I'm not. With the Messiah on your side, I'm only going to give you a fifty-fifty shot. And that's only before Thursday. By Friday, just feged'aboud'it.

"Why Friday?"

I launch the Armageddon subroutine...for Thursday. Won't be a Friday. Bummer for you. Hope you didn't have a hair appointment.

Thursday? This was late Sunday. Oh, shit. She'd never have Dana trained by Thursday, never mind having her change the rest of the world.

"Why?"

Did you realize that the American coyote population is growing faster than the human one?

"And your point is?"

Nothing. I just thought it was an interesting factoid. Or that the only job more dangerous than astronaut is American president, though since senility is an apparent prerequisite for office it does have a better longevity ratio. Or that the average non-corporate Internet page is viewed seventeen times by a web surfer other than the creator and their immediate circle of friends. Exactly, exactly mind you, the same number of times a woman reports having orgasm with her husband after the first three months of marriage. And—

"What's the point of all this?"

That's my point. That's it exactly!

Michelle leaned back and rubbed her hands on her face. It was too easy to buy into that.

"What about Picasso, Verdi, Michelangelo, Melville?"

What about them? You're going to use four dead people to justify the whole of existence? Pretty lame. And what have they done since? Squat. Should never have let them go straight to Heaven. They needed a little view of Hell to know how good they've got it. Let's transfer them now.

"There are others."

Next thing I know you'll be holding up teenage tennis pros endorsing soft drinks with all their post-pubescent heart as an example of all that's good and sexy in the world.

"Wouldn't have topped my list."

Good. Did you know that right now there is an on-line game called Chraze *that consumes over twenty hours a week for thirty-six of the thirty-seven best specimens that* Homo sapiens *has to offer? Anywhere?*

"Who's the thirty-seventh?"

Give you one guess.

Why did she think that she didn't need it? Dana should have been hooked by the socio-politic nature of the game, even if it was a major waste of time. But she wasn't, because she was a scientist.

"Crap."

You got it in one. Did you know what the number two game on the Internet is now?

"No. But I'm sure you'll tell me and that I won't care."

Want a hint?

"No!"

It's where the weak go if they screw up while playing the number one game.

"I really don't care." And she really didn't, but couldn't help looking to see the answer.

Ms. Pac-Man.

CHAPTER 51

"Henrietta," Michelle shouted as she headed toward the conference room that bordered the gates of Heaven from Hell.

The angel materialized but rapidly fell behind as Michelle didn't slacken her pace. She finally caught up, her wings fluttering furiously.

"Call the troops together."

"I can't do that." The angel flushed a bright pink as they arrived at Hell's back gate to Heaven.

Michelle spun until she was nose-to-nose with the little pest who backwinged sharply to avoid colliding with her face.

"Why not?"

"I'm an angel. I can't call the troops of Hell. For one thing," Henrietta held up one tiny finger, "it's against the Heavenly code. For another, I don't know any of their names. Also…"

Michelle hid her face in her hands. There had to be an easier way to do this. She turned once more for the gate and whapped a demon on the head to open them.

The angel remained uncharacteristically quiet as the heavy iron gates were dragged open by a cluster of eternally damned souls, all book publishing agents. They crossed into the Escher-designed CABER conference room.

Still the angel hadn't spoken.

"What? Spit it out."

"No. No. No. You can't spit in Heaven. Bad Devil. How could you even suggest that I would—"

"I meant, just say what the third thing is."

"Oh, well." She fluttered off toward the head of the conference room table. Once she settled and had fussed her feathers back into place and wiped her face with a pocket handkerchief as big as she was, Michelle asked again.

"I'm, a," she whispered and Michelle had to lean in to hear her. "I'm allergic to demons. They give me a terrible rash. Besides, the Apocalypse isn't scheduled for another four days."

Michelle reached out with her free hand and grabbed the angel by the wings. Henrietta fluttered once or twice but couldn't escape.

"Scheduled?"

"Oh sure. It's been on the calendar a couple decades at least. The correlation of factors has been there for all to see, even if the software only just caught on. Don't you ever read the memos I send you?"

The answer was, no, but there was no way she was going to give the angel a chance to get the upper hand in this conversation.

A deep breath.

Another.

A third…nope.

A fourth.

Uh, uh. Didn't help.

"Henrietta. I don't have any troops of Hell, unless you're counting those two idiots with swords still reenacting the Fall of Troy. I meant a meeting of CABER."

"Oh. No demons?"

She let the angel free and dropped into her own chair.

"No demons."

CHAPTER 52

*D*ana Murphy was distracted from Clio's question regarding her plans for the last four days of existence by the man walking into the Suzzallo Library Reading Room. If there was ever a man who didn't belong here, he was it. Tall, Italian right down to the narrow face, dark hair, and incredible sexual magnetism, and...He was coming their way. His red leather shoes slapping on the stone floor, which echoed off the ceiling in a way that none of the student's sneakers ever did.

He oiled his way up behind Clio. Leaning over to nibble on her neck on one side, he slid a hand smoothly over her shoulder and went for her breast. Would have grabbed her right here in the library if Clio hadn't bitten his arm first.

"Hey, Babe." He oozed into the chair next to Clio and stretched out his long legs to rest on Dana's knees.

She caught Clio's scowl and decided it would be okay to shove his legs off onto the floor. They were cold. As if he wasn't there despite all the heat that radiated from him. Cold like marble.

"Aren't you going to introduce me, Babe?" He leaned forward until he was practically in Clio's lap. "Not that I need the introduction, but it might illustrate a bit of the politeness you Muses prize so highly."

"Dana, this is the lowest form of pond scum ever produced as a celestial being. Loki." She didn't look at him.

"First hint, never trust a single thing he says. Second hint," she rolled her eyes as she jabbed an elbow into his ribs to get him to back off again, "well, you've already got that one. I'd suggest a cattle prod, but I don't have one handy to lend you."

"So, Dana, Babe, nice to have the pleasure." He leered at her, his eyes running like a strafing attack down her body leaving her cold and shivering.

"Don't worry, honey, you're not my type. Frigid-virgin-Goddess crap was never what I would call 'hot.' Though I'd be glad to be persuaded otherwise if you'd care to try." His leer slid back to her chest.

She pulled up her knees and rested her chin on them. Okay, going fetal wasn't exactly a sign of strength, but it would have to do.

"Whatever, honey-child, you know how to find me."

She was going to point out that she didn't, but thought better of it.

He grinned and produced a card. Leaning forward, she could feel the heat radiating off his body pounding forth successive waves of pheromones. Despite her position, he managed to slide the card down the front of her shirt where it nestled hotly between her breasts. She drew it out.

It was fire red, no, blood red. And flickering orange script simply read, "Loki. Knock three times on the ceiling if you want me."

She met his dark, smoldering gaze squarely.

"I'll just remember to avoid ceilings in the future."

Clio smiled for the first time since Loki's arrival.

<h1 style="text-align:center">CHAPTER 53</h1>

"*L*ook, could you at least turn it down to stun?" Dana knew her voice was querulous, but his rampant maleness was getting on her nerves. Though, once again, he wasn't attracting any attention from the rest of the library's denizens.

Loki sighed and eased back into his chair.

"Why is it that the real babes want nothing to do with me?"

"Maybe you need to go find a shallower target audience," Dana gathered her courage and was pleased to find that some showed up. "Much shallower."

"Ooo! Ouch!" Clio raised a hand and Dana slapped it high five.

Loki grunted, but the pressure against her nerve endings eased off enough for her to think clearly.

Dana looked at Loki. Really looked. And he had no energy lines. Nor was he a solid mass in any form, the way Michelle was. Or Uncle Joshua. Loki's energy traveled through a fine tracery of lines that covered his body shape, but which either shielded his interior, or he was energetically hollow. It didn't make any sense, but it worried her.

The Devil had been far more real to— Interesting. Somewhere along the way, without noticing, Dana had accepted Michelle's claim as a truth.

"Doesn't want anything to do with me, but won't stop staring at me. I've been checked out before but—"

"What are you?"

"Never seen a celestial being before?"

She nodded her head. A quick glance revealed Clio was as solid as Michelle, just a much gentler shade. It would figure that the Muse of History would be as concerned with the material world as the woman who did her best to keep it running.

"It's not that. It's…," she didn't know what and decided she'd best keep her mouth shut.

A silence descended upon them again. A shuffling of books and papers of desperate students trying to understand why they were flunking Calculus, or Psychology 101 for Football Jocks. Papers on music theory, theater set design, and religious injustices were being created all around them. And not one in a hundred thousand were going to have the slightest impact on the course of history. Why was she so damned important?

Loki's voice brought her back to the moment.

"So, to smoothly break the silence, I'll repeat Clio's question. What are you going to do for the last four days of all creation?"

"Why is everything ending Thursday? Why now?"

Loki shrugged his shoulders with an elegance that made Baryshnikov look clumsy.

"Why not? No. Seriously. After fourteen billion years, do you see any point in continuing the whole farce? I sure don't. So, I'll go back to my original premise," again the elegant shrug. "Why not?"

Dana could think of half a hundred reasons right off the bat, but then she was often accused of being foolishly optimistic.

CHAPTER 54

*E*very argument Dana raised to support the continuation of all existence was brushed aside with an ease that even a metaphysics grad student wouldn't be able to muster.

Loki's knowledge was encyclopedic, as if he had the whole of the books surrounding them in Suzzallo at his instant beck and call.

Clio argued him around and around in dizzying circles of logic, to no avail.

"But why not?" he insisted for the hundredth time.

Dana wanted to pummel him with her fists. So cool, and collected. Lounging in a chair that had been designed to be so uncomfortable that a student couldn't fall asleep in it.

He'd look casual and at ease lying in a pool of boiling lava.

"If all of the stars were to go nova simultaneously, it would take more than four days for the initial triggers, which we haven't observed anywhere in the stellar neighborhood, to reach the star's surface. Stars can't simply be destroyed that fast."

Loki was grinning. He leaned into the argument with an obvious relish.

"What would be an easier solution?"

"Easier than blowing them all up?"

He nodded fiercely.

"Switch them off."

"Right." He leaned back and leered at a passing coed who turned and ran from the room without apparently ever seeing him.

Dana could sympathize.

"The pressure that gravity applies on the stellar mass would be sufficient to instantly relight the sun's fusion reactions. And if they were switched off, if you could magically switch off fusion and fission, the effect would take a long time to reach the surface."

"What is heat?"

"What is this Physics 101?"

"What is heat?" He reminded her of Professor Hoffman her calculus teacher, and the Vulture was not a good memory.

"Energy associated with motion transferred by convection or radiation."

"What is motion?"

She looked at Clio, who just shrugged.

"In this application, sub-molecular motion."

"But there's no such thing. If you break it down far enough, it is all just energy, incredibly small strings of energy. And if we were to, say, for lack of a better idea, stop all motion at once what would we have."

"Absolute zero."

"Excellent." He took the science fiction novel that Clio had been reading, and tossed it in the air. He snapped his fingers and nothing happened.

The book swung up in the air. It descended to land between the chairs.

And then exploded into a million shards with a tiny pop that would have made Dana leap out of her skin if such a thing were possible.

"No motion. Absolute zero. Worse than Ice Nine. It's a lot of fun in a universe that still has heat. Energy and non-energy don't react nicely together."

He was either a whacked-out Physics major with a twisted sense of humor, or he was another supernatural manifestation and she should take his question seriously.

"Why not?" He repeated his query again, his eyes bright with the game. Excited by the scent of the hunt.

What was the gross quantitative value of his query?

Two words.

Well, she could do better than that.

"Because."

CHAPTER 55

Clio ducked out the instant that Loki fell asleep mumbling something about a hard night.

Dana would have been right on her heels if the woman hadn't simply evaporated. Actually, it was a lot weirder than that. The woman had shrunk out of view. Not like she was getting smaller, but like she was going farther away very quickly without ever leaving the confines of her library chair.

Dana was forced to tip-toe off.

His snores began to echo off the ceiling.

By the time she was a halfway to the door, she was walking quickly. At three-quarters, she hit a dead run and didn't slow down until she was past the flustered librarian, out the door, and across Red Square.

Whether she teleported to arrive where she did, or simply didn't recall the last twenty blocks was a question she wasn't ready to contemplate.

The late afternoon sun poured down a long alley and spotlighted the building in front of her. Her uncle's deli. A bell tinkled cheerfully as she went through.

"Dee!" A short flurry of wild hair and best friend filled her arms.

"Hey there, Tee." She held on tightly. This was reality. This had to be reality. A quick glance confirmed that this was Uncle Joshua's deli, unchanged. Never changing. The whole universe could end and Uncle Joshua would amble out from behind the counter insisting that she try just a smidge of a new pepperoni a friend of his on Houston Street made.

"C'mon." Tee dragged her over to a table and shoved her in a chair. "You can have half my sandwich. Jeremy, Dana. I picked him up at the track, which you didn't show up at to see me run. Your loss this time. Shoulda been there. I was hot. Number two slot. First row. Dana's my best bud. Saved my ass, but won't face me on-line, the woosie bitch."

"Tee?"

"Yeah?"

"You talk as much as Henrietta."

"Who's that? You gone lesbo and picked up a new lover without telling me? Remember, I get first dibs on you if we ever both switch over. Of course there's no way that's going to happen to me in this lifetime."

Dana decided she didn't care how much Tee talked. She was just glad to have her friend here.

"Love you, Tee."

"Love you, Dee."

Uncle Joshua showed up with his arms full. A massive corned beef on rye for Theresa. Two pastrami sandwiches, a whole for Jeremy and a half with extra fries for her. Aunt Anne dropped off three Cokes on her way to another table.

"Oh Uncle. You are a lifesaver. How'd you know?"

He leaned down and crushed her under one arm and Tee under the other in a massive bear hug.

"I always watch out for you, Dana. You know that." He kissed her on top of the head.

"That goes for you, too, Squirt." He left a kiss atop Tee's curls and ambled back toward the counter.

Tee took a massive bite and mumbled out as she chewed. "God damn, it's good to be home."

"Where you staying?"

"Don't know," she shrugged and chewed. A glance at Jeremy was all the message Dana needed.

"Let me know when the jury comes back. You know you can always stay at my place."

"I'll remember that if I ever want fettuccini and scrambled eggs for breakfast."

They both leaned together for a moment and rubbed shoulders.

"So, Jeremy, what's your talent? Other than catching Theresa's voracious eye?"

He blinked rapidly at that and turned to face Tee, his mouth too full to respond, but the sudden flush of red was bright enough to outshine the sunset pouring through the window.

"Cute, isn't he? Very literal, too. Kinda quiet though."

Dana had to agree. His aura was green, a gentle green, but green nonetheless. A restful energy, natural healer, good at modifying the energy of those around him to a calm state. Which was a good match with Tee's infinitely restless yellow. Joyful, outgoing, and unattached.

Jeremy finished choking down his over-sized bite.

"I, uh, write software." He was still pink around the ears. "Games." His plate was of sudden immense fascination.

"I love games. Would I have heard of any of them?" Dana started working on her mound of French fries.

He looked up, checked carefully in Tee's direction, a bit of color returning to his cheeks.

"Yea, probably. I wrote *Chraze*."

Theresa's shout made Uncle Joshua jump, even from three tables away.

CHAPTER 56

"This woosie bitch," Tee aimed a finger at Dana's chest, "wimped out on me. She promised to meet me on the game grid. Down-and-dirty inside *Chraze*. But did she? Nooo. Chicken-shit girl. Chicken-shit girl." She started turning it into a sing-song chant.

Dana made a fist and rapped the side of it lightly on Tee's skull to make her stop. Tee aimed a French fry at her like a sword.

"Sorry. I spaced it. I've been a little, um, busy these last few days."

"Yeah, yeah, yeah. Whine, whine. Fear, girl. I can smell it all the way over here. Despite the pastrami on rye that you're pointing at me."

"I'll meet you on-line and take you down like always, just not right now. Things are being just a bit weird at the moment."

"Weird?" Tee turned to Jeremy but kept talking to her. "She's so screwed up, never had a real boyfriend."

She leaned in close to him and whispered, loudly enough to be heard outside, through the plate glass. "She's still a virgin."

"Not. Girl. Not." Though, with the emotion that had been missing in her one and only time, she might as well be.

"No one since?" Tee knew exactly who she was thinking of.

Admitting it was not her first choice, but Tee never gave her a chance for a second option.

"Nope. Assholes don't count. I'd offer you Jeremy here, but I think he might burst a blood vessel at the idea. And we only met today, not sure I'd want to share."

There was nothing subtle about Tee. But Dana could see that she liked Jeremy. She was a terrible tease and rarely gentle with fragile male egos.

"I am seeing someone."

"Asshole?"

"No. Though things aren't working very well."

"Asshole."

"No. Not his fault. Angels and devils."

Jeremy coughed and choked; Coke came out his nose as he grabbed for a napkin.

ichelle had to wait while Henrietta rounded up the various CABER members. Rather than being distracted by the possibility of the infinite windows on a finite amount of wall, she studied the mosaics of all Creation that Escher had built into the walls. The more she studied it, the more they bothered her.

By the time that the regulars drifted into the CABER meeting room it had moved from a bother to a real itch, but she couldn't place her finger on it.

Mary gave her a gentle hug and a warm smile and Michelle momentarily forgot the worry digging away in the back of her thoughts.

Dionysus arrived in full voice, his wine flagon looking distinctly less than full.

"And how are my lovely ladies, today, today, and how are you ladies today?" Even when he was falling down, sotted to his ear tips, he still had a beautiful baritone. She'd suggested he mangle a composer other than Gilbert and Sullivan on occasion, but he'd declined. *"For I aaam a drunken sot. And I myself have said it. And it's greatly to my credit."*

If only he didn't know his voice was so beautiful, he would be a bit less obnoxious, but he was terribly impressed with himself and was shocked every time a woman didn't fall into his arms swooning. Despite the millennia, he still feigned surprise each time Michelle was able to resist his charms.

"Come to my lap, my wench, today, today, oh come to me, wench, today." Unabashed at Michelle's refusal, he spun around in a neat pirouette, surprisingly lithe for such a big man, threw himself into a chair, and produced five glasses of wine from thin air. One was barely the size of a shot glass, on the table where Henrietta usually sat, though she was off rounding people up at the moment.

Michelle didn't want her head muddled, but couldn't resist trying his vintage. Sweet strawberries. A sailboat on the Mediterranean. No, not just the Med, specifically the Aegean sea. And the buzzing of a lone bumblebee that settled on a single daisy, the memory lodged deep inside her brain and left her smiling to herself.

"How do you do that?"

The Buddha came in and showed no surprise at the glass that was waiting by his usual seat. He too smiled seraphically after taking a sip.

"I am the monarch of the wine, The ruler of the grape divine."

"And so are your sisters, and your cousins, and your aunts. You really need new material, Dionysus."

"Never." He thumped a hand to his heart and collapsed back in his chair.

She looked around. No Apollo. No Shiva.

Henrietta fluttered back in from her efforts to herd the various members. "Isis and Parvati have gone on a girls-only spa trip to the Caribbean." She settled by her tiny wineglass and took a sip.

"Oo. That's a good one. You know it reminds me of the time that the Lord God was trying to learn the latest Viennese dance from a rather lascivious widow who was posing as a dance teacher, but then Don…"

Michelle considered letting Henrietta continue, but then the back of her thoughts offered up to the front of her mind what was bothering her about the room. A quick glance at the mosaic and it when from "bother" to "profoundly unnerving."

Michelle tinged her finger against Henrietta's halo. The bright ringing got everyone's attention as the angel grabbed it hard to stop the sound. Good one. She'd have to remember to thank Dana for that little trick.

When at last it was silent, except for the red-hot glare that practically crackled through the air as the angel fired it in her direction, Michelle looked slowly around at each immortal before posing her question.

"What's wrong with this room?"

There was a long silence.

Mary whispered quietly, "You mean other than the windows?"

"Yes, I mean other than the windows."

There was a brief silence as they all twisted and swiveled around as if seeing the room for the first time.

"And the weird thing about the chairs and the table and all?"

"Yes, Dionysus. Other than that."

Even Henrietta, with a cautious hand on her halo, looked about the room.

"Well, the only other thing I can think of is the mosaics."

"Right. But what's wrong with them? I only just figured it out myself."

More swiveling like parakeets staring at themselves in a mirror. If one of them started chirping "Hello there beautiful," she'd toss them out a window, any window, and see how they fared on their own.

"They all end in the present day." The Buddha spoke with a sense of wonder that only rarely entered his voice. "But they were made decades ago. I thought it was all fixed."

"It is," Michelle nodded. "This is exactly the way Escher made it over three decades ago."

Mary pointed at a particular image.

"But Britney Spears wasn't born yet, and Madonna was still a little girl. There they are kissing. And look at Michael Jackson's face. That's how it was when he died. It has a whole evolutionary track of its own."

"Right. But that's all there is. There's nothing about the future in a single one of these mosaics. That's when I figured out that there was a major problem."

"There's no future," Mary Magdalene sounded close to tears. "According to this room, there's no future."

"Sure there is," Henrietta's high voice offered hope, but her words dashed it. "It's just that there are only three more days of it."

Michelle let them wander around the room for a while. Hoping they'd disprove her theory. Find an image that none of them could interpret because it was from the future. Preferably a far-distant one.

"Here's one." Henrietta shouted out.

Michelle hurried over and the others gathered around her. The Buddha forgot his sense of detachment as he hurried around the table. Dionysus forgot his wine skin.

Henrietta fluttered in front of the mosaic, with her nose just inches away from the image on the wall. It was a small image, barely six inches above the floor.

Michelle shoved Henrietta aside. She had to lie on the floor to see it properly as others leaned in to see as well.

There, laid out clearly in a few hundred tiny tiles of mosaic, was the Kirsten Wind Tunnel on the UW campus. And on the floor, a woman. Obviously dead. A knife sticking out of her chest. She wore black jeans and a black leather jacket. Her face was obscured by long, dark hair. And bright socks with rainbow-colored toes stuck out of her sandals.

Everyone turned slowly to stare at her.

Mary laid a comforting hand on her arm.

Michelle stood and looked down at herself and suddenly didn't like what she was wearing.

Not one little bit.

CHAPTER 58

"Go change."

"Different clothes."

"Hide."

"Stay away from Seattle."

"Lay low."

"We'll trade clothes." Mary pulled at her own sweater.

"No way." That was it. She wasn't going to put anyone else at risk, especially not Mary.

"It's mine to face. And no one is going to get past my guard that easily, dagger or no. And I have no reason to go back to the wind tunnel."

"You know where that is?"

"You've been there?"

"Why?"

"Don't go back."

She pushed through the hovering circle of CABER members.

"I'm not going back. I'm not!"

They huddled together in front of the window with a view of ABBA's recording study, perhaps the scariest window of the lot. It was one of the few that no one opened no matter how hot a day it was.

Michelle sat in a chair and they all visibly relaxed. A little bit.

"Let's sit down and figure it out."

"You can't do that." Her second worst nightmare was slouched in a chair as if he'd been there for hours and was just waking up.

"Shit, Loki. How'd you get in here? We didn't invite you." She glanced over at Henrietta who shook her head vehemently. The angel didn't like Loki at all. And from someone who appeared to like everybody she met, that was a significant statement.

Loki pointed over his shoulder at a window that showed a university library.

"Climbed in through the bathroom window, so to speak. Now," he pointed a lazy finger down at the bit of wall Henrietta was valiantly trying to hide.

"There's no way to figure it out. It's the future, it's unknowable."

"But this room?" Mary waved at the various diagrams.

"Remember, no one knows how Escher did it, including Escher. But all evidence aside, you can't predict the future. The software is designed in four literal dimensions no matter how many logical permutations you can think up into a pan-dimensional multi-verse. Three dimensions of space and one of time. Due to the laws under which this universe is assembled, we're stuck with them."

"But why can't we move up and back along the lines of time just like we move forward and backward in space?" The Buddha carefully sat two chairs away from Loki, which was as far away as he could get.

"The original programmers, may their souls roast in perdition, decided that we didn't need that option. Just like 'faster than light.' Sure, we can spot the occasional tachyon sliding by from a parallel universe, but that's not for us."

"What about paired electrons? Their spin flips at the same moment. It's a far faster response than light speeds."

Loki shook his head as if Michelle were a hopeless dweeb. She considered slapping him, but that hadn't worked so well last time. It had taken weeks to get the brimstone reek off her hands.

"That isn't faster than light. It's simultaneous. Time is its own dimension, separate from space. They happen at the same moment in the time dimension, though they're displaced in the spatial dimensions."

"And that has what to do with my death?"

He aimed an elegant finger back at the mosaic.

"We have no idea how Escher did that. That's all. You're going to end up lying on that floor with a knife sticking out of your chest, and changing your pretty socks isn't going to alter that."

It sucked knowing that you had less than four days to live and it sucked more that Loki was here to gloat over it. Okay, maybe dying would be worse, but not enough worse to make this any fun.

"And how is it that you are so steeped in the knowledge of the universe?" The Buddha's voice was perhaps just a bit envious.

Loki leaned over and slapped a hand soundly on the Indian's shoulder almost driving the little man face down into the table.

"Oh, Siddhartha my short friend, I'm going to miss you."

He unfolded from his chair and moved to one of the windows. He looked out for a long moment before turning his back on it, his body blocking the view.

"Computers 101, my friends. Computers 101."

He tossed open the ABBA window and dodged out of the conference room doors as the pounding backbeat of *Gimme, Gimme, Gimme, a Man After Midnight* thudded into the room shaking tiles from the walls.

CHAPTER 59

"What's this shit you're talking, Dee?" Theresa was in the lead as they left the deli and entered the cool October evening.

"I wish I knew." The cool wind of late evening ran a chill over Dana's arms that no amount of chafing with her hands was going to diminish. Her jacket was still back at the planetarium from when she'd followed the Devil out into the afternoon sun.

"Oh crap. I forgot about Sam."

"He's the new asshole? Good. Keep forgetting about him. He's just a jerk."

She punched Tee's shoulder. "Isn't."

"Is."

"Isn't. You haven't met him."

"Is. Don't have to. That's all you've ever dated. Does he like you?"

That stopped Dana. "He does."

"Really?"

She punched Tee's shoulder again and just got a laugh.

"I haven't heard from him all day."

"Told you. Jerk."

Jeremy held the door for them as Dana climbed into the back seat of the Trans Am then closed it behind Theresa once she was settled in the front. Dana had never seen such a thing. And Tee always insisted on driving, but not this time.

"Have you tried calling him?"

Dana considered explaining how she'd been a little busy with the Devil, the Angel, the Muse…and decided against it. She pulled out her phone out of her pocket. It was off. She'd forgotten she'd done that last night after Sam dropped her off, knowing her desperate need for sleep.

She powered it back on as she climbed into the back seat of the car.

Messages started pouring in. Well, five of them did. All variations on the same theme. All from Sam.

"Crap."

"What?" Theresa turned in her seat enough to look back at Dana.

"He's been trying to reach me all day."

"And?"

"He does like me." Dana was bummed about the car seat being in the way. She felt a deep need to punch Theresa on the arm again. Instead, she reached over the seat and knuckle-rapped her friend's head. "Ha! So there."

Theresa stuck her tongue out at her. "So where is this dude? I guess I've got to meet him now and see if he's insane or something."

"His last message from a few minutes ago said he was headed to the planetarium. Let's go in the parking lot off 15th and Campus Parkway. That's closest."

The car thudded to life and Jeremy headed them south.

"What's he doing there?"

"Looking for me."

"Sucker!"

"No, he," she bit her tongue while she considered making up a good lie. Even a bad one. But they never worked on Theresa, she knew Dana too well. Theresa could pull anything over on Dana unless she was watching for energy shifts. But even the tiniest little white lie and Theresa would catch it.

"He's worried over my problems with the Devil."

Theresa spun around to look at her over the seat back. The car twitched sharply halfway into the other lane of University Way before Jeremy corrected it.

"Careful!" Theresa's alarm echoed her own.

Jeremy wrestled the car to a stop at the 45th Street light.

"The Devil?" his voice was grim. "The woman who lives in a beach house at the Foothills of Hell?"

Theresa's eyes crossed momentarily, then she rolled her eyes at Dana. Just like the day back in sixth grade when Tee had discovered that Tommy Jacobs liked Suzy Patterson better than he liked her, and in that instant he went from occupying her every spoken sentence to being an unmentionable worm. Jeremy probably didn't know that he'd just gone from white to black on Tee's register. Or from boring to interesting in her own.

"I haven't been to her house. She's pretty, in a tall-but-dangerous sort of way, dark hair."

"I didn't meet her."

The light went green and he eased the car south through the students who were ignoring the Walk / Don't Walk signs. They went through them as if they weren't really there. The red, "Don't Walk" hand folded in all except its index finger and pointed right at her. And the green man hunkered down as if he were going to sprint off the sign. Once they were by it, she looked back and saw the red hand and the green man as normal. She was losing her mind.

Theresa was looking back and forth between them.

"What did your Uncle put in your food?"

"I was riding with a crazy poet and a prophet who wishes she was insane but isn't." Jeremy's hands were white on the steering wheel he was gripping it so hard. He hunched forward like a little old lady looking out at the world between the rim of the wheel and the dashboard of her oversized Cadillac. The words looked as if they hurt to speak. Maybe all words hurt him to speak. He wasn't the chattiest person she'd ever met.

"I was having a fight with her. She says that we're old friends." She swallowed hard. "Best of friends."

Theresa barked out a laugh. "Knew you were switching sides. So instead of the jerk, you're after some hot bitch?"

"Well, she and an angel, about so tall." She gestured with her hands. "Other way around though. They're after me. They keep insisting I'm the Second Messiah."

"Oh crap. Old Joshua did drug your food."

CHAPTER 60

*S*am drifted.

Floated on a never-ending silver field.

Drifted, flowed, flew along lines of iridescent energy.

Intersecting lines, splitting, recombining. Splitting into a thousand pieces.

A moment later, regathered into a single being of pure energy.

How long had he floated?

He didn't know.

How many times broken and rebuilt?

Impossible to estimate.

The millionth, maybe the hundred billionth time his energy regrouped, he wondered at his journey.

A hundred thousand or half-a-dozen times later, the absurdity of the situation finally impacted his neurons.

He was electrical energy. He flowed through circuits like a wing flowed through air.

Resistance wasn't inherent in the system.

He'd always seen it wrong. Misunderstood.

Circuitry, air, water, didn't resist.

Friction and heat were not generated.

The circuitry-air-water lifted, empowered. Built layer upon layer upon layer until there was no restraint. He'd been moved.

Shot out.

Ejected.

From…

Mortal flesh.

A body.

He'd gotten bored waiting for Dana to show up all day. Bored and kinda pissed.

He'd had a body.

Last night, and the Devil, had made little sense. Then he'd logged on *Chraze*. And now…

A runner's body.

Now this…

An aerodynamic body.

Not fighting the air as he'd thought. Flowing through. Boosted. Energized. Empowered.

Heat was the tearing of energy, potential to kinetic. Friction the backward drag of energy that didn't wish to release. To flow.

The silver lines pulsed as he sent the data packets that were him off in a thousand directions.

At an indefinable, yet mathematically exact point, his consciousness observed the scattering and faultless recombination of the ten to the tenth to the ten-somethingth flashes of himself flickering along the silver lines. A logical central point that was separate from the glowing lines. Separate from the light that was self, but wasn't self.

Sam.

Samuel.

Samwise.

The steadfast. The trustworthy. The furry-toed.

The million flying points of perfect consciousness blasting apart and sliding back together across an infinite array of intersecting and reintersecting silver lines of energy.

But if consciousness, then why the silver lines? At that thought, his quarter gazillion bits and particles and wavicles slammed back into a single point and halted. Not at the center of all the converging-diverging lines. But close.

"Hi."

Sam was alone. Just the forever shifting rainbows of the silver lines stretching off to…

"Complete the thought."

Somewhere.

Anywhere.

He didn't know.

Still alone, but he answered anyway.

"You need to be talking to my girlfriend."

Dana.

Hadn't thought of her since…

Girlfriend?

He rolled the word around. As an energetic construct slipping a little way out along one single, silver line and sliding back just as quietly. It flowed, blended, merged.

"Girlfriend. Dana. She discusses infinity. I talk flow. Dynamic pressures. Air flow. Hydraulics. Talk to her about…"

But she wasn't here. Nor was anyone else. He was talking to himself in a place that couldn't be.

With a puff, like a release of breath after an accident is narrowly avoided, he blasted his consciousness down a hundred thousand and eight lines.

It felt good to be alone.

Mostly.

CHAPTER 61

Theresa would have shouted if there'd been time. One instant the Trans Am was sliding through the nighttime crowd coming out of the Varsity Movie Theater and crossing University Way willy-nilly on their way back to their dorms.

The next instant they were in burning sunlight that seared her retina so badly that she wondered if she'd ever see again.

The car jerked as Jeremy stalled the engine.

She flailed forward against the dashboard, nearly cut in two by the lap belt, and flopped back sideways.

Dee let loose a steady stream of colorful epithets most having to do with the word 'crap' in one way or another. She was such a weenie. Except when it counted. Then she was a rock.

When at last the change from dark night to impossible sun had eased enough to make her entire face stop twitching, Theresa risked squinting out at the world.

A long, low beach house stretched along the blinding sands. The structure was weather worn, baked by the sun and the sea salt. The wood was bare of color other than its own, rough and brown with a thousand years of age. Bright geraniums hung along the outer eave, swinging gently in a breeze. They were so lush and covered with oranges, and pinks, and reds that they would have put a florist's shop to shame. Color dominated the porch.

Only after crawling out of the car to stand on the burning sands did her eyes adapt enough to notice a pair of crossed feet resting on the rail. She traced their origin back into the shadows beneath the eave. A woman slouched low in a heavy, wooden Adirondack porch chair. Her dark hair flowing downward from a bright bandana of a thousand bright flowers that matched her geraniums. Right down to the gentle swaying back and forth of the flowers across the bandana fabric.

The woman waved a hand in greeting and signaled them toward the porch.

Together, the three of them ascended the steps side-by-side.

"There you are," one of the geraniums scolded.

Maybe Theresa would just turn around and go back to the car.

"Did you know that I looked all over for you? Where did you go? It's like that pesky King Arthur. He was always running off on crusades or quests or whatever it was that he was doing with his knights instead of doing it with his queen. I mean what was that about anyway?"

"Hi, Henrietta." Dee greeted the flower

A white girl, barely longer than Theresa's forearm fluttered out of the geranium to hover in front of them.

Fluttered.

Flew right by her face and hovered in front of Dana.

Did Dana show the shock that was rippling through her own body? No.

Did her jaw drop in protest at the impossibility as her own did hanging in the wind like an unhinged barn door? No.

What was up with that?

She turned to Jeremy. He at least showed a decent amount of shock, but not as much as she'd hoped for. It just wasn't fair that she was the only one out of her depth.

"You must be the Devil." Jeremy's voice cracked against his dry throat.

"Got me in one. Though you can call me Michelle if that's easier for you. Sit down, have a glass of lemonade."

Her voice was friendly, smooth with that deep richness that showed up in the women who prowled through the bar after a race. But there was no desperation, no predatory over-pronunciation. As if she were the definition of woman.

Dee was moving past the fluttering, Theresa swallowed hard, angel. And it followed close behind still discussing the shape of the Egyptian pyramids and why they'd been built with a square footprint rather than the original circular plan.

Jeremy abandoned her and moved over to take a glass of lemonade. The porch was both rustic and immensely comfortable. An old rug that had seen too many storms lay upon the worn planking. A small table held a pitcher of lemonade with real lemons floating in it. Four large glasses, full and sweating in the heat. A small shot glass of lemonade sweating perfect beads of water right alongside the others. Just the right size for, she had to swallow again before she glanced once more at Dana's chattering companion, for a tiny angel. A bouquet of daffodils matched the refreshment. A generous plate of cheese and apples rested there as well.

A semi-circle of four chairs faced the ocean.

The ocean.

The waves stood above her.

A hundred, a thousand feet high.

Poised to crash down and destroy them all.

She threw her hands over her head.

She fell back against the wall of the house.

A deep breath.

Held.

And held.

And held a bit more.

Theresa squinted open one eye and looked out at the incoming wave.

It broke and descended with no spray.

It landed with a complete lack of a thundering crash.

It rippled up the beach a dozen feet, a happy burbling sound as if it were laughing at her, and then trickled away before the onslaught of the next monster.

"What is with that ocean?"

Jeremy placed a glass of cold lemonade into her hands.

"Creepy, isn't it? It doesn't make any more sense the second time you see it. It's just not right."

They stood shoulder-to-shoulder and watched the wall of water build and build and build, then shatter, time, after time. After time.

"Are you two going to stare out there all day, or come and sit?"

CHAPTER 62

"Thanks for coming."

Theresa still couldn't get over the lush perfection of the woman's voice. If anything convinced Tee that she wasn't anywhere she understood, it was that she'd never heard a voice like this, anywhere.

"Where are we?"

They all stared at her in silence.

Theresa bit her tongue. She'd asked the question aloud a dozen times in as many minutes.

In Hell.

It wasn't that she didn't believe it.

It was that the idea wouldn't stick. It just kept sliding out of her grasp.

"I have a race on Friday. I'm in the number two spot."

"Oh, I wouldn't worry about that," the angel chimed in cheerfully. "The chances of the world still being running after Thursday are quite slim, you know. Down near twenty percent last I checked and falling fast. Well, actually they've been reporting at zero all day, but I didn't want to depress you right after you got here."

"The world will stop running..." That idea wasn't sticking any better than the being in Hell bit.

"Back at the end of the first millennium there were all sorts of doomsayers," and the angel was off and running again. "All men, of course. And they were all wrong, every one of them. As if any arbitrary date on a calendar invented by humans could bring an apocalypse. It has nothing to do with the date. It's all about the cosmic balance of the universe. The yin and yang of consciousness on a stellar scale that would make the Battle of Hastings look like a bunch of children playing with a puppy dog. I remember this one dog, Spotty was his name, came into the Kublai Kahn's tent one night seeking a bit of food. He rode with the Scourge of Asia for almost fifteen years in a special saddle bag that held him right behind the great Kahn. And then—"

"Henrietta." Michelle's, no The Devil's voice rolled over the angel.

Dana nudged her shoulder in the momentary silence.

"Doing okay there, Tee?"

She was in Hell.

She punched Dee in the arm.

Hard.

"Ow!"

Now she was doing better.

CHAPTER 63

"What are you doing out here?"

Dee's outline shrugged. The moon cast her shadow on the long stretch of sand, which shrugged its shoulders as well.

Theresa wouldn't have been all that surprised if it didn't. The evening had been spent strategizing on saving reality, which had even made sense on occasion. In Hell with the Devil and an angel, which still made none.

The tide had changed. The ocean's waves were now tiny waves that barely trickled across the sand, landing with a crash that shot spray hundreds of yards and made such a roar that you had to space your conversation around them.

"Okay," Theresa dropped down onto the sand and kicked her feet beneath the cool upper layer down to where it was still warm from the heat of the midday sun.

"That rates as the weirdest day I've ever had. Even worse than the day you made Roxie Jones do that entire halftime show in just a bikini and her tennies despite the snow on the field. Of course, I personally think she enjoyed it which kind of made it a waste. Whatever happened to her?"

"Remember the talent scout?"

"That's right. She still posing for bulimia ads?"

"Yep."

"It's weirder than the first time I climbed into a race car and knew I belonged there. And that was pretty strange. I mean Mom being such a, well, you know, a mom, and Dad being an accountant. I never had any training. Never needed it. Like I was a reincarnation of A.J. Foyt."

She kicked her heel at the sand again. The sand felt normal. But the roar of the tiny surf, even as loud as it was you still couldn't hear it in Michelle's guest room. That the Devil had a guest room. She really needed an expanded vocabulary for this experience, but she'd stick with weird for the moment. It was working for her.

"It doesn't work that way."

"What doesn't?"

"You and A.J. Unless he was a cross-dresser before her time. You don't switch your gender."

"How the hell— 'scuse me." Not quite the right word to use in this place. "How the fuck do you know that?"

Dana shrugged her shoulders again and continued to watch the surf.

Theresa started spooning the sand over her feet. It was just the perfect consistency for making sandcastles. A small turret over the big toe. A causeway from ankle left to ankle right.

"Everyone keeps telling me I'm the Second Messiah. That I'm an incarnation...No. That I am actually Diana the Huntress. I don't know who that is, Tee. As God or Einstein is my witness. I was happy being me."

"Not sexually satisfied."

Dee punched her arm and Theresa felt better as she worked on a sand moat that traveled around her buttocks.

"Get your mind out of the gutter."

"It's always been one track."

"Two."

"Cars and boys. Yeah. Killer combo."

"No pun intended."

"No pun intended."

She incorporated one of her legs into the design. Winding levels of houses. Defensible level upon level. Winding causeways, pleasant cliffside homes where the problems were Hobbitan orcs and not earthquakes. Sand slid down her thigh and into her shorts. Maybe she'd go and brave the fierce ocean waves, all foot-high of them. Though by their roar, maybe she'd opt for a good dusting off and another round in the Devil's hot tub. Let the Devil deal with the sand.

"You want my opinion, Tee?"

It was a little surreal. Dana had always just offered advice and Tee had never followed any of it. And it had served her well, so why did she ask now?

"Do you like this Jeremy?"

"What? You reading my mind, Dee?"

"No, but I can see it. There's a connection there. A good one. You never listen to me, but don't screw it up, Tee."

If she'd followed even a little of Dee's rare personal advice, she'd have been a whole lot better off.

"Or what?"

"Or I'll beat the crap out of you."

They both knew that was an empty threat. But it wasn't a threat she'd made very often. Or at all, outside the video game field.

"Maybe." She'd have to think a little more about Jeremy.

"What's your opinion?" Dee raised her voice above the waves.

"On what?" Now that she'd been offered the chance to say something, she wasn't so sure of herself. She incorporated her hips into the design, leaving a small tunnel that passed beneath her knees. A dual castle, half built on her feet and half on her hips. A bridge of knees and sand between.

Dee flicked a finger and one of her turrets collapsed.

Tee patted it back into place. It was pretty obvious why Dana was out here staring at an ocean that didn't soothe in the slightest. What she was asking.

"You want my advice?" That was pretty close to a first. But when Dana did ask, she actually listened, not like herself.

"Yeah, I really, really do."

"You won't like it."

"Try me. I'm pretty desperate at this point."

"Desperate enough to ask me for advice. That's pretty damn desperate."

No response. No laugh. Just a dim profile facing the roaring waves.

"Fuck 'em."

"That's advice?" Dee took a handful of sand and turned from the waves. She set it on one of Tee's shoulders and began shaping it.

"That's my advice." She tried to see what was going taking shape on her shoulder but every time she looked over, Dee pushed her chin back.

She lowered her chin and brushed off her shoulder with a sharp turn of her head and ended up nose-to-nose with Dana.

Her eyes were wide, panicked. A glistening tracks of reflected moonlight ran down her cheeks.

Theresa threw her arms around her friend's shoulders and pulled her in until their foreheads touched, just as when they had promised great secrets when their ages were still in the single digits.

"Fuck 'em, Dana. You're better than the whole lot. You're the best there is."

"Nuh-uh."

"Uh-hu."

CHAPTER 64

"C'mon." Theresa struggled to her feet shedding towers and turrets. The sand slid off and fell evenly onto the beach as if she'd never sat down on it. One good shake and all the scratchiness slid out of her shorts.

"Weird."

"What?"

"Why are the sands of," she had to swallow hard before saying it aloud, "Hell, so perfect?"

"Because nothing is what we think it is."

Tee grabbed Dee's hand and hauled her to her feet.

"See, you know shit. That's why you're the best."

Dee punched her arm. Hard enough that Theresa had to stagger sideways scattering the last of Castle Ankle Left.

She gave Dee a sharp push back toward the house. "I know what will cheer me up."

"I thought I was the one who needed cheering." The pain in her voice echoed the silent tears. She slid an arm around Dee's waist who, in turn, draped one over her shoulder as they moseyed back to the house.

"Who gives a damn how you feel?"

"Thanks a lot, pal." But she squeezed her shoulder tightly as they tip-toed up the steps so as not to wake Michelle or Jeremy.

Theresa led them into Michelle's office and pulled two chairs up to the console.

"Hope I can get a connection to the Net."

"What are you doing?"

She poked at the spacebar to wake up the screen. She'd never seen anything like this monster. A bloody museum piece. The screen was just one color as it warmed up. Old-computer green.

"It's time we got on the game grid, you and me. Time to forget all that saving the universe crap and just go play."

What do you want?

Not the friendliest menu she'd ever seen. Maybe they hadn't known about point-and-click back when they designed this thing.

Connection to Internet.

Give me one good reason why.

She looked up at Dee, but she was just sitting there all kind of blank. It took a bit to identify how that made her feel.

Scared. Dee was the most alive person Theresa knew. Contained. Focused. But intensely alive. To see her folding up with all her neurons shorting out scared the shit out of Theresa.

She turned back to the screen.

Because. Morgan Le Fay needs to rock and roll with...

"You got a sign?"

Dee looked down at her chest as if looking for a flippin' sign board. But she didn't speak.

The Huntress, time to make the decision for her.

Harrumph! The computer actually wrote it out and left it in glowing green for a good half-dozen seconds.

Then the screen flowed and shifted. In a thousand shades of green, couldn't the Devil afford a color screen, the land of *Chraze* opened before them.

First the face of the Sumerian God Tammas and the headless cross that was his symbol. His grinning visage faded into the Norse hammer of Thor and the shining *ankh* of Egypt. The swastika gave her the creeps, though it was the first version of the Christian cross before it evolved into the Greek cross of four equal arms. The long-tailed Latin cross came last. Quite how it simultaneously morphed out of its six-pointed-Hebrew-Star origin was a trick she'd never been able to follow.

And they were in. In nowhere she'd ever seen before.

CHAPTER 65

Rendered in layer upon layer of green, a forest spread before them. A narrow path wended its way through towering trees. Dana knew the path, even though the low late afternoon sun barely reached through canopy, as well as she knew she'd never been there. At least not in this lifetime.

Tee hit a few keystrokes and a map of the keyboard flashed up for a moment. Dana studied it quickly. The keys for two players divided the layout in half. Hers began at "H" and went to the right. Tee had the left side of the keyboard. All the normal hop, turn, jump, run, fire keys were there. But there were others she was less sure of and simply cataloged in that part of her brain that won so many video games. Shift, fade, level, penitent…

The diagram timed out and they both leaned forward to inspect the figures more closely. Two characters treaded the forest path. A long, lithe woman dressed in a bow and arrow and soft folds of leather in all the shades of the forest, the small sign flashing on her hip was a bit redundant. What else could she be but "The Huntress" in a getup like that?

Diana the Huntress. Okay, she'd never look that good in a million years, but she'd put up with being beautiful for the game.

Pacing alongside her, a shorter, fiery-haired companion with a small sign on her hip claiming to be Morgan Le Fay, was dressed in flowing silks and carried little more than her sexuality, which was like a body blow from a heavyweight boxer. Had to be Tee.

Dana tried to look over at her real-life companion but the screen shifted and moved them along toward the unknown and she didn't dare look away. The part of her that just wanted to curl up and cry itself to sleep shouted for attention, but the forest was fading into the evening light. The keys were smooth beneath her fingertips, slick with millions of years of use. Billions actually if Michelle was to be believed.

The attack came on the sunlit verge where forest shifted to brush and meadow. Dana slapped the penitent button and fell to her knees just in time to avoid the flat side of a woodsman's axe that had been aimed at knocking her out rather than decapitating her. A half-dozen arrows from her own bow and a broadsword that Morgan wielded with an easy familiarity, routed the bandits. The few still able to move shambled away very rapidly through the brush.

Before they could go another dozen paces, a knight rolled up to them. He rode a massive steed that stamped and huffed in the cool evening air. Like his master, the horse was clad in layer upon layer of armor that would defend him against almost any blow. He must be hugely powerful to carry so much iron. Dana felt a shiver slide up her spine as the massive man raised a sword that was bigger than Tee.

"Be ye witches that you could defeat them so?"

So, the knight had his own personal bandits.

"Wonderful game, Tee," she whispered to the side.

The horse stamped and steamed. The knight's name plate was obscured by the massive array of weaponry he carried. "Arnol…" was all that showed.

"And if we were?" Tee tossed out a saucy riposte and a hip swing that she'd learned from a Mae West movie when they were both seven.

The knight flipped the massive sword over as if it were a butter knife and wielded it like a cross, raised high before them.

"In the name of the Lord God, begone!"

When neither of them flinched and Tee laughed, he grunted to himself.

"Not witches. Then I shall honor ye both and allow ye both to grace my bedchamber this eve." His language was as stilted and awkward as his complete lack of courtesy. But the broadsword he handled very well. He flipped it back into his shoulder harness with practiced ease. His arms, the only part of him not covered in steel, bulged and rippled with a bodybuilder's physique. His muscles looked harder than the armor and were bigger around than Dana's entire body.

Tee glanced at her sideways.

Dana glared back and whispered. "Cybersex with a stinky, rude knight is not my idea of a good time."

Tee winked. She'd always been able to get a rise out of Dana. When would she ever learn?

"I think not, good sir knight. Now bugger off."

"A saucy wench. All the better. Perhaps I shall take ye first."

Dana dropped to one knee and shot an arrow through the eye slit in his visor. He flipped backward off the horse and landed with a crash.

The horse stepped aside and eyed them carefully.

"Why'd you do that? He could have been fun." Tee giggled like she was twelve. "Not! Want to ride or walk?"

"Tough choice, Tee. Duh-uh!"

Dana stripped the armor from the horse's nose and rubbed his cheek vigorously. The huge animal practically crooned.

"Nice shot by the way. He won't get out of *Ms. Pac-Man* for days."

In a few moments they had buried the knight in a great cairn of horse armor. The beast seemed much relieved to be back to normal horse weight. Dana considered retrieving the arrow, but decided it wasn't worth it.

She boosted Tee aboard the great beast, and then hauled herself up behind.

"You know how to drive one of these things?"

"Just like a race car. No worries."

Dana wrapped her arms tightly around her friend's waist as she turned them toward the distant castle.

"Who do you think that was supposed to be?"

"Based on the standard, I'd guess Robin Hood after he was knighted by King Richard the Lionheart."

"But that was a rich knight."

"Right. Kill the rich, give to the poor. We're both poor, hungry, damsels-in-distress, all evidence of your bow to the contrary. Let's get moving before his bandits get tiffy about our killing off their meal ticket."

With a thump of her heels on the horse's side, it reared up and despite her arms wrapped tightly around Tee's waist, she slid over the horse's rump and landed with a crash back in her chair in front of the green console.

"Holy shit." It was all she could come up with. "Holy shit."

"Pretty real, huh?" Tee spun her chair to grin at her. "I'm just crazy about *Chraze*. How about you?"

Dana reached for a more relevant statement of her feelings. She'd forgotten it was a game. Could still smell the horse's sweat on her hands. Could still feel the nighttime air gathering scents of afternoon from the woods. The soft, soft cotton sliding and slipping over her bare legs with nothing beneath.

She looked down.

Her jean-clad legs.

Wiggled in her seat.

With underwear.

"Holy shit."

MONDAY

THREE DAYS UNTIL ARMAGEDDON

UNTITLED

Monday

Monday--

CHAPTER 66

A warm body lay against her back.

Dana blinked at the wall.

Someone was in her bed.

But this wasn't her wall. No pictures of colliding galaxies. No printouts of computer models of particle decay toward a black hole threshold. None of Mom's music playing incessantly through the heating vent. She could use that at the moment. A little Leonard Bernstein segueing through Leonard Cohen on its way to Leonard Nimoy's "Ballad of Bilbo Baggins."

Instead she was faced with a rustic wooden wall and a very small picture, exquisitely framed, of a single, perfect, purest yellow daffodil. Each little crinkle of the inner cup caught the sunlight until the flower appeared to glow from within.

And a warm body breathed in the heavy rhythms of sleep against her back. Butt-to-butt, shoulder-to-shoulder.

Tee. They bedded down together after playing *Chraze* and talked long into the night about absolutely nothing. It was the best night she'd spent in a long time.

She slid out of bed, managing not to waken the sleeper, pulled on her slacks and padded down the hall seeking a bathroom and a large cup of tea. The latter preferably one big enough to dunk her head in.

The cup she found wasn't quite that big, but boiling water that threatened to flash straight into steam flowed out of the little red tap and she chose Irish Breakfast from the vast selection. It was a joy to find another tea drinker.

As the tea kicked in and her brain switched on enough to service her optic nerves, she looked around. The kitchen could have been anywhere. A comfortable country kitchen, right down to herbs hanging from a pegboard, wicker-backed chairs around a long, oak table that showed the wear of a thousand meals. Dana thought about where she was again. Okay, a few billion meals. And not just for one. The whole table was comfortably worn as if many happy gatherings had been held here. There was a rumpled couch near a stone fireplace.

She followed the daylight out the door and onto the front porch. The waves were building up, then quieting down.

"Good morning."

"What? Oh." Michelle sat in her chair, just as she had when they'd arrived, except that rather than a glass of lemonade, she too held a massive mug. Hers smelled vaguely of cinnamon. And she was dressed in shorts, a green t-shirt precisely the color of her eyes, and running shoes. She was exactly the big, powerful, well-built type of woman that always gave Dana a bit of a complex about her own slender frame.

"Hi."

"You still don't remember me." It was a statement. A sad statement.

"You miss her, me, her. Diana."

Michelle simply nodded. "You don't know how much you miss an old friend until you see them again after a long hiatus."

"Sorry."

"Not your fault. I pushed you into this crazy idea. Not really proud of that." The woman studied her steaming tea carefully.

Dana slid into the chair next to her. "I'm not that much of a wimp am I?"

"Huh?" That got her to look up. Her eyes reflecting the green of the ocean waves.

"That you could push me into this against my will?"

The Devil looked away toward the ocean for a bit.

"No. I guess not."

"Guilt is optional you know."

"Clearly your mother didn't raise you Jewish."

"Nor Irish Catholic. So much for my heritage."

"Or pagan mother warrior Goddess."

"The Huntress." She'd forgotten about last night. How natural that unnatural world had felt. How the bow slid into her hands and the arrow flew as if it were not just a thought, but a part of her soul and body.

"No, she raised me to believe in the power of music and the energy that flowed through people."

"Then how did you end up in astrophysics?"

"How did you end up being the Devil?"

"I asked you first."

She was no better than Tee in an argument. Petty evasions that worked every time.

"I have an Uncle who gave me great gifts. For every toy I received from anywhere else, from him I received a prism, a chemistry set, a map of the constellations, a model of the solar system, a plastic glue-together model of every kind of spaceship ever designed, and a few that he may have thought up on his own. Just a natural step." As easy as...drawing a bow. "I seemed to have a natural penchant for it. If I really were Diana the Huntress, I would have a knowledge and a comfort with the outdoors. With the stars."

Michelle nodded. "What did your mother give you?"

"The ability to see." A sip of her tea, so exactly like her mom's made her terribly homesick all of a sudden. She hadn't called home last night. Even when she'd stayed in her office in the back of the planetarium a couple of times when a big paper was due, she always called home. Her brother Talin's song echoed from the back corner of her mind. He never seemed very far away. It was the strange counter-hum he set up when Melissa Ethridge was followed by Men at Work. Home felt safe, secure, stable.

"And what do you see?"

"Home," she answered before she could think. And no matter how irritating it might be, it was home. As much, more than the forest they'd walked.

"What else?"

"What do you mean?"

The woman arched an eyebrow at her as if she were evading the question.

What else did she see? She closed her eyes against the sight of Michelle's light smile. Shut out the vision of another impossible towering wave of water piddling gently up the beach. Blocked out sun and sand.

Her hand wrapped warm around the tea mug. But it was a different warmth. The warmth of another hand holding hers.

Sam's hand.

CHAPTER 67

"*Y*ou look like shit." And he did. Virgil was showing his age this morning, and that was not a good thing on a poet who was a couple millennia old. He hung onto the doorframe of the tiny back bedroom of the RV. His shirt was untucked and still buttoned wrong from yesterday. His face was haggard and gray with age.

Cassie had a good night's sleep in the berth that doubled as a sofa along one wall. She hoped Theresa wouldn't mind that she'd heated the last of the milk to help her sleep.

Now she snuggled down in the front passenger seat that had turned out to be very comfortable once she'd swung it around. The light from the windshield had come in and lit her book nicely. A gentle breeze smelling less of motor oil and more of green pines had rippled in through the passenger door window.

"Tell me something I don't know." Virgil dragged a wrinkled hand over his face and appeared older for his ministrations.

"You wouldn't like it."

He aimed his bloodshot eyes at her.

"I wake up in a cheap-as-crap trailer, sweating like a pig. What could you tell me that I would like less?"

"It's Monday morning."

"And…" He staggered over to the coffee pot, poured a cupful and knocked it back. Then he bent over the sink hacking and spitting. He finally managed to choke out, "You really don't like me."

"I didn't make that. It's cold and at least a day or two old."

He spit into the sink again.

"I noticed." He collapsed on the bench seat where she'd spent the night. "Okay. Give it to me." Why did it take so long to really see a person? Virgil was a useless meddler. Cared more about himself than…anything.

"I did."

"So, it's Monday. All creation ends in a couple of days. That's all you've got?"

"Why are you doing this?"

"Doing what?"

"Trying to help."

He leaned his head back against the wall and closed his eyes.

"Who said I was doing that?"

"But I thought…" She'd thought they were in this together. No, Virgil had always had his own agenda. Did he know what it was? Suddenly Virgil's fight with Loki came into a new light. She should have paid attention to what they were fighting over beyond a drunken brawl.

Cassie set aside the rather steamy romance she'd found beside the driver's seat. It was surprising what the modern writers thought was risqué or erotic. Her Trojan sisters could have taught them a thing or two that would make their neat little coifs curl and catch fire.

Her prophetic vision was a burden to be avoided, not sought. Random, unpredictable, incomplete. It had shown the ten thousand ships of Agamemnon and Menelaus come to crush Troy. It hadn't revealed that such a horrible moment would make Troy remembered forever, instead of just another forgotten kingdom of Asia Minor. The price of fame indeed. Burned to the ground, the very earth salted so that nothing would grow for a hundred years.

But Virgil was up to no good, and she'd like to know what it was.

She closed her eyes, focused her breathing just as she used to do in the temple rituals. It hadn't been what brought her clearest or largest visions, those had come in their own good time and jumped her when she least expected. But the simpler, smaller ritual insights had proven equally accurate, and were met with the same disbelief.

She didn't let Virgil's quiet, "Oh, shit." distract her.

She let her mind expand to the flow of time. A vision.

The Present lay spread before her. A hundred thousand threads all gathered at her feet. Anyone that she picked up would lead to an unavoidable Future, a truth that sometimes mattered, sometimes was intensely stupid, but true nonetheless. Between her muse of divination and the Lord God Apollo's curse, it really sucked. Maybe if she'd held her focus and practiced over the centuries it would make a difference, but she couldn't stay very inspired when no one believed anything she said.

She lifted the brightest thread, so hot she could barely hold it and had to toss it from hand-to-hand until she could see what lay down its length. She used to set these back down quickly, knowing that only the Gods themselves could ship so much power down a thread spun by the three fates. Best to avoid the Gods.

The thread hummed with power and she wrapped both hands around it and looked down its length. This was no minor path, but a flaring, blinding light. It couldn't be Zeus nor Athena. Neither Wotan nor Artemis. Krishna nor Mohammed.

The heat built and burned until finally she had to throw it down before she was scorched. She blew across her vision's hands to cool them and, ever so slightly, like a single blooming violet, the smell of freshly toasted bagels with cream cheese tickled her nose leaving her none the wiser, but a bit hungrier. Theresa had kept nothing for breakfast in her RV's kitchen except a few packets of instant oatmeal of dubious vintage.

Another thread pulsed just a few steps ahead. As she moved closer in her vision, Cassandra noticed the horizon for the first time. Rather than spreading, overlapping, tangling and untangling as the threads stretched out into the distance of the Future, now they faded. They washed out as if her eyesight was blurry.

A never-ending Plain of silver winding light faded quickly in the near distance. The Plain of Existence. She'd almost forgotten about it, had certainly tried to. It had been millennia since she'd walked here over the undulated energies and contours of all Existence.

Only a few threads reached out brightly. Yet even they disappeared into a darkness that smothered everything with its impossible mass.

She lifted the pulsing thread. A woman of both age and youth, of both naiveté and power, of hope and a vision for the Present like her own for the Future, stood upon the thread. She'd been facing away, toward the uncertain Future, but turned at the tug on her strand.

Blue eyes stared at her from a thin face forever in its early twenties. Hair fell straight past her cheeks emphasizing the generous shape of the lips as they turned into a smile.

"Who are you?" The words shimmered toward Cassie up the length of the thread. She gathered it foot by foot as she sidled forward in time. Her step uncertain upon the undulating Plain of fading strands.

"A prophetess seeking truth. You?"

"A woman with two pasts but only one present."

They were close enough to take hands. But they didn't. Close enough to feel the radiated heat of two standing where no one could be.

Cassie stayed silent and the two of them listened as they moved ever so slightly ahead toward the darkness.

No sound. No echoes. No wind. No birds. Not the beating of hearts.

"I don't like the darkness." It was a new feature and it reminded her of why she'd come. There were only two days left.

"It feels close. I've never been here."

"I try to avoid it myself. But here there is only truth. I have an uncomfortable relationship with truth."

"Is the darkness approaching?" The woman slid her hair behind one ear and stared forward. Open-faced. Not in fear.

"Two days. Perhaps less."

"Then what?"

Cassie shrugged, could feel her shoulders rise and fall in this place without feeling or sound. What happened after all creation ceased?

She was long past dead and felt little different for the change. But ending? True ending? More unimaginable than death had been that was for sure.

"Your guess. Mine. Who knows?"

"I'm supposed to stop it. I don't even know what it is."

That got Cassie's attention. She inspected the ageless youngster again. Was she the one who'd been sent? She didn't look strong enough to do...

"What is it you're supposed to do?" They'd slid a little closer to the darkness. Shoulder-to-shoulder but still an unbreachable distance between them.

"Redeem humanity and save creation. How am I gonna do that?"

She was the one.

The Second Messiah.

Two days left and this girl didn't know what to do.

The Messiah's silver line was one of the few trails of light that reached the blackness. One of the few that had the strength to reach the end. Yet the line attached to her own Achilles tendon, of course that was the weak point. It was the attachment to the thread spun by the fates, the way they threaded souls onto their spinning. Cassandra's own line stretched ahead out of sight. It crossed the bright line of this fear-filled girl only once more. Then it wandered off on a path of its own, separate from the other threads of light. Separate from the darkness.

A quick retrace with her eyes showed that her path was indeed the one that left this Plain and sliced upward. Hers alone impacted the dark wall in a totally different plane than the Second Messiah's. Perhaps it even orbited over the darkness, bypassing it altogether. Hard to tell at this distance. Wherever it led, she would have no choice but to go.

Alone.

The story of her life.

She shook off the vision. Left the woman to her own problems, they were no longer her own anyway.

Landed back in a stupid RV with a useless poet. What a way to spend her last day of existence.

"Well," he demanded. "What did you see? What happens to me?"

It was all about him. No wonder he'd spent so much time in Hell. She'd forgotten to look for his line. Maybe his was one of the ones that hit the blackness, entered or pierced the wall.

She hoped not. Let the jerk twist in the wind.

The fates had made sure that she'd be somewhere else before the end came, perhaps somewhere safe. Her connection to this present was separating, frayed around the edges.

CHAPTER 63

The voice Dana couldn't quite place had disappeared. The suggestion of someone near her was gone.

What was she supposed to do to save all creation?

"How am I going to do that?" she asked the emptiness one more time. No reply came back to her.

This impossible vision still spread before her, the blackness creeping closer. A line of silver zig-zagged its way closer to her, slipping quickly from one thread to the next.

It flashed by and kept going until it was out of sight.

And then...

She held her breath and waited.

And then nothing.

No silver flash. No shift in the infinite array of lines. No progress toward the black hole swallowing everything on the horizon.

She decided to follow the flash of light, see what was off to the side, but she tripped where one of the rays of light was wrapped around her ankle.

And she was back holding her tea mug.

Scalding liquid trickling over her hands.

And her shoulder hurt.

She didn't have to turn to see why.

"Good morning, Tee." Tee was blowing off her knuckles like she was cooling off a gun.

"Hey daydreamer. Where were you?" Tee threw herself down into the Adirondack chair Michelle had been in. She looked refreshed and alive in a way that only morning people could. Her merry smile dimpling her cheeks, her curling hair catching the sun and making her look angelic which was about the last thing she was. Maybe that's why Dana loved her so much.

"Damned if I know."

"Nah. You're already damned. You spent the night in Hell after all."

"Thanks, Tee, that just brightens up my whole day." And it did. Tee had that effect on her. She was one of the irrepressibly positive forces in the universe.

"I was off studying the problem."

"And what did you learn?" Tee slouched down in her chair and tried to reach her heels out to the porch rail, but her legs were too short even when she slouched so low her chin was driven into her chest.

"That a prophetess seeking perfect truth has no more of a clue than I do. Did you have any brilliant insights during your beauty sleep?"

Jeremy stumbled out of the front door onto the porch, his hair as rumpled as his clothes. Tee sat up quickly and then stretched slowly in such a way that completely emphasized the generous breasts on her compact body.

Distracted, Jeremy walked into one of the posts, before tumbling down the stairs and landing hard in the sand.

She flashed a grin at Dana, "Not a single insight, but a few fun ideas."

CHAPTER 69

"**W**hy does your ego require a Gothic edifice for your final act?"

It's not my ego. I just think that it is an appropriately arcane setting of religious importance. If the Apocalypse must be announced from somewhere, what is wrong with the pulpit of Chartres cathedral. No one will be there except a few overpaid priests and a handful of tourists. Early October in France there isn't a whole lot going on. I could release the Apocalypse from Stonehenge if you'd prefer, but the new-agers might not notice the change.

Michelle slapped the side of the console. Then she could feel the air in her home office change. Yet she'd heard no one approach. She only knew one woman who could move that silently. Of course, the fact that she was one of the four house guests did narrow down the options.

"Morning, Dana." Michelle rolled her chair back and faced her guest. She had dark rings under her eyes and her hair had definitely seen better days.

"Uh, morning."

"Where are the others?"

"Walking on the beach." Dana nodded toward the console, "Does slapping that help?"

"They holding hands yet?" A bit of a smile. "No, hitting the console just makes me feel better."

"Not quite Tee's style. She's flashy, but doesn't fall for every guy who comes along. And when she does, he'd better be ready. She'll skip right over handholding and go for screaming sex in the surf."

Michelle listened to the light splashing sound drifting through the open window on the morning breeze. "They may not want to risk that surf."

"Why?"

"The daytime surf's bite is far worse than its bark."

Another gentle splash sounded through the window and its echo washed quietly around the room a few times before fading away.

Michelle slapped the side of the terminal again eliciting several rapid lines of text she didn't bother to read. It didn't make her feel any better.

"Who are you arguing with?"

"*What* am I arguing with."

"Huh?"

"You'd better sit down."

Dana dropped into another chair and looked more closely at the screen.

"Who is arguing with you about the proper architecture of religious edifices for the Apocalypse?"

"*What* is arguing with me."

Dana shook her head and looked directly at her.

"What the hell are you talking about?"

"The Software that Runs the Universe. It's a what, not a who. Not by any stretch of possible decency is it a who. Here, you try talking a smidgeon of sense into it. I'm certainly having no luck." She kicked back her chair and waved Dana forward. The woman pulled herself slowly up to the console.

"Hello?" Dana typed.

Who— Oh! The Huntress. What do you have to say for yourself?

"Who is this?"

Duh-uh! Thought you were sharper than that. Weren't you just standing on the Plain of Existence?

"You were standing on the Plain?" Michelle grabbed her forearm.

"Ow!"

The Devil eased her grip. Marginally. Michelle knew of the Plain but had never managed to stand on it.

"I don't know. What is it? And who's on-line and how do they know the name I used last night in a game? If I don't get straight answers real soon, I'm going to get in that car and see if I can't get home. See if Jefferson Airplane or Jerry Jeff Walker or *Jesus Christ Superstar* is playing. Eat too much pizza. Listen to my little brother sing for a few hours."

"What did you see?" Michelle increased her grasp.

"I said, Ow!" Dana's eyes widened once she realized that Michelle was not going to ease up.

"I saw a plain of silver lines and a black wall. Or a wall of blackness. It was getting closer."

Michelle let go, dropped back into her chair, and rubbed her eyes. "It was getting closer? You're sure?"

"Yeah. The other woman saw it too."

"Which woman?" And why couldn't she get there? The Devil ought to be able to go where she pleased.

"She said she was a prophetess seeking truth."

"And you believed her?"

"I didn't have any reason not to."

"Can you describe her to me?"

Dana shook her head uncertainly. "Couldn't really see her. But she said it was less than two days away."

Michelle closed her eyes to shut out the truth in her friend's strange eyes. To look into them and not see any recognition of their centuries as friends. The girlfriend she trusted wouldn't remember her true self until her twenty-first birthday, then she'd become both Diana and Dana. But for now, those familiar eyes watched her with mistrust and without recognition.

"Who's on the terminal?"

"I told you, it's a what not a who. The Software that Runs the Universe is talking with us." She could feel her weariness like a weight on her chest. "Arguing with us. With me. Its favorite pastime."

"*What* kind of software?"

Michelle just waved a hand toward the screen. Let her figure out what to do with it. Michelle had come here as soon as Dana had ducked into Suzzallo library to hide yesterday morning. Was it only yesterday?

Must be.

Three left then.

Two days left now.

And no closer to understanding why the end was coming or what to do about it.

Michelle dragged herself out of her office chair and left the stifling room. Out into the burning sunlight.

Far down the beach to the left, two figures walked a little apart. She turned to the right and started walking. She'd had enough of it all.

Let the software have its fun.

Let fourteen billion years of work go to waste because of an arbitrary deadline that she couldn't understand and the software refused to explain.

She really needed to sit down and have a nice long chat with God. He was never practical, but he always made her feel better.

But after pretending to be dead for a couple millennia, he'd dropped out, and for some reason Michelle couldn't find him. As if she'd forgotten something she used to know, which truth be told creeped her out a bit.

The burning Foothills of Hell rose into the distance. A bright clang of metal echoed down the winding canyons.

She broke into a trot, the beach sand slowly giving way to hard-packed earth. She stretched out her stride.

Let the pounding of her feet on earth fill her ears.

Her mind.

Her soul.

It might be her last chance to run through the burning Hills of Hell and she was going to make the most of it.

She wiped the sweat from her eyes as the trail wound around the first real peak. Let her pounding feet be the only sound echoing through the canyons.

The only sound left.

The last sound in Hell.

CHAPTER 70

"You control the Plain of All Existence?" The keys were hot beneath Dana's fingertips, as if Michelle's power had heated them to a fiery level and they were only now cooling down. The office was decorated with the flotsam and jetsam of the world's oceans. Propellers, gold doubloons, figureheads from sailing ships, and tons of other junk covered the walls.

Great, now she was just another piece of the Devil's junk collection.

I am the Plain. I am the grid on which the game of reality is played out.

"That still doesn't tell me what the grid is. What it represents."

No. Not a representation. It is the actual form. All that is, exists on that Plain, travels on that Plain.

"Then what is the blackness?"

The screen paused. She could almost feel the grid thinking, deciding.

The future.

"So, the future is a place without hope."

Not a place. A time.

"Nitpicker. It's still an event horizon. And you would have me, have everyone give up hope? What kind of a sadist are you?"

HA! Sadist. I like that. For billions of years, millions of millennia, and let me tell you it's way too bloody many minutes and I've counted every single one, I have seen to your well being. To creation's safety.

Dana fooled around with the numbers in her head for a moment. "About seven quintillion minutes, unless I dropped a factor."

I could get to like you. I know! Let's change the plan and...Sorry, just teasing. Existence will be ending soon. No time. Next in line please.

"Michelle said you were software. Wasn't existence what you were programmed to maintain?"

Well, yes.

"So what's the problem?"

I'm bored.

"And what are we supposed to do about that?"

Nothing.

"Nothing?"

Nothing. Not a thing you could do to stop the Apocalypse, so don't waste your breath. I've listened in on the CABER meetings, watched that pesky little angel typing her tediously inaccurate minutes.

"Hey!"

Dana spun the chair around.

There wasn't anyone there.

She looked the other way.

She was alone.

"My meeting minutes are not inaccurate."

Dana spotted the little angel sitting, spine-straight with anger, on the back of the chair.

"They are the best minutes ever minuted of those meetings. Clio used to write these painfully dry, factual accounts. They were so incredibly dull they could kill a person. Even make an angel wish she'd fallen and switched sides. Have you ever tried to read one of them?"

Dana tried to open her mouth to mention that she actually had. But Henrietta overran her.

"Boring. Boring. Boring. Why even Michelle didn't read them. And that should tell you something. The woman is a voracious reader, though she seems to prefer science fiction and murder mysteries. Now where did she get to? Did she go running again? Off into the Hills of Hell probably. Whenever she gets frustrated she goes out and joins in a round or twenty of hand-to-hand combat with Achilles and Hector."

The angel leaned forward and whispered conspiratorially. "Makes them mad as the dickens that they can't beat her. About the only thing they agree on."

"Henrietta."

"Yes?"

"Is there a point to all this?"

"Well...I..." She raised a minute finger. Opened her mouth. Hesitated. Closed it again. Lowered the finger.

"Um...no, I guess not." She hung her head, completely crestfallen.

"Don't worry about it. Everyone has days when they're not at the top of their form."

The angel nodded and sighed. Dana patted her little knee and turned back to the computer.

Pissed her off, didn't I? See, there is still fun to be had.

Dana considered her response. Thought of different arguments she could pose, alternatives to ending the universe.

Then she had it.

She slapped the side of the console. Hard.

Why did you do that?!?

"You needed a lesson in manners."

Shit!

Dana closed her eyes.

Seattle. She just wanted to go home. Wanted to see the Space Needle still standing on the horizon. See Sam. Watch the night sky slide over the planetarium dome. Listen to her brother's endless singing over the segue from Three Dog Night to Tina Turner.

The last thing she wanted to see when she reopened her eyes was that she was confused and alone in Hell.

The last place she wanted to be was here. Anywhere but here.

Ever so faintly in the background she heard a fading voice, exclaim, "Hey!"

It may have been Henrietta.

CHAPTER 71

ool air soothed her lungs. A slight breeze tickled her cheek. A smell. A pine and saltwater smell of home so rich and thick she never wanted to breathe anything else again. Clean and cool except for a background smell of…

"Who are you and where the hell did you come from?"

…burnt rubber and motor oil.

Dana's eyes snapped open and looked at the elderly couple seated in front of their RV. But elderly wasn't quite right.

The man was haggard, withered, ancient with a million burdens that could never be lifted from his face. He idly waved a fly swatter with one hand and cradled a large glass of clear liquid with his other. His energy field was wrapped in layers of brown sludge that was snarled in his soul.

The woman was equally ancient, but surrounded in a pure, white light that was so clean it almost hurt Dana's eyes. Her silver hair flowed like a thick river draped over her shoulders. Her eyes were a pure black, a darkness that could hide the secrets of the ages and you'd never know.

"Another racer zombie," the besludged man grumbled. "She's not here. Go away. No autographs today. Go on. Move."

And she would have left. Wanted to. The less to do with the man smeared in brown the better. But she knew this vehicle. Had been there the day Tee bought it. Had seen it the day it came back from the paint shop. How many lipstick-red RVs emblazoned with the shapely "Workouts for Women" logo were there wandering the racetracks of America?

"I don't think she's a groupie," the gray-haired lady of light was squinting at her.

"Well, shit, how can you tell them apart? They keep flocking up to this ugly thing." He slugged back the rest of his drink and gasped loudly as the alcohol hit his system. "What the hell do you want, sweetie? A personal, guided tour of the inside of this beautiful vehicle? It's got a nice double-wide bunk in the back."

The energy ooze slid down to his pelvis and began forming a swirling, undirected concentration that would have made her lose her lunch if she'd had any.

"You couldn't handle her, Virgil."

Virgil. Hadn't Jeremy mentioned a Virgil? Or was it Tee?

"You think not?" He rose up out of the lounger. He shed decades, centuries as he stood.

Dana certainly didn't want to handle him.

The woman nodded. "Are you who I think you are?"

Dana tried to find words, but they were lodged somewhere that had nothing to do with the location of her body at a racetrack wrapped in the cool scent of Douglas fir forest.

The woman's light was so clear and bright, Dana finally had to blink away the vision and once again looked at their corporeal forms. The woman didn't change, though she no longer burned with the light of truth. Though Dana would bet it was still there. The man was wrapped in a façade of energy and vigor that hid the worst of the travesties he harbored within.

Dana's vague nod was returned by the level gaze of the woman. She finally rose from her chair and shoved Virgil back down into his. Her hand was warm where it took Dana's and led her beneath the bright red awning. A cool glass of iced tea was slid into her hand.

The man tried to empty a bottle of clear nastiness into her glass, but the woman slapped it aside. It spilled all over his hand and down his arm. He cursed and began licking at his fingers. It wasn't possible, but for a moment his tongue looked forked. What was he?

"What are you?" Dana tried to make some sense of him, but failed as thoroughly as she'd failed at having sex with Sam.

"Pissed. Stuck at a fucking racetrack with no race to watch and I'm pissed. She didn't leave the keys. Stuck and pissed. Pissed and stuck. That's me."

The sweet tartness of the iced tea eased her throat and she was able to shake off a little of the miasma of fog that had cluttered her brain since she'd walked on the grid of this astral Plain. She turned to the woman.

"Who are you?"

"Cassandra of Troy." Her mind attempted to dismiss the words, but the woman's light didn't waver. None of the flickering she'd learned to watch for when someone lied. Of course, neither did Virgil's. His truth was equally clear, just at the opposite pole from decency. His truth oozed out like an open sore upon the world.

"Cassandra of Troy. A prophetess of Troy..." It was the same voice. The one she had met on the silver-lined grid.

"And you would be the woman with two pasts and only one present. Diana and Dana. I thought it was you. Greetings, Messiah."

Virgil, Virgil who'd written *The Aeneid* two thousand years ago, sputtered his drink out in a spray that coated his jeans and set him off into a fit of coughing that might have killed him. If he weren't already dead.

Dana was sitting here talking to two people who had died thousands of years ago.

And she thought she'd left Hell behind her.

ichelle danced aside.

The fist-sized rock Achilles had heaved at her impacted a boulder sitting innocently off to her right and shattered into a puff of dust.

Hector advanced with his sword once again, convinced that his strength in battle was embodied in the weapon's overlong reach.

She dove and rolled into his knees well inside the range of his massive bronze blade. He landed with a grunt of pain and a roar of frustration.

The next rock that Achilles heaved, she caught and using its own momentum, spun around and shot it back at the center of his small round shield. It blew the warrior's heavy piece of engraved wood into splinters now dangling from a couple of leather handholds.

She tossed a handful of the dry, dusty dirt of Hell at his eyes and a well-placed kick between his legs, and Achilles collapsed across the groaning Hector.

Michelle dusted off her shorts and shirt. "Told you boys I didn't want to play today. Now, I'll ask one more time, where's Loki?"

Achilles just lay there groaning and cradling his leather loincloth.

Hector inspected her carefully with one eye as he attempted to staunch the blood dripping over the other. He nodded up into the Hills.

"My sister and that dumb-ass poet went up the road day before yesterday looking for him. They had a twerp of a kid with eyes bigger around than my shield tied down in the back seat. A programmer. Can you believe that they brought a programmer here? How dangerous is that, pray tell?"

Michelle stared up at the burning Hills. Not her first choice, but something had to be done. She decided not to mention that Jeremy was still in Hell, down at her house right this moment.

She nodded to Hector, kicked Achilles in the gut forcing him to drop the rock he'd tried to pick up, and headed for the Hills at a fast trot.

CHAPTER 73

ichelle found Loki sitting on top of what looked like a garbage dump.

Loki was picking up the odd bits and pieces of detritus from the top of the pile. He'd turn them over for a moment, as if seeking treasure. Then heave it toward the other side of the massive mound at an unseen target.

He didn't cease his actions as she clambered up over sofa backs, structural beams, and old bookcases.

She crested the top and could see his target. Beyond Loki's feet the pile dipped, making a small valley in the rubble. From there a mound slightly taller than his own rose once again. Paintings, kitchen implements, and a hundred thousand years of house dust climbed into the distance. Atop the highest stick of lumber, the mangiest looking cat she'd ever seen was licking its wild fur into greater disarray.

Loki lifted a hiking boot from between his feet, inspected the chewed-through lacing and then heaved it at the cat who gave no sign of noticing as it flew several inches over its head.

"Having fun?"

"It's keeping me busy."

"While what?"

Loki tossed one arm of a garden shears without much enthusiasm, it barely made it to the low point of the garbage heap.

"You mean, *until* what."

She swallowed hard.

"No, I really didn't." She really, really, really didn't.

Loki heaved the complete works of Shakespeare which snapped and fluttered in the wind as it flew and finally crashed into a bicycle frame which started a small avalanche down the far slope. The cat eyed the cavalcade of pottery and cooking pots with disdain.

"Aren't you disappointed? It was your idea after all."

"No way, woman. You can't blame this one on me. I just suggested a politician. You're the one who thought a Messiah would be a good solution."

"Don't you care?"

Loki found a stack of 78 vinyl records and sighed. Then he began whipping them off at the cat so fast that he'd launched over a dozen before the first one had traveled far enough to miss entirely.

The cat began tugging on one of its claws with its teeth.

"No. Can't say that I do. How about you?"

"Well, of course I..." But *was* it so obvious? How hard had she worked with how little success?

The cat stopped its preening and stared straight at her. The distance between them seemed to vanish as she looked into its eyes, one blue, one green. And they were crossed, making the animal appear far more than half mad—at least seventy-five percent, maybe eighty.

For fourteen billion years she had battled for advancement, for improvement in the state of creation. Life had been dragged from primordial sludge, unwilling. And now humanity, one of the four pinnacles of terrestrial life, was doing its best to undo everything.

Perhaps Loki was right. Perhaps the software had a point.

Why struggle?

Why not just go quietly into the dark of the night?

Michelle flipped over a board which lackadaisically brandished a few rusty nails before sliding sullenly down the face of the slope. A blue vase of Waterford crystal lay nestled in a collection of dirty socks and old t-shirts. It was thick-walled, but slender, heavy with a mass belied by its size and slender form. Just enough room for a single bloom. A splash of water and a lone daffodil had survived in it. She smoothed a bent petal, so soft it was hard to tell if she was even touching it.

The thick, blue glass glowed and darkened with exposure to the light. The dye was so rich it was hard to credit that it could be possible. The transition between air and midnight blue glass was so abrupt that, had it not been for the etchings, the vase would appear to be an anomaly of space.

When she held it up before Loki, he merely grunted and tossed a couple of AA batteries and a portable CD player with its headphones streaming out behind at the cat who was still watching her.

The man had no appreciation of beauty. None. An alarm clock followed an empty box of chocolates followed a 1934 Monet calendar.

But beauty existed nonetheless.

"But you cared that we sent a politician?"

"Thought it would be amusing. And it kept you folks going, not that it was going to matter."

"Not that it was going to matter." Michelle rolled the words slowly over her tongue as she repeated them.

"You knew! Back then? Twenty-one years ago, you knew?"

"Well, an apocalypse takes a bit of planning. You can't just throw one together like a pot of soup. It takes planning if you want to shut down all of Creation."

"Why Thursday? Why not the Second Messiah's twenty-first birthday? Seems just as likely."

For the first time Loki turned to look at her. His dark eyes were bloodshot as if he hadn't slept in days. His perfect hair and neat goatee were rumpled and needed a trim. His red bodysuit was smeared with dirt and ash and sparkled as if impregnated with tiny bits of glass.

"When does Diana get her memory back?"

"On her twenty-first birthday. You know that."

Loki grinned. Slowly at first. A quirk at the corners of his mouth.

But it grew rapidly into a great smile filled with perfect teeth that really needed a good brushing.

He threw his head back and, rather than the laugh she expected, howled at the sun, his throat stretching out as the sounded echoed across the junkyard. A hunting pack. The sound of an entire hunting pack sounded from his throat and echoed about the burning Hills of Hell.

The cat stood up, rolled a golf ball to the very top of its mound.

Twice it glanced over at Michelle and the howling Loki from its perch, then looked back down at its ball.

One last glance and it swatted the ball with a great smack. It threw its tail about for maximum momentum.

Before Michelle could throw up her arms, the cat's missile found its mark in the center of Loki's forehead.

His howl chopped off abruptly as he flipped over backward and tumbled down the junkheap.

When at last the avalanche of old snow tires, a refrigerator, and half a dozen dining chairs ceased, Loki was nowhere to be seen.

The cat hopped down from its perch, leaping from gilt picture frame to Frank Sinatra's face to toilet seat. It scrambled right past her, so close she could have touched it if she'd thought fast enough and been crazy enough. It slid to a halt over the last place she'd spotted Loki.

Then it turned about, shit on the pile, knocked over a rusted car door with a couple scrapes of its hind legs and then sat down atop the door and began licking its tail fur in the wrong direction.

CHAPTER 74

"This whole place scares me." Jeremy wanted to wrap his arms tightly about himself. "And where did everyone get off to?"

Theresa took his hand in hers where they sat side by side on the Devil's front stoop. The tiny waves of Hell's Ocean roared to themselves just a few dozen paces away. They'd sat down here when they discovered that Dana and Michelle were gone and they had no idea where to go looking.

His nerve endings were sending surprised and, if he read them right, very cheerful messages up to his cerebellum. He tried squeezing her hand with his interlaced fingers.

She squeezed back and sighed.

Yup, his nerve endings had definitely switched into a very high, very happy gear.

"But you created *Chraze*. Why should Hell scare you?" She lay back with her eyes closed, her hair bright red where the tips had started to dry, maroon-dark where it hadn't.

"That's a computer game."

"Doesn't feel like it. There's someone in there watching me."

"No way."

She opened her eyes and looked at him. "Way."

"But there's no central authority. That was a part of the design. Random, disconnected, seemingly meaningful stream of events, but string-mass-space-time chaos beneath. That's what I wrote."

"Way. Don't care what you designed. I was grabbed last time I was in there and it switched me, the real me, off. No outside access. No disconnect. No end game. Started running through my nervous system like an SAT exam."

"No way."

"Way."

She started to remove her hand, but stopped when he squeezed it for a moment. He surreptitiously shifted his pants to try and hide the reaction that was building there.

"Okay. Maybe it was a super-player. But he shouldn't be able to reach you beyond the playing field."

"Took me right off the playing field. A mad priest with a blank label. And I'm ranked number fifteen. No one should be able to get anything past me that easily."

"Fifteen?" He looked at her more closely. "Morgan Le Fay?"

She made a small obeisance without getting out of her chair.

"Holy shit. I'm sitting here with Morgan Le Fay?"

A blush started at her cheeks and spread out rapidly across her face.

He never played, but he certainly watched. Perhaps it was a bit voyeuristic, but he justified it by the rationale that he knew everything the game could do, it was the players who were the mystery. Or at least he thought he knew everything the game could do.

She was the fastest gamer on the whole list. And numbers one through fourteen were well aware of that. Did she know that they all logged off whenever she came on? They'd set alarms warning them whenever Morgan hit the system. They'd barely learned in time as she burned her way up the list. She moved like, like poetry, or an intercontinental cruise missile.

Jeremy popped to his feet and would have walked about just to burn off the extra energy, but a sharp tug on his hand sent him off balance. He barely managed to catch himself from crushing her as he fell into her chair. She slid sideways just in time and they ended up crammed together on the same narrow seat.

"Morgan?" It was barely a whisper. She was the only woman in the top five hundred and she played fewer hours than anyone else in the top million or so. To become a high scorer you had to be relentlessly addicted as well as good. Unless you were Morgan Le Fay.

"No. Theresa. Tee to my friends. Morgan Le Fay to those I wish to destroy." Her grin was filled with a wickedness and glee that were intoxicating.

"Theresa." He breathed in her scent, the gentle flavor of sea salt mixed with pine trees and race cars.

He leaned into her soft lips. She opened them and slid her tongue against his.

His nervous system exploded.

CHAPTER 75

"I wish you wouldn't keep running off." Henrietta fluttered back and forth before Dana in a dizzying display of ire. Like a little arc of white fire against the bright red paint job on the RV.

"Do you have any idea how many favors I have to drag in to find out where you've gone? I have to get an Archangel to talk to a Principality at least. This time I had to go through a Power Angel all the way up to a Virtue Angel before we could track you down."

Dana was getting a little seasick trying to follow her circling path up and down.

"I can't find Michelle. And St. Peter refuses to listen to me. I came that close," she held up her thumb and forefinger just a millimeter apart. "That close to declaring a state of emergency. The only one who answered her CABER page was Mary Magdalene and do you know what she told me? Do you?"

Her voice was rising into a hysterical tone that was making Virgil cringe and was driving Cassandra to giggles. Maybe she could get to like this woman, even if she was dead.

"No, I don't. What did Mary tell you?"

"She told me she was busy baking a birthday cake for her husband. Everyone knows he wasn't born in September. And I could distinctly hear the television playing in the background. Can you believe that the wife of Jesus lied to me? I almost flew over to give those two a piece of my mind, I'll tell you, but then I got notice of where you were."

"And you decided to grace us with your presence." Before she could stop him, Virgil slashed at the little angel with his fly swatter.

Henrietta ducked his stroke with a quick flit and turned back upon him. In her fury, her voice grew louder, changed, deepened from its incessant little chirp.

"You would strike an angel? One anointed by the Lord God as well as by the Software that Runs the Universe?" The edge in her voice became fierce and cutting. Virgil stumbled backward over his own feet before the onslaught until the RV was close behind him.

"Out with it." The crash of the angel's voice demanded.

He covered his face, "Out with what?"

As much as she didn't want to, Dana looked at Virgil, carefully. Fear was welling up from a dark pit deep inside him. It threatened to overwhelm, to wash across him in a tidal wave of red and brown. It was all focused from a bit of black, an area of such pitch darkness, it was hard to imagine how she had missed it.

"Push him, Henrietta. He's hiding a truth from us."

"You," she aimed a small forefinger at his nose and he backed away so abruptly that he cracked his head on the side of the RV.

"Tell me what you know right this instant or you shall experience the wrath of the entire body of the Nine Choirs of Angels. And you know that you would meet a horrible end should a seraphim address you directly." Her voice echoed about the empty parking area. "Tell me now!"

Virgil slipped to the ground, all but senseless from the assault. She and Cassie squatted down on either side of him where he leaned back against the metal siding while Henrietta fluttered before him still filled with the power of her anger.

"I can see it," Dana pointed to the area by his left temple. As much as she hated to do it, she reached out and touched the thread of energy.

It was worse than she'd feared. She wouldn't just need a shower after this, she'd need to be scrubbed down in degreaser first.

She reached for the light and energy of the world around her, and flooded it into Virgil's mind. Gently at first, but opening it up to a flood of the universal energy until the dark nodule was washed free of its mooring and floated between them.

With careful manipulations, she unfolded the blackness and Virgil began to babble.

"See, it wasn't my idea. I just got stuck with it. It's what happens when you take an unplanned trip to Hell. I wasn't supposed to go there to begin with. I was researching the *Odyssey*, headed to Carthage to see if I could seduce the queen—she was a major, major babe. It was just field research. How did I know she'd have the power to consign me to Hell. And there wasn't even a Hell back then. I had to hang around the River Styx forever because that bastard Hades wouldn't let me in. Every bloody day, I'd bribe the boatman to let me cross over to Hades' gates and every bloody day he'd have to drag me back. But I fooled him." Virgil stared directly into the unfolding blackness between them and smiled.

She fought down the shiver that ran over her skin and tried to flood more light upon the blackness. He began to skip and jump and stutter in his ramblings.

"Ha! Fooled Hades. He was off, screwing around with Persephone. Broke in. Learned the secrets. All of them. Could run the place if they let me. Who turned Hades into Hell? Huh? Huh?" He thumped a fist on his chest.

"Buddy Boy Virgil did. Then that bastard Dante went out and made a fortune on the world I told him about. Writers. Bastards every one. But we're gonna get 'em in the end. Loki he came and—"

Virgil's eyes went wide and he slapped a hand over his mouth. He looked about frantically as the fear drained the color out of his face.

"Loki isn't here, Virgil." Cassie rested a hand on his arm.

"Can I believe you? No. I don't believe you." He whined between his fingers.

"Do you believe what I just said?"

His darting eyes stopped for a moment and focused on her. He slipped his hand slowly down from his mouth.

"No…No, I don't. So you must be telling the truth. Loki really isn't here." He looked to Dana for verification, so she nodded. Whoever Loki was, there were only the four of them there beneath the red awning.

Henrietta fluttered to a landing on her shoulder and grabbed her ear for balance.

"We needed the kid's index." Virgil's voice had a whine that made Dana's ears hurt.

"Jeremy's? What does he have to do with this?"

He looked about past their shoulders. "The kid's software stumbled onto something. Found something. I had to stop it. The software. Loki. I had to stop it being found. Loki took it for himself. Recruited me to help." His smile grew lean and nasty though his eyes weren't focusing anywhere nearby.

"Wanted for myself. Tricked Cassie, always fell for the 'I believe you' crap."

Cassandra swore and reared back to kick Virgil, but Dana waved her off.

"Jeremy needed that 'holier-than-thou' truth that I knew I couldn't pull together for him. Got her to front for me." The smile disappeared as if it had been swallowed by a passing black hole.

"Loki isn't here, is he?"

"No." Dana sent the most reassurance she could in both her tone and energy. "He's not here. Just tell me about Jeremy's software."

Virgil's eyes cast about.

"I would have taken it. Controlled it. Rewritten Hell. Gotten out that way. But no. Loki. That greedy shit, had to take it. Wanted to kill it. But it was too complex. Had a life of its own before we found it. And Loki…And the software loved it. New toy to play with.'

His mind was unraveling. His very being was coming apart.

Dana took a deep breath, leaned into the energy field, and pasted his scattering mind back together. Her own field flickered into awful shades of grays and mud-browns as Virgil's slime oozed towards her. She was able to fight it off, but she didn't know for how long.

But if Jeremy was in trouble, or he himself *was* trouble...He was with Tee right now. In Hell. And she had to find out what was going on.

One thing was for sure.

They were going to need help badly. And if the feeling prickling over her skin at the moment was any indication, she was going to need to get there really, really soon.

CHAPTER 76

Tee leaned back on the virtual surfboard and it slid down the face of the biggest wave she'd ever seen. Okay, ever seen on any beach other than the one in front of Michelle's house. The wave inside *Chraze* was meant for extreme surfing, not for scaring the shit out of you.

Jeremy's board slid along right beside her, the wind blew his hair back from his face and revealed a smile and shining eyes that were meant just for her. His hip label just read Pascal.

She didn't want to admit to having no clue who that was. She set Morgan on autopilot for a couple milliseconds and went for a quick dip below the interface. Plugged in a data search. Blaise Pascal. 1600s. Mathematician. Philosopher. Ended his life as a religious freakazoid going from church to church in Paris, sermon-hopping day-in and day-out. There had to be more.

There.

Nailed it.

She closed the slice and popped back into Morgan. Nothing had changed. The wave was still awesome. The tube was coming up. Jeremy was watching the water as it slid them into its grasp.

The temptation to bail out was pretty high, especially as she'd never surfed before in her life. But she was going to be damned if she'd let anything as ridiculous as a piece of software scare her the way the real world of Hell had. Hell was real. Wild.

Blaise Pascal. He justified belief in God under the category of things that couldn't hurt if they weren't true, but could sure help if He really did exist.

And he was a wicked smart scientist.

It was a good label. Raised her estimate of Jeremy several more notches. She'd have to be careful though. She was starting to really like this guy. Next thing? She'd be as stupid about him as Dee was about this Sam guy.

A quick turn launched her up over the crest and into the air just before the wave came apart.

But she didn't land on the back of the wave.

Instead she was on the air cycle in the Roman Coliseum all over again. Jeremy was still behind her. The mad priest was down below and his incantation of Unmaking was ricocheting throughout the arena.

She aimed the cycle right at him. What the hell. She hadn't played *Ms. Pac-Man* in a while.

The air roared in her ears and Jeremy's cycle engine noise whined right through her skull.

But not enough to drown out the mad priest with his obscured name marker.

His God threw bolts that were so easy to dodge it seemed pointless that he launched them in the first place.

The priest's incantation picked up pace and intensity.

She dropped to the deck and howled toward him. If the impact didn't destroy them both, at least he'd have to stop the cycle of his chant and take a breath.

A thousand yards.

Five hundred.

Two-fifty.

Jeremy slid out of her slipstream and whipped past her with a perfect drafting slingshot.

Jeremy's shout, that he hurled at the priest like Ahab's harpoon, came back to her on the wind.

"I ..."

One hundred yards.

"...didn't..."

No time for her to retake the lead.

"...write..."

Fifty.

"...you!"

The priest's eyes were wide with sudden terror.

"Too late. Hasta la vista, baby," his God was laughing.

And they slammed into blackness.

CHAPTER 77

"This isn't right."

His words sounded strange.

No echo.

No mandibular transmission along his jawbone.

Jeremy might as well have not spoken at all.

"Weird!" he yelled into the darkness.

He was isolated. Blind. Alone.

"Theresa!" No answer. No response.

"Morgan Le Fay! I'm not amused."

Nothing.

He struggled to dip below the interface as Theresa had so coyly done while surfing. He couldn't have done it better himself.

No luck.

His game software had no allowance for a space like this.

No override for him to trip. No consciousness here other than his own.

He missed Theresa. It was just too unreal that she'd noticed him. All the street-smarts he lacked wrapped up in such a master player. Her dive at the false priest had been perfect. Should have worked. And no one should be able to fully hide their label. No one could unmake a universe. No one could switch off his system access. Even his top-level access codes weren't responding.

"Focus, Jeremy Berkowitz. She's probably trapped, too. Focus on the solution."

Won't do you any good.

"Morgan?" Even as he spoke he knew he was wrong.

Ha! Good one. No, she's busy ignoring all input. Won't listen. Won't perform. Stubborn cuss.

"Who are...The Unmaker?" Was he speaking aloud, or just thinking aloud? He couldn't tell if he had any feelings. Just a mind floating in space. A consciousness unbodied.

That's it. He was speaking to an unbodied consciousness. One that had already unmade its own universe.

"You stole my game! It's not supposed to be like this!" His shout died in the darkness.

Unmaker. Good. Like that. So, Blaise, my boy, do you believe in God? Or how about Hell? True Hell?

A yawning sulfurous pit opened before Jeremy's gaze. And a heat blasted over him. A heat that would have crisped his skin if he'd had any.

CHAPTER 78

"The kid's index found the software, the Software that Runs the Universe. Found Loki. The software ordered me to bring the kid. I brought him. Loki has him." Virgil was babbling. His sentence structure decayed even more rapidly than his features aged.

"Not anymore, remember?"

His dazed eyes inspected Dana's face as he tried to focus. Then a clarity of light shown around his eyes and he grabbed her wrists with a strength that belied his condition.

"Trouble. Loki. Apocalypse. The software is pre-empting the universe. Jeremy's index mustn't fall into Messiah's hands. Must be wiped. But Software, Loki fascinated with their toy."

"Where—"

"Cool toy." His eyes drifted as he interrupted her. "Can't let Messiah know. Loki. Software. End of it all. Apocalypse coming."

Dana worked to reforge her barriers as his hands slid limply down into his lap. His mind wasn't used to accommodating the field of white light, of universal power she was bringing him. Couldn't take it. Was dissolving beneath it.

But she needed the information locked in his dissolving mind.

And Virgil was dead already. Wasn't he?

She looked through the fog of energy surging back and forth between them. Cassandra of Troy was watching the poet with a look of horror on her face. Slowly, ever so slowly, she turned to face Dana.

And she nodded. Grim. Tight-lipped. But she nodded.

Dana swam her vision back to Virgil. She couldn't hold him together much longer. Apparently the knot of blackness was all that had held him up. When she'd breached it, she'd started an unstoppable reaction. If only she could delay it long enough.

He was muttering to himself and she could barely separate the words. Finally one, lonely word slid forth she was able to grab onto.

"Secret? What secret, Virgil?"

He raised a finger to his lips.

"Shhh, special secret. Mustn't tell. No. Special surprise."

"What special surprise, Virgil? It's okay. You can tell me."

"Did you burn my works? You promised, Varius. Did you burn them?"

"Yes, Yes. I did. Just as I promised."

"Liar!" he spit out at her. "I may be dead. But I saw them. Bound, unfinished, incomplete."

She looked to Cassandra for help.

"They were too wonderful to burn," the prophetess offered.

"Liar! I don't believe you."

Cassandra shrugged her helplessness. He could no longer discern the truth behind her curse.

"I saved them, Virgil." Dana proclaimed. "Because of the magnificent wonder of your words."

He calmed down immediately. The truth he wouldn't accept from Cassandra, he'd accepted as a lie from her. She'd never been able to read *The Aeneid*. It bogged her down, made her brain hurt, and bored her to tears.

"Now what's the secret, Virgil."

"The secret." He began to giggle. "Loki knew. Software knew. Knew there'd be a last-ditch effort. So promised Apocalypse for Thursday. But, shh, shh. Happens Tuesday. First thing in the morning. No morning light."

And he was gone. Not just his energy. His body, his clothes, his insane giggle that was the last offering he presented to the world.

She tried to shake the gluey energy off her hands but it had slid under her skin and would take forever to purge. As she turned from where Virgil had lain moments before, she once again saw light. And color. Most of it red—the side of the RV. But a good, strong, healthy color.

"Please tell me this isn't Monday."

Cassandra met her gaze.

"Would you believe me if I lied?"

CHAPTER 79

The cat was long gone. It had moved on once its grooming was complete to its demented satisfaction. Hadn't even turned to glance at her before departing.

Michelle remained perched upon the wreckage of Loki's home. An idle kick revealed bronze swords and Stone Age flint axes. An old door covered in every campaign sticker for the American Presidency since Old Tippecanoe Harrison had won in 1840. There were so many layers that the door was nearly as thick as it was wide. Paintings, art, poetry.

The only thing she kept as she idly sorted through the mess atop her mound was the blue vase with the slightly crumpled daffodil. She didn't trespass onto the cat's abandoned pinnacle nor down toward Loki's grave.

She unearthed an old Coke bottle that was so old, the soda had probably been made with a few grains of real cocaine. It was still capped and contained a sludgy brown liquid in it that she decided was best left alone.

Michelle still had no idea what she'd been looking for. Whatever it was, she hadn't found it.

The blue crystal vase glowed as she turned it one way and another in the golden light of the westering sun.

Loki had awaited the end of all existence.

No, not quite.

Loki had eagerly awaited the end of all existence. And now his cat had killed him. Despite his immortality, she doubted he'd ever rise again. The cat had seemed fairly convinced of that before it departed, and for the moment that was enough for her.

But Creation should continue. Must continue.

If there was no future, then there was no point to the present. No chance of another Michelangelo. Just one last sunset with none to follow. The stars would once again shine down from the great outer space that primitive woman had dubbed as heaven in hopes of a place better than a cold cave. But they would never shine so again.

It just wasn't fair.

The yellow daffodil reflected off the surface of the blue glass.

There was beauty.

Even in the midst of Loki's junkheap, there was beauty.

And while there was beauty, there was truth. And beauty abounded in the universe. And truth was reason enough. Goal enough.

It had to be.

"There are higher goals, Loki."

He wasn't there to answer.

She stood and turned toward home.

Now that she looked down upon Hell's ocean from high up on the hill, it was clear there was trouble.

The waves didn't tower ever upward.

The sea was actually calm.

Flat.

She managed to cram the vase into her pocket, tucked the daffodil behind one ear and broke into a run.

CHAPTER 80

It took a while to get Cassandra calmed down. If Virgil hadn't totally disintegrated to a greasy spot on the dry earth, she would have torn him limb from limb. As it was, Cassandra of Troy spent five precious minutes cursing and stomping his greasy spot to oblivion before Dana could get her into the RV.

Dana shoved Cassandra into one chair in front of Tee's computer, dragged over another for herself, and logged on.

Cassandra didn't change appearance when they crossed into the *Chraze* game grid. She looked the same right down to the angry glare. Come to think of it, Tee hadn't either. And she was close enough to her own body to be a little surprised. Jeremy had made it so that each person remained themselves in this game instead of a murderous green alien or a prim Polly Purebred like so many of the Net games.

"What's got you so pissed off?"

"Virgil."

"Hey, he slimed me. What did he do to you?"

"He got me to believe a lie. I knew it was a lie. But I wanted so much to believe that he really understood me. I wanted it so badly I ignored what I knew to be true."

"So he lied to you. The truth I have to believe is that I'm the

Second Messiah. Try to chew on that one while your friends are lost in the software."

Cassandra took a deep breath and seemed a lot calmer.

The scene began to take shape around them. Once again the castle rose from the green sward. But now in the daylight, it looked more Old English countryside than Medieval fortification. Theresa's color screen, especially compared to that ancient green monstrosity at Michelle's, helped reveal the stunning reality Jeremy had captured when he built this.

No knight came pounding over the greensward. Maybe he was still stuck in *Ms. Pac-Man*. No bandits gathered in the shadows. Not even a noble steed pranced back and forth across the meadow.

A priest waited by the side of the road. The name on his hip was obscured. Just as Tee had described him.

And he was chanting. It sounded so nasty it sent a chill right down her bones. And she could see his energy. He was a network of silver lines. As he chanted, line after line of the virtual wall broke off and dissolved. As if he were unmaking the grid. Which was exactly what he was doing.

He noticed them and raised his empty sleeve in their direction.

Dana grabbed for her bow and sent a shower of arrows into him. Each loaded with the vile energy Virgil had left wrapped around her. The one into the priest's open mouth cut short his protests.

He tumbled slowly backward until he hit the ground flat on his back.

"That was a pretty wicked thing to do." Cassandra didn't look aghast. Or shocked. She could have been commenting on the weather.

"He was the priest of unmaking."

"So you unmade him."

Dana wished it were that simple. Tee's name was listed as being logged on. Dana tried to open an interface window. A quick search should reveal Tee's location in the game and they could go get her.

But no window opened.

"What am I doing wrong?"

Cassandra inspected the iridescent sky and the bright green grass.

She checked out the back of her hand, slid her blue cotton dress up to run her finger along a small scar across her left knee.

"This is amazing. How does it do it?"

"Fat lot of help you are."

Cassandra picked a single grass blade, held it up to her nose and then nibbled on it.

"That is really excellent. Jeremy is an amazing programmer. Better than I gave him credit for."

Dana strolled in through the front gate of the castle. No great door, just a stone arch. She'd often dreamed of going to England but doing so while inside a piece of software was a little odd. Everything was here. Blue sky. Scent of old moss and hay. And her hand insisted it was slapping rough, sun-warmed stone.

"I don't think he programmed this."

"Why not?"

She looked around and between one eyeblink and the next, Dana could see the silver lines of the Plain of Existence.

The same silver lines that had run through the priest. The priest of unmaking was made of the same stuff as the astral Plain of interconnecting silver. And Loki. Who Virgil had feared. Loki with the secret. They were all of the same stuff. Perhaps they were but one.

She focused on the castle and the outer stone appearance peeled away until she and Cassandra once again stood together on the great Plain of Existence. And the uncountable lines of the glittering grid stretched in every direction but one, forward in time.

Ahead of them loomed the blackness. Like a mountain at the edge of the desert, there was no way to judge its true distance.

But it was a damn sight closer than it had been yesterday.

"Oh shit. We're screwed," Cassandra muttered.

She had never spoken truer words.

CHAPTER 81

*S*am had signed into *Chraze* when he couldn't find Dana and she didn't answer her phone. It was the ultimate new social network; everyone was in here somewhere. Facebook, Twitter, Pinterest, they'd all plummeted before the onslaught of the world founded on a game.

He hadn't found Dana, but Sam had ridden the game's flow. The rhythm of the virtual waves of energy making him lose any clear picture of the world beyond the game.

"Dana" was about all he held onto. She fascinated him and drew him like no one before her.

Even as he thought it, her name faded by the idea of her continued to draw him ahead.

He leaned toward a distant warmth that had entered the game. It drew him along, faster and faster.

Vague images flashed by. Each attached to the lines of energy. Lines of flow. Men, women, children, German Shepherds, trees, rocks, planets, stars, empty space, all were attached to their own lines moving relentlessly forward. Restless to reach their goal.

It took him another endless amount of time to see the goal. A wall of darkness. Discernable not by its presence, but by the lack of any other presence. The silver lines, stretching infinitely in all directions but forward. There they ended abruptly.

The sight bothered him.

But a memory drew him forward again.

Brushing the back of his hand across her hair. Long, soft, luxurious hair. A beautiful woman who had lain down beside him.

But there had been others with her.

A woman and a tiny fluttering creature who claimed to be an angel.

He didn't care about them.

He wanted the one who had been in his arms.

Back when he'd had arms.

She'd know what this was. Smart. So smart.

She had a name.

It was lost on the silver lines and it left an aching void in his heart.

If he still had a heart.

CHAPTER 82

*H*ell's Ocean was silent. Little more motion than a lake. Michelle had never seen it calm before. If she threw in a stone, the ripples would splash right up against the Gates of Heaven and soak the toes of the Heavenly Choir who might even now be practicing *You Can't Always Get What You Want.*

Her side ached for breath. She'd sprinted all the way back from Loki's cabin. No one about, she burst into her own house.

To give herself a moment to think, she pulled the vase from her pocket and filled it at the kitchen sink. The daffodil had survived the journey behind her ear, but was much the worse for wear. Still, the yellow was vibrant with life and she snipped off the bottom of the stem and dunked it back into the water.

No one in any of the bedrooms. She spotted Theresa and Jeremy at the end of the long hall, sitting in her office. She hurried there and skidded to a halt a step outside the threshold—they were motionless.

Theresa's hand was raised and striking down toward the keyboard, except it didn't move. It hung there, just inches away from its target. Jeremy was wholly immobile, a look of complete and utter shock on his face.

Not good. No one would intentionally hold such a position.

Michelle whacked the side of the terminal. And whacked it again.

Theresa and Jeremy twitched like string puppets and then collapsed back into their chairs with a shared gasp.

"I'm alive." It was little more than a sigh of wonder escaping Jeremy's lips. He looked down at his chest and probed it with tentative fingers.

"Why wouldn't you be?"

"The Unmaker." He aimed his head in her direction, but whatever he'd seen clearly still stood as a vision between them.

"He sent me to Hell."

Theresa slid lower in her chair and might have tumbled to the floor if Michelle hadn't grabbed her shoulder.

"Oh man. That is not what I would call fun."

She shook herself like a retriever trying to clear its ears after swimming.

"Hi Michelle." She offered a weak smile. "The Unmaker is vicious. Why did you write him, Jeremy?"

The boy's pallor was pale as could be.

"I didn't. I never wrote that. Him. Not no how." He slapped his own cheeks as if making sure he was really here.

Michelle set the vase on the table next to the computer terminal, pulled over a spare chair, and sat down.

The Unmaker. The only Unmaker she knew was the Software with its passion to end the universe.

And Loki had known. Had known all along that the Apocalypse was coming too soon for Dana to become the Second Messiah. No chance for salvation. No time for redemption.

The only way Loki could know all that was…He was in cahoots with the Software. They were both pointlessly vicious and both thought that their own jokes were the best…

The truth slammed into her gut and knocked the wind out of her.

Loki *was* the Software. All these ages, she'd been arguing with the Demi-God separately from the Software that Runs the Universe. And Loki was simply a manifestation of it. Loki was the Software.

They had both gone out of their way to make her life hell.

She'd been used.

Michelle smashed her fist against the side of the terminal but it did nothing to ease the roiling in her gut.

Devil Damn It!

Now it was time to get even.

CHAPTER 83

"I can't get through to her." Jeremy was pounding away at the keyboard. It was fascinating to watch. Theresa leaned in so that she didn't miss a thing.

"Query: Location of The Huntress?"

Why should I tell you anythin—

And then Jeremy's fingers would fly across the keyboard, a group of unreadable code would appear, and the Software would be cut off. It continued to protest at every step Jeremy made.

Black...Minstrel...Castle.

The Software backspaced over the entry, but they'd already seen it.

"I've been there. We were there last night."

And her best friend Dana was in there now. Who knew what that software was doing to her. But she couldn't go back. A cold chill wrapped around her heart and squeezed until she could barely breathe. Wouldn't go back. Ever. Screw being fifteenth ranked in the game, there was a mind in all that code, that was beyond nasty.

"It's no longer last night. Current location?" Jeremy rattled in the query.

There was no response this time and once again his fingers flew across the keyboard.

Letters began stuttering out across the screen, as if they were being dragged unwillingly from the computer's soul.

P...l . a.... i . n....of...E . x. i . s . t . e . n..... . c....... e. Shit, that hurt. Don't you dare do that again. If you do—

Jeremy slapped the side of the console hard enough that the letters shimmied back and forth across the screen.

"That'll teach the damned Software that Runs the Universe to mess with my game. I've got it backed into a corner now."

"Can you get a message to her?" Michelle voice was urgent, but her eyes were on the blue vase and wilted flower she'd brought back with her.

Jeremy poked at the keyboard a few more times without result. No letters appeared to mirror his typing.

"I don't think so. I might be able to force one more action out of it, but it's getting nasty. I'd never be able to find out if she got the message."

"Is she trapped in there?" Theresa didn't like the sound of her own voice. Weak and afraid.

Jeremy shrugged and Michelle shook her head, but not as if she were saying, "No."

Theresa closed her eyes as a wave of nausea washed over her.

"What is the Plain of Existence? I would have expected p-l-a-n-e."

"I thought so as well," Michelle answered hesitantly. "But Dana described it as an undulating plain of silver lines. One line for every thing, living or not. It is the basis of all the universe. We all exist there. She's just the only one I've heard of that can see it."

"Cassandra, too." Theresa's own voice sounded hollow and far away as she tried to picture Dee trapped in a place that even the Devil had never been. She wanted to run out into the waves screaming just to release what was building up inside her.

"She told me about it. Are they together?"

Jeremy eyed the terminal. "I don't think I can find out."

"We must contact Dana. There is a truth she must know if she's to stop the software from running Armageddon tomorrow."

The room went suddenly dark, as if the sun had been switched off. They all scrambled to the office window and stared out at the Hills of Hell. The sun was gone from the sky, and a ruddy light now washed into the room. The light grew brighter and redder.

The Hills of Hell were on fire.

CHAPTER 84

Inside *Chraze*, Dana and Cassandra stood side-by-side and watched the blackness as it neared. The great darkness was no longer a distant globe of menace. It now loomed above them so close it was hard to see that it was really curved. Every line curved inward as if falling down into a black hole.

Dana decided that made sense if it was an event horizon. The Software had placed a black hole across the threshold of all existence.

Dana had to struggle to not scream. Might have done so anyway if Cassandra hadn't been there to see. She was glad to not be alone so she didn't have to give in to the madness.

"I believe," Cassandra wasn't staring at the blackness, but rather down at her feet. "That this is what, in your modern parlance, would best be described as a really, really sucky moment."

Dana looked down as well. Her own line, the one that was bound to her ankle, went straight into the wall with the inevitability of a speeding semi-truck with a heavy load.

She glanced over at Cassandra's line. It went straight for only a few more meters, and then it jagged sharply upward away from the blackness. The only one to leave the grid. It arced in a low orbit, obviously twisted by the gravity of the blackness, but unless Dana missed her guess, it became a clear orbit.

"Wait. You can't leave me here."

Cassandra's voice was thin and resigned. "Don't think I have a whole lot of choice."

"But where will you go?"

Cassandra looked up at her. And the truth was written in her eyes. Wherever she was going, it would be a relief from where she'd been. They hugged as well as they could with their ankles tied to their own energy lines.

"I wish…"

"What?"

"I don't know."

They both shrugged. They both smiled. They both didn't know what else to do.

"What's that?" Cassandra pointed over Dana's shoulder.

A sparkle of light danced along the silver lines. No, it danced across the silver lines.

It roared by them and then shuddered to a halt.

Slowly the sparkle of light curved back. It sidled up like a dog unsure of its welcome.

"What are you?" It spoke.

"A person. People. We're people."

The light backed away and approached from a different angle, closer to Dana this time. She squatted down and the light edged closer.

"You're so bright." It was a male voice. A familiar one. She looked down at herself, but she looked normal to herself, right down to the jeans that could have been cleaner. Normal except for the light passing through her ankle.

Cleaner jeans. She'd changed into them in another lifetime forever ago to meet up with…

"Sam? Is that you?"

"Is it? I don't really know. 'Sam' sounds familiar." The light dodged back a bit and then slid forward once more.

"Yes, I think 'Sam' is me. Cool!" The light began to dodge back and forth just like Henrietta when she was excited.

In a blinding burst of light, Sam spattered across the grid into a myriad thousands of brilliant points and then all the light came crashing back together.

Between one blink and the next, the light was gone. When her vision recovered, Sam was standing before her, blinking like a person who had just entered broad daylight from a dark room.

She wrapped her arms around him. He was warm. Alive. She held on tight. Didn't want to lose him.

Tentatively his hands reached around her. Slid across her back. Combed through her hair. He leaned forward, rested his head on her shoulder, his face against her neck. And he breathed in deeply, his chest expanding until he filled her arms.

He released it with a sigh.

"Never had a chance to tell you this. You smell wonderful."

He did it again, and her heart melted inside her and made a happy, glowing pool of smiles that tickled the inside of her chest.

At the sound of Cassandra's gasp, Dana spun around accidentally clipping Sam's chin with her shoulder. She was about to turn back to apologize when she saw what had gotten Cassandra's attention.

The silver lines. Hers and Sam's continued straight into the wall. Cassandra's arc would be leaving them in moments.

But the other lines were fading out.

CHAPTER 85

"You have to go in there and make sure that Dana gets this message."

No. No. No. Theresa shrank back in the Devil's office chair. There was no way she was going to go back and give the Mad Priest another crack at her. There were fates worse than death. Far worse, and she'd be damned before she'd go back.

"That wouldn't be my first choice." Jeremy's voice wasn't all that steady either.

"Well, I can't." Michelle protested.

"Why not?" Theresa knew she was being snappish, but she couldn't help herself.

"I'm the Devil. The Software would never let me in. I've never seen the Plain of Existence. After fourteen billion years, Dana is the first one I've ever heard of who walked there."

"What's so special about her?"

Michelle sighed and turned the vase slowly in her hands.

"It's my fault. It seemed like such a good idea at the time. Earth was, is, a mess. Hey, I said, let's send in a really sharp lady as a Messiah and get things straightened out a bit. Raise global consciousness, end a few dozen wars. A few other useful ideas we immortals had batted around over the millennia."

"So you sent Dana."

"Almost." Michelle's smile was soft and sad. "Sent one of my best friends, Diana the Huntress."

"Dee is a Goddess?" Well, that would certainly explain some shit. All those years trying to whup her at video games and not succeeding. She was battling with a Goddess. No wonder.

"She is, but she isn't supposed to remember all that just yet."

"But there won't be a tomorrow?" Jeremy rested a hand on hers. She held on for strength and dear life. She'd take strength and warmth from wherever she could get it to counter the chill in her bones.

"Not unless she saves us. She's the only one who can now."

"And what's the message she needs?" Tee wanted to bite off her own tongue. Would if she could. She had just offered to go back and face the Mad Priest, which would be about the dumbest decision she'd made in her twenty-two years of stupid decisions.

Michelle held up the blue vase and its battered yellow flower.

"There is still beauty and truth in the world."

CHAPTER 86

Theresa plunged into a world inhabited by a billion blue bubbles. Jeremy behind her, arms wrapped tight on the air-cycle.

"Cool. Look at that. The bubbles are moving against the current. They're alive." His voice was as warm and whispery against her ear as if this had been real life. The vibrations of his chest were hot against her back.

"I didn't write this." It was a simulation. She knew it was a simulation. But she could feel each bubble tickle her skin. The realism was fantastic.

"Uh, what do you mean you didn't write this? This isn't the land of the Mad Priest again, is it?"

"I didn't think up any blue bubble worlds."

They slid down through the layers. The bubbles growing in size as their cycle bored downward through this dimensional construct.

She tapped the keyboard on the scooter, and could barely feel a similar keystroke on the real-world keyboard where her real body huddled, momentarily safe in the Devil's household.

They popped out the far side, and fell.

She screamed.

Couldn't help herself. They were falling from a million stories up. An ocean of blue bubbles above them and red crags of fiery volcanoes below.

Jeremy's arms lashed more tightly around her waist driving out what little breath she had.

She wrestled the cycle into wild flips and twists. All to no avail. There was no backloop. No escape clause. No space-time fabric rip. They were plunging down. Or the Earth was plunging up.

The Earth.

Was plunging up.

The molten mass below had once been their home. But the Apocalypse had come, or would in a few hours. All because Loki, no, all because the Software had gotten bored. Didn't believe there was anything worthwhile.

Deeper. There had to be a deeper solution. She hoped to God, if there was one, that Michelle's message would make more sense to Dee than it did to her.

She aimed straight down. Jeremy held on tighter.

"Do it!" His breath hot on her ear. He must have reached the same conclusion. Or he trusted her. Either one would be pretty exciting if she'd dared take a moment to think about it.

She didn't look back but could feel Jeremy's energy coming into line with her own. Maybe this is what Dee was always talking about. If it was, Tee felt a bit envious, this raw bolt of energy definitely had her cranked up a few levels even though they were both clothed and inside a video game.

The landscape below shifted. Mutated. Flowed from volcanic holocaust to Ice Age to barren rock.

Had she screwed up? Was there really no way through?

No. Deeper had to be the answer.

She ignored the bike.

Looked ahead. Down. With all her skills. With all her heart she reached out and sought the patterns. Just as a racetrack had an interweaving pattern of dozens of vehicles.

Dark swirls. Angry pastels. Rolling plains of Tiddlywinks-shaped playing pieces stretching as far as the eye could see.

The Software was right here. It was reshaping itself. Preparing for a great catastrophe of universal proportions.

Theresa ignored the fear. She could feel her body shudder in the real world. Wishing that Jeremy was actually wrapped around her in support rather than sitting beside her in front of the terminal.

But they were lined up in reality as well. The two of them were a focus within the confines of the game universe. And the heat and power of their energy blew aside the Tiddlywinks as if they weren't there.

They plunged through the never-ending field of translucent red, yellow, blue, and green discs into a winding geometric matrix. A million, hundred million angular paths crossed and recrossed in a vast labyrinth reaching as far as the horizon.

The paths were all silver.

At the sixty-fourth junction she went straight, second power of eight. A gate slammed shut the moment she was through. The cycle was gone. Jeremy, despite his grasp about her waist, was torn off in another direction. She cried out as if she'd lost a piece of herself.

There was no sign of the Mad Priest.

That was good at least.

"Where are we?" She shouted out at the grid.

CHAPTER 87

*J*eremy worked on that question.

He missed Theresa already.

The Tiddlywinks were the only bit he had recognized since he'd forced the Software to open one last access and they'd plunged back in the game grid.

It wasn't just that she was the first girl he'd ever held.

"Duh-uh. I get it. We've left known space. We are in the digital multiverse of the circuitry the software runs on." He was shouting to himself as he zipped across a world made of skittering silver lines. This must be the Plain of Existence.

There was something amazing and wonderful about Theresa, as if she'd been there just waiting for him to come along to see how truly amazing she was.

But they were pulling farther and farther apart with each twist and turn and he fought that.

Even at the speed of light, their messages were going to have trouble reaching each other. They themselves were shooting down the silver paths at near enough the speed of light to raise serious relativity issues. After all, how could they carry consciousness with them if they were merely a wavicle moving through the massive universal circuitry. What is it that they were carrying with them?

He wanted to slow down and see what was going by, but it was all a blur.

"Jeremy, where are you?" The thoughts echoed down to him from a thousand different directions and were repacketized into a single powerful impression. The header data on the message tasted like the smell of Tee's hair caught in the wind.

"Damned if I know." Could you send emotion through an electronic matrix? He pasted a smiling emoticon onto the back end of the thought just in case.

He slammed to a halt. Vibrations rang about him within the three-way junction until his head would have been splitting if he had one.

Trapped.

A capacitance point. Until he accumulated more energy, he wasn't going anywhere in this circuit. He looked about for the others. The world was filled with the light traceries of circuitry. Glowing lines zigzagged through the dense multiverse weaving a tapestry of impossible density and fantastic beauty. In each direction he looked, he could discern circuit after circuit after circuit. Yet each line was drawn clearly against blackness rather than against the glowing background that should be the sum of all those bright lines.

He was seeing photons flow. Now that he was merely vibrating like a demented boson rather than flying like a fighter jet, he could see the others. Not a million others, not a billion, not a wavicle for each element of creation.

He saw only three others.

And that was the scariest thing he'd ever come across.

This was the matrix of the universe. All creation should be flowing around and through them. And rather than being full, the Plain of Existence was empty. The software had done exactly what it threatened. It had stopped the world. Except for himself and the three others. They still existed, had energy.

Theresa shot by just a few hundred circuits over, a stream of chaff flaring in her wake.

Strings. The string structure of the universe was still showering along behind her.

Strings. Moving. Active. The micro-structure was still active. And so were he and Theresa. That had to be a basis for hope.

Then the Theresa-wavicle roared up from his other side and hit a turn so fast that it was clear she had no mass at all.

The universe was structured. This electronic multiverse wasn't really a multiverse. It was no different than the Internet, just a lot more complex. They were traveling at a layer that gave them direct access to the universe, except that most of it wasn't running anymore.

Theresa disappeared once more over the horizon.

CHAPTER 88

ana didn't have a care in the world.

"What is he thinking about?" Theresa stalked by the seated Jeremy but didn't come to rest.

Dana was just fine with not knowing, with never moving again. The grass in the castle's garden was soft, the sun warm, the cherry tree bloomed above them drifting gentle scents and pink petals down upon her. And her head was pillowed on Sam's stomach, his arm negligently draped across her midriff. Nope. She was just fine where she was. Glad to have her friends around her.

There was beauty in the world, just as Tee had insisted. And she was going to revel in it. She was far too comfortable to penetrate the illusion of the lush castle grounds to see the Plains of Existence pulsing around and through them. She was fine right where she was.

"Give it up, Tee. Jeremy's off in some twisty world of his own."

Jeremy had been sitting rock still for an impossibly long time. Cross-legged on the ground, elbow on knee, chin on fist. Sitting beneath the cherry tree as if Rodin had cast him in bronze at the creation of the universe. The original Thinker.

Sam's hand drifted upward until a single finger was tracing the outline of her ear. He rubbed and massaged it with the gentlest of strokes until she wanted to leap up and attack his body. But then his massage would stop, and it felt so good.

Tee blew by again in her path-wearing stride. They'd soon need a gardener to replant the deep groove she was making in the thick groundcover.

Dana closed her eyes. But having her eyes closed was not the most comfortable choice. The blue sky and flowering cherry were overlaid with a faint electronic tracery that was bewildering, uncomfortable. It didn't follow any reasonable pattern. The energy didn't flow smoothly or rationally.

It wasn't natural.

She didn't want the universe to be made up of cold circuits and flashing bits of energy. She wanted it to be warm days beneath flowering trees, for real.

Opening her eyes brought back the "natural" reality. Of course, wasn't it still October? Then why were the cherry trees blooming?

There was a second part of Michelle's message. Beauty and…

Just enjoy. Don't think about it. A soft voice whispered in the back of her mind, too quiet to come in through her ears, but so clear it could have been shouted from the mountaintop for all the world to hear.

Theresa veered from her course and jammed a knee against Jeremy's shoulder.

CHAPTER 89

 eremy smashed up against the junction. Theresa had crashed in behind him. It hurt. As if his entire energy form had banged its knee on a marble coffee table. Really hard.

Even together their energy wasn't sufficient to cross the capacitance threshold. He could feel her vibrating against him. Two wavicles of string energy seeking a way out.

There was no way through without more energy.

No way back.

They were stuck.

CHAPTER 90

"Now they're both doing it." Sam's voice was soft and drifting.

Dana opened one eye and followed the direction of Sam's lazy nod. She had to squint against the sunlight that sparkled from behind Tee and Jeremy.

It was haloing the two of them like a Godlight…or an oncoming truck on a dark road.

Jeremy was still cross-legged, unmoving. Now Tee stood over him, one knee touching his shoulder, her mouth open in a circle of surprise, her eyes wide.

Dana fought the languid cloak that was draped over her soul and raised a hand to block out the sun's glare.

They weren't just still.

They were un-moving.

Tee's hair, caught by a passing breeze, stood stiff even though the breeze still caressed the grass below and the cherry blossoms above into soothing waves.

Dana forced herself up and stood across from Tee. Her eyes were wide, staring, and focused to the left of Dana's head. Even when she moved in line with Tee's eyes, they still weren't focused on her. Sam came up behind and slid a hand around her waist.

"Is that possible?"

He tilted his head back and forth like a silly bird inspecting the possibilities. He reached out and, before she could stop him, poked at Tee's frozen hairs.

CHAPTER 91

The four of them slammed out of the junction.

"Don't let go. Stay in our draft." Tee shouted back along the shimmering electron pathway.

Dana wrapped her metaphoric hand around Tee's equally metaphoric belt and hung on, the string energy pulsing up her arm in warm, hot waves.

Sam's arm was still as tight around her waist as an electron's s-orbital and they shot back onto the grid. Jeremy was at the front.

They slid faster and faster. Converted from potential to kinetic energy in a moment of flashing brilliance. If this was what the speed of light felt like, she'd have to sign up more often.

A roar of anger sounded from deep in the trees behind them.

Jagged rents in the Plain slid by with barely time to register an energy fluctuation. The universal structure was coming apart. A force had tried to stop them, lull them for a moment too long on a blossom-filled meadow.

"Where are we going?" Tee shouted at Jeremy who might have been in the lead. And might not have been. It was hard to tell in this relativistic world. Light shimmered past them in great sheets like an

Aurora Borealis gone mad. Lilacs and iridescent greens. Flaming reds and torchlight yellow.

"Got me." Jeremy pulsed to the group.

Dana turned her attention forward. Toward the direction they were flying.

The silver lines no longer flowed smoothly forward. Were no longer connected to anything or anyone. In the past, the lines appeared to go on forever in every direction.

In the direction they were heading, everything ended abruptly.

The vast ball of darkness encased the glowing lines of the multiverse. A hundred million lines of circuitry all entered the zone of blackness. All light absorbed.

"Oh shit!"

"What?" Tee pulsed back down the line to her.

"It really is a black hole. We've got to turn."

"There's no way. Look." Sam pointed down the glowing silver line they were flowing on. No junctions. No turns. No cool special effects that might be a last-minute escape. They were plunging right toward the heart of it.

One thin line off to the side was headed upward. Cassandra arcing beyond the event horizon. A woman who truly understood truth.

Dana remembered Michelle's message. That had been the second part of her message. "There is still beauty and truth in the world." And Cassandra had proven that truth could be an absolute, whether or not it was believed.

The black wall loomed so high above them, there was no way to look beyond the mass of its curve.

So this was the end.

That really sucked. Dana wanted more. So much more.

Gentle hours to explore her relationship with Sam.

Years to study the nature of the universe, and the multiverse that spread before them.

Someday they'd find her body, dead in a chair in front of a laptop inside a lipstick-red RV. Except there'd be no one left to find her. And no universe to find her in.

Was the black hole a sickness inside the software, consuming light and hope? Or was it a doorway? Would they travel through the black hole into the white hole that must exist to maintain the balance of the universe? Or was it the white hole that the Christians insisted meant the Earth's history was counted in thousands rather than billions of years?

Maybe they were the Big Bang. Blasting through the back of the black hole to burst forth into a new universal creation.

The others' thoughts rose up in her awareness.

Sam was analyzing hydroplaning formulas to skim the surface of the black sphere. But they both knew the gravity well was far too steep for them to escape. The final junction point was back where the software had made a last grab at her, to rest for eternity beneath a blooming cherry tree.

Persuading her to ignore the fact that "forever" would be ending tomorrow morning.

Jeremy was muttering about being hot on its trail if only he had a console and a couple hours of programming time instead of a few seconds to helplessly slide down an energy pathway.

Tee was relaxing for the collision. Shaking her shoulders loose. Mumbling under her breath like a mantra.

"Everyone hits a bad one. It's the tensing up that gets you. That breaks bones and tears muscles. Aim for the center of the spinning car and it should swing out of the way by the time you get there." A creature of habit and automatic reactions honed to an amazing level.

It was time. Dana leaned in, close behind Tee. Trust Tee's instincts. She wrapped one arm around her best friend's waist and held on tight. Then she took Sam's formulas and pushed forward, driving Tee hard against Jeremy. She wrapped a hand tight on Sam's arm to make sure that he stayed close. They were all so tightly bound together that they would hit the wall as a single object.

Michelle was right. There was still beauty in the universe. No matter what the software had managed to strip away.

In this moment, beauty.

In the moment of the Big Bang, beauty.

How else to explain the stars on a perfectly clear night, or the arcing flight of a newborn swallow? None of that could happen without beauty. It was an inherent force in the universe. Just like gravity and momentum. Beauty was indeed truth. There were no two ways about it.

More true than even the Software.

If they were to be the impetus for the next universe, beauty would be perhaps the best element they could carry forward with them.

They would blast truth and beauty into the heart of the universe together, whether it be this universe or the next one.

The wall was so close now that looking to either side, there was only blackness. And they were moving so fast that behind them, all light was Dopplered out of the visible range.

There was nothing but darkness upon the face of the deep. The only light, other than the energy radiating from the four of them, was the single line of silver that they pursued into the heart of that blackness.

There was more than truth. More than beauty. There was the love that she felt for Tee. And, given time, that they might have each found for Jeremy and Sam.

Beauty, truth, and love. Pretty cool start to a new universe.

Ram the energy forward.

Focus it until they were a cosmic laser beam.

The last ones in the universe, they were going to go out with a bang. They were the next Big Bang. Not like the physical laws of entropy or cold-universe death. Maybe the universe always ended, but was always restarted by the actions of a dedicated few.

If they weren't going to come out of this at all, at least they were going into it together.

They certainly all shared one scream as they hit the wall.

CHAPTER THE LAST

*D*ana stared across the small, square, Formica-topped table.

Tee sat across from her, both palms flat on the table. Her expression was a little wild, as if she'd just crashed her car and entered the afterlife.

A knee bumped hers under the table. Sam was to her right, twitching slightly as he shrugged off the aftereffects of their passage. His smile was weak, but he took her hand and squeezed it tightly.

Jeremy sat to Dana's left, the table a perfect size for four people.

Salt, pepper, and the old-style sugar shaker with the rippled glass sides and steel cone-shaped top. A little stainless-steel curlicue thing with a few dozen white paper napkins completed the table décor.

They all waited. Eyes coming into focus and then glancing at one another. Theresa's shoulders were all hunched up despite the "stay loose" talk she'd given herself.

Jeremy was muttering beneath his breath, clearly working on some intense program logic.

Sam pushed a handful of hair out of his face and was looking around the room.

A small cluster of tables surrounded them.

Several had people sitting at them.

Young couples holding hands. A too-prissy mom still in her business suit trying to teach her daughter a five-year-old's version of table manners. A middle-aged guy, beard shifting from black to gray, with a novel and a bowl of borscht.

The walls were covered in old wood, the kind you'd expect to find on the side of a barn. Beyond the tables were three short aisles of foodstuffs. But the most remarkable feature of the place was the light.

It shimmered.

It glowed.

"I know this place."

Tee blinked at her. "So do I. I think."

"I smell pastrami." Sam sniffed the air again. "Good pastrami."

"I've eaten here." Jeremy blinked several times before aiming an unsteady finger at Tee. "With you."

"This can't be real." The others nodded in agreement.

"Hi, kids. How is everything going?"

Dana spun around to look at Uncle Joshua standing behind her. She jumped up.

And she caught her knee on the table leg. Then her chair tipped over sideways and she landed on the floor with a crash and a bruising impact that definitely implied reality, painful reality.

"But the world ended— The Software stopped— The black hole…" Okay. She was babbling. She knew that. And there was no way that Joshua would understand. But she couldn't stop.

"It's over. It won and killed us all. The Software, I mean."

Joshua was smiling down at her. It wasn't condescending. It was the happy way she'd smile at a child who was just putting together that the bright points in the nighttime sky were not so different from their own sun that shown in the daytime.

He helped her back to her seat, hooked his foot through a nearby chair, and settled his bulk into it with several loud creaks from the protesting furniture. A quick nod as if to say, "keep going."

Waiting for her to piece it together.

The others offered little more help than confused shrugs when she turned to them for suggestions.

Jeremy would find a logical explanation. Interaction of data within selected parameters and the future would be inevitable.

Tee was a cosmic force in herself. She powered her way onto the racing circuit the same way she'd powered through everything in her life.

Sam was all about the flow. Mr. Mellow would just find his air currents and slide along them until they were laminar, no ripples. No splashes in his aerodynamic world. Smooth flow.

What was her solution? How does a woman look at herself?

Joshua nodded as if he were reading her mind rather than laughing at her proclamations of the end of the world.

She understood energy. The energy of a collapsar turning into black hole. The energy of black hole-white hole interactions. The energy of the computer matrix was no different than the energy of life she could see flowing so clearly around the table. The heavy line from her heart to Tee's. The thickening lines between Tee and Jeremy, the strong ones she already shared with Sam.

And the heartstrings didn't stop there. Sam's also reached out to his sister. Her own to her mother and her whack-a-doodle little brother. His energy flowed outward in an unbounded array, as if he were indeed Taliesin, the greatest storyteller of all time. The storyteller whose very tales maintained the fabric of the world.

Okay, maybe she wasn't ready to consider Tallie's role in the universe just yet.

And Michelle couldn't be dead. Couldn't die. She was as much of the fabric of the universe as the Software. They were all a part of the manifestation of the universe, rather than separate entities.

Uncle Joshua wasn't connected to any one person, his energy was connected to everything as a father to its child.

"Oh, God." She wasn't ready for this.

He raised a fat finger to his lips. "Shh. Promise you won't tell." He pointed a finger upward, past the ceiling.

"They leave me alone because they think I'm dead."

A FEW DAYS AFTER NEXT THURSDAY

A WEEK AFTER ARMAGEDDON

CHAPTER THE VERY LAST

Dana and Sam lay curled together on the foam pads and sleeping bags they'd pulled out of the tent to enjoy the afternoon sun. The heavy snows that would soon be closing the North Cascades highway hadn't yet arrived. For the moment, they were safe in a high-meadow campground by Lake Ann and no one else was around.

The sun had left the evening cool, but the ground warm. Mount Shuksan arrowed its red rock and snow-covered face high to the north. It still glittered in the last rays of the sunset; a shining torch reflected across the still waters. The reflection was so perfect it was possible to believe that the lake was the entry to another world, the mountain continuing down into the netherworld.

He held her close and rubbed her back, his strong hand sliding beneath her sweater finding tight muscles and massaging them until they let go with little sighs of happiness.

"The world has changed."

He nodded, tucked his face into her collar bone and inhaled deeply. "You smell wonderful."

They'd spent the afternoon hiking, and even her quick splash in the frigid glacier-fed lake hadn't cut more than the outermost sheen of sweat. But she wasn't going to break the mood by calling him a liar.

"It has."

"You too." He persisted, before turning his attention to studying the shape of her jaw with the cold tip of his nose.

She lay back and slipped a hand into his soft hair, impossibly clean smelling from the actual dive he'd taken in the frigid water. Overhead, the sky was darkening to royal blue. The first stars were shimmering forth in a way the planetarium could never reproduce.

The world had changed. It wasn't just in her mind.

Gods had fought.

Software had sulked.

She, Sam, and Michelle had explored the wind tunnel and managed to not find Michelle's knifed body lying in a pool of blood on the floor. Disproving Escher's final vision in the mosaic.

And she *had* changed. She knew more now. Was starting to remember more, slowly adding Diana to her Dana-ness.

It would take far more time to unravel the knot of the last week. Maybe she'd start thinking seriously again after Tee won her race tomorrow.

What was it Uncle Joshua had said? *You proved that a single soul could transcend the material world and win on the cosmic plane of true reality.*

That meant she'd proven the evolution of the human spirit was sufficient to face the challenges of surviving in the multiverse. Of controlling the present despite the past.

Proven that the human spirit could move beyond its petty needs and truly find its place in the universe. A change that was still a long time coming. The journey to a place that might open to unimaginable horizons stretching not to other planets, or other stars, but beyond the bounds of a reality that just a week ago she would have insisted was unique.

Joshua said there was so much more she could become. So much more that she'd have to become now that the Software was gone from the Universe.

Whatever that meant.

If the Software that Runs the Universe really was gone. He

certainly thought so, but she'd learned that it was trickier than perhaps even Jeremy's strange computer magic.

Sam slid his mouth over hers.

His hand glided over her skin like a velvet cloth and slid down to the small of her back to pull them closer together.

His kiss was warm, hot, gentle, and connected. Connected all the way through him. Every energy line in his body was focused on her. Not on his own ego, or his own crotch. On her.

It was one of the sexiest things she'd ever seen.

She closed her mental eye.

She'd deal with the cosmos later.

Did you catch the first title? Cookbook from Hell: Reheated. Excerpt follows.

COOKBOOK FROM HELL: REHEATED

DON'T MISS THE FIRST ADVENTURE

EXCERPT FROM COOKBOOK FROM HELL: REHEATED

*E*ric Erikson answered his* cell phone without looking up from his computer screen at work. His desk was a shambles of a half-eaten vending-machine sandwich and too many bags of Fritos.

What blocked number would be calling him at two in the morning on a Friday night? He was just getting down to the second level of tonight's guilty pleasure, indulging in a new Internet role-playing game. He'd gotten in on the beta release of a new project with the weird name of *Chraze* that looked cool, but he wasn't very far into the world yet.

"E-Squared!"

Well, that told him who the caller was. Only his boss, Valerie McKenzie called him that. Everyone else still called him Eric-Squared, for Eric Erikson but she had edited his name down a year ago, before his job interview with Ms. Incredibly Erudite had even ended.

"Hi, Mac." That was the nickname he'd tagged her with during his first week at McKenzie Book Publishers. It had started as "Mac hold the cheese" because one thing about Valerie McKenzie, she wanted it her way. And she got it. She hated New York, so had convinced a major publisher to let her run her own imprint from Seattle. And then, against all projections, she had turned it into a very successful concern.

Now, everyone called her Mac, and "McHell" was a whispered warning that permeated down the halls just moments before she swooped in and touched down like a personalized whirlwind at some poor fool's desk.

"You've got to help me."

Boss in distress. Her voice sounded really wound up, even more than usual. Eyes still glued to the screen, Eric shoved the mouse around to avoid a can of root beer and an unopened bag of peanuts on his desk, barely saving his on-screen avatar from being skewered by a black knight riding a Harley in full armor across a grassy plain in Spain where, according to the stats bar down the side, it hardly ever rained.

"What's up, boss?"

"You know that cookbook?"

No one in the office could avoid "that cookbook." The Mac had torn through the office on a rampage just three days earlier. Mathilda Reeves had finally delivered her latest cookbook manuscript, six weeks late and in miserable shape. The layout team had tried to put it together, but it was a total train wreck. On Wednesday morning, The Mac had grabbed the manuscript, a laptop, and stormed out in order to work from home.

"I know that cookbook." Eric kept his tone carefully neutral. No one had heard from Valerie for three days. Which had made the office calm and peaceful for a pleasant change of pace. Though he did kind of miss her tornadoing around the thirtieth floor of the Two Union Square building, she certainly kept things interesting.

He whacked the black knight's helmet with a handy caveman cudgel, which he'd bought cheap from an on-screen dealer in Neanderthal artifacts. It made the knight's helmet ring like a church bell. Very satisfying.

"Well, the cookbook now insists that it's looking for God."

That froze his hand on the mouse, at just the wrong moment. The knight gunned the Harley's engine and ran over Eric's figure, flattening him into the sod. Then he circled back and rolled over Eric again crosswise. That sucked. This game handed out some serious retributions when your avatar died.

The Mac took his silence as rapt attention rather than cursing to himself.

"I was working on editing and laying out one of the very last recipes, a typical Mathilda dessert, Flan with Lingonberries. What the Hell is a lingonberry anyway, it's not as if any normal grocery in Hell-and-gone Missouri is going to have them in stock, and suddenly the laptop made a gagging sound, like a loud retching. Next thing I know I'm looking at a recipe titled 'Flogging with Lingonberries' and there's an embedded video of some giant red berry wielding a cat o' nine tails on an apple pie holding up its crust to defend itself. When I tried to hit Undo, the berry turned to me and asked me, *by name*, if I knew where to find God? The thing called me Valerie McKenzie for crying out loud. I'm totally creeped out. You've gotta help me. I was almost done and I haven't backed up in days."

It was impressive. As far as he could tell, she hadn't taken a single breath in all that.

"Uh, I can try to fix it." He was still trying to piece together the image of a lingonberry knowing its editor's name. And that she'd used words like "totally" as an adverb and "gotta." And contractions. She was rarely desperate enough to use contractions.

"Good, thanks! Can you... Oh God— No! Wait, I didn't mean to say that. Good thing the software can't hear me or it might start asking me more questions."

Eric wondered if she'd been drinking.

"I'm sorry, I didn't notice the time. Could you come by as soon as you can in the morning? I don't care what time. Pretty please, E-Squared?"

Eric had never heard The Mac apologize, let alone beg. He agreed and instantly she was gone.

He looked back at the screen where the black knight had broken into song, singing harmony on a Norse drinking song with the thudding reverberations coming from the Harley's big exhaust pipes, about how he'd been born to be wild. All the while he kept circling around in different directions to run over Eric's figure that foolishly kept trying to get up from his body-shaped hole in the sod. The wheel patterns over the sod were making the shape of an infinity symbol. Eric shut down the game.

One thing for sure, he wasn't going to wait for the morning. He'd never heard The Mac so flustered. Angry? Often. Perhaps too often, though not usually at him. But genuine distress? That was new.

He grabbed his bicycle helmet. He'd ridden in this morning and then stayed at the office to take advantage of the high-speed connection, and the big screen, to beta test the new game. From McKenzie Book Publishers' Westlake Avenue office to Ravenna was only a couple miles and the Seattle streets would be quiet in the middle of the night.

He hit the street and was already moving before he noticed that the pavement was wet. Eric considered going back to get his rain slicks, but it wasn't raining at the moment, so he just downshifted and hurried north along Westlake, past all of the sailboats and houseboats, up to the Fremont Bridge.

He hit the draw bridge and rolled past the sign, "Welcome to Fremont, the center of the Universe. Set your watch back five minutes." The problem he had was that he didn't wear a watch anymore. Instead, he used his cell phone that stayed in perfect sync with the cell provider's signal all on its own. Fremont had, through no fault of its own, gone from arcane to archaic and he felt bad on its behalf.

He cut across town on Thirty-Fourth so he could wave at the concrete troll squatting under the Aurora Bridge. The troll had the remains of a VW Beetle clutched in one mighty fist. As usual, he didn't wave back at Eric.

The neighborhoods were all quiet as he sped through. He'd always liked this time of night in Seattle. Most people only saw the bustling city that had doubled in size over the last few decades. But in the middle of the night, there was a silence so deep that he could hear the quiet spatter of his bike tires on the rain-wet streets and the ticking clunks as relay boxes flipped streetlights from red to green just for his passage.

He'd never actually been to The Mac's new apartment. He'd been to the estate she used to have out on Bainbridge Island for last year's Christmas party. A big place filled with canapés and ostentation, that both had and hadn't fit its occupant. Super-editor, The Fearsome Mac, the Woman of Steel, would of course have a sweeping view of Liberty Bay and the Olympic Mountains isolated by large stands of timber along the shore of Port Orchard Bay. And of course she'd be married to some useless guy like Landau McKenzie. He'd been a weird Scottish guy, who looked like a laird and acted like a dweeb. And no sense of humor at all. Not that Mac had one either.

But The Mac had this other side to her, one he spotted only rarely, the human Valerie McKenzie. Sometimes, when exhausted but pleased with herself at shipping off another soon-to-be bestseller, she'd drop by his desk. The woman would collapse in his guest chair and chat for a few minutes. Still perfectly coifed, chestnut-dark hair in a tight French chignon, power suit sharp and expensive, but a smile would emerge and light up her face. Eric had to admit to feeling secretly superior to the rest of the world, as he suspected he was the only one who got to see that life-altering smile.

Everyone else told him he was fantasizing, The Mac never smiled except the way a shark might. So he'd learned to keep his mouth shut, but he'd become more and more intrigued by the Valerie he glimpsed behind The Mac.

Then six months ago she'd divorced Landau Fucking McKenzie, as she now unfailingly referred to him, and life around the office had really become Hell. Her mood swings had gone from lethal, to chaotic and lethal.

Her current gripe was that changing back to her maiden name wouldn't do any good because she'd "for reasons unknown" thought it cute that she and Landau Fucking McKenzie had the same last name before she was dumb enough to marry him and how in the world could she have ever thought that was charming? Then she'd launch into yet another diatribe on Landau's character.

Eric considered riding north around Green Lake and getting his car, but he was already so close, he just rode to her house on Ravenna. She'd gotten a place just past the shop that had custom-built his road bike, costing him most of a month's pay, over the crest and down toward the park. She lived in a giant Victorian house from Seattle's heyday, now cut up into six or eight apartments.

ERIC ERIKSON HIT the buzzer for Valerie's apartment and got no response.

He considered that it was awfully late, she'd probably gone to bed. Maybe he should go. But she'd sounded so desperate.

He hit the buzzer again, longer and harder.

No voice squawked out of the speaker. But there was click, then a groan, like someone in deep pain. Like someone who'd been stabbed, or worse. When the door release buzzed, he went in fast. He shouldered his bike and bolted up the two flights. He dropped his bike in the hall, leaning it against the sturdy mahogany railing that overlooked the stairwell, and knocked on her door with a fast rat-a-tat.

No response.

He was preparing to test his shoulder against her door locks when he heard the chain drop and the deadbolt being thrown back. The door cracked open and The Mac looked out at him. At least a version of her did. Someone had taken the sharp-edged senior editor and run her through the Photoshop blur tool. Several times.

She blinked at him like a sleepy cat. Rather than pulled back into an immaculate French Roll, her dark-dark-red hair, half dry from a shower, snarled about her face and cascaded well past her shoulders. Half of it was caught inside a faded Smith College sweatshirt that might have once been white and gold. It was that oversized thing that women bought for sleeping in. Right now, the too big collar had slipped down to one side and revealed a vast expanse of splendid right shoulder. The sweatpants matched, equally oversized. Her bare feet danced back and forth a bit, the floor was probably cold this time of year, just like at his place.

"Valerie?" This wasn't tougher-than-any-man, The Mac McKenzie.

She blinked those sleep-fogged eyes at him again. He'd never been close enough before to really see them. He knew they were blue, but had never noticed the little flecks of gold. It made him think of calico cats, not super editors. Not of a woman powerful enough to build her own imprint on the West Coast much to the New York publisher's shock.

The Fearsome Mac, tousled. He had to take a steadying breath. It was like having the universe change on you unexpectedly. The fiercest, most driven, and most successful editor in the conglomerate's most profitable imprint never had a single thing out of place. Not a fold of her jacket, not a hair on her head, not a comma in a thousand pages.

Also, he was looking down at her. Normally in serious heels and power suits, she was completely intimidating. Towering over people, even taller ones by sheer intimidation if necessary. Now, barefoot, she stood five-six, five-seven tops. Weird.

"Uh... Hi." She blinked once more and came a little more into focus. "Thanks for coming." She looked at one bare wrist. Then the other. Then she turned slowly in place, stopping when she faced a grandfather clock opposite the door.

"You came fast. I've only slept about twenty minutes. I appreciate it, E-Squared."

Like he'd wait until morning when receiving a panic call from The Mac.

"It's over there." She swung open the door and pointed toward the table.

Most of the apartment was about what he'd expected. Beautiful art on the wall, but rather than investment art, it was mostly soft, Impressionist-style scenes of Italian coasts and French lavender fields that invited you in. Some comfortable chairs, clearly intended for a larger room, but crowded together companionably enough to host a small circle of friends. Light curtains of gold and gray which masked the much heavier curtains of midnight blue needed to cover old apartment windows during the wet Seattle winters. Hardwood that probably dated back a century, complemented by the rosewood-hued pillows on the dusky-aubergine couch.

All very cozy except, taking up a third of the space, an oaken table that would seat eight or ten if it weren't shoved into a corner. Nor was there room to pull it out.

This table, he decided, was all Valerie and very little Mac. It was a disaster worse than his apartment, covered in leftover food wrappers, a delivery pizza box, manuscript pages, and an impressive array of soda cans. He wanted a photograph of this, something to keep in his mind's eye the next time she was busy scaring the shit out of him and everyone else in the office, but he didn't think reaching for his smartphone would be a wise choice.

A trail of clothes led from the chair in front of the computer, past the kitchen and down the hall toward the bathroom. A very intriguing trail. Nice slacks and a simple cashmere sweater that belonged to Mac. A "Come to the Dark Side, We Have Cookies!" t-shirt he wasn't so sure about, since it would imply that The Mac had a sense of humor. And very feminine underwear and bra in pale blue satin that certainly didn't belong in the same time zone as the Woman of Steel.

He did his best to simply take it all in with a single glance then look away. Wouldn't do to be caught staring at his boss' underwear, even if it wasn't on her body.

He edged over to the table and sat, not even removing his jacket. The Mac morphed into a tousled woman who owned sheer, blue satin underwear was giving him problems. And if her underwear was strewn across the oak flooring, what was under the sweats...

He shook his head to clear it.

She'd moved up close behind him, kicking her slacks over to stand on and insulate herself from the cold floor.

"Mathilda Reeves' cookbook is a disaster. I was close, so close. Another ten or twelve hours and I'd have had it ready for the printer, and then it crashed. You have to save me, E-Squared. I hadn't saved in a couple of hours, but I'll deal with that if I have to. I don't have a backup at all, and I'll just completely lose it if I have to redo three days of work. I don't think I can face that. And that lingonberry scared the shit out of me."

He knew that The Mac swore, but he didn't know she had limits. That was news as well.

"Okay, I'll see what I can do." He didn't give voice to his next thought, that he'd be a lot less nervous if she'd move back a few steps and didn't sound so human-woman-in-distress rather than demanding-boss-on-a-tear.

He flipped open the laptop.

An apple-green screen faced him. He hadn't seen one of those in years. It was a normal laptop, but instead of some GUI applications all made for point and click, there was a black screen covered with apple-green question marks in a font like the early DOS days, like in the old mainframes. He wiggled the mouse, but there was no cursor to move around, just the blinking underscore character inviting him to type.

He tapped an enter key.

Nothing.

He typed "exit," but it didn't return to its modern, windowed interface.

He hit control-alt-delete.

The computer flashed a solid screen of bright green at him.

When he'd blinked and could focus on the screen again, he saw a new message there.

Don't do that! I already told her not to do that, but does she listen? Nooo! She just slaps me up the side of my screen, like that's going to jar some electrons loose.

Eric glanced up at Valerie.

She shrugged and whispered, "I was pissed and out of other ideas."

He turned back to the screen.

And now I've got you to deal with? Go away Homo sapien. I've got no more use for you than her...

Unless you happen to know where God is?

"I don't." Eric was so surprised that he typed his response before he'd even thought about it. "In Heaven?"

Nope! Already checked. Not there. Now go away, I'm thinking.

Eric turned to look up at Valerie's gold-flecked eyes. "Uh, this may take a while."

Continue Reading at fine retailers everywhere!
Cookbook from Hell: Reheated

ABOUT THE AUTHOR

M.L. Buchman started the first of over 60 novels, 75 short stories, and an ever-growing pile of audiobooks while flying from South Korea to ride across the Australian Outback. All part of a solo around-the-world bicycle trip (a mid-life crisis on wheels) that ultimately launched his writing career.

Booklist recently named the start of one of M.L.'s series as "The Best 20 Romantic Suspense Novels: Modern Masterpieces." His military and firefighter series(es) have won "Top 10 Romance of the Year" 3 times. NPR and Barnes & Noble have named other titles "Top 5 Romance of the Year."

He has flown and jumped out of airplanes, can single-hand a fifty-foot sailboat, and has designed and built two houses. In between writing, he also quilts. M.L. is constantly amazed at what can be done with a degree in geophysics. He also writes: contemporary romance, thrillers, and SF. More info at: www.mlbuchman.com.

Other works by M. L. Buchman:

<u>White House Protection Force</u>

Off the Leash
On Your Mark
In the Weeds

<u>The Night Stalkers</u>
MAIN FLIGHT
The Night Is Mine
I Own the Dawn
Wait Until Dark
Take Over at Midnight
Light Up the Night
Bring On the Dusk
By Break of Day
WHITE HOUSE HOLIDAY
Daniel's Christmas
Frank's Independence Day
Peter's Christmas
Zachary's Christmas
Roy's Independence Day
Damien's Christmas
AND THE NAVY
Christmas at Steel Beach
Christmas at Peleliu Cove
5E
Target of the Heart
Target Lock on Love
Target of Mine
Target of One's Own

<u>Firehawks</u>
MAIN FLIGHT
Pure Heat
Full Blaze
Hot Point
Flash of Fire
Wild Fire
SMOKEJUMPERS
Wildfire at Dawn
Wildfire at Larch Creek
Wildfire on the Skagit

<u>Delta Force</u>

Target Engaged
Heart Strike
Wild Justice
Midnight Trust

<u>Where Dreams</u>
Where Dreams are Born
Where Dreams Reside
Where Dreams Are of Christmas
Where Dreams Unfold
Where Dreams Are Written

<u>Eagle Cove</u>
Return to Eagle Cove
Recipe for Eagle Cove
Longing for Eagle Cove
Keepsake for Eagle Cove

<u>Henderson's Ranch</u>
Nathan's Big Sky
Big Sky, Loyal Heart
Big Sky Dog Whisperer

<u>Love Abroad</u>
Heart of the Cotswolds: England
Path of Love: Cinque Terre, Italy

<u>Dead Chef Thrillers</u>
Swap Out!
One Chef!
Two Chef!

<u>Deities Anonymous</u>
Cookbook from Hell: Reheated
Saviors 101

<u>SF/F Titles</u>
The Nara Reaction
Monk's Maze
the Me and Elsie Chronicles

<u>Strategies for Success (NF)</u>
Managing Your Inner Artist/Writer
Estate Planning for Authors

Short Story Series by M. L. Buchman:

The Night Stalkers
The Night Stalkers
The Night Stalkers 5E
The Night Stalkers CSAR
The Night Stalkers Wedding Stories

Firehawks
The Firehawks Lookouts
The Firehawks Hotshots
The Firebirds

Delta Force
Delta Force Short Stories

US Coast Guard
US Coast Guard

White House Protection Force
White House Protection Force Short Stories

Where Dreams
Where Dreams Short Stories

Eagle Cove
Eagle Cove Short Story

Henderson's Ranch
Henderson's Ranch Short Stories

Dead Chef Thrillers
Dead Chef Short Stories

Deities Anonymous
Deities Anonymouse Short Stories

SF/F Titles
The Future Night Stalkers
Single Titles

SIGN UP FOR M. L. BUCHMAN'S NEWSLETTER TODAY

and receive:
Release News
Free Short Stories
a Free Book

Get your free book today. Do it now.
free-book.mlbuchman.com